"Tom Bailey respects his characters too much to simplify them, and his readers too much to condescend. *The Grace That Keeps This World* is a work of beauty, dread, and honest suspense, poetic in its language and complex in its apprehension of family love and forgiveness. I was nailed from page one, and hope Mr. Bailey has more in the works."
—LEIF ENGER

"A compelling first novel about love and rivalry in the Adirondacks builds towards a shattering conclusion."
—*PEOPLE*

"A haunting, sharply observed novel about a family struggling to live in harmony with each other, their neighbors, and the natural world. In the lyrical, crystalline prose of a master stylist, Tom Bailey has written a book that will break your heart and linger in your mind long after you put it down."
—TOM PERROTTA

"Like some modern-day version of a Greek tragedy . . . a chorus of narrators . . . moves this story about a family in the Adirondacks . . . slowly and beautifully [towards] an indelible disaster. . . . This is, after all, a story about a man forced to expand his moral imagination, and in the end it inspires the same sympathy from us."
—*WASHINGTON POST BOOK WORLD*

"Tom Bailey has a great (and lyrical) imagination." —ANDRE DUBUS

cotton song

cotton song

a novel

TOM BAILEY

THREE RIVERS PRESS
NEW YORK

Copyright © 2006, 2007 by Tom Bailey
Reader's Group Guide copyright © 2007 by Three Rivers Press, an imprint of the Crown Publishing Group, a division of Random House, Inc., New York.

Published in the United States by Three Rivers Press, an imprint of the Crown Publishing Group, a division of Random House, Inc., New York.
www.crownpublishing.com

THREE RIVERS PRESS and the Tugboat design are registered trademarks of Random House, Inc.

Originally published in hardcover in the United States by Shaye Areheart Books, an imprint of the Crown Publishing Group, a division of Random House, Inc., New York, in 2006.

Library of Congress Cataloging-in-Publication Data
Bailey, Tom, 1961–
Cotton song : a novel / Tom Bailey. — 1st ed.
1. Race relations—Mississippi—Fiction.   2. Mississippi—Fiction.
3. Infants—Death—Fiction.   4. African American women domestics—Fiction.
5. Lynching—Fiction.   6. African American girls—Fiction.   7. Children of murder victims—Fiction.   8. Social workers—Fiction.   I. Title.
PS3552.A3742C68   2006
813'.6—dc22   2006012852

ISBN 978-1-4000-8333-6

Printed in the United States of America

Design by Lauren Dong

10 9 8 7 6 5 4 3 2 1

First Paperback Edition

In memory of my grandmother

We would like to think the whole starry universe would curdle at such a monstrosity: the conjunctions of Orion twisted askew, the arms of the Southern Cross drooping. Of course not: immutable is immutable and everyone in his own private manner dashes his brains against the long-suffering question that is so luminously obvious. Even gods aren't exempt: note Jesus's howl of despair as he stepped rather tentatively into eternity. And we can't seem to go from large to small because everything is the same size. Everyone's skin is so particular and we are so largely unimaginable to one another.

JIM HARRISON,
Legends of the Fall

Acknowledgments

THANKS FIRST OF ALL to my editor and publisher, Shaye Areheart. Shaye's enthusiasm, generosity, graciousness, keen book sense, and lionhearted ferocity (at least when it comes to sticking up for her authors) make her a formidable ally—and a cherished friend. I would also like to express my appreciation to the members of Shaye's "team" with whom I have worked closely on this book: Sibylle Kazeroid, Melanie DeNardo, and Joshua Poole. My continued gratitude goes to my agent, Jane Gelfman, whose savvy and experience have held me in such good stead through the years. The 2006 Mississippi Institute of Arts and Letters Award for Fiction given to me for my first novel, *The Grace That Keeps This World*, brought me home in more ways than one. I remain thrilled at the honor of being claimed as a native son.

For their willingness to read and respond with heartfelt honesty to early drafts of this book, I would like to express my gratitude to my father, Carl Bailey, and my in-laws, Geraldine and Peter Herbert. My wife, Sarah, pored over every word as if she had written the novel herself; her passionate contribution to our shared life's work (including the raising of our three wonderful children, Samuel, Isabel, and William) makes ours a perfect marriage in more ways than one.

Jeff Lazar, once a creative writing student of mine, now a doctor serving his residency in emergency medicine at Yale, patiently taught me my medical facts. I had the pleasure of serendipitously meeting Patsy Sims at a summer writing workshop where we were both teaching. Her daring and insightful nonfiction book *The Klan* proved invaluable in writing this work. I would also like to note my indebtedness to David M. Oshinsky's *"Worse Than Slavery": Parchman Farm and the Ordeal of Jim Crow Justice*, William Banks Taylor's *Down on Parchman Farm: The Great Prison in the Mississippi Delta*, John Dollard's *Caste and Class in a Southern Town*, and Marie M. Hemphill's *Fevers, Floods, and Faith: A History of Sunflower County Mississippi, 1844–1976*.

Thanks to Susquehanna University for supporting my twined loves of teaching and writing, and to Gary Fincke, director of the Writers' Institute at SU, for running such a terrific creative writing program. I couldn't imagine a better place to "work." As ever, Kathy Dalton, research librarian at Susquehanna University, rooted out the facts I needed to nail down the truths in this book. She is a treasured resource.

Thanks, too, to my mother, Elizabeth Bailey, for telling her tales of growing up in the Delta, and to my aunt, Eleanor Failing, for hosting me on more than one visit back to Indianola to research this book. Sonia Fox, recently retired as director of the Welfare Department in Sunflower County, Mississippi, was kind enough to regale me with stories about my grandmother's long tenure as her boss. I would also like to express my appreciation to my cousin James Failing for his discourses on, among other things, the relative differences (or lack thereof) between water moccasins and cottonmouths. I found our conversations over beers that were always *just cold enough* every bit as entertaining as they were enlightening.

Finally, I would like to remember again my grandmother Mary Steele Nabors—*indomitable to the last*—to whose memory this book is dedicated and upon whose character this story is based.

Author's Note

THE LYNCHING OF Letitia Johnson is a strictly fictional account of such acts of vigilantism that have in fact occurred in Mississippi. Hushpuckashaw County and the names and locations of certain towns and hamlets in the Delta have been fictionalized, while others are true, in an effort to create for this book its own place in the state. Facts about Parchman Farm, the state's infamous penitentiary, as well as those concerning the state's welfare agency and the resurgence of the Ku Klux Klan as a home guard during World War II, have been used as they have best suited the story. The characters also are creations of the story, and while they may have been inspired by certain figures, they are not intended to represent any persons, alive or dead.

cotton song

chapter one

THE ROAD TO Ruleton ran dry and dusty. Baby Allen negotiated the ancient Model T as best she could, the loose gravel sliding her tires side to side as if she were skating on ice. Though it was shy of 10:00 A.M. the Mississippi Delta heat already wavered in gaseous, evil-looking shimmerings before her, ghosting the cotton fields that stretched to either side of the straight two-lane divide of U.S. Highway 49. On the horizon the sun squatted—the bloody yolk of a fat, frying orb.

The story of Letitia Johnson's lynching plastered the front page of the Monday, July 17, 1944, edition of the *Hushpuckashaw County Tocsin* that lay on the seat beside Baby, beating out the usual headline designated to naming the local soldiers fighting overseas who'd been chosen for the Hushpuckashaw County Victory Valiants and the quotes for farm prices, not to mention the "11 Musts for Peace Given to Business by the U.S. Chamber" carried by the AP wire, and the war news of Montgomery's attack on Gain, below Caen.

Letitia Johnson had worked as the mammy for the Rules, the founding family of Ruleton. The baby girl of the youngest daughter, Sissy Rule Tisdale, had been found drowned to death in the bathtub of their home Friday morning. Sheriff Dodd had arrested Letitia Johnson on suspicion of infanticide that same afternoon, but before she could even be indicted for the crime she'd been swept away by a mob and hung. Her body had been tarred and then set on fire. It burned all night and into the next day. Such acts of vigilantism, rampant before the 1930s, had grown almost rare since the state had bought a new portable electric chair, which could be transported to perform executions in the county where the crime had been committed, but Letitia Johnson's grievous act, the paper's publisher, L. B. Ware, wrote in an accompanying editorial, had been so heinous as to "earn the support of the God-fearing public for what had been done to her. For though we may be against the gruesome public hangings that have beleaguered the good name of the state of Mississippi in the recent past, we must be able to entrust the care of our most valuable treasure, our children, the heirs of all we hold precious in this world, to the aunties who raised us all."

The article did not point out that Letitia Johnson had been the mother of a girl herself, a twelve-year-old daughter. Now that child was orphaned. Mr. Brumsfield, the director at the welfare, had laid the responsibility of her file on Baby's desk. As a county agent, it was that orphaned girl, Sally Johnson, whom Baby was driving to Ruleton to find.

On the north side of the hamlet of Boyer, halfway between Eureka and Ruleton, she was forced to slow before a cloud of dust that signaled the long line of a chain gang working with picks and shovels to smooth and grade that stretch of the bumpy highway. The convicts wore pants and shirts rung around with horizontal black and white stripes, yellowed with sweat. All the prisoners held at the state penitentiary, better known as Parchman Farm, were busy serving years of hard labor for the profit of the state. The majority of the men worked off their crimes at toil chopping cotton on the twenty-two thousand acres of fields that made up the old plantation-style "farm," but a few work gangs like this one were contracted out to labor for the railroad or public works. Leg irons dragged behind them, and their faces were dripping wet. All eighty or so men at work swinging their picks and shoveling rock were Negroes. The six men guarding them were Negroes, too, convicts as well. As an officer of the newly mandated parole system that had fallen under the auspices of the welfare in Hushpuckashaw County, Baby had come to recognize these men as trusties. Handpicked to carry guns by the sergeant who ran each work camp, they stood at a distinct remove from their fellow prisoners, called gunmen, who worked within range of their aim—the levered rifles or double-barreled shotguns the trusties carried trained directly on them. All the while, the sergeant strode up and down the line, driving them, while a squat, barrel-chested convict wearing a striped prison cap like a grinder monkey's shouted out the chant that paced the rise and fall of their picks. Baby rolled to a stop, elbow on the edge of the open window, and leaned her head on her hand at the delay. The swell of the man's big voice and the chorus of the call thundered back from every convict on the line, all at once, and with the gathered *umph!* and the ringing strike of their picks.

> Ridin' in a hurry.
> *Great Godamighty!*
> Ridin' like he's angry.
> *Great Godamighty!*
> Well, I wonder whut's de matter?
> *Great Godamighty!*
> Bull whip in one han', cowhide in de udder.

Baby climbed out to look for the overseer. A dark-green state car sat tipped at the angle of the ditch in the lane facing her, but no one was in it. She shaded her eyes with her hand. Before her, in the first of the three cotton trucks that had been used to transport the convicts, she spotted khaki trousers attached to a pair of boots sticking out the window of the opened front door, heels crossed. The boots showed dusty brown, the soles squashed hard to the outsides. Baby ducked back in the car and pulled up beside the first truck. She had to lean across the newspaper that was faceup on the passenger seat to see up into the cab.

"Excuse me. Sir?"

When the man sat up from his nap, wearing dark sunglasses, pushing back at his hat, Baby recognized Jake Lemaster, Boss Chief's son. Boss Chief was the appellation of authority granted the superintendent of Parchman Farm, and though Jake Lemaster hadn't been branded with such an omnipotent-sounding title at the prison yet, which Baby took as a good sign, he did have the reputation of being his daddy's right-hand man. This was ironic, seeing as how Jake Lemaster was a one-armed man himself.

"I hate to disturb your sleep, Mr. Lemaster. But some of us have work to do this morning. I'd like to pass by, if you don't mind."

Jake Lemaster peeled off his sunglasses and thumbed the sleep from his eyes. "Morning to you, Mrs. Allen. Thought I recognized that dusty old car. I wasn't sleeping exactly, just resting my eyes. And how is our local angel of mercy today? On dove's wings to do some good up our end of the county, I hope."

Even for a Mississippian born and bred, Jake Lemaster had a heavy accent, which he slathered on country thick, sliding in extra syllables to ease his drawl, his vowels full, and consonants with the edges rounded off. His "morning" sounded like "ma-haw-nin," "car" like "ca-ah." He was still thin and youngish, though not exactly young anymore, certainly no boy, although there was still something boyish about him. He wore his rust-red hair unusually long, curling out from under the back of his hat, and he remained tall, broad-shouldered. His fabled freckled left passing arm looked hard beneath the short-sleeve shirt of his khaki uniform, but she could see a little pooch over his belt the way he sat hunched in the truck with his legs bowed out—a drawn pistol, she saw then, resting in his lap—and he had hard lines drawn down at the edges of his mouth.

Baby had met Jake Lemaster's father, Boss Chief, exactly once, on her first visit to the prison. Boss Chief sat tipped back behind his big desk in the living-room-sized office of the Victorian mansion, called First Home at Front Camp, where he lived and which served as the administrative center for the prison. When she'd been escorted into the room, he'd run his yellow eyes up and down her body, from her legs to her breasts to her face and then back to her breasts and legs and face, before settling on her hips, never meeting her eyes. While she spoke, informing him of the state's new parole law and what her job would be on her visits to Parchman Farm, he pivoted his chair to stare out the window, his thick fingers steepled before him. Nor did he venture to say one word to her during their entire interview except to acknowledge its conclusion by barking his son into the room. Boss Chief mumbled in his growl of a voice to his son, with an accent so guttural and marble-mouthed that she hadn't understood one word. But Jake had. He said, "Yes, sir, Mr. Boss Chief." With that, Boss Chief had apparently washed his hands of her, turning over to Jake the responsibility of dealing with "that woman from the Welfare Department" whenever she made her visits to see the convicts.

The fact Baby remained sharply aware of was that Boss Chief was not a professional penologist—nor had the governor appointed him to act like one. Convicts were sent to Parchman to be *punished* for their crimes. At Parchman no distinction was made between ax murderers and thieves. The cages, as the dormitories in each work camp were called, had no individual cells. Hardened fifty-year-old incorrigibles slept side by side with fifteen-year-old first-time offenders. A mental incompetent was not separated by the state. Insanity was not recognized as a defense for committing a crime—a crime was a crime. All the prisoners at Parchman were treated the same: the common denominator simply that they had all been convicted as guilty. Reform was not the state's goal. Boss Chief had been hired years ago because he was a proven old-style plantation farmer of the first rank. His qualifications proved he could grow cotton on an immense scale. He could "handle niggers." Boss Chief ran Parchman as if the convicts were slaves in antebellum times and he was their "Marse"—except if a convict died there was no loss for Boss Chief. Judges from around the state sent the fodder of new labor Boss Chief's way every day in droves, hauled in from the town and county jails by the white man feared far and wide as Long Chain Charlie. There seemed no end to the number of men—and women, too—who shot and knifed and did personal injury and bodily harm and stole. So there was no real incentive for Boss Chief to keep the prisoners alive or even well. As a parole officer for the state, Baby had met men who'd killed and who had been killed, who were simply no longer *available* to talk to her when she went back for their next interview. As a home visitor for the state, she came to know their families equally well while they served their time in jail.

It was on one of these visits to Parchman Farm that Baby had worked up the temerity to ask Jake exactly what had happened to his right arm. She'd heard the common rumor that he'd lost it in some sort of farm accident. He told her he'd fallen off the back of a tractor when he was a boy. He said he was lucky the trailing disk hadn't diced him to ribbons. The mangled arm had been sawn off neatly above the elbow. Fortunately, he still had full use of the stub, which he'd become adept at using like a flipper. And though Baby was sure the loss of the hand and forearm had cost Jake Lemaster in more ways than she could imagine, she also knew that as a young man he'd shown the determination to overcome such a crippling. He'd risen to play tailback in the single wing for the University of Mississippi's championship-bid football team of 1935—the squad that had taken Ole Miss to its first bowl game. Baby didn't follow football, but everyone else in the Delta seemed to. She happened to remember the facts because everyone had so bemoaned the 20–19 Orange Bowl loss to Catholic University. Still, 1935 had been a great year for the great state of Mississippi, people said. And Jake Lemaster was still remembered for the all-American-honors-winning part he'd played in it. For many, Baby knew, "Red" Lemaster would always remain the fiery-haired, one-armed captain of the Rebels who'd been praised by sportswriters for his speed and quick wit—

Jake Lemaster was a regular red fox they said—and the color of his hair had forever sealed their nickname for him.

"Thank you for asking, Mr. Lemaster. Your local angel of mercy is just fine this morning. Though I'd venture to say it feels more like afternoon."

"Yes, ma'am," he said. "It surely does. 'Cepting it's going to get hotter 'fore it gets cooler. You can take that to the bank. Who we visiting this morning? You heading Parchman way? Daddy didn't say anything to me. We expecting you?"

"Not today, Mr. Lemaster. I'm on my way up to Ruleton. I have an orphaned girl to see." And then Baby just said it—usually she wouldn't have even disclosed that it was an orphan she was going to visit. That was official welfare business. She didn't know why she said it or why in heaven's name she would say it to Jake Lemaster, the Boss Chief's son, of all people. She couldn't keep the anger and bitterness out of her voice either: "Letitia Johnson's daughter. You may have read about her mama, Mr. Lemaster." She waved angrily down at the newspaper on the seat between them.

Jake Lemaster absorbed her tone and the information with a straight face, looking directly back at her, the blacked glasses blanking his expression.

"Now that you mention it, I did hear something about that," he said slowly. "Truth be told, Mrs. Allen, that's all I been hearing about for three days now. Would you believe, Mrs. Allen, that there are Christians in Hushpuckashaw County who still stake their faith on the rock of the Old Testament belief of an eye for an eye and a tooth for a tooth? The murder of the murderer for such Christians isn't enough it seems. Justice must be done. If a child died, such Christians believe, a child's life has got to be paid. They believe that's the only way to even the scales and set things straight."

Baby looked carefully back at him. She nodded slowly, believing she'd heard what Jake Lemaster was trying to tell her—Letitia Johnson's daughter was in danger. This horridness wasn't over yet. Since Baby had heard about the lynching of Letitia Johnson she'd felt a lot of things, but this was the first time she'd felt the rush of fear. "I want to thank you for this confidence, Mr. Lemaster."

When she said that, Jake Lemaster's face changed again. He leaned forward and tipped down his glasses to look at her with his sky-blue eyes. He stretched a flat smile.

"My 'confidence,' as you call it, Mrs. Allen, is nothing more than a statement of fact. You best understand that. What we're having ourselves here is merely a theological discussion." He pushed his sunglasses up the bridge of his nose, blacking his light eyes from her again.

He stood on the running board of the truck. "Joe!" he called and waved his pistol for the trusties to hold back the line of gunmen so that she could pass.

The shooters shuffled the chained convicts at gunpoint into two raggedy lines across the drainage ditches on either side of the highway. Baby glanced back up at Jake Lemaster, but he was focused on the line. She put both hands on the wheel. "Good day, Mr. Lemaster." She faced forward and let off the clutch.

As she drove slowly between the gauntletlike lines, Baby could feel the trusties and gunmen looking into the car at her without looking as if they were looking. Not one of the convicts dared meet her eye. The sergeant stood close by, Black Annie, his wide, short strop of a whip, held at his side. From her visits, Baby knew how bad it was. You did not want to go to Boss Chief's Parchman—no, you did not. The reprisals were legend; murderers were sent to Parchman, real killers. And if you weren't a murderer when you went in, you were a killer for real when you got out, or chances were you were just plain dead, buried in one of the unmarked graves for unclaimed prisoners at the swamp edge of the penitentiary.

Baby drove the length of the line. As soon as she'd passed, the trusties put the gunmen immediately to work again, the gauntlet of picks she'd run already rising and falling, ringing with each swing, and the chant of the caller fading inside the mounting cloud of dust she left behind:

Well you won't write me, you won't come and see me.
Oh!
Say you won't write me, you won't send no word.
Oh!
Said I get my news from the mockingbird.
Oh!
Said I get my news from the mockingbird.
Oh!

In the rearview mirror, Baby could see Jake Lemaster still stand-ing on the running board of the cotton truck holding on to the door with his good arm, pistol in hand, looking after her. His black eyes stared through the glare. Baby touched her hair, and a shiver ran down her spine. At the time, she could not have said why.

THE DUSTY ROAD ran another twelve miles before it reached the outskirts of Ruleton. Though Baby could go as fast as the shaking Model T would take her now on the open highway, the wind that grabbed at her did not make her feel one iota cooler. Hushpuck-ashaw County hadn't been blessed with a rain since the end of May. Her throat felt as parched as the cotton in the fields looked, the mitt leaves drooping, wilted from thirst, the plants stunted, just knee-high, and forced to an early blooming, the yellow and pink flowers of the budding bolls cast across the rows like a dusky skyful of bright, hot little stars. Baby flicked on the staticky radio and lis-tened to a garbled report of the Red Army's storming of Grodno. It seemed inevitable now—the war would soon be over; it was merely a matter of time, though she imagined many more would still die. Baby wondered what peace would bring home to them. After all the talk about the country's struggle against tyranny and subjugation, the fight for freedom . . . She flicked the radio off.

A rolling trickle of sweat slipped between her breasts, and she pressed the flat of her hand against the front of her dress, absorbing it into her bra, and dabbed her forehead with a handkerchief. Baby glanced again at the grainy photograph of Letitia Johnson's body. It didn't look like a body at all really—she looked as if she'd been co-cooned, until you realized that she was burned, charred beyond human recognition by the fire. The picture was framed by the tree from which her already hung body had been chained for that final indignity; the hats and caps of the heads of onlookers could be seen looking up, tilted back, unidentifiable as their guilt in her murder. The safety of numbers. Anonymity. No one was to blame. Letitia Johnson's murder would go unsolved, of that Baby had no doubt, and so the question of whether she'd actually done what she'd been accused of would never even be investigated. She'd been sentenced, her punishment pronounced and carried out without benefit of a trial. And so the matter of Sissy Rule Tisdale's drowned baby girl would be put to rest. No questions asked. And for that, they were all of them guilty, she thought. *All of us.*

Baby slowed and turned left off the gravel onto a dirt road just outside of the city limits of Ruleton, feeling the sickening, woozy, light-headedness flash over her again, shifting her off-kilter. Out of sight of the main road, she pulled over and fumbled at the door's latch and stumbled into the field through the cloud of dust she'd raised, where she leaned as far forward as she could to keep the string of vomit off her dress. She ended up dry heaving; she had thrown up in the toilet that morning trying to get ready quietly in the dark while her girls, Claire and Jeana, slept, and her head was still swimming. She knew from experience that what she needed was to eat, but she hadn't been able to keep any breakfast down, not even coffee, and there was nothing in her stomach to come up. There was cold fried chicken and potato salad in a greasy brown bag on the floorboard of the backseat—leftovers from Sunday dinner that she'd packed for her lunch—but even the thought of meat made her retch again. She dabbed at the edges of her mouth with the handkerchief still clutched in her hand, looking down at the smear of red lipstick she'd wiped off. Slowly, she straightened.

The fried cotton stood in neat rows, raying out like spokes on a giant wheel from the hub of the point where she stood under a blue sky. At the end of the horizon a winding, well-watered explosion of trees, water oaks and cottonwoods, sycamores and locust, willows and persimmons, lined the banks of the Hushpuckashaw River. She followed the line with her eye until it came to rest on the weathered gray of Letitia Johnson's shack, still tiny in the distance. Baby dabbed her mouth again and parted the neck of her cotton dress to try to snare a breeze.

It seemed there was no end to trouble in this life.

"Goddamn you, Gabriel Allen," she said and felt the dam burst of tears she'd caught back talking to Jake Lemaster begin to well and spill. It all came down on her again then. It had been two weeks since she'd sent her husband packing. Trouble enough that he was gone and now she had their two girls to raise all on her own, but the fact that she'd let Gabe get her pregnant again at the age of forty-one while he was cheating on her with that awful Franks woman drove her to the brink of distraction.

Baby trudged back to the car, the door left hanging open. She sat back in the ovenlike cab and pulled her legs inside to fix her lips in the rearview mirror, reapplying the mask she'd turned to face Jake Lemaster. She smacked her lips together and put her lipstick back in her purse. As she shifted the Model T into gear again and started to drive, she wondered what she'd find at Letitia Johnson's when she was let inside. As a visitor for the welfare, she knew: You *never* knew what you'd find. She'd learned to expect just about anything in her official inquiries into other people's lives and so was no longer as surprised by the doings of others as she was by her own.

chapter two

FOR THREE DAYS and three nights Sally Johnson hid in the brush and trees that grew along the banks of the river. From there, if she had to, she could shimmy back on her belly and slip silently into the yellow waters of the Hushpuckashaw River and disappear downstream. Just like a water rat. Water rat was the game they used to play, her and Marky and Charles and Caroline. She could swim. And she knew the way to hold a reed and breathe through the tube of it. There were reeds all along the bank. You couldn't tell which reed she was when she laid herself down underneath them. If she had to she could breathe there all day, cool as could be. *Don' let them snappers snap you!* Marky always said, wide-eyed, grinning. Mama always said Marky was full of mis-chif. He said there was carp in there big-enough mouthed to swallow a dog. He'd seen it! He didn't want to even tell about the alligators lived in there. And, worser even, *swear*, the crocodiles. Usually Marky could get to her. But she was more afraid of the po-lice. Or the carloads of white men who'd come out to their home looking since. She would risk the snapper, any hard-mouthed carp. She did not know what had happened to her mama other than that she'd been taken away.

When the po-lice pulled up in the car early that morning, her mama had peeked back the red-and-white-checkered tablecloth curtains she'd made to look at them. She turned quickly back to Sally with blaring eyes and said, real sternness in her voice, "You come out from neath that bed no matters what you hear I'll whip you black and blue, you hear? I'll whip you til you can't stand up." That had scared Sally almost as much as the po-lice with no necks and razored hair, pink-scalped. Her mother never talked like that. She wasn't like that. And then she'd felt truly afraid because she knew then just how scared her mother was. Sally felt that fear again, holding close onto the reed now, clutching it for dear life, lying flat on her hollowed belly watching the old car drive up into the yard beside their house—drive up and stop just the same way the po-lice had that morning three mornings ago and almost in the exact same spot, too. And she lay still, not even daring the flicker of motion to wave away the dauber that hovered near the coat of yellow mud she'd smeared on her arms and legs and face to keep the mosquitoes off.

The white woman climbed out. She was wearing a dark-blue dress. Stockings. Dressed like a church lady. One of them ones with yellow hair and blue eyes, though she couldn't see the white lady's eyes from there. But she knew her kind. The air rasped with the shucking adze of cicadas. The morning air cooked. Against the smoky green of the cotton, Sally saw the flicker of a red fox, black nose in the air. The fox went stock-still, caught out in the open, watching the woman who was stepping up onto their boarded porch. Her shoes were hard-heeled, clumping. The woman looked around. Sally didn't move, her heart thundering. The woman turned back to the door and knocked and the fox darted into the cotton and disappeared. Sally listened to her own breathing.

"Sally?" Sally heard the woman call. She didn't move.

The woman knocked again. She opened the door and stepped inside. When she came out, she turned and scanned the cotton and the line of woods where Sally hid.

"I don't blame you for hiding," the white woman called. "My name's Mrs. Allen. I work for the Welfare Department. I'm here to help, Sally."

The woman held her hands clasped before her, clutching a swatch of white cloth. She stood still. She called, "Sally!" After a while, she sat down on the top step of the porch. Every once in a while she would dab her forehead with the cloth. She was a white woman, Sally thought, who looked even more white-faced than most white women looked. The sun shadowed across the trees, sending them long into the yard. It angled the roof of the house shorter and shorter the hotter it climbed.

When the shadows said straight up and down noon, the woman stood. She had to reach for the wall. Her mama had told her how white women fell out all the time, wilting like cut flowers in the heat. Sally waited to see for herself. But the woman got her balance back. When she did she stepped down the stairs and walked through the dust of the yard to her car. She opened the back door and leaned in. She came out with a brown paper bag, greasy dark on the bottom. Sally watched her shut the car door and walk the bag back onto the porch. The white woman held the bag. Sally watched her hold it, her own stomach talking to her, asking what food might be in the bag. The woman turned and looked out over the cotton and the woods again, angling the flat of her hand over her eyes.

"Sally, are you out there?" The woman scanned the fields and woods again. "How long's it been since you've eaten? You need to eat, Sally. I'm going to leave this bag of food for you—fried chicken and potato salad. Eat and stay hidden as good as you are now, you hear? Don't come out again for anybody else but me. You've got to trust me, Sally. I'll come back by for you on my way home this evening. I imagine you'll be hungry again by then. I'll bring supper with me."

The woman continued to search the fields. Sally lay still, holding on to her stomach to keep it quiet waiting for her to go. Finally, the woman gave up. She set the bag on the top step and clipped back down the stairs into the yard. She started the engine and swung the black car about in a wide circle, sending up a ring of dust. Sally trailed the tail of dust she made driving away until it faded from sight. She knew it couldn't be a trick, because she could follow the woman's car in the dust for as far as it went. She waited while the dirt settled back to earth and the sky cleared blue. Sally looked down in time to see the fox, following his nose, trotting for the porch.

"Hey!" she yelled, stumbling up and slipping, her legs and arms locked from lying still for so long. She jumped up again, scrabbling after two rocks, which she held tight in her fists—suddenly feeling hard carp-mouthed enough to eat the fox herself. "You ain't nothing but a little dog noways!" The first rock she threw puffed dust behind the fox. The fox hunkered still, ears perked, spotted her, and ran. The second rock chased after him.

Sally raced for the bag.

SHE BIT HUNKS out of the chicken and then used her fingers to spoon the potato salad into her mouth. She chewed it all together and gulped to get it down. When her hunger had calmed, the breast cleaned, she gnawed each fine bone until it gleamed. She licked the sweet dressing from the bowl. When that was gone, she peered again into the empty bag. She left the ripped bag and the empty bowl forgotten on the step at her feet and stood, wiping her hands down on her dress.

Only then did Sally smell something wild, feral. She sniffed and realized it was her. Out back at the well, she slid back the boards and splashed the bucket down. The water in the cedar bucket that she cranked up had an orange color to it and tasted strongly of iron. It tasted so good. Sally used the rest of the water in the bucket to wash herself as best she could. She took off her dress and draped it over the well. She was still wearing her britches. Her mama had rowed her hair just the day before the po-lice took her, but now it felt nappy, stuck with twigs. Frizzed.

After she'd dunked her head and then her dress and twisted and hung it on the line to dry, Sally threw the remains of the bucket on her mama's burned-looking beans. A grasshopper whirred away. She hooked the bucket back in place and replaced the boards. Sally scanned the fields. White folks didn't walk. Dust meant cars, which signaled they were on their way, but the woman had driven off and there was no dust for as far as she could see. She decided to risk the house.

Nothing inside had changed. The windows had been left open and the checkered curtains hung straight down without a breeze. Her mama had just been getting ready to fix breakfast for the two of them and their places were neatly set. A pot of water waited on the bellied stove. The fire had been kindled, but hadn't been lit. Her mama's white uniform for work hung neatly on a hanger from a nail in the wall. Her clean shoes sat side by side beneath the white dress. The shoes were clean because Young Miss Rule insisted on such things. "Don't muss them" were her orders. To keep them white, Mama slipped them into her bag and walked home along the dusty road the three miles from Ruleton barefoot. And her mama always hung up her uniform first thing to keep it clean, just as she'd hung it up that day—her big breasts spilling loose from her bra as she stripped it off. Lines cut across the beef of her back. "Whew! Free at last," she laughed as she slipped into the cotton dress made from the same bolt of cloth as the one Sally wore. "Too hot for underwear," she joked.

There was only the one room. The two of them ate in that room and changed in that room and slept in that room, too. Sally had never met her daddy. But the man Alfonse came by to visit with her mama some nights and sometimes he stayed on for a couple of days or even weeks. He seemed to Sally a giant. His mama smiled: Bigger is how everybody else called him, but she liked the ring of his whole first name. *Alfonse!* He had to duck to step through their cabin door. His skin shone so black it gleamed a sheen of blue. He didn't talk much, his eyes always on Mama. His big hands reaching out every time she passed, her shooing him and laughing. When he sat in the room with his ham thighs making the chair disappear underneath him, there wasn't much room to pass. He had the sweating body smell of a man close in their woman's vanilla-scented house. He had one front gold tooth and one silver one, too. He was proud of his *teefs*. And at night there was nowhere to go and so Sally lay wide-eyed listening. Watching, too. And feeling something good between her own legs. And her little nipples would tingle and perk up. She'd touch down there. She didn't know what she was doing, but now that she was nearly twelve she knew what felt good. The rubbing made her hold her breath. And then she'd shudder with the power of it and feel content and go straight off to sleep. It was like magic. Alfonse used the magic to make her mama feel good—good as the good-time sounds they made—and that was good enough for Sally.

"Do you love him?" Sally once asked and her mama laughed and put her hand on the back of her neck. She arched like a cat against it. "Alfonse? I guess I do love him," she said. "But he's a rascal. Like your daddy. I just love them rascally kind, I guess." But Alfonse hadn't been around all summer. Mama said they had him on Parchman Farm for some rascaliness. She visited up Parchman way Sundays, as faithful now about it as she'd been a believer in going to church before. The Boss Chief let all the wives and girlfriends in. If Sally made the trip from Ruleton with her and the other women, she waited outside on a green bench while her mama and Alfonse made what her Mama called their *conjul visit*.

Mornings before the morning the po-lice came for her, Young Miss Rule would come pick up her mama. Mama had raised Young Miss Rule from a baby herself and Old Mr. Rule had sent Mama with her when she got married and moved into a house with her new husband, whose name was Clyde Tisdale: Mr. Clyde. And then Young Miss Rule was Mrs. Clyde Tisdale, but since Mama had raised her she still called her Young Miss Rule. It took Young Miss Rule awhile but then she got pregnant and Mama took charge of their baby, whose name was Robert: Young Mr. Robert after Old

Mr. Rule. And then after some more time passed they had a little baby girl. Because Mama was leaving for the day Mama said Young Miss Rule let her walk home evenings. But in the mornings she came to pick her up first thing because she wanted her to take care of her baby girl right away. Young Miss Rule would sit in her shiny car outside in the yard and beep the horn. Sometimes she'd show up early. If it had been a bad night of the baby's crying, it might still not be light. They couldn't figure out was wrong with the baby. Sometimes she'd cry all night after Mama left. Young Miss Rule would sit out in the car with her headlights shining in the cabin window and honk four or five times. "I'm comin', I'm comin'," Mama would say, bumping into things as she walked slowly about, getting dressed and gathering her things. Her mama always said to Sally before she left her on her own, "You do good at school today. I don't want you growin' up to be no white person's maid."

Sally stood inside the cabin. And then she started to cry. The sound of it surprised her. She put her hand to her face. Somebody was wailing. It was her, she heard. She had a bad, bad feeling. That white woman coming after her was saying something. Where was Mama? The po-lice hadn't brought her mama back. Sally's stomach opened up and swallowed her. She cried and she cried. She didn't know it but she knew it not knowing how for sure: her mama was not coming back to their cabin for her.

It was dark when Sally woke. She lay perfectly still. Frozen in fear. For a moment she had no idea where she was in time. She'd fallen asleep on the comfort of her own bed. She'd only meant to rest there a minute. And then she saw headlights flash bright across the curtains. She heard the creak of the brakes, the idling engine. She dropped to the floor and rolled under her mama's bed, where she'd hid when the po-lice came in.

Sally scooted back so that she was pressed against the wall. She hugged her knees up so that her feet wouldn't show. The car door squeaked and slammed. Sally looked out, horrified. She hadn't closed the cabin door.

The white woman walked up shining silvery in the glare of the headlamps, her yellow hair haloed gold behind her. Sally watched her bend and pick up the bag and bowl she'd left on the step. The lady had a white bag in her other hand. Even from there Sally could smell the food. The woman faced the open door.

"Sally?"

Sally was too scared herself to hear the touch of fear in the woman's voice.

Sally heard her stomach grumble. She pressed it hard, trying to hush it. The woman stepped forward and reached in to press the door back flat against the wall. "Sally?" She stood looking in and then she stepped all the way into the dark cabin. The woman had a match, though, and she found the candle on the table. The room flickered and glowed. Outside the crickets were going *creeker, creeker, creeker*. A bullfrog throbbed. Sally watched the woman's hard shoes. They were blue with white on the toe. The shoes turned and the candle she'd left on the table cast the woman big and black against the far wall.

"Now I don't guess it could've been that fox I saw this afternoon that ate that food, but maybe it was. You've got to be quick and smart to beat a red fox."

Sally watched the shoes step away from the table. The white woman clipped across the floor to stand before her bed. The woman bent, her stockings stretching, and Sally saw the sheet move. The sheet straightened from where she'd been lying on it.

"And speaking of foxes and food, you must still be hungry. I brought you some supper. I hope you like hamburgers and fries. Have you ever had a burger from Delaney's? They're something. Best burgers in the Delta. We'll taste them together, if you want. To tell you the truth, Sally, I haven't been able to eat all day myself. I'm about famished."

The shoes walked over and stood before her mother's clean white shoes. The woman stood before them, facing her mama's hung-up white dress, and then she turned back into the room. "I know you wish your mama were here. I wish she were, too. I'm here to help you as best I can. You know, I have two little girls of my own. My youngest, Jeana, is right about your age. I'd like for you to come home with me tonight and meet her. Tomorrow I'm going to help you find a new home. Why don't I leave your food out here and go out and get your dress? I saw it hanging on the line. That'll give you a chance to come on out from under that bed. All right?"

Sally was still holding her breath. The woman walked out of the cabin and down the steps into the glare again. A moth fluttered into the room. With the bright light behind its wings, the moth looked as if it were fanning the flame. It hovered about the candle, but didn't get burned. Sally crawled out from underneath the bed. She stood looking down at her skinny self in her burlap shorts. Her knees knobbed out and she had long toes. She didn't have any other clothes. The white woman came in again carrying her dress. She smiled when she saw Sally. "It's dry." She handed the dress to Sally and turned her back, setting out their food on the table while Sally slipped it on over her head.

"I even snagged a bottle of ketchup for us. Big Daddy Delaney won't mind."

Sally stood waiting for the white woman to sit. She had never in her life eaten at the same table with a white person.

"Please," the woman said. She pulled back the chair beside her for Sally. "For the record, I'm Mrs. Allen from the Hushpuckashaw County Welfare Department, but between you and me I'm strictly Baby."

Sally sat stiffly. "Is my mama comin' back?"

Baby looked at her. "I'm so sorry, Sally."

Sally sat with her hands in her lap. The room blurred and swam before her. The white Baby woman beside her pulled her close. "It's okay to cry," she said. "Feeling sorry's what crying's for."

Sally took her mama's white shoes, but she left the maid's uniform behind for good. They closed the windows and blew out the candle. They latched the door behind them.

Baby drove with her lights shining on the gravel road before them, the wind and the crickety creeking and bullfrog groaning of the night whooshing by on either side. Sally had never ridden in a car at night. She wondered if this was what it felt like to fly. She sat in the front seat looking over the dash. Something in the road flashed red and Baby slowed before a possum crossing the road, three babies clinging to its back. She waited for them to cross and then Baby lurched forward again. Sally watched as shacks and houses loomed darker in the dark, massing closer and closer, until they were there in the headlights and then just gone, that quick, left behind, given back to the black fields that stretched into the bluer night. Out her window she could read the same stars she knew above her own home. Before them a quarter-moon curved sharp as a silver scythe hung in the sky. They seemed to be driving toward it.

Sally thought about Marky and Charles and Caroline and she wondered if she'd ever see them again. She didn't know where she was going to tell them she was going with this white Baby welfare woman even if she could have told them. She had no idea the world was such a long place. They traveled straight through the dark like the whole night's journey of a dream. But this wasn't no dream, she knew. Wherever she was going now she was headed there fast.

chapter three

FRIDAY NIGHT WHEN Letitia Johnson had been dragged out of her cell and swept away on the tide of the mob and hung, and then cut down, tarred over, burned, and left chained up to dangle as a charred, smoldering example, Jake Lemaster had been at home in bed. Earlier that evening he'd stood visibly alone under the yellow bulb of the porch light of Second Home at Front Camp with his hand set on his hip, his boot on the rail, watching as a line of five cars led by the captain of Camp 5 Calvin McGales's rattling pickup swept by. They hardly bothered to slow for the armed trusties at the gates of Parchman Farm before swerving out onto the southbound lane of U.S. Highway 49 and racing straight for Ruleton. Since they'd first gotten word that morning that Sissy Rule Tisdale's daughter, Dorothy, had been drowned by her own mammy the night before, the switchboard had been lighting up all day with reports of the crowd that had begun to swell the town square within a bottle throw of the jail. Jake knew: McGales and his boys had been in a lather to make Ruleton before the "fun" was through.

That Monday night Calvin McGales's night man came knocking on the back door of Second Home. It was nearly 11:00. Old salty-haired Mason—whom Jake's wife, Jolene, insisted on calling their "manservant" even though what he was was a sixty-three-year-old

convict serving the twelfth year of a twenty-year sentence for shooting his wife's boyfriend in the back—found Jake in the study with
his third drink in hand. He was still wearing his khaki uniform. From
long experience, he knew the dust in his hair from the day he'd
spent on the road made him look as if he had on a powdered wig.

"Mr. Jake, Sergeant Shepherd's here to speak with you."

Jake wondered, what now? Since they'd gotten the first call Friday morning, Letitia Johnson had been all anyone on Parchman
Farm talked about, captains and convicts alike. And only that morning that Allen woman from the welfare had stopped on the road to
glare at him with the newspaper faceup on the seat between them as
if he, Jake, were responsible or had had anything at all whatsoever to
do with any of it! He'd been in bed, for Christ sakes!

News from Calvin McGales that couldn't wait until morning
could not be good news. Worse, Assistant Sergeant Shepherd, the
night man in Camp 5, was a truly nasty piece of work. An ax murderer with the crafty intelligence of a five-year-old, he would have
been deemed unfit to stand trial for the horrors he'd committed in
any other state. At Parchman Farm he'd served eighteen years of the
first of his two consecutive life terms. An imbecile like Shepherd
knew no bounds, and the gunmen he oversaw in Camp 5 were absolutely terrified of him and what he was capable of doing to them if
McGales ordered it done.

Jake stood from the deep comfort of the wingback chair he'd just
sunk himself into, feeling the first two slugs of bourbon he'd bolted
down as soon as Jolene had gone up to bed. His wife had left in a
snit that he'd missed the noon dinner that she'd had their house girl,
Calpurnia, fix—lamb with all the trimmings, including a special
mint sauce Jolene had read about in one of her magazines. Now it
was nearly 9:00 and three-year-old Lee and little Jakey, who was
five, were already in bed, and Jolene hadn't wanted Jake to wake
them to say good night—the price for his thoughtlessness. After Jolene had fallen asleep, Jake would sneak in their rooms and ruffle
their sweet sweaty hair and kiss them in their sleep.

When he'd come in from work, Jake had left his dusty boots before the back kitchen door where Jolene insisted he leave them. Shepherd waited for him there now. He stepped out of the study and scuffed through the brilliantly lit dining room in his socked feet. He'd left the drink on the sideboard, and he pocketed his empty hand, using his stub to stiff-arm past the flap of the double doors that led into the blacked kitchen. Mason had flicked on the orange painted bug bulb over the back porch.

Jake found Shepherd hunkering in the shadows, shying back from the bright. "Well, what is it?"

"Sorry to 'sturb you, Boss, but de main boss man he say come straight on to you quick and so I come!"

Shepherd stepped up to the light, dragging the inside arch of his left foot flat behind him. He appeared all but white. His skin looked as if it had been burned by bleach, a raggedy pale pink. A mottling of liver-colored birthmarks covered his face and arms. Shepherd had always reminded Jake of an overexposed negative.

"Cap'n McGales say tell you dat Mr. Alley been cut bad. Dat giant new nigga, da one de boys all call Bigger, he da one dat done it. I never seen nothin like it afore, Boss. Big as he is and he had 'im a shank. Blood on the walls! Plates come crashing! It happen in de cage once dey all got home from the fields to eat so's I's right dere to hear. Mr. Alley was telling agin about da hanging of dat woman dat happen and jes how dey done done it and all wid da rope and den da tar and dat first flicked match what set fire to her and den *boom!*"

Jake listened with his hand propping him against the frame of the door. The lynching of Letitia Johnson again. He felt himself weaving, the bourbon swaying him. He wanted to make it stop. Alley Leech served McGales as his first assistant sergeant in Camp 5. And if Shepherd could be seen as a walking abomination, Alley Leech could be viewed simply as the worst sort of white trash. Everyone at Parchman knew that Alley Leech had been sent to the state prison for forcing unspeakable acts on his own nine-year-old son before he'd slit his boy's throat in an attempt to hide his guilt.

Alley Leech was serving the first of three consecutive life terms and would get no sympathy on Parchman Farm, nor would he give any—that's why McGales had handpicked him as an assistant sergeant from among his trusties. McGales considered the willingness to inflict cruelty an asset in his sergeants. More to the point, Alley Leech had no one else to turn to; the white gunmen despised him and the Negro gunmen dreaded him. Alley Leech lived the life of a hated man. The real miracle was that some gunman hadn't gone off and killed him long before this. Without McGales's protection, Alley Leech would have already been dead. Just so, his allegiance to McGales's authority remained absolute.

Jake recognized the new man Bigger from Camp 5 who had cut Alley Leech only because he was so uncommonly huge—a head again taller and a size again broader than the next biggest big man in the yard. He'd arrived on Parchman Farm earlier that summer, hauled in by Long Chain Charlie for something to do with razoring another man. Over cards maybe? Or dice? Jake couldn't recall his case exactly, but he did remember that the judge had sentenced Bigger to five years on Parchman Farm to think long and hard about what he'd done. And here he'd gone and done it again, except this time he'd gone and cut a sergeant—and, worse yet for him, a white one.

A black prisoner could not be allowed to get away with cutting a white man, and especially not a white sergeant or captain. That was Rule Number 1 on Parchman Farm. The commandment had been passed down from on high. If such a thing happened, Jake's daddy the Boss Chief firmly believed, it would throw everything off-kilter. Who knew what might happen next? There was, Boss Chief held, a natural balance to things, an order. McGales seconded his belief. Of course, Calvin McGales was the very "Christian" Jake had heard gloating about the lynching of Letitia Johnson over his milk and molasses turned coffee in the staff kitchen of First Home that morning before he'd left to work on the road and met up with Mrs. Allen. McGales who'd made the comment about *an eye for an eye and a tooth for a tooth:* that the scales of justice had not been weighed level until Letitia Johnson's daughter was offered up to Him in the after-smoke smolder of a lamblike burned offering, too. From any of the other captains or sergeants on Parchman Farm, Jake might have shrugged off such talk as bunk, hype, or bull, but McGales was capable of initiating such a deed and of actually carrying it out—the rumor that Calvin McGales would not confirm but did nothing at all to deny was that he now held the Grand Dragon's standing in the county's klavern of the Invisible Empire of the Ku Klux Klan.

Ten years ago when Jake had graduated from college, he'd been approached about joining the Klan. The man who'd approached him had been a well-respected lawyer in Oxford, a wealthy booster of the university's football team. Jake remembered the ring he wore with a red stone and gold-embossed A, which the man had explained, smiling, trying to win Jake over, stood for AKAI, "A Klansman Am I." Until he'd heard the rumor about McGales, Jake had thought the Klan had died out in the Delta—especially now with the focus of fighting on the war against the Germans and Japanese overseas. When the idea of an unmasking law had been raised in the legislature the year before, the *Jackson Daily News* had shrugged, "Why kick the corpse?" Now Jake wasn't so sure. It seemed McGales might be working to revive the membership and grow it any way he could—such as spreading the word that the history of the Klan, since the aftermath of the Civil War, had always been as a home guard—the idea being that the men who'd been left behind, like Jake, were *needed* now. Given the size and fervor of the crowd that had gone after Letitia Johnson, Jake imagined that an event like a lynching must be a good way to recruit new "ghouls." If he could, McGales would keep the fire stoked by going after Letitia Johnson's daughter. Mrs. Allen was right to be afraid.

Jake pushed away from the door to stand straighter. He spread his feet wide as if the planked kitchen floor were the rolling deck of a ship in a storm over which he had no control.

"They've taken Alley Leech to the infirmary?" he thought to ask.

"Doc Evans sewin' 'im up right now."

"He going to live?"

"Can't say about dat, Boss. I done tole you 'bout all dat blood."

"And Bigger?" Jake was thinking about having Quirt Hanson set his dogs. "He escape?" Visitors always exclaimed their surprise when they first caught sight of the field camps that housed the prisoners on Parchman Farm. Separated from the freedom of open space by a single harmless-looking show of barbed wire, Parchman didn't look like a prison. It *looked* like a farm. The gunmen in each camp raised chickens and pigs and grew their own vegetables. They did laundry in tubs in the yard and hung it to dry on lines strung from the walls between the cages—open barracks with barred windows—which in the summer were covered with screens to keep the hordes of mosquitoes at bay. Visitors believed it must be the easiest thing in the world to simply "walk" from Parchman. And it was. But the twenty-two thousand acres of the plantation covered forty-two square miles, practically the entire northern third of Hushpuckashaw County, and whenever a prisoner walked, the trusties immediately put Quirt Hanson and his dog boys with their yelping hounds on the trail. Those blueticks and redbones and beagles and bloodhounds could nose down a man—or a woman from the women's camp—before he made it a mile down the road. Quirt Hanson's dogs would find him even if he hoofed the twenty it took to make it to the prison's borders from any of the camps, so long as they caught his scent within five hours. Nights of an attempted escape, the happy baying of the hounds could be heard across the fields and down dirt roads and across ditches.

Every once in a great while a prisoner made it to the river that bordered along the crude baseball diamonds that offered the camps their prime Sunday afternoon entertainment. More than a few escapees had drowned in the yellow waters of the Hushpuckashaw. These deaths could most often be attributed to the fact that few gunmen could swim rather than the swiftness of the current, which flowed by at a slow, drowsy-seeming meander. And there was always the fear of snakes, the waters rumored rife with cottonmouths and water moccasins and plain water snakes eight feet long that would drop down on you from the low-hanging branches of the trees, copperheads crawling the banks.

"Oh, no, suh. Dat nigga ain't got nowheres," Shepherd said. "He didn't escape. We fixed him up, big as he bees. He had da two front teeths, a gold toof and dat silver. Now he gots da silver one. Maybe someone grabbed dat gold one. Or he drunked it with all dat blood." Shepherd grinned. "But what else I 'spose tell you is Cap'n McGales gone give him a whole day in dat box. Dat's what he sent me to tell you. He gone start him in at dawn."

Killing a wayward convict outright was too easy; it didn't leave the proper impression—Jake knew how McGales's mind worked— and though ten licks from the strop of Black Annie could certainly get a gunman's attention, the box was Captain Calvin McGales's punishment of choice. The box was shaped like a coffin, but made entirely of tin with an envelope-sized slit set over the mouth. The slit let in air enough to live, but it wasn't nearly big enough to let out the broiling heat that built up inside that box during the day. In the cool before dawn, the manacled prisoner was forced to lie down in the box, which was situated in the center of the dirt yard where no shade could reach it all day. Once the prisoner was lain inside, the lid was banged closed and the latches on the box were shot through and locked. As soon as the red sun peeked up and the first rays touched the tin, the box would begin to heat up as if a fire had been kindled underneath it. By noon, the one-hundred-plus-degree sun blazing straight down on the box would have raised the temperature inside to over two hundred degrees. Bigger might just wish he was dead lying in the coffin left to cook him under the Mississippi Delta summer sun thinking about what he'd done, but he wouldn't be dead. That would be his only consolation. Though it wouldn't seem much of a consolation, Jake knew.

Jake had seen other gunmen raised like the living dead from the eternity of having spent three afternoon hours in the box. After four hours in the box, Bigger's already too big body would begin to swell, his guts boiling to get out of his skin with nowhere to go. Already too big for the box, his bare arms and legs shoved against the frying metal, Bigger would begin to split at the seams like a boiled frank. By noon he'd be bleeding from his nose or his ears or the inside edges of his eyes. The longest a prisoner had ever lived being baked alive inside the tin box during the day that Jake knew about was five hours. In effect, by giving him a fourteen-hour day in the box, McGales had sentenced Bigger to death. That's what McGales wanted Jake to know. Part of Jake's job as the number two man on Parchman Farm was to oversee the overseers. Ultimately the responsibility for McGales's actions would be his own.

"All right," Jake nodded and Shepherd turned to go. He flipped off the light and closed the door behind him.

Jake wandered back through the kitchen and dining room into the study and stiffened his drink. Maybe it would help him sleep. The whole thing sickened Jake. He was sick to death of all of this. But somehow he couldn't see his way free of Parchman Farm. When he'd left Ole Miss riding high on the tide of victories that had taken his team to the Orange Bowl and made him a local hero, he'd had his pick of offers. The fledgling NFL's Brooklyn Dodgers, so called after their brother team in baseball, had drafted him in the first round, but Jake had felt finished with football, done with sports—even now he rarely attended a game or thought to tune the radio in to hear one. At twenty-three, he'd felt he wasn't getting any younger; he'd wanted to get on with his life. He could have put his bachelor's degree to work in New Orleans or Memphis, if he'd cared to. He could have run an insurance agency or been the front man for a company that sold farm equipment or negotiated cotton futures. He had given serious consideration to going on to law school at the university. Given his popularity and his daddy's reputation throughout the state, his own eventual career in politics had seemed a more than likely future. But he hadn't chosen to do any of these things. Instead he'd bowed to a temptation that had been proffered since boyhood—his daddy's wish that he return to Parchman.

The plantation that the Boss Chief promised him would one day be his.

The immediate enticements his father had used to lure Jake from the other choices he might have made upon leaving Oxford and Ole Miss were the beautiful old Victorian-style mansion called Second Home on the quad of Front Camp, the staff of ready servants, the second-in-command position, and the wand-waved and guaranteed immediate wealth of a considerable salary that he and his bride, Jolene, had begun to draw on the first day of June after they graduated and were married and left on their all-expenses-paid six-month graduation/honeymoon trip to Europe.

Thinking back now, Jake wondered why he'd done it. Why, *really?* But back then, he remembered, life had seemed so good, damn near perfect. He'd been on a roll, riding a long streak of wins, and had had the sort of confidence—the arrogance born of a successful youth and not having the hard-earned experience to have learned— that things could never change. One-armed though he would always be, he still felt charmed. He, Red Lemaster, couldn't lose!

But after having been back on the farm for a few years what Jake found was what he'd always known from growing up at Parchman as his daddy's only son: Boss Chief had a lock on the place. He might have been training Jake to take the reins, but Jake couldn't make a single change without his okay. Boss Chief left no room for reforms—reform wasn't part of *his* plan. There was nothing for Jake to build—except roads, of course. He'd shored up and grated and graveled more of them than he cared to consider, the map work of them like a spider's web stuck in his head. The fact of his job was that he could sleep all day long in the truck if he wanted. His own second in command, his sergeant, the legendary brawler Joe Booker, was more than capable of running a road crew. Even as the number two man in command of the fifteen other camps and captain of Camp 1, Jake felt underused, his potential for leadership wasted. Because of his missing arm, even the army wouldn't take him on as cannon fodder. Dr. Jenks, who'd examined Jake, was a staunch

Rebel fan; he'd acted as team doctor during Jake's gridiron years, and he knew Red Lemaster could be a formidable foe in a battle. He was sympathetic. If it had been the Civil War all over again, Dr. Jenks had assured him, not only would he be certified as a soldier, with his record for leadership and his daddy's political power he'd have been given a vital command—he could have been a one-armed Stonewall Jackson! But this was the U.S. Army, and there was nothing anyone in Mississippi could do for him. Jake Lemaster had been classified 4-F.

Now, nearly ten years after making that initial crossroads decision to return to Parchman Farm, Jake had come to feel as confined to the twenty-two thousand acres that surrounded the penitentiary as any of the convicts whom he was paid to guard. At the age of thirty-three, Jake knew he was no hero—no matter what his potential for heroics may once have been. He was no longer the flamboyant red-haired, one-armed tailback who'd led his team to the championship game and gotten the beautiful girl and left college to live happily ever after—a rising star in the royal blue firmament of the Southern social order. The fact was Jake Lemaster felt plain useless. Lately, he'd begun to see himself as a different kind of one-armed man—not as the hero who overcomes all odds to succeed, but as a cripple beset with all the limitations such a disability seemed to beg him to be.

Jake kicked back the last of the bourbon and stumbled for the stairs. Mason would turn off the lights behind him and take care of his glass. The next evening Jake knew he would find the decanter filled, waiting on him when he got home from work and Jolene had left him downstairs in a huff for what he couldn't imagine this time. He'd deal with McGales first thing in the morning. He'd take the case straight to the Boss Chief.

In bed, Jake again had the dream that had come back to him now three nights in a row since the night Letitia Johnson had been lynched: in it, he led a screaming charge into the face of a faceless enemy waiting hidden behind a great stone wall that stretched before them for as far as they could see. But in this dream, instead of brushed Confederate gray, he found himself outfitted in his old grass-stained red-and-blue Ole Miss Rebels uniform—number 7 on his chest. Instead of a saber in his left hand, he held a football cocked to throw. The dream began with Jake leading a well-ordered march toward the wall. The men behind him remained close-ranked at first, but as they drew closer, in sight of separate rocks, the distinct reds and yellows and grays and browns of fieldstones, they began to jog, and the lines thinned out. When the waves of men had jogged within range of the bristling muskets, close enough now to see the chinks in the rocks, faces squinted, tersely white, aiming, Jake gave the order, tucking the ball, and they began to run, charge, letting go the howl of the Rebel yell. In these dreams Jake ran as fast as he'd ever run in his life. His men tried to keep close behind him, but he was faster and soon he was far out in front, racing. When the hail of bullets from behind the wall was unleashed, he was the first man to meet them.

He woke sitting straight up in bed to the realization that he'd been killed—looked up to see his left arm rigid over his head. He glanced around the dark bedroom, the cherry hutch, his wife Jolene's dresser with the white doily spread neatly over the top, and the moonlit green wingback chair, the lace curtains hanging straight down, no breeze. Jolene lay with her back turned beside him, her bare shoulders and arm showing snow whiter than the ivory shimmer of her silk nightgown. He listened for Jakey and Lee. His boys lay silent, sleeping peacefully, undisturbed, safe in their beds at the other end of the hall—as they'd been when he'd stopped in to check on them on his way to bed himself.

Exhausted, sweating, and dry-mouthed, his head pounding from the bourbon he'd drunk, Jake eased back on the pillow beside his wife feeling as if he really had raced to give his life for the third night in a row in a final futile charge at that wall.

chapter four

JAKE CAME TO the breakfast table the following morning nursing the nick he'd given himself using the shaking blade of the stropped straight razor. The blot of paper soaked red and dripped. He licked it and plastered it to the cut on his neck again. Jolene had already assumed her chair at the end of the long mahogany table, sitting straight up with her hands in her lap, waiting on him before she asked Calpurnia to serve the meal.

For breakfast, Jolene wore a willowy green dress and the strand of pearls he'd given her for their first anniversary. She could've been dressed for Easter Services at church. A Presbyterian, Jolene never missed a Sunday service, towing Jake and the boys along to sit with her in the pew, but today was only Tuesday. His Orange Bowl queen dressed like this every day of the week, even when she never left the house. And most days she never had occasion to leave the house. Parchman Farm remained largely self-sufficient. It had its own sawmill, a brickyard, a slaughterhouse, gardens, a vegetable canning plant, and two cotton gins, even its own railroad depot to bring in visitors—the wives and girlfriends and husbands and boyfriends of the prisoners for their sanctioned Sunday visits. Ruleton, twelve miles south, with its bank and grocery stores, and row of shops on Main Street, was the closest town. To keep up with the season's latest fashions, Jolene made quarterly trips to Memphis, where she stayed at the Peabody Hotel. Everybody from the Delta on up to Memphis knew who Boss Chief was and wherever she went she was afforded special treatment. Though she would have portrayed herself differently even five years ago—certainly ten, when Jake was at the height of his football fame—nowadays everybody knew who Mrs. Jake Lemaster was because she was sure to tell them: She was Boss Chief's son's wife.

Jake reached out and ruffled little Jakey's wet-combed hair and nipped Lee's ear between his thumb and first finger. "Daddy!" The boys ducked and tried to wrestle his left hand, but he snatched it back from them.

"Watch out now! Watch out! You don't know who you messing with! It's that one-armed man!"

"Jake!" Jolene said, her face tight. He could see the powder touched with rouge on her cheeks. She sat poised prettily perfect as any china doll he'd ever seen. It seemed to Jake a shame. She hadn't always been like this—so fragilely beautiful, only to be looked at, not touched. Green-eyed and svelte with a bouffant of honey-colored hair and sassy to boot, Jolene Ina Anderson had been the number one attraction on her float at the bowl parade before the big game, and for Jake she'd been the prize to top off the team's championship bid. Jolene was not a virgin when they became engaged, nor did she pretend to wish to always remain one like many of the other sugar-coated Southern girls Jake had dated.

By now, his wife of ten years had long since perfected playing the part of an attractive wealthy white Presbyterian woman—a member of the Daughters of the Confederacy, the Altar Guild, and the Ruleton Garden Club—but that wasn't the way Jolene had been raised. Her uncle and his wife had been croppers and she'd grown up absorbed into their brood of ten kids on their hardscrabble little forty-acre farm in Alligator, Mississippi. She onced joked that her uncle worked like a mule because they were too poor to own a real one. She'd worked hard for the scholarship she'd earned to go to Ole Miss and she'd worked even harder to make up for the social graces she felt she lacked growing up. She'd accepted a bid at Chi O and become the jewel in the crown of the glee club, class secretary, and coed student adviser to the president of the university and its board of directors, a white-skirted and blue-and-red-lettered cheerleader. That she became the belle of Oxford—without the benefit of being part of the Delta's designated debutante crowd—had been her greatest victory, and she used it to step up from campus to statewide fame as the third runner-up in the Magnolia State's contest to send a beauty to the Miss America Pageant in 1933.

In those early days Jolene's forwardness and carnal knowledge had excited Jake beyond reason, and there were moments now when he thought with some bitterness that must have been the *reason* he'd married her. These days they made love once a month, in a good year. Her disappointment in him manifested itself in their every interaction. To be fair, Jake guessed he had failed Jolene. When they'd married, her determination to succeed had matched his will to win. They no longer seemed to share the same social desires. But she was the mother of his two sons, which was a fact that no matter what else he felt nowadays about their relationship he simply could not escape.

"Morning, dear," he said and bent to kiss Jolene on her turned cheek.

"What in heaven's name did you do to your face? Now don't get that blood on me."

"I'm bleeding like a stuck pig. I damn near cut my head clean off."

"Jake. Please. You know I won't tolerate vulgarity at the table."

Jake pulled back his chair and sat. He tucked his napkin in the neck of his uniform. He winked across the table at Lee and picked up his fork.

"You're worse than the boys. Truly."

Jake set down his fork. His wife glared at him before she

lowered her head. The boys dipped their chins, but peeked back up at him. He winked at both boys.

"Dear Lord," his wife began. "We thank You for this day and for these and all our bounteous blessings. We thank You for this food, which You have given us. And we pray that You will help us think of others today as we think of ourselves. In Jesus Christ's name we pray. Amen."

"Amen," the boys echoed.

With that cue, the swinging doors to the big kitchen parted and their house girl, Calpurnia, dressed in an iron-stiff starched white dress, who was six feet tall and just shy of matching Jake eye to eye, bustled in with their food on a silver tray, followed by Mason. Calpurnia and Mason worked solely for Miss Jolene. They performed her bidding the livelong day, "sentenced" to her express command and discretion. Jolene held them to such a schedule of dusting and mopping that it was no wonder Second Home remained immaculate—the giant old house never had a chance to get dirty, no matter the dust from the parching dry outside that constantly floated in through the screens. When Jolene tinkled the little bell on her nightstand, Calpurnia appeared immediately as if materialized by that silvery sound. In her three years on Parchman Farm, Calpurnia had twice tried to turn this ability to suddenly appear into a disappearing act. Though initially sent to Parchman Farm to serve a mere six-month term for vagrancy, upon being returned she'd had the term of her sentence doubled and then quadrupled. Each morning that he came down and saw her in the stiff white dress, Jake felt surprised. Nearly three months had gone by since her last escape attempt. He figured she was about due to make another break for it.

All through breakfast Mason hovered just over Jake's shoulder, stepping up to heat his coffee before he could drain the steaming cup halfway down, and when they'd finished eating, Calpurnia reappeared to help clear off the plates.

"Will that be all, ma'am?"

"That will be fine, Cal," his wife said. "Oh, maybe I will have one more of those little muffins."

"Yes'm."

Jake didn't wait for Mason to take his plate. He glanced at his watch. It was nearly 8:00. His sergeant, Joe Booker, had the odious responsibility of hustling the gunmen out of their bunks at the sound of the steam whistle at 4:30 A.M. After feeding them a breakfast of hardtack biscuits slathered with syrup, he and the trusties loaded them into the cotton trucks. They'd been hard at work on the road since 6:00, but Jake still had to speak with Boss Chief, who would now be in his office.

Jolene pointed to the spot on her cheek where he could kiss her safely without smudging her makeup. "We're counting on you to be here for dinner at twelve thirty, aren't we, boys? Now, please, Jake, let's not have a repetition of yesterday's debacle."

Mason brought him his hat and fixed him with the left-handed brown leather holster while Jake held his arm away from his side. He tied the strap around Jake's thigh to keep the pistol from jouncing. "Boys, I was thinking maybe we'd go down to the bayou, do a little fishing this evening. Catch a perch or bluegill or two. Maybe Joe Booker and his boys'll want to go, too? How's that sound to you?"

The boys were still sitting at the table. They had yet to be excused. They glanced at Jolene, waiting to see if she said no. "Yes, sir." And despite the control Jolene had haltered them with, both Jakey and Lee beamed.

"No hats in the house!"

Jake touched the brim to the boys and walked back through the kitchen and out the back door, where Mason had left the dusty boots he'd kicked off the night before setting side by side, gleaming again.

ON HIS WAY to see Boss Chief, Jake decided to stop in at the infirmary and see for himself what Bigger had done to Alley Leech—such firsthand information might prove useful in swaying his daddy to his point of view. The infirmary resembled most of the other cages at Parchman Farm, a long, white painted wooden barrack—the only difference that the windows were simply screened. They were not barred. It was one of the peculiarities of a place like Parchman that no prisoner who had been sent to the infirmary for the treatment of an ailment had ever tried to escape. Of course, Jake thought, more to the point might have been the fact that a prisoner had to be nearly dead to get off work to be sent to the infirmary in the first place. The likely step after their departure from the screened building at Front Camp would be a ride in the back of the wagon to the prison's cemetery.

Jake stepped up loudly on the boxed wooden stairs and yanked the screen door, trying to slip in quickly without letting inside any more flies.

"Morning, Mirabel."

Nurse Hankins carried a tray of pills and medicines in her hands, but she paused in passing to glance back at him. She wore plain black-frame glasses and a starched white uniform with white stockings, a perfectly proper white nurse's cap.

Without so much as a greeting, she turned back to her duties.

Jake grinned. Mirabel Hankins was one tough old bird.

In all his years at Parchman, Jake had only seen Nurse Hankins without that hat properly pinned in her hair two or three times. She wore it like a crown she deserved, and she ruled her infirmary with an iron fist. In her thirty-seven years on the job at Parchman, she'd seen it all, from a raging black-plague-like epidemic of yellow fever that had wiped out over a hundred prisoners, to the killing curse of smallpox and bouts of malaria, as well as the common gun wounds and knifings, gouged eyes, broken bones and shattered teeth, stoved fingers, and hoed-off toes. From what Jake had seen, Nurse Hankins seemed every bit as knowledgeable in practical medical procedures as old scaly-armed, tortoiselike Doc Evans, who stopped in at Parchman twice a week, on Mondays and Thursdays, unless he was called in for an emergency as Jake suspected he had been last night.

Nurse Hankins also served as Parchman's resident dentist. She had become expert at the yanking of teeth—the unlikely size of her man-haired forearms proved she had the grip to do the job.

The two gunmen who worked for Nurse Hankins as her assistants pulled open the screen door carrying stacks of bleached sheets from the laundry. Jake stepped aside to let them pass.

"Mornin', Cap'n."

Jake scanned the beds on this side of the dormitory, where the white male prisoners were housed. Three of the fifteen beds lay filled. The convicts watched Jake like nocturnal animals, their eyes big with seeing and filled a little with fear, swimming up out of the hollows of their faces, worried about why he was there and what might happen to them next. Jake nodded to them to try to set them at ease.

"Alley Leech brought in last night?" he asked Nurse Hankins.

"He's right there in the back, Mr. Lemaster," she answered as she bent over the first of the sick prisoners. "Behind the curtain."

Jake walked the painted planks to the back of the building. Behind the curtain that separated the regular white convicts from the trusties and sergeants, Alley Leech stretched boy-skinny under a single sheet. His naked chest had been bandaged in a Union Jack flaglike crisscrossing mess of white surgical tape. His arms and hands were bandaged, too, no doubt from where he'd been slashed trying to protect himself. A shank! Good God, it looked more like Bigger had taken the hacking slash of a two-foot-long machete blade to him. Alley's face drooped slacked, asleep. But he lay so still it might well have been that he had indeed been killed. The loss of blood he'd suffered had left Alley grub whiter than he usually looked, even albino-like—if he'd have opened his eyes Jake would have expected to see that his pupils were pink. In fact, he looked like some form of sharp-faced rodent—not like a white lab rat exactly, that would've been unfair to rats, but a mix maybe between a kept rat and something wilder, a fledgling badger maybe. His long, tobacco-smoke-yellow hair hung down about his hollowed face, while straw-yellow hairs sprouted on his chin, sticking straight out stubble-stiff as a whisk broom. Jake thought he should feel sorry for the man, but he couldn't stop the thought that came to him: Alley Leech was ugly as sin.

Jake turned to Nurse Hankins, who had parted the curtain behind him.

"Doc Evans still here?" Jake asked quietly.

"You just missed him."

"How many stitches he give him?"

"Forty-three just across his chest. Came within a hair of his jugular. Dr. Evans says it's a miracle he's alive. The wonder is he didn't bleed to death before they rushed him here from Camp Five. And there's no need to whisper. He's been injected with enough morphine to fell a horse."

Alley Leech twitched troubled in his sleep as if he were trying to raise his arms again before the onslaught of Bigger's blade. He groaned and collapsed back into the dead rest of a too-still sleep again.

"You think he's going to live?"

Nurse Hankins bent and checked Alley's pulse. She looked at her watch matter-of-factly, counting silently. She dropped his wrist. "I knew Alley Leech before he arrived at Parchman, Mr. Lemaster. My people are from Ita Bena, too. My professional opinion is that he'll live, more than likely. My personal opinion of Alley Leech is that he's way too mean to die."

Nurse Hankins looked at him then. Jake had known Mirabel for years—as a boy he'd been scared to death of her, believed her a witch, and he'd raced past the infirmary just to feel the heart-thumping rise of fear—but for the first time, Jake recognized that old and tough as she looked on the outside, behind her glasses she had a younger woman's eyes. He noticed that they were hazel.

"What about the man who cut him, this man Bigger? McGales's sergeant, Shepherd, said they fixed him up good. McGales bring him by, too?"

"He wasn't brought here."

Jake glanced at his watch. Bigger had been in the box now for at least two hours, but the test of real heat was still to come. "He's been put in the box for the day for what he did to Alley Leech."

"Well," Nurse Hankins said and turned abruptly away from Jake. She bent to straighten the sheet. "If he's left in that box for an entire day I'll see him yet, one way or another, won't I?"

Jake settled his hat to go. "If Mr. Leech here dies I'd appreciate it if you'd send word to me straightaway. If he dies and Bigger somehow does survive that box I don't want this thing to get out of hand any more than it already has." And then he added, almost as an afterthought, "I mean after what happened to Letitia Johnson and all."

Nurse Hankins didn't respond. She stepped away from Alley's bed and yanked the curtain open for Jake to leave. "I'll try to keep it in mind that you don't want to let things get any more out of hand, Mr. Lemaster."

Jake slapped out of the infirmary and cut diagonally across the grassy quad of Front Camp toward the wide steps and wraparound porch of First Home. It didn't seem possible that First Home could be more immaculate than Second Home, but it was, for a fact—something about the great old Victorian-style mansion always being scraped or painted or swept or polished or repaired or built new. Jake stepped past a convict prying up a perfectly fine-looking plank to replace on the front porch and pulled the screen door to meet another gunman pushing a broom across the cleanswept floor of the entranceway.

When Jake stepped inside, his daddy's secretary, a young woman by the name of Betsy Reed, turned her brown eyes up at him from where she sat behind her desk set in the middle of the wide entranceway that doubled as Parchman Farm's administrative front office. Dressed in a severe black skirt and a crisp white blouse, her dark hair swept up in a bun, looking at him from behind the cat-eyed glasses she wore, Jake recognized that Betsy could be seen as attractive in a kind of deliberate, rather-ordinary, no-nonsense, and straight-backed sort of way. She'd married Van Reed, the blocky coach of the Ruleton

Cougars high school football team, who every time he ran into Jake pumped his hand enthusiastically, telling him again what an honor it was to meet Red Lemaster. Betsy had married Van earlier that summer, but she'd worked for Boss Chief since she'd graduated from McCall's Secretarial School in Tupelo three years before. Over that record-breaking length of time she had proven over and over again that she had the fortitude as well as the feminine wiles necessary to negotiate a position at the prison that had left a long list of Boss Chief's previous secretaries weeping hysterically as if they'd been keelhauled in his rather formidable wake.

Betsy turned from Jake and glanced significantly at the grandfather clock. Her eyebrows arched.

Jake removed his hat. "He's expecting me?"

"He said to tell you he wants to see you first thing, Mr. Jake—if not sooner."

Jake rapped on his daddy's double doors and waited. The superintendent's office had once been the sizable sitting room of the plantation home. There was no answer.

Jake glanced back at Betsy.

She nodded.

Jake reached down and turned the brass handle.

Boss Chief stood before one of the wide windows that overlooked Front Camp, shouldering back the light. Boss Chief was a good six feet four inches tall and as of this past fall, when, as a joke, he'd stepped up on the cattle scale at the Avery's Feed, weighed 278 pounds—a solid 83 pounds heavier than Jake, who'd weighed 195 in his best shape during the height of his playing days. His daddy wore the uniform he always wore in his role as the superintendent of Mississippi's largest state prison, a gray summer-weight worsted wool suit and black bolo string tie, clasped by a sterling silver rattlesnake with jade green eyes, a gift from one of the parade of dignitaries— wardens from other countries and states, as well as politicians from far and near—who visited Parchman to marvel at the way "the

Farm" worked. Boss Chief's white shirts were made of prized Egyptian cloth cotton and tailored to thirty-seven inches at the cuff, though the inseam on his trousers was a mere thirty-two inches— Jake knew this because he was the person Boss Chief entrusted with the care of carrying his pinned suits and trousers back and forth from his tailor's in Ruleton. Boss Chief gained all of his height from the hips and shoulders on up. His legs bowed squat and thick as if bending under the weight of his huge upper body, his feet wide as paddles to support him. He had a massive head, granite-like in its sculpted magnificence, a broad nose and wide cheeks, a low, brooding forehead, and an eagle's eyes, the oddest color of amber. His once-black hair, which he slicked straight back from the brow, had streaked dramatically with white in the past few years. Jake didn't know if women found his daddy exactly hand-some. Perhaps it was his commanding size and distinct features that proclaimed the raw power of the man that attracted them. Certainly Boss Chief was never at a loss for what he indelicately called "poontang."

It was simply another part of the story that bound Boss Chief and Jake tightly together as father and son that Jake's mother had died giving birth to him thirty-three years before. Catherine McCrae had been the only woman Boss Chief had ever loved enough to marry, and Jake had grown up lamenting the fact that he'd never known her. As a boy, he could only guess who she'd been at all by sneaking into his daddy's bedroom on the second floor to take out of his top drawer the sepia-yellowed photographs of her that Boss Chief trea-sured so much he would not give up a single one of them for his son to keep as his own. It was in those pictures that Jake had first glimpsed a likeness and so had known for certain that he hadn't been picked up floating in the bulrushes that bordered the bayou or ar-rived all bundled up, deposited at First Home by a stork.

The photographs revealed that while Jake may have been his daddy's boy, he was undoubtedly his mama's son. It was his mother, as a McCrae, who had given him his red hair and sky-blue eyes. In another studio photograph where she stood beside his daddy, wearing a close-fitting formal black dress, his shape appeared to be her pleasing shape, in a man's form—with long legs and wide shoulders, a slim waist. On his daddy's shoulder rested a smaller copy of his own delicately boned hand, and his mother's smile had turned out to be Jake's smile. They both had the same thin, aquiline nose. The bridge of her nose and her cheeks were also lightly freckled. At times, growing up, Jake had caught his daddy staring at him with those eagle's eyes of his, brooding. One night late, when Jake had stopped by the big house muddy and tired out from trailing the hounds with Quirt Hanson to give his father the news that they'd caught the escapee they'd been hot after all day, Boss Chief had waved the importance of the information away as if to say, *Of course.* He'd been dressed in a long white nightshirt, brooding over a glass of Canadian scotch in his hand, and he'd said, suddenly, apropos of nothing, "Your mother was the most beautiful and intelligent woman I ever met. I might even've been a different man with her at my side. She fucked me over when she died. I'll never forgive you for it, boy."

That had been when Jake was twenty-three—his first year back home on the job.

That night Jake had stood before his father, who lost himself once again in contemplation of the whiskey, and then he'd let himself out, feeling shaken at the yellow-eyed malevolence leveled at him in his father's gaze. What Jake still couldn't fathom was why, if his father hated him so much, he'd tempted him to return to Parchman Farm. Some days he believed his daddy had wanted him to come back simply so that he could continue to punish him for being born and taking his wife from him. Jake had never told anyone that the day of the accident when he was five—the day he'd lost his right hand and forearm when that tractor lurched forward and he'd lost his balance and been thrown off the back—that, in the instant before Boss Chief let off the clutch, his daddy had turned and looked straight at him with those eyes of his. Then the tractor jumped.

Now, standing before the big windows, Boss Chief swiveled his great streaked mane from the goings-on in the yard beyond, offering him his strong profile. "You ain't getting enough poontang at home, is that it, Jake? That pretty little wife of yours not puttin' out for you like she used to?"

Jake waited with his hat in hand. He had long since learned to ignore his daddy's barnyard crudities when it came to matters of the flesh with the opposite sex. Jolene had never received an exemption from such references, and so Jake stood his ground, not as shocked by his father's way of talking to him about his sexual relationship with his wife as he was unsure where his daddy was leading him with the question. Betsy had said Boss Chief wished to see him "first thing." Naturally he'd expected to be asked about Alley Leech. Jake was no lawyer. But he'd do what he could. He'd come to plead for Bigger's life.

Boss Chief turned all the way around to face him. "I would think maybe she's a little old for you, son. Not that she's got a bad shape on her—for a mature woman. I can tell you I took a good look when she came up in here, checking her out for my own self. A full ripe woman like that can surprise you. Voluptuousness is a virtue of age, as is experience, son. You can't underestimate the power of experience. Appetite for the act is another matter. Once they go through their time their blood can cool. But there's something about her. Maybe it's all that yellow hair. Hair tells. And a woman's hips. She's got good hips on her. Big enough tits."

Jake shrugged. "What are we talking about?"

"What!" Boss Chief snorted. "It's *who*. As if," he said. "Why, you are a fox aren't you, Red? That visitin' woman from the welfare. I hear you two whiled away an entire morning talkin' yesterday when she passed by. I wonder what you two could've possibly had to say to each other. You talkin' her up, Jake? Tell me that's it, son. Because if that ain't it, then it has to be something else. What could that something else be, Jake? That's the mystery. You tell me."

Jake had learned long ago never to lie to his daddy. Boss Chief had eyes and ears all over Hushpuckashaw County. When it came to knowledge about the goings-on at Parchman Farm, he seemed unnervingly omniscient. Still Jake felt himself bristle at the insinuation in a way that he hadn't when his daddy had talked about his sexual relations with his wife.

"We were working on the road and she couldn't get by. She asked to pass. I know you don't believe in the work the welfare does, Daddy. Did you want me to keep the highway barricaded so she couldn't get up this way and waste your tax money?"

Boss Chief stared at him. "You sassin' me, boy?" Jake did not look away. "You're takin' this a little too personal, aren't you, son? That makes me even more worried about you than I already am, Jake. I hear things."

Boss Chief turned back to the window, his meaty hands clasped behind his back.

"What I hear is that you lay up in the cab of that cotton truck napping all day. I hear you're drinking up half a decanter of bourbon 'bout near every night. I hear Jolene's got your balls in a vise over everything from dirty boots to missing dinner. I hear that niggrah Bigger cut Alley Leech last night. I hear Letitia Johnson had a daughter and that welfare woman you were busy talkin' up found her out to her mama's place and took her home with her back to Eureka. And that ain't all I hear. I hear other things, too."

It was Jake's turn: "Like 'an eye for an eye, a tooth for a tooth.'"

His daddy glanced quickly back back at him. "Hmmpf." He laughed. "Don't be a simpleminded moralist. You sound like a goddamn Baptist, Jake. That's a black-and-white Calvin McGales way of thinking. Naw, that ain't what else I hear. I hear there's important folk think we ain't done with this one yet quite. It's the principle of the thing. The rule, if you will."

Jake quit fidgeting with his hat. "Rule as in the Rules?" The thought stopped him cold. "What are you saying? You mean Letitia Johnson didn't drown that baby girl? Then who?" Jake met his daddy's yellow eyes. He couldn't imagine. He shrugged. "Sissy?" he tried—as far off the mark as he could think to go. Boss Chief held his gaze. He did not flinch. Jake felt the blow. He'd known Sissy Rule his entire life. They were the same age, and the potential for a union between the two of them—and the two families—had been the talk of Delta society at the time Sissy made her debut. Jake and Sissy had been an item for almost a year, and for a time things had gotten hot and heavy between them. They'd tell her parents they were off to the movies and then, unchaperoned, make straight for the turn rows along the river or park Boss Chief's car in the high grass that hid the bayou. Jake imagined the Sissy he knew again. She was slight, beautiful, fair, with auburn curls, a bit flighty—"high-strung" people called her. The image of her holding her baby girl, Dorothy, underwater until she bubbled out of breath would not come. It was far easier to imagine that her mammy, Letitia Johnson—whom Jake had never met—had done it. Startlingly horrific as that thought was, he found he could believe that Letitia Johnson had committed such an act, even if he disagreed with the vigilantism of the mob. But it had never even crossed his mind that she hadn't done it. The realization that he'd never even considered the possibility of her innocence shocked him almost as much as the fact that Sissy could be guilty of drowning her own child.

"I wonder if Sissy Rule Tisdale came to stay with us if maybe Old Robert Rule or maybe her husband, Clyde Tisdale, at the bank would donate a third home in Front Camp to keep her comfortable for life." That made Boss Chief smile. Boss Chief rolled back the leather chair from behind his table-sized desk and sat. He leaned forward and clasped his hands before him, giving Jake his full attention.

"I got ears and eyes all over, but you're my right-hand man, Jake. You see that welfare woman again I want you to find out where she places that girl. Once we know where she is all we have to do is throw out the bait. The rednecks'll do the rest. I'm sure you heard about McGales. He's been recruiting heavy from the camps. He'll jump at the chance to go after that girl. An eye for an eye and a tooth for a tooth! Fanning the hate ain't nobody got time to think this thing out straight. Fact is that most white folks are just like you, Jake—they don't really want to know the truth."

Sometimes talking to—or, rather, listening to—Boss Chief was too much for Jake. Like trying to stare into the sun, hearing him he glimpsed infernal truths that left black spots before his eyes. Dazed, Jake turned to go.

"One more thing. I want that stretch of highway combed and graded up by Friday this week, hear? You're costing me money, Jake. It's July and there's choppin' to do. I need all my lines back in the fields. Wake up, Jake. Get your ass out of the truck and fill a pothole for a change. Make it happen. I damn sure didn't make this place what it is sitting behind no desk or in no truck with my feet hangin' out the window hiding from the sun."

As if he'd been slapped, Jake suddenly remembered why he'd come. He turned back to face his father. "Truth is I'm shorthanded," he ventured. "I could use that man Bigger from Camp Five. I want McGales to give him up."

Boss Chief raised his chin. "He cut a white man, a sergeant. Can't stand for that. There's a balance to things. He's got to be punished."

"Better to make an example of him then where the other gunmen can see him suffer. Put him on the road with me. I just come from visiting Alley Leech, and Mirabel Hankins assures me he can't die. But Bigger's going to die in that box, sure enough—especially after the way I hear they beat him up. Strong as he is, no man can stand a whole day in the box. You know it as well as McGales and me. He aims to kill him."

Boss Chief thought about that carefully, eyeing Jake. "I don't like to get between a captain and his job, you know that. I like to give my captains as much autonomy running their camps as possible. That's what makes this system work." He leaned forward on his elbows. "But it's your authority, son. You're the number two man on Parchman Farm. You oversee the overseers. One day you got to take over this place yourself, and you might as well learn about taking responsibility for such decisions now. But, Jake, you got to know you ain't winnin' that big niggrah much. He might end up cursin' you for takin' 'im out of the box and not lettin' him go on and die and get this over with, not McGales for puttin' him in it. And McGales won't exactly be thankin' you neither—you know that, don't you? You'll be goin' directly against the authority of his command as the captain of Camp Five. I wouldn't take makin' enemies with him too lightly either. McGales may seem like a ludicrous figure to you and me, Jake, but he's a fanatic and don't you forget it. Fanatics like McGales ain't got a proper sense of scope. They only care to understand their own warped view of seeing things. They'll do anything to make that vision come true. But that Bigger is a specimen, for a fact. It's your call. He just got here and I agree it seems a shame to waste 'im. Unless Alley Leech dies, that is. Then we got no choice."

Boss Chief rocked back in his chair, hands clasped in his lap, and put one heel and then the other up on the edge of the desk.

"So, it's your decision, Jake. But let me give you a little *advice*, 'fore you go off half-cocked. Here's what you do: You leave Bigger in the box until after lunch—one o'clock—that'll give him six hours in there to think hard about ever cuttin' a white man again. You got to show you're not going soft. This is the price of his life.

"If you free him, then no matter how bad a shape you find him in he goes straight to work on the road without being taken to the infirmary. He gets no water and no lunch. He swings a pick and moves his own dirt at the head of the line for the rest of the week. He wears irons on both legs and manacles on his wrists. If he falls out in the heat, nobody—and I mean nobody, Jake—touches him. Leave him on the side of the road. That's the deal—I figure it gives that Bigger as least as good a chance at surviving as he had in that box—but it's your call. You think about it, son. It may make no dif-ference a'tall in the end, and you'll have to deal with McGales on your own. Don't come cryin' to me, Jake."

"Yes, sir, Boss Chief."

Jake topped his hat to go and stepped out the door, catching Betsy behind her desk peering closely into a compact as she powdered her nose. When she saw Jake, she quickly snapped the case closed, the model of efficiency again, sitting bolt upright in her chair, absorbed in her work, her cheeks blushing rouge.

"Mrs. Reed," he heard his father call. "Could I see you in here a moment, please."

Jake stepped out onto the porch without letting himself glance back, angling his hat against the glare.

chapter five

THE NEWS FROM Camp 5 had already been passed down the length of the line by the time Jake arrived at work on the road that morning. The word that made its way back up the line to him through his sergeant, Joe Booker, was that Letitia Johnson had been Bigger's woman. Bigger had been Letitia Johnson's man! Now Jake understood why he'd cut Alley Leech, talking the way he had about what had happened to her. Alley Leech was lucky to be alive.

> One! . . . *he's a gitten' de leather,*
> Two! . . . *he don't know no better,*
> Three! . . . *cry niggah, stick yo' finger in yo' eye,*
> Four! . . . *niggah thought he had a knife,*
> Five! . . . *got hit off 'n his visitin' wife,*
> Six! . . . *now he'll git time for life,*
> Seven! . . . *lay it on trusty man!*
> Eight! . . . *wham! wham! He gotta wuk tomorra,*
> Nine! . . . *he gotta chop cotton in de sun,*
> Ten! . . . *dat's all, trusty men, you's done.*

After hearing that Bigger had been given an entire day in the box, not one of the gunmen seemed to want to test his luck by slacking off. They kept their heads down and the count of the chant up. And with Jake out of the truck striding up and down the dusty highway, dust from the flurry of their picks and shovels continued to rise. They managed to break up and then grade level and smooth off two hundred yards of the baked concrete-hard gravel road before lunch— the most they'd done at a stretch in weeks.

Jake walked over to where his sergeant had taken up a wide, arms-crossed stance in the middle of the road, keeping careful watch over the gunmen as they worked to comb up the shoulders. Nearly all of the gunmen who were chosen as trusties or assistant sergeants on Parchman Farm were serving life sentences for murder, and Joe Booker had been a cage boss and a trusty and then an assistant ser-geant. A professional boxer, he'd killed a man in a bare-knuckle fight. At the time, Joe Booker had been boxing his way across the Delta, taking on all comers. He'd never lost a bout—not officially— until the Saturday night when he'd pummeled his challenger, a thick mulatto man from Yazoo City, to death and been arrested for it. Whenever one of the white sergeants asked Joe about that night, he'd give a halfhearted shrug. It didn't mean a thing to him; it hadn't been personal. He hadn't even known the man. He'd never laid eyes on him before that night in the makeshift ring. But the fights had been unsanctioned, illegal to begin with—simply country carnival entertainment—and the judge had made no distinction between the harm Joe Booker had done with his fists to earn a living and the bru-tal kill-'em-with-my-bare-hands sort of murderer he'd become used to sentencing people to life at the state prison for. Twenty years after he'd come to Parchman as a twenty-year-old man, Joe Booker had received a pardon from the governor. Forty by then with half his lifetime at Parchman Farm under his belt, he'd remained at the prison as a "free man" who could come and go at will. He'd accepted the sergeant's position that Boss Chief had offered him—the only Negro full sergeant on Parchman Farm.

As a sergeant, he'd been given his own cottage on the place to live in, and he had his own family now. Joe Booker's living on the grounds of Camp 1 allowed Jake to live in Second Home in Front Camp and to take on other responsibilities, such as the program in public works and the administrating of the other captains in the fifteen camps. Jake needed an inside man like Joe Booker—he was the sort of center he could run the ball behind—and Jake trusted him completely. And because of Sergeant Joe Booker Camp 1 ran the most smoothly of all the camps with the least amount of brutality. It wasn't that Joe Booker wouldn't resort to Black Annie if he had to, but he'd lived by his fists all his life and so rarely had to stoop to the strop of the whip. All the gunmen knew about "Cap'n Bukka." If a gunman really got out of line, Joe Booker might choose to go a few "practice" rounds with him. There wasn't a man in camp yet who'd been able to stay in the ring with him to begin the third round.

Jake leaned his hand on the butt of his pistol and squinted at the sun, straight up and down over them. "Why don't we go ahead knock off for lunch?"

"Yes, suh, Mr. Jake." Joe Booker gave the order and a trusty yelled: "Leaves your tools where they lays!"

"All right now," the trusties started in, rifles raised—forming the line to move out. Under the cover of the trusty shooters, the manacled gunmen shuffled fifty yards and dropped under the spreading shade of a single gnarled pecan—that little spot of cool worth the extra work of the walk. Jake had ordered the cook to set up his pot there, the water cart in tow. But some of the men lay still, too hot and tired even to line up for one of the day's three allotted drinks. Even in the shade it must have been more than 90 degrees. Out on the open road the temperature had soared to 101.

Jake wondered if Bigger was still alive.

The cook rang his gong, sounding dinner.

The men groaned and cussed, clanked like ghosts called to Judgment as they rose out of the rest of their welcome graves in the shade to form into yet another line.

"I got a little business to attend to on the farm, Joe. I should be back later this afternoon," Jake told him, aware that in the past few weeks he'd taken to arriving on the road later and later for work each morning before leaving to go home for a sit-down dinner with Jolene and the boys at noon and taking an afternoon nap before returning to the line just in time to knock off for the day and heading home, where he knew the filled decanter awaited him. Boss Chief had been right about what he'd heard about his son, at least when it came to his performance on the job. He *was* costing them money. Jake had let this highway roads project fall inexcusably far behind schedule. Hell, he probably spent more time driving back and forth on the highway these days than he actually clocked in at work on it. Going back and forth certainly couldn't be worth the precious pass for the closely rationed gas and tires he raced through. If he'd been on straight rations, he would have been forced to stay in one place all day. But Jake couldn't seem to help himself. Lately he'd taken to watching his own behavior as if he were separate from it. He himself was curious to see what he thought he was up to.

Joe Booker absorbed the news of Jake's leaving the line again with a noncommittal nod, "Yes, suh." Joe Booker had never once asked Jake where he'd been—or where he was going. Certainly he would never think to chastise Boss Chief's son for shirking his share of their duties. Jake understood that it wasn't his place to; as far as Joe Booker was concerned, Jake Lemaster could sleep all morning in the cotton truck if that's what he chose to do. Still, they were friends, at least as close to a thing called "friends" as two men living and working so closely together in such unequal positions could be on Parchman Farm. But now Jake wanted Joe Booker to know what he was up to—that he wasn't just going home to a sit-down dinner and an hour in the hammock under the cool of the porch fan. It was somehow important to him that Joe Booker knew.

"I'm going for Bigger. He'll die if he's left in that box all day long."

Beads of perspiration stood out on Joe Booker's forehead. He swiped the sweat with the broad slab of his right hand, and Jake noticed again the brick-sized block of his fist. "That right, Mr. Jake?"

Joe Booker said. The Ping-Pong ball pop of his eyes always made him look as if he'd just been surprised. "Scuse me for sayin' it, Boss, but might be best for us all if he jes did go on and die in there if you know what I mean. No disrespec', suh."

Jake looked at his sergeant from behind his dark glasses, which turned the hard yellow sun blazing down on them into the welcome lie of a lake's cool blue. Jake respected Joe Booker and he trusted his judgment in all matters regarding life at the prison. Jake took what Joe Booker said into account—he knew what his sergeant said about leaving Bigger in the box might well be true. Boss Chief had warned him to think carefully about what he was getting himself into, too. He nodded. "We're going to finish this stretch of the job by the end of the week Friday. I want another two hundred yards before we knock off tonight. You can tell the men they'll get another drink of water when they give me another hundred yards. No rest till then. I plan on bringing Bigger back to help."

Joe Booker nodded at this new news, no more or less surprised looking than he had been before. "You the boss," he said.

AT THE FRONT gate of Parchman Farm, Jake waved his way past the armed trusties and drove by Second Home without slowing to stop in and tell his wife that he was going to have to miss dinner again. Jolene had a fundamentalist's belief in the righteousness of her ordered routine, and she brooked no challenge to her authority as first in command of their household, her domain. He imagined her behind the jalousies, peeking out to see where he could be, already angry that he was late. Hadn't she *told* him *again* just that morning? And, there was no use trying to deny it, not showing up for dinner in person at all was worse than being a little late. The table in the dining room would be laid out, linen tablecloth and fresh-cut flowers and all, and the boys would have been cleaned up, wearing knickers and button shirts and hard shoes, hair combed back neatly again from when he'd ruffled it rousing them at breakfast, and sitting up with their pink-scrubbed hands in their laps, waiting for him to arrive and their mama to offer up a blessing so that they could dig in. There was no way he could stop in and explain to Jolene what he was up to since he wasn't exactly certain himself. Hat in hand, standing just inside the back screen so that he wouldn't have to take off his road-grimed boots, Jake would have to bear the brunt of relating the bad news that he was skipping lunch for no better reason than he was working to try to save a Negro gunman's life. There were knives on the kitchen counters. Pots. Pans. Dishes. No telling what Jolene might throw—or what she might scream no matter who was listening if she got riled enough to say it, instantly transformed into the Alligator-raised hellcat he knew his wife to be, no matter how hard she tried to act the model of a lady nowadays.

Jake followed the grid of dirt roads that led him back to Camp 5, which lay at the geographical heart of Parchman Farm, and turned into the yard. Calvin McGales's trusties had marched the gunmen who made up his line into the fields at dawn. They wouldn't return until dark. The camp was all but deserted except for two gunmen who'd been left behind to tend to chores, busy now hoeing listlessly at the garden. He saw the tin box set out in the center of the yard. Jake waited for the dust to settle before he climbed out of the car. He saw Shepherd coming, stumping down the steps of the cage, and rubbing his eyes—the night man slept during the day unless he was needed.

"Help you, Boss?" Shepherd asked. Shepherd hauled himself across the yard to stand blinking before Jake.

The two gunmen in the garden took the opportunity to lean on their hoes.

"Captain McGales around?" Jake asked.

"De main boss man lyin' down a little in de house. He said no one s'posed to 'sturb 'im agin after last night. He need his sleep."

"I come to get Bigger."

Shepherd's eyes blinked rapidly at that, as if what Jake had said was bouncing around like a pinball launched up through the round oh of his mouth into the space between his ears. Finally the thought sparked a connection. The blinking stopped and the penny size of his eyes lit up, growing round as nickels. "I better get de cap'n!"

Jake watched Shepherd hustle off, gimping surprisingly fast now that he knew what was afoot.

Jake turned toward the box. His watch told him it was exactly 1:00. He was following Boss Chief's "advice." The sun gleamed over the heat-warped tin, making the metal look molten.

McGales came storming around the cage working hard at the baseball-sized chaw of tobacco wadding his cheek, hustling as hurriedly as if he'd been roused out of bed to answer the alarm of a fire, leaving Shepherd behind. The red thermal underwear top McGales wore for a nightshirt hung down to his knees, and he was barefoot. He hadn't bothered to take the few seconds necessary to pull on his pants and lace up his boots. He obviously hadn't shaved in three or four days. Jake had seen cartoon depictions of rednecks in the Northern papers—as if such caricatures could tell the truth about the peoples of their region—and he'd been offended by such representations of Southerners. But as McGales came chugging toward him, getting up a full head of steam, Jake couldn't help but think there *he* was—right down to the cud of tobacco. Boss Chief had called McGales a "ludicrous figure." To Jake, McGales seemed the very parody of a redneck—chaw-chewing, slight, hardscrabbled— his face tanned and deeply cragged from years of weather, the nape of his neck sun-spanked the color of a freshly butchered steak from bending over all day in the fields, and his graying hair cut so short Jake could see the red irritation of chigger bites on his skull.

But though he might've looked beat, McGales was not beaten. He had mean, bright, ice blue eyes, quick seeking as a ferret's, and his arms underneath that nightshirt, Jake knew, were sinewy strong, thin and blue-veined, the forearms bulging. The thumbnail on McGales's left hand had been permanently bashed black, his remaining fingers wired strangely askew as if already long beset with arthritis, ruined from hard manual labor—McGales liked to brag that he'd gone to picking cotton as good as a "full-growed man" since he was six. But it wasn't just McGales's appearance that portrayed him as a redneck; being a real redneck rooted deeper than that. McGales held to certain fundamental beliefs, which included the supremacy of the Protestant white race, with the tenacity of a hog-sized loggerhead snapping turtle. Once he got clamped around an idea you could lift him up by it and even beat him to death to get him off. McGales would not let go.

"You got no right! You got no right!" he hollered at Jake as he stormed up to get in his face. "This is *my* camp. *My* authority. You gitten your nose in bizness where it don't belong, Jake. Your daddy know you here? Or this your own big idea?"

Jake touched his sunglasses. He was a head taller than McGales. He spoke calmly down to him. "Bigger's no longer your concern, Calvin. You're to release him to me. I'm taking him to First Camp. He'll be out of your way. And don't worry, he's not getting off easy for cutting Alley Leech. I'll see that he's punished. But he's been in that box long enough. He's under *my* authority now."

McGales worked up his cheeks and spat hard. "The fuck."

Jake rested his hand on his pistol again. "Boss Chief says it's my call."

At that, McGales looked as if he might really go for his throat. He kept clenching and unclenching his fists. The blood vessels in his eyes looked as if they'd burst, seething red, and the jag of a single thick vein charged his forehead like a lightning bolt going to ground.

"You ain't heard the last of this. You best goddamn understand that, Jake Lemaster. Your daddy can't save you from everything. You know who I am."

With a last gathered spit of tobacco juice in the dust at Jake's feet, McGales turned and raged away, steaming past the gunmen in the garden, who began to hoe with real vigor, heads down.

"You two," Jake called to them and walked the other way across the dusty yard toward the box. "Shepherd," he said, ordering him to follow.

"Unlock the box."

Three clasps sealed the box. A thick chain ran through the two-inch clasps. Shepherd had the key to the lock on the ring jangling from his belt. Jake stood back and waited for him to work it. Standing in the yard under that bald and burning sun looking down at the blistering coffin, Jake wondered if he wasn't already too late. No sounds came from inside the box. He waited to see. The lock clicked and the chain slithered through and thunked into the dust.

Shepherd flipped down the clasps and creaked the lid open with a stick he found so that he wouldn't have to touch the metal with his bare hand.

The smell hit Jake first—piss and shit and the iron taste of blood and scorching flesh. Instinctively he raised his left arm and buried his nose in the crook, peering down.

"Gawd a'mighty," one of the gunmen said.

Bigger lay bunched in the box, his legs bent strangely akimbo to make him fit in the coffin that was far too small for him. He hadn't been attended to after the beating the trusties had given him and the purpling of bruises remained terrifically swollen and unbearably painful looking. His top lip had been slashed, showing the gap of the missing front tooth, his face cut, and his right eye blacked shut. His uniform had tinted red, the sweat-soaked cotton sponging up the blood. The manacles that bound his legs were linked to the handcuffs on his wrists, holding his arms down behind his back so that he was forced to lie on them. Steam rose from the body in the box. Bigger still hadn't moved. He stared blindly past them.

"He done dead," the other gunman said and swiped down his hat.

Jake reached out to touch Bigger's bull neck and snatched his hand back—his flesh was that hot—gone cooked from the inside out. Jake tried again, sliding his fingers down Bigger's throat until he found the deep-down bass-drum beat of his pulse.

"We got to cool him off. Let's get him up and into that trough."

The bathtub-sized rinse trough for the laundry stood under the shade of the trees. The dirty water hadn't been dumped, gone an algae green. The gunmen grabbed under Bigger's arms from either side of the casket. Shepherd pulled from the front and Jake cradled the back of Bigger's head so that it wouldn't hang down. He was just plain too huge to carry and he could not walk himself and so they had to drag him to the trough. Bigger's body sizzled when they slid him into the water, like a smithy's heated horseshoe being dunked.

Bigger groaned. He let out a moan and then he threw up, but there wasn't much, yellow bile.

"Get him some of that water from the well.

"Careful now," Jake said, "just a sip. Not all at once. Don't let him gulp it."

Jake stood while the gunmen dipped more water for him. Bigger was coming around. He wasn't going to die, though Jake wasn't exactly sure what he was going to do with him. Jake couldn't imagine how he was going to put him to work on the road that afternoon. What he needed was to be rushed straight to the infirmary—*immediately*—but Boss Chief had told him he couldn't take him there. Jake thought about that; he'd made his choice. He pushed back his hat and looked about. The yard stood empty. Shepherd had disappeared after he'd helped lift Bigger over the edge of the tub. Jake hadn't noticed him shuffle off. Calvin McGales was nowhere to be seen either. The silence that surrounded him had the sort of razor's edge to it that Jake had managed to cut himself with that morning. The sun continued to beat down, and it was only going to get hotter.

"Okay," Jake said to the two gunmen standing behind him. "Now help me get him out of there and fit him in the back of the car."

chapter six

SPRUCED AND COIFFED, her hair freshly washed and picked and newly plaited to make the right sort of impression on her family-to-be, Sally waited with her hands in her lap on the hard-back wooden chair across from Baby, who sat perched before her Remington typewriter, pecking out the paperwork she would need to file in order to officially find Sally a foster home. Even while Baby focused on the keys she didn't want to miss as she typed out the forms, she let her gaze slide back to Sally's wide-eyed watching out the window behind her.

The new County Welfare Office, constructed before the war, backed up against the train tracks that drew the clear boundary between the white and black halves of Eureka, and her small office, where she could interview her clients in private, looked over the depot. Baby had learned to ignore the intermittent roar of trains coming and going, huffing, the bells loudly clanging, and the porter's yelling, "All aboard!" Now, with Sally there to remind her of where she was, Baby glanced up at the screech of metal on metal—that long first slow pull, the couplers banging and then yanking, clanging tight, as the train chugged out of the station. Together they watched the individual faces framed inside the windows of the passenger cars blur as the train gained speed, sliding away.

"Where them folks headin' off to in such an all-fired rush like that?" Sally asked. It was the first she'd spoken all morning and there was wonder in her voice. They'd breakfasted with Claire and Jeana, Baby's girls chattering away, excited to have anyone stay with them, but Sally wolfed down two stacks of blueberry pancakes, and then kept her eyes down on her plate, hands in her lap. She hadn't even dared to speak to Ruthie, who lived in the cabin at the back edge of their lot and who cared for the girls during the summer days while Baby was at work. Jeana and Sally were the same age, and for her interviews, Baby had fitted out Sally in one of Jeana's school outfits, a light-blue gingham dress with a bow at the back and a simple white lace collar. BEST FOOT FORWARD: ALWAYS MAKE SURE A CLIENT LOOKS CLEAN AND NEAT read point number three on the director Mr. Brumsfield's "Points to Pay Attention to When Taking a Client to a Prospective Foster Family Home."

Baby smiled to encourage Sally's talking: "They're headed north through Ruleton and Parchman. That's the nine fifteen to Memphis." Baby looked at her. "Do you know where Memphis is?"

Sally shook her head. "No ma'am. I can't say I do. But I heard of it, I think."

"It's a city. Across the border. In the state of Tennessee."

"It must be some kinda place to want to get there as fast as that."

"It's a busy place all right," Baby said.

Sally thought about that. "Am I goin' on that train there to live? Is that why I'm here?"

"I hope we're going to find you a foster home right here in Hushpuckashaw County. As soon as I get this paperwork done, we'll take a drive. There are some families who'd like to meet you. Would you like to meet them?"

Sally continued to stare out the window. She shrugged, her eyes filling again.

Baby reached over and squeezed Sally's leg. "We're going to find you a good home, Sally," she said. "I'm not just going to drop you off with some family. You have to want to live with them, too. All right?"

Sally nodded, wiping her eyes with her arm. Baby handed her a tissue.

"I'm almost done here."

LETITIA JOHNSON read the name under PARENTS; the box MOTHER checked DECEASED in the choices to mark under it. Baby dabbed to cover the black X she'd struck; she'd managed to miss the box. She broke into a cold sweat. Baby glanced back through her name on the door: MRS. ALLEN stenciled backward on the scalloped sea-green glass. She reached quickly for the trash can underneath her desk, leaned over and retched into it, giving up little more than a splatter of coffee, which was all she'd been able to stomach that morning. She heaved again and then again, gagging. She kept her head down between her knees.

Sally was sitting straight up, gripping the arms of the chair. "Are you gonna die?" she asked.

Baby rummaged the purse underneath her chair for a hand-kerchief. She smiled greenly at Sally and sat back, patting her mouth. "I only managed to make it sound as if I am." She pressed the sweating palm of her hand against her clammy forehead. The fan blew directly on them. She scooted back her chair and stood to aim it to blow the sick smell out the open window.

"Forgive me," Baby said, returning to her seat. She released the form from the Remington and slid it inside Sally's folder and set the file on the right side of her desk, trapping it underneath the brick-heavy paperweight with the edict THESE MUST BE PAID.

Finding a foster home for a ward of the state wasn't the kind of work Baby could manage on the phone sitting behind her desk at the welfare—most of her clients didn't even have phones, not to mention electricity, or running water, or indoor plumbing. She and Sally would have to go on the road in an effort to find her a family.

They had a lot of territory to cover, and she'd hoped to get an early start. By 9:30, the mists of the morning would have already burned off. She fully expected another long, torrid day. While Sally sat patiently, Baby bustled about, gathering the other pertinent paperwork and the armload of the files on the families they'd visit.

"Ready?" she smiled.

"I reckon so. I can't think of no other place I gots to be today."

Gladys Pointdexter, another agent, rapped on Baby's office door. Baby could tell it was Gladys by the height of the silhouette she cast against the glass. Gladys remained the tallest woman Baby had ever seen. She appeared to be storking around on stilts. She had to have been at least six feet five inches tall and her face was so thin it appeared to be constantly in profile.

"Please, come in," Baby said.

Gladys ducked her head inside the door. Baby saw her sliver of a nose wrinkle involuntarily at the smell. She glanced at Sally and then at her. "Everybody feeling okay?"

"I think I may have caught a little stomach bug," Baby explained.

"Maybe you should go home and get some rest."

"That would be nice, but I'm afraid that wouldn't help. It's not that kind of bug."

Gladys looked sideways at her. Her eyebrows arched. "No. Oh, Baby. Say it's not so," she said. "And on top of this mess with you know who."

Gladys was Baby's confidante—the person she'd first told about Gabe and that Franks woman—and now the first person to know about her "predicament." She had as yet hardly dared admit the pregnancy to herself. At the confession, she felt her own eyes welling. Baby grabbed for the tissues on her desk. "I'm afraid so. And don't fret. I promise to come sob on your shoulder later. First we need to find Sally here a home."

"Of course. You poor dear." Gladys shook her head. "Mr. Brumsfield sent me down here to request you stop in to his office and see him before you go on the road this morning."

"All right." Baby set the files and paperwork on the edge of her desk. "Would you stay with Sally?"

"Both y'all, dearie. He wants to meet you, Sally. We'll have that talk later," she said pointedly to Baby and slipped out, leaving the door open. Before following her out of the office, Baby leaned over and straightened the collar of Sally's dress. She licked her finger and swiped at her cheek.

"Perfect."

Tall windows brightened Mr. Brumsfield's large office from three sides, but Mr. Brumsfield kept his back to the view, his massive partner's desk barricaded before the door. Mr. Brumsfield was always ready to go to battle for the good of the welfare, and he was no stranger to conflict. William Harding Brumsfield had achieved the rank of captain of artillery in the First World War. On the wall directly behind him hung a framed photograph of the then Captain Brumsfield in a steel doughboy's helmet standing with his high-laced boot up on one of the old artillery cannons in the battery he'd commanded. Another photograph showed a different Mr. Brumsfield altogether, the avid student. He posed in a three-button suit and bow tie on the steps of Massachusetts Hall with his fellow classmates at Harvard College. Mr. Brumsfield had attended school in Cambridge for one year after the war before answering the call to duty once more. He'd withdrawn from school and returned home to Eureka to run the family hardware store for his father, who had had a stroke and who would finish the last years of his life paralyzed in bed. Running the family hardware store while raising three boys with his wife, Eleanor, whom he married the year after his return, he hadn't had time to continue his education.

Over the next several years, taking classes now and again, whenever he could, Mr. Brumsfield had finally finished his bachelor of arts at Mississippi State in Starkville. Of all the accomplishments in his life mounted about the walls of his office, Mr. Brumsfield seemed to be most proud of that one. The degree given him at graduation hung professionally matted behind glass in a large golden frame on the wall directly opposite his desk, where, when he did look up from his work, it was the first thing he saw. But Mr. Brumsfield hadn't stopped there. Armed with the undergraduate degree he'd earned, he'd finally sold the hardware store to help finance his three years of law school at the University of Mississippi. First in his class, he'd accepted an offer from the state district attorney and spent the next five years working in the state prosecutor's office before his interest in public service led him to seek a political appointment as the first director of the then fledgling Welfare Department of Hushpuckashaw County.

Under his capable command, the welfare had gone from operating out of a tiny storefront on Main Street in downtown Eureka to the large new office building they now occupied. Baby knew Mr. Brumsfield to be an extremely capable administrator. He never forgot a fact. He could quote the statistics on placements for aid-dependent children from six years before up to the moment and, taking those growing numbers into account, quickly extrapolate trends, projecting from such a rise in responsibility, for instance, the increase in their total costs of operation by using the 3 percent rise in the price of such department staples as powdered milk.

The year before, Mr. Brumsfield had begun to actively exercise what in the past had been merely his hobbyist's interest in state politics. He had seemed an ideal candidate for the state legislature. He had a law degree, and from his subsequent years of work at both the state prosecutor's office and the Department of Welfare, he knew well the political system—he'd been tussling with the legislature in Jackson for years and he'd come out on top more often than he'd been pinned. He had served his country and he'd made enough money as a merchant acting honorably with his family to earn a reputation as a good and generous man. He even worked a tithing of his time as the accountant of Highlawn Methodist Church, where his family had always attended. Because of his work at the welfare office, Negroes and poor whites alike throughout Hushpuckashaw County knew Bill Brumsfield by name. His constituency had seemed to span a broad base. In his attempt to win that election, he'd hiked his way all over the county, through each of its little dog-dry towns and crossroad hamlets, its bayous and backwaters, going door-to-door, shaking hands, taking the stump at every little podunk fair or church picnic to which he could manage to get himself invited. He should have won his bid for the state legislature by a healthy margin but the Negroes had not the vote; instead he'd lost in a landslide. He'd fallen in defeat to a good ole boy named Lance DuBon, a crony of the governor's, who'd had no platform worth arguing about at all except for his playing the ace of the race card—promising to fight tooth and nail to assuage the general fear that Jim Crow might one day be repealed and "the niggers could drink at a water fountain or use a bathroom or eat at a lunch counter as good as if they were me or you!"

Since that landslide loss to Lance DuBon a year ago, Mr. Brumsfield seemed to have adjusted his sights, if not his views. He'd modified the scope of his political ambition. Now Mr. Brumsfield had his heart set on being mayor of Eureka. While he awaited the next election, he'd volunteered to function as the blackout inspector for Eureka's home guard. Once a week the fire station sounded the air-horn moan of a general alarm and the residents of Eureka had to blanket every shimmer of light in preparation for a potential air-borne bombing attack by the Germans or the Japanese. Mr. Brumsfield patrolled the block in the pitch dark, donning the authority of a pith helmet and a long-handled MP's flashlight. Baby had received one of the inspector's unofficial warnings during a weekly "raid" the previous August—a sharp rap on the glass of her kitchen window—because she and Ruthie had been up late trying to stew and can the abundance of tomatoes they'd harvested from their Victory Garden before the rot set in. She hadn't pulled the quilt down all the way, trying to let in a little air so that they could breathe.

Baby knocked. "Mr. Brumsfield?"

"Mrs. Allen," Mr. Brumsfield said without looking up. He sprinkled sawdust across the document he'd been scratching at with a turkey feather quill pen and raised the page and blew it off onto the floor. He quickly scanned his signature and then peeled off his round wire reading glasses and laid them on his desk. Mr. Brumsfield was not a handsome man. He had an overlarge head and a bulbous nose that showed his pores, and he still wore his now white hair clipped militarily short. His eyes, which were an unusually warm shade of brown, saved his face from appearing severe. Mr. Brumsfield's eyes revealed him to be kind.

"So," he said, pushing back his chair and rising to meet them. "This is Sally Johnson."

"Sally," Baby said, "this is Mr. Brumsfield, director of the welfare."

Mr. Brumsfield cragged a smile. "Don't worry, Sally. I know I'm ugly. You know what they called me in the election I lost? Ugly Abe. I found the comparison quite flattering—in my opinion Lincoln was the ablest politician this country's ever known—though, of course, my opponent was trying to draw the parallel in our height and visage in an effort to distort the appearance of my record in the eyes of the public. I'm no Republican, God knows. I'm a yellow-dog Democrat through and through. Given the way the politics of this state have evolved since Reconstruction, if Lincoln was alive today he might be, too. At least I'd like to think so." He stepped around the desk and shook her hand. Then he leaned back against the edge of his desk and crossed his arms. He wore a wrinkled white button-down shirt and a Rotary Club tie. The slightly too-short trousers from his khaki suit didn't quite touch the tops of his cordovan-waxed wingtip shoes. It wasn't yet 9:30, but Mr. Brumsfield had already shed his jacket and rolled the sleeves of his shirt up to his elbows. He studied Sally.

"I wanted to tell you myself how sorry I am about your mama. I wanted to say that."

Sally herself was studying the wide-plank pine floor as if she were trying to memorize the placement of every nail. Baby put her hands on her shoulders.

"You have some good prospects?" he asked Baby, still watching Sally.

"We're going to start with Mrs. Brim in Clark and work our way across to the Samsons in Magnolia."

Mr. Brumsfield nodded. "I have the highest respect for Mrs. Allen's ability as an agent in the field, Sally. She'll do right by you. All you have to do is put your best foot forward. Look them in the eye and smile." He reached forward and gently raised her chin. She held his gaze. He laid his other hand on her head as if he were blessing her for the trip.

He stood and Baby turned Sally to go. "Mrs. Allen," he said and she turned back toward him. "I ever tell you about the time I debated Lance DuBon at the Blackberry Fair outside Tutweiler?"

"No, sir. I don't believe so."

"Mr. DuBon tried to accuse me of being a blue blood for having been lucky enough to attend Harvard College for two semesters. He told me in front of that crowd gathered under that hanging tree to hear us that I didn't know diddly-squat about the common man in Mississippi. I looked him in the eye and said to Lance DuBon that in my role as director of the Welfare Office for Hushpuckashaw County I'd come to know many ordinary men and women facing hardship in Mississippi, but now knowing him I knew far more than I ever cared to about what a common one was."

Baby held Mr. Brumsfield's gaze.

"The most important thing is that you and Sally here take care. Don't hesitate to call if you need me, Mrs. Allen." He turned his attention back to Sally. "It's been my pleasure," he said, shaking her hand good-bye.

BABY DROVE AND Sally sat in the backseat as if she were being chauffeured. Riding into a town sitting side by side in the front seat together during the light of day would have caused too much of a stir, the craning of necks, stiffening chins, elbows nudging to quick look see for yourself. So Baby drove with her papers and files on the passenger seat beside her and Sally had the big backseat all to herself.

The first home they came to sat within sight of the highway outside the city limits of Clark. Baby slowed to turn off the road and rolled to a stop in the ruts from the last long-ago rain left baked fossil-hard in the dirt yard. At the edge of the property, a trash barrel sent up a black smudge of smoke. A crowd of kids sat on the steps. Baby counted nine of them when Mrs. Brim stepped up to shadow the screen with a screaming baby in her arms.

Baby turned to Sally looking out at the children still on the porch looking uninterestedly back at her. "Wait here. I need to talk to Mrs. Brim alone for a moment."

"Mrs. Allen," the woman said when Baby stepped up onto the porch carrying her clipboard. "Didn't 'spect to see you here today."

"Mrs. Brim. How are you?"

"We gettin' on."

The little girl, Charmaine, whom Baby had placed with Mrs. Brim the year before, had swipes of dried mud on her bare chest. She huddled with the others. Baby didn't see her brother, Franklin.

"How are you, Charmaine?"

"Fine, ma'am."

"Is Franklin around?"

"Oh, he down by the creek lookin' for crayfish's where I bet he is," Mrs. Brim said. "Is that where he gots to, Raymond?"

"I reckon," Raymond said. He was a young man of about twenty-five. He rocked sullenly in a battered-looking cane chair, smoking what smelled like a home-rolled corn-silk cigarette. Baby realized he must be Mrs. Brim's oldest boy—so, counting the new baby, five of the children on the porch were hers. Raymond had been listed as an independent when Baby had made her initial investigation. The state paid twenty-nine dollars and eighty-five cents a month to a foster family for the support of a first foster child. For each additional child, the state offered additional assistance of eight dollars and eighty cents. Baby was sure Mrs. Brim was using up that money trying to support the entire brood. When Baby placed the children, Mrs. Brim had had the three and a job working for a woman in town.

"Looks like you've got your hands full. I didn't know you'd had another baby. You ought to've let me know."

"I didn't know I's goin' to neither," she sighed. "It was like this one drop out of the sky. These other chillen I just watchin' for a while. I figure I could make a little extra sittin'. I done lost that other job on account she said she didn't need me no more now that I has this baby with me all the time."

Baby touched the infant's head. He was sucking hard at a breast that looked to Baby as used up and shriveled thin as a stretched balloon. "You really interested in taking on another child?"

"You still payin', I'm still interested," Mrs. Brim said and laughed, hacking up some phlegm. She launched the lugee into the yard and smiled, showing a front tooth as brown and shriveled looking as a raisin. "I 'mit I'm feeling a mite tired with all these I'm s'posed to watch. But my oldest, Raymond here, he a big help with them since he come back home to live."

"I can see he is," Baby nodded, turning to look at Raymond, who continued to rock as if she weren't even there. He leaned his head back and blew smoke.

"I meant to come see you next time I'm in town anyhow," Mrs. Brim said. "We can't drink no more that powder milk you brung us. It make Raymond here some kinda ill. Chillen won't drink it neither. Give 'em all the runs. We all runnin' from it."

"I'm sorry. That's all we can get. With the war on, there's no fresh milk to be had. I drink it myself."

"I was wonderin' then, could I get an advance on my checks? I'm a little down and out jes now. This no-good man I been countin' on done run out. And I loss that job. I need to get back on my feets."

"Mrs. Brim."

"I know, but maybe jes this once. Jes this once maybe."

"I'll see what I can do about some milk, but I can't promise anything. I'll be back later in the week. We're going to have to talk about how many children you can take care of. My first responsibility here is to the children I've placed in your care. Perhaps we can file for some other funds."

"Then I can't get another one, noways?" Mrs. Brim followed Baby back to the car. "I could sure use one," she said. "It would sho' be a help." She looked in the back at Sally and grinned through the window. "Ain't you a pretty one? What your name? You come on back live with Auntie Brim, hear? Come on back play with all my chillen. Raymond, he love chillen. You can go down to the creek, hunt crayfish with Franklin. We have lots of fun."

Baby started the car. "I'll stop by later this week."

"Say bye-bye," Mrs. Brim said to the baby to say to Sally. She waved the baby's hand. The baby started to cry. The baby began to wail.

Baby bumped the car out of the ruts in the yard she'd rolled it into, looking over the backseat past Sally. "I had no idea Mrs. Brim was in such straits."

Sally turned to the side window and leaned forward to watch the other children sitting on the porch. They still hadn't moved. Raymond was still rocking and smoking. Mrs. Brim walked slowly after the car as Baby and Sally backed down the dusty drive. She walked holding the baby to her chest and waving her raised arm over her head the whole time as if she'd had some emergency and was trying to flag them down.

"Don't I have nuff troubles? What I need that sort of trouble for?" the mother of the fourth foster family they visited that morning told Baby, hands on her hips, peeking around behind her to sneak a look at Sally, who was sitting straight up in the backseat to try to make a better impression this time. The last three foster families who had filed an interest at the welfare in taking on the care of another child and who had seemed to Baby acceptable during the interview had balked when they recognized Sally Johnson for who she was. The story of how Letitia Johnson had drowned Sissy Rule Tisdale's baby daughter and the details of how she'd been lynched and burned after being arrested for it were far too fresh in everyone's mind, especially in the consciousness of the families Baby was taking Sally around to meet for the first time.

"That sort of trouble ain't worth no eight eighty a month. I got three other mouths to feed and keep safe for the state. I can't be risking it all for just that one, tho' I am awful sorry what they done to her mama."

"That lady don't want me neither?" Sally said when Baby climbed back in the car. They could both see the woman and kids peering out at them from behind the bedsheets they used to curtain the windows of their cabin.

"It's not you," Baby heard herself lie. "She already has three children. It's my fault. I should've thought of that."

Sally sat back and Baby started the car.

"Miss Baby, may I ask you somepin?"

"Certainly, Sally."

"What my mama do so terrible they gone and killed her for it?"

Baby felt it all tumble down through her. She stumbled, hearing how lame her explanation sounded even to her: "We don't know that she did anything wrong, Sally. She may have just been someone to blame."

Sally nodded. "Yes ma'am. I know my mama loved me much as I love her. But I'm feelin' so terrible alone inside. I blames her, too."

INTERVIEWING EACH FOSTER child was part of Baby's duties as an agent for the welfare, but Baby preferred to ask her questions as they came up naturally rather than to sit the child in the hardback chair in her office and interrogate them. On the road, she wondered aloud about an approaching sign: "How many miles to Tutweiler?"

Sally looked at the sign as it flashed past. "Eleven," she said. "Why, Miss Baby, can't you read?" she said. "Or you got the poor eyes, too? Mama was a fiend about me readin', but she couldn't see what she called 'diddly-squat.' She use to say you gots to git your education 'cause it's the one thing can't nobody take away from you. But I can't read but a little bit yet." Sally sighed, apologizing, but Baby was pleased to find she knew her alphabet and she could read the book of *Dick and Jane* Baby had left on the backseat of the car if she sounded out the words slowly.

"'See Dick run,'" Sally read. She looked up. "I don't know about these books you gots here, Miss Baby," she said. "I mean, ain't that Jane got nothin' better to do than watch that Dick?" she asked.

In questioning Sally about her family, Baby volunteered information about her own life. Her given name was Mary Bascomb Gavins, but her mama's first name had been Mary, too, and so she'd been called Baby from day one. She told Sally what a pistol her own mama had been. She'd been born and raised on a farm in London, Kentucky. After college at Western Kentucky State Teacher's College, she'd moved to Vicksburg to take a teaching position, and that's where she'd met Baby's father. She'd known about Vicksburg because her own great-grandfather had fought there in the Civil War—for the Union under General Grant.

"Most of the men in town were flat terrified of Mama. She didn't fit the mold. She had 'opinions.' Mama made it a practice to say exactly what she thought. She was a crusader for every sort of cause, from suffrage to better schooling for the children of sharecroppers around the county. Mama was working for people around Hushpuckashaw County before there was any such thing as the Welfare Office. I admired her so. I guess it was just natural that I'd follow in her footsteps."

Baby went on to tell Sally that her own father had died when she was fifteen. "He was a pharmacist. We owned Eureka Drugs in town. I remember he came home from the pharmacy one evening and said his chest felt tight. Mama found him sitting in his wing-back chair with the paper in his lap. At first she thought he was just asleep. He was such a kind man. Gentle. I still remember the moth-ball smell of his suits. And the little cigars he smoked. He had a soda fountain at the drugstore and I used to sit at the counter under the ceiling fan summer afternoons. I'd always order the peanut parfait. Daddy made a mean peanut parfait. We boiled the peanuts ourselves."

Sally continued to stare out her window at the rows of the fields flickering by. "I never knew my daddy," she said. "I don't think he died, but he was always good as dead to me. I don't even know what he look like 'cept Mama said he look like me. Same eyes. Mama said he was a rascal. She always said she guessed she jes liked them rascally kind. Like Alfonse."

"Alfonse?"

"That's his called name Mama liked to claim him by. He mostly go by Bigger, which jes natural on account of his size. *Bigger* than a bull or a ox even. Stronger, too. Sweet, tho'. He the kind likes to smile. He has a gold front toof and the other silver always gleaming at you."

They drove in silence for a time. Sally turned away from the fields and settled back in her seat. She folded her hands in her lap.

"Alfonse was always good to Mama. Couldn't keep his hands off her. He and Mama had the magic, for a fact. They worked it all the time. But this summer Alfonse had to go up to that farm to stay awhile. She was waitin' for him to get out and come back to her. I went with Mama to do her conjul visit a few times. I didn't like that place no matter what they say. They say it's a farm, but it ain't. Men wid guns make you work. Mama said that's the way you pay off your debt to the state, but it wasn't the state Alfonse owed even. That man he cut owed him's the way Mama told it. But it got messed up so that Alfonse ended up being the one who paid."

When she asked Sally the last question designed by Mr. Brumsfield to test the client's self-esteem—"What do you want to be when you grow up?"—Sally looked out the passenger side window, watching the field row by, considering her answer before she raised her chin and turned to meet Baby's eyes in the rearview. "I don't know. I ain't had too much time to think on it. I ain't thought on it too awful much. But lately I been thinking maybe I'll grow up and go to college. Work for the welfare, just like you."

chapter seven

B Y THE TIME Baby and Sally made their last visit and zigzagged
their way back and forth across the grid of gravel roads and
pulled the gasping Model T into the shed at the back of the
house at 12 East Percy Street, it was well past dark and Sally lay
stretched across the backseat, sound asleep. Baby killed the engine.
When the headlights blacked, the hot, summer swarm of silence—
the chorus of crickets and the distant croaking of bullfrogs from Indian Bayou, only one block away—swelled the cab. Baby sat stuck
for a time holding on to the wheel as if both her hands had been
glued there. Beginning with Mrs. Brim that morning, they'd visited
a total of twelve families. They'd received the final—by now—stock
answer from the Samsons in Magnolia. Even if a family like the
Samsons checked out in every other respect, Baby had grown to expect the reservation about Sally when she revealed the fact that she
was Letitia Johnson's daughter. They'd exhausted every name on
her list. Baby couldn't begin to imagine where she would turn next.

She sighed, gathering herself in the dark, decided to leave the mess
of paperwork on the seat, and felt for her purse before she leaned
into the door and shoved out. Baby pulled the strap of the purse over
her shoulder and turned to open the back door. Long as Sally
was for a twelve-year-old girl, she rose as if her bones were hollow,

bird-light in Baby's arms. Baby jutted her hip to shut the door and carried Sally down the worn path that bordered the street side of the house.

The kitchen light shone brightly behind Ruthie, who stood waiting with the screen held wide. A mosquito floated clearly into view and disappeared indoors. "Let me help you with her, Miss Baby."

"Thank you, Ruthie."

At fifty-four Ruthie was already a great-grandmother, though she did not have even one gray hair to show for it. Her skin beamed a healthy, bright coffee color and her white teeth looked made of ivory.

Baby followed Ruthie and Sally up the stairs into the kitchen.

"I'll just go on and put her right to bed," Ruthie was saying. "Then I'm goin to sleep myself unless you needs somepin. The girls went down jes fine though Jeana waited up on the porch swing for you until late. I fixed you a plate, and I wants you to eat it. You gots to keep your strength up now you know, Miss Baby. You eatin for two!"

Baby stopped. She hadn't told Ruthie she was pregnant. For a second she wondered if Gladys Pointdexter had stopped by after work.

Ruthie turned with Sally in her arms. "You think I's born yesterday? Don't I have ten chillens my own self? Men! Get you big and leaves you. They's a caution. If it's troubles you want to talk about now, Miss Baby, we can talk anytimes you like!"

Baby laid her hand on Ruthie's arm. She did not want to talk about it—she didn't even want to think about it—but if she did she knew she could talk straight with her. Ruthie would say what she thought, and you didn't have to like what she said. That was part of the bargain in having a conversation with her.

Baby touched Sally's cheek. "I'm afraid we didn't have any luck today. We'll have to try again tomorrow, first thing—though where it is we're going to try I have no idea. We visited every name on my list."

When Ruthie stepped out to put Sally to bed, Baby dropped her purse on the table. The glow of the overhead light made her kitchen look dingy, old. The waxed yellow vinyl was beginning to buckle. Ruthie had left the newspaper out on the table for her and Baby rolled it tight to thwack after the mosquito that had drifted in, bashing a red blotch against the painted cabinet. She unrolled the paper and stared down at the bloodied face of the governor, who, when asked if he was going to order an official inquiry in an attempt to find out the identities of Letitia Johnson's killers, had scoffed. "I have neither the time nor the money to investigate two thousand people," the *Tocsin* reported him as saying.

Baby dropped the newspaper onto the table. Then, on second thought, she picked it up and buried it in the trash can under the sink.

Ruthie bustled back into the kitchen and began to gather her things, her shopping-bag purse and the floppy cast-off pink straw jamboree hat that she always wore whenever she stepped out, day or night.

"Don't you fret none, Miss Baby. You'll find a family for her. You always do. Folks they just scairt right now's all. We thought we was done with this kinda foolishness once we got the NAACP down here. And now here they go again lynchin folks just like in the olden days. Folks sayin it was them Kluxers had a hand in this."

"The Klan?" Though Baby had grown up hearing stories about the presence of the Ku Klux Klan in Mississippi, she had never had occasion to lay eyes on a member—at least not in regalia. Who was actually a member in the Klan and who wasn't, one never knew. The Invisible Empire they called themselves. The name gave her the creeps. "You think it's foolish having Sally stay here at the house?" Baby asked, thinking back to the "theological discussion" she'd had with Jake Lemaster on the road the morning before: *an eye for an eye and a tooth for a tooth.* Maybe it was the Klan he'd been warning her about. They considered themselves to be Christians, Baby knew, though how she couldn't begin to imagine. But there was no doubt in her mind that they were the sorts of "common" men that Mr. Brumsfield had been cautioning her about when he'd told her his story about Lance DuBon. "I don't mind the danger for myself, but I hate to think I might be putting you and the girls at risk."

"Don't you worry 'bout us," Ruthie said, straightening her hat. "The girls and me with you no matter what. And you all Sally gots."

Ruthie parted the screen and Baby stepped up to watch her go shuffling sideways stair to stair before lumbering off into the dark. Her stomach grumbled underneath the palm of her hand, and she turned back into the kitchen. She opened the icebox and took out the plate Ruthie had fixed and left covered for her, forcing herself to pick at the cold chicken and making herself eat half of the clump of mashed potatoes and two bites of the collard greens. Before leaving the kitchen, Baby made sure she closed and locked the side door and shut the windows, hot as it was. She flicked off the light as she stepped out into the hall, the sound of her heels clicking after her through the dark.

She paused before her older daughter Claire's room and silently turned the knob. Moonlight flooded through the opened windows. Humid and hot as the house felt to Baby, Claire remained coolly on her back, her blond hair framing her face, her hands folded peacefully before her on the snow-white sheet—a fairy-tale princess waiting to be kissed awake. The bathroom buffered between sixteen-year-old Claire's and twelve-year-old Jeana's rooms, and after straightening Claire's sheet even straighter Baby let herself through both doors. She found her younger daughter twisted in the sheets, turned upside down on the bed, lying on her stomach with her arms flung wide, cheek smooshed against the mattress, her pillow kicked off onto the floor. Jeana had inherited her father's bottle-green eyes and jet-black hair, the mess of curls teased straight from burrowing the covers. Baby flipped her daughter around and tucked the sheet in at her feet and then pulled it to her chin. She leaned over and planted a kiss squarely on Jeana's forehead.

She let herself out into the hallway, already reaching to unzip the back of her dress. Baby guessed it must still be at least ninety degrees in the house—night offering no relief from the hours of sun, which would force the temperature the next day even higher, turning up the heat as if they were stuck baking in an oven. Without turning on the light in her bedroom, Baby slid the straps down off her shoulders and stepped quickly out of the dress—feeling immediately cooler. She picked up the dress and draped it neatly over the back of the rocking chair. When she unclipped the catch on her bra, she found that her breasts were sore, tender to the touch. She stepped into the center of the room and waved for the string of the ceiling fan in the dark, caught the cord and gave it two quick yanks. The blowing air gave her goose bumps, cooling her skin. She pulled down the shades, then leaned over the bedside table and switched on the lamp.

Because of her state job as a home visitor, she had an essential services pass for gas and tires, but coupons for luxury items like real nylons were nearly impossible to come by, and Baby could not afford to ruin even one pair of stockings, no matter how hot and uncomfortable they made her. To take them off, she sat on the edge of the four-poster bed that Gabe and she had bought together after they were married—their first piece of furniture. Only then did she let herself kick off her heels, not willing to risk a snag on the plank flooring. She massaged the sole of her right foot, then her left, before unsnapping her garter. Baby set the rolled pair of stockings on the bedside table.

Baby laid both hands on her tummy; she didn't remember feeling so sick with either of the girls. What she remembered was that she'd enjoyed her first two pregnancies, and that the queasiness of the first three months hadn't troubled her unduly. She'd welcomed the feeling of the life growing inside her body. But back then, she thought, she'd been newly married. She and Gabe had been happily in love. She'd been twenty-five when she'd had Claire. Twenty-nine when Jeana was born. Her twenties were gone. Her thirties! It struck her again: She was forty-one. When she'd last been pregnant, her and Gabe's life together as man and wife had still been happily unfolding—not sadly unfolded. Done.

Baby ground the heels of her palms into her eyes. She would not let herself cry. She would not.

She stood suddenly, swiping hard at her cheeks, and reached down for her shoes to put them away inside the big closet. When she raised her arms to slip into her white cotton nightgown that she'd left hanging on the back of the door, she caught the glint of the silver, pearl-handled .22-caliber revolver hidden on the highest shelf between her two winter sweaters and a stack of colorfully striped and ribboned hatboxes. When she'd first taken the job with the welfare as a home visitor, Gabe had bought the pistol for her. His thinking, as he'd explained it to her when she'd opened the "gift" and stared down at the pistol in horror—as petrified for a moment as if she'd unwrapped the birthday-bright box on her lap and peeked back the lid to find a brown recluse spider waiting to leap out on her—was that the gun would keep her safe. Baby couldn't imagine how; just the thought of touching the thing scared her absolutely to death. And—she had assured him—she certainly wasn't going to *shoot* it!

Later, after the shock wore off, trying her best to reconcile the gift, Baby had told herself that her husband had bought the pistol thinking of *her*. She'd tried to see the pistol from his point of view. She attempted to understand it as a gesture of his thoughtfulness— his love for her. His care. He was worried about *her* welfare. She'd gone so far as to practice loading and unloading it while he watched, coaching her how to slip the bullets into the cylinder. But she couldn't shake the feeling that his furnishing her with a weapon had less to do with her safety than with his protecting himself against his own fears and prejudices. Baby was not at all afraid of her clients, who needed the help she offered and usually welcomed her into their homes. She did fear the pistol falling from the shelf and accidentally going off, even though she kept it unloaded. She had never taken it on a visit to a client's home, but she couldn't figure out exactly how to get rid of the thing either. You didn't simply throw a gun in the kitchen trash! And she didn't want to be responsible for giving a weapon to someone else, directly or indirectly. The thing had become something of an albatross. And so for lack of a better idea she'd kept it, the bullets in a separate box in the back of the underwear drawer of her dresser, the .22 as safely stowed as she could think to keep it without losing sight of it and therefore possible control. Baby reached up on tiptoe and nudged the pistol a touch farther back on the shelf. She shifted the nightgown about and smoothed it down over her hips. Clicked the closet door.

Seated before the bank of mirrors at her dressing room table, which showed Baby to herself from three separate sides at once, she reached up to pull the bobby pins out of her hair. Her blond hair fell in phases, the bun coming undone, and then unwinding, dropping to her shoulders, and, with the yanking of the last pin, the length of her back. She picked up her mother's silver brush. Holding her hair above the knot, she pulled straight down, leaning back against the snags.

As she commenced counting out her ritual hundred strokes, Baby fell to dwelling again on Gabe's affair with that Franks woman. What did his fornicating with another woman mean about their life together as man and wife—the lovemaking they'd shared all these years? she had to wonder. She had always suffered a weakness for Gabriel Allen and there was nothing she liked less than feeling weak. Baby valued her strength more than any other thing about herself. But she couldn't say she hadn't known all along about Gabe Allen. So far as that went she had no one to blame but herself. Big as he was, Gabe was only a beautiful, weak man. When they'd married, he'd had a good job as acting postmaster, but after his term had run out he'd lost the position to a more "industrious" applicant. He hadn't held a job for longer than a year since, trying his hand at everything from selling Bibles to cars to shoes.

Gabe's inability to hold down steady work had been the big reason she'd gone back to the welfare sooner than she would have liked after Jeana's birth. Even with the labor shortage brought on by the war, he had not settled into full-time employment, though employment was certainly available. It just depended on the type of work one was willing to do. Gabe always had an excuse: a temporary slowdown at the munitions factory, a hurt back lifting cotton bales, the prospect of a cushy office job just around the corner. In lieu of gainful employment, Gabe had made it his business to keep abreast of the news down at the Masons' Lodge; he'd made a career out of playing cards with the boys at the barbershop or going off to the deer camp to hunt for weeks at a time.

What had saved their marriage in Baby's eyes and made it worth working so hard to keep all these years was that Gabe had always been sweet. He loved Claire and Jeana and the girls doted on him—they all did. He had always been kind—thoughtful in genuine ways that the ambiguous gift of the pistol didn't begin to reveal: a spray of fresh-cut jonquils left on her bedside table, a surprise family picnic that he'd fixed himself and sprang on them under the guise of driving to church. Gabe Allen had always been charming. And, goodness, was he ever handsome! Everyone had always said that Gabe Allen looked more like Clark Gable than Clark Gable looked like himself.

Even now, furious and hurt as she still felt about his infidelity, even after being married to the same man for so many years, she could feel the sway he still held over her—the strength of his hands managing the rhythm of her hips. With Gabe she'd happily indulged desires that before she'd met and married him she hadn't even known she'd possessed. Losing herself in the reflection before her now, she could picture her legs over his shoulders again then. The way she'd let herself call out his name when she had an orgasm—to lose control like that in all-consuming desire—was the most luxurious feeling Baby had ever allowed herself knowledge of. Unadulterated lust. *Pure wantonness*, her mother would have chided, as much embarrassed for her as she'd been disappointed in her for her choice of Gabriel Allen as her husband.

What pained Baby most about the whole affair, though, was that she could no longer let herself believe that May Franks had been the first. And with that understanding came the knowledge that she wouldn't be the last either—even if Baby had been able to bring herself to forgive him and take him back. Baby was convinced now that Gabe had been cheating on her for years. Looking back, all the hunting expeditions he'd gone on, countless afternoon and evening Rotary meetings, his very membership in the Masons, all became suspect, not merely another chance to get up a game of cards with the boys, but countless opportunities for assignations. Before she'd married Gabriel Allen, sex between a man and a woman had seemed to Baby as straightforward as other aspects of a simple and useful life. He'd gone and made everything complicated.

One hundred.

Baby clapped down the brush and turned away from herself. She folded back the white cotton bedspread, climbed in under the covers, and turned off the light without bothering to reach for the latest novel Miss Honey from next door had smuggled on to her—a well-thumbed copy of James Joyce's *Ulysses*. In the dark, she pulled up the sheet and then shoved it back down. The heat in the room clung to her as heavily as a wet blanket. She lay staring up at the ceiling, listening to the clocklike ticking of the fan, forgetting her own troubles to fret again now about Sally's. Whatever in the world was she going to do? In the darkness, she felt the shadowing of a thought. And then, as if the bulb light in the lamp beside her had been flicked on again, she had the bright idea of the Reverend Charles Beasley in Rivers Bend. In her years as an agent for the welfare, Baby had met all kinds. She believed Reverend Beasley to be one of the very few true saints. Reverend Beasley and his wife, Victoria, had founded and still directed Children's Home, a group charge begun exclusively for dependent Negro children that they ran as an experimental farm and school. Children's Home had been sanctioned as a private alternative to State Home, the government-run orphanage in Jackson. Reverend Beasley's wards had always greatly impressed

Baby. Not only were the children under his care clean and well be-haved, most important of all they seemed happy. Sally could be happy there, too.

It could work—if Reverend Beasley and Victoria had room for Sally. Therein lay the glitch. They limited the number of children they could work with effectively to twelve—the count of Christ's disciples who had spread Christianity throughout the world. Rev-erend Beasley had high hopes for the work his charges would go on to perform after they left Children's Home, even if their greatest ac-complishment was to successfully have a family and raise children of their own, planting again the precepts they'd been raised by. When one of his charges graduated, Reverend Beasley brought an-other child into the fold he called "the Family." He always con-tacted the Welfare Office himself to schedule an interview when he had space for another child. Reverend Beasley hadn't contacted them. If he had, Baby would have thought of Children's Home first off as the best choice for Sally.

Still, at least they could try. She'd run the plan by Mr. Brums-field in the morning. He'd tell her to follow procedure and call first. Baby would've gladly called to ask before she and Sally drove all the way out to Rivers Bend, but she knew the reverend didn't believe in the distance phones placed between folks. If you wanted to talk to Reverend Beasley, you had to meet him face-to-face. Of course, she'd have to explain the danger he might be putting himself in. But Reverend Beasley had been through a lot himself, Baby knew. He was not an easy man to scare. The possibility of an answer to Sally's problems was the sedative Baby needed. Exhausted, she fell fast asleep.

BABY DREAMED THE scream. It seemed to begin in the cave-deep of her consciousness, the sound drawing her up and out of herself, the screaming—death, destruction, fire, rape—until she woke, already throwing back the covers—*Claire!*

"Mamamamamamamama!"

She saw the flickering of the flames on the curtains, and then she heard the revving and racing of engines, feet slapping across pavement, car doors slamming.

"Let's go!"

Baby grabbed back the shade. She counted three carloads. And then from the front of the house she heard the shatter of glass. Jeana was screaming now, too, adding to the din.

"Maaaaama!"

Baby raced into the hall. Claire was running toward her room and she gathered her into her arms. She pushed into Jeana's room and pulled her close, too. Stumbling across the hall together, they burst into the little guest bedroom where Sally slept. Sally was gone. Baby scrambled down on her hands and knees and grabbed her arm from under the bed.

"Quickly!"

The flames leaped tall along the walls. She could smell the reek of kerosene, but the air breathed clear. The house wasn't on fire, Baby realized. The fierce shadows thrown by the flames came from the front yard. She hustled the three girls into the hallway, away from the danger of another window being broken, the drill they'd rehearsed in case the black-funneling cloud of a tornado tore past the house. She pushed them together into a crouch under the telephone table. "Stay down," Baby said. Peeking into the living room, she caught a glimpse of the brick that had been thrown through the front picture window lying on the rug amid glittering shards. Looking out through the jawlike, gaping jags of glass, she saw what she had half-expected to see but would never have been quite able to believe without having witnessed such a thing for herself: A burning cross had been touched off on their lawn.

"Who is it, Mama?" Claire asked her as she hurried past the girls, heading straight for her bedroom.

"Just stay down," Baby said. "Don't come out until I tell you to."

She yanked open the closet and scrambled the shelf with her

fingertips, on her tiptoes, knocking the hatboxes down, the sweater flopping onto her head. Just as she snagged the butt of the pistol another window shattered. The girls shrieked again.

Baby yanked open her underwear drawer and raked it clean looking for the box of bullets. She fumbled at the cylinder, dropping two of the .22's shells. She managed to load three.

"I mean it," she said to the girls on her way back past them down the hall. She opened the front door. A battered pickup screeched as it turned the corner, braked, and revved in reverse. The two other cars followed suit, racing forward, squealing, and stopping short, screeching to a stop, before spinning their tires again, terrorizing them with the noise, trying to make the most of the fear. The smell of burned rubber mixed thick with the suffocating black smoke from the kerosene. The men packed into the cars wore white robes, their faces hidden behind white hoods—night riders. In the blaze from the burning cross the rounded cutout holes of their eyes seemed to scream red, glaring hard at her in her white nightgown standing on the stairs.

"There's that bitch."

"Bring out the pickaninny," the driver of the pickup yelled. "Else we'll burn her out of there for ourselves."

Baby raised the pistol, pointing it blindly at the pickup truck in front of her, and began pulling the trigger. Under the close low-hanging roof of the porch, the loudness from the echoed report of the shots going off surprised even her—*Pow! Pow!* click click click *Pow!*—sounding as if she had a cannon on her side. The front tire on the closest car popped, whistling air. A puncture puckered the door of the old pickup truck, warping the metal.

It seemed a sudden vacuum of silence followed the shock of the shots, sucking up the sharp slaps inside it—a silence that grew somehow louder still with waiting to see what would happen next. Baby knew she'd only loaded three bullets into the revolver, but they didn't. She raised the pistol again, looking to aim this time, pointing the barrel at the driver of the pickup. The three vehicles roared off in a line led by the shot truck, the popped tire of the wounded car thumping as it limped away on the rim. Another window shattered as they sped by down that side of the house past the shed. The darkness left lit by the jagged shapes of flickering flames filled in behind them. The wood of the torched cross crackled. Baby stepped barefoot down the stairs into the dewed grass to stare up at it, the pistol hanging at her side. From next door, Miss Honey emerged from her dark-screened porch with her arms crossed over a tent-sized yellow muumuu. "I saw the whole thing," she said. Mr. Howard Crosthwaite from across the street came gimping as fast as he could, carrying a double-barreled shotgun with him. He stood looking after the cars. "They gone? Damn these old knees! Y'all all right?"

"Mama?" Jeana said and came running down the front stairs. Baby knelt to meet her and hugged her up, held her hard. Claire ran into her arms. Baby knew Sally would not dare the terror of the yard.

"Shhh," Baby said, holding them both. They were hysterical, weeping.

"Shhhhhh. It's okay," Baby said again and again, petting their hair. "They're gone. It's all right. They're gone. Everything's going to be fine."

SHERIFF BURGESS DROVE out to the scene immediately, wearing a pair of overalls and a white T-shirt, his face unshaven. He wore his moccasin slippers and hadn't even thought to bring his hat. What was left of his hair stuck straight up curlicued like a question mark over his broad forehead. Sheriff Burgess had been a close friend of Baby's mother—he was Uncle Al to Baby.

They stood on the porch.

"Pretty fine shooting from what I hear. You're just lucky they didn't start shooting back. It's about Letitia Johnson's girl, is that it? She staying here with you?"

"Yes, she's staying here," Baby said. She crossed her arms over the robe she'd gone back inside for. "Are you saying she shouldn't be staying with us, Uncle Al?"

"I'm saying I'm just surprised those boys went so far is all. "

"You know those men?" she asked.

"You probably know some of them, too. I just mean I haven't heard of any of them going night-riding in some time."

"Why now?"

"I don't know. I guess this lynching has got them stirred up—or they stirred up the lynching. Way I hear it there's a fellow named Calvin McGales folks are saying named himself the new Grand Dragon."

"But they can't go around terrorizing people. They can't take the law into their own hands."

"No, they can't. In Ruleton, Tom Dodd's supposed to uphold the law. Eureka's not Ruleton. I'll have a talk with McGales."

A sleek black Oldsmobile slid up on the other side of East Percy Street in front of the house, and Mr. Brumsfield climbed slowly out. He surveyed the scene, wielding the authority of his long-handled MP's flashlight. As blackout inspector, he'd been alerted by the fire department. A night fire stood in clear violation of the blackout laws. But it was as director of the Welfare Office that his face turned grim at what he saw.

"Are you all right, Mrs. Allen?"

Baby nodded. "I'm fine. I half-expected something like this, but I admit it caught me by surprise."

They watched as the volunteer firemen axed the guy lines that held the skeleton of the charred cross and pulled it down. It fell with a groan of the joined timbers, and the men quickly stepped up and doused it with buckets of water, the charred wood hissing, roiling gray smoke against the blacker sky.

chapter eight

REVEREND BEASLEY had his own story to tell. He preached it daily in the form of encouragement. Of self-improvement. His church, a one-room schoolhouse the size of a cabin, stood alone in the cotton fields within walking distance of his farm outside of Rivers Bend. The church remained staunchly undenominational. Reverend Beasley had named it simply Blood of the Lamb, and inside it he preached his own brand of religion. Sundays, the folding chairs filled from the front first all the way back to the door. People who arrived too late stood against the walls to hear him speak. In the warmer months, he left the windows and front door open so that those who couldn't jam their way inside could sit under the shade of the eaves and hear what he had to say. Blood of the Lamb had no choir. People came to hear the little man's great big voice go booming. Most of the audience was made up of Negroes, but a few whites made regular pilgrimages to hear Reverend Beasley, too. All were welcome. Baby had taken Jeana and Claire to Blood of the Lamb just as her mama had taken her when she was a girl. Reverend Beasley preached less against sin than he did against what he called the *abnegation of the self.* "Believe in you!" Reverend Beasley thundered, his big head barely rising over the lectern. "Don't be a slave to yourself! Set yourself free! You going to wait for Jesus to do it? Jesus is IN you! And you got to do it! If you don't, that's your sin!"

Baby's mother had loved him. She clapped her hands as they walked the dusty road back to the car. "Pure heresy! Now that's my kind of preacher!"

Charles H. Beasley—he liked to joke that because he'd never met his mother or father he never did find out what the H. stood for—had grown up orphaned himself, an aid-dependent child at the government-run State Home in Jackson. Baby had visited State Home when she was in school, during her training to become a social worker. But she'd heard the horror stories of the place long before she arrived: weevils in the grits and the favor the director showed for the rule of the rod were the least notorious of them. A twelve-foot brick wall enclosed the "campus." State Home itself had the terrifying aspect of a medieval castle, made of gray stone, complete with buttresses and spires. As she'd toured the first floor, Baby tried not to imagine the dungeon of tortures she feared housed below.

When he told his story of growing up at State Home, Reverend Beasley said that, yes, it had been bad—"hell on earth"—but he had *persevered.* That was the lesson he wished to impart. At the age of fifteen, he'd executed his plotted escape from the place by clinging to the underside of a delivery wagon. As Baby had heard him preach it, the reverend had dreamed up the crafty plan upon reading in *The Odyssey* how Odysseus held on to the belly of the sheep to sneak past the blinded eye of the raging Cyclops. The boy that was to become Reverend Beasley had held on as long as he could, his biceps cramping into knots, his grip feeling permanently clawed, before dropping off a mile or so outside of the walls and rolling into the muck of the drainage ditch beside the road. He hid in that muck until long past dark when he heard the whistle of the midnight train. For months before the day of his escape, he'd lain awake in his bunk figuring the schedule. He'd timed this moment and he raced to hop one of the thundering boxcars. He said he'd never run so fast in all his life; he didn't know he could run so fast. "But I nailed her drag on the fly!

And pulled myself up!" All he knew as he sat heaving in the open door, the shadowed country clacking past with only the spacing of telephone poles passing to mark off the miles, was that he was heading east, across the state, toward Alabama. At State Home, Charles Beasley's goal had been to read every single book in the dusty and ill-kept old library. Not only had he found the key to unlocking his escape plan hidden inside the pages of *The Odyssey*, he discovered for himself, without any clue from the white teachers who were hired to teach at the home, that there was a school—a *college*—founded by and for *Negroes!*

Using the big atlas, he'd traced a map to Tuskegee, Alabama. Nightly, as he waited to time the lonely whistle of the train, he'd studied it.

"I didn't know *anything*," Reverend Beasley boomed from the pulpit, pausing to scan his congregation, their fans bobbing and heads nodding, meeting his parishioners eye to eye. "I was as ignorant as the day is long, as the world is wide. But I knew one thing: I was *going* to that school."

He showed up on campus at the end of the summer, having slept in boxcars and walked who-knew-how-many miles over the course of nearly two months to find his way there. The one thing he hadn't been able to glean from his books was an accurate conception of such a distance. His clothes and the treasured map of the directions he'd drawn of how to get there hung ragged in tatters from a nasty fall he'd taken on the cinders chasing after a speeding train he'd caught only to be thrown off by a Pinkerton guard. He arrived at Tuskegee covered with soot as if he actually had work as a chimney sweep, though in fact he was jobless and didn't have a penny to his name. He informed the secretary behind the desk of the first big building that confronted him that he was "here." She took a long look at him and excused herself. It turned out that Charles H. Beasley had had the good providence to stumble into the administrative building that housed the office of the president himself.

The president stepped out of his office buttoning his three-piece suit. He invited the young Charles H. Beasley into his grand office—Charles entered with slack-jawed awe; he'd never seen such sumptuousness, not even in a white person's home—and offered him a seat. The president took the chair directly across from him and crossed his legs and rested his hands in his lap to hear Charles out. When Charles H. Beasley finished the story of the home and his journey, the president nodded. He tapped his chin, appraising him again.

"You understand, Mr. Beasley," the president began, "that the usual course for a prospective student to be accepted into a program of study at Tuskegee is that he first apply."

Reverend Beasley said he felt suddenly foolish—the joke entirely on him. He saw his one hope slipping away. A sweat heated up the back of his neck, going cold down his spine.

"Yes, sir," he said, sitting up even straighter in his chair. He gripped the arms. "But let me say that I think I have shown great *application* in planning my escape and making my way here all by myself."

The president looked at him and then he smiled. Then he laughed. He stood up and offered Charles his hand. "Yes, Mr. Beasley," he said. "I'd say you have."

The Reverend Charles Beasley became part of the "Tuskegee Tradition," graduating from the university summa cum laude. As class valedictorian, he rose to speak at the commencement, where he first told his story—the trail of tribulations, he said, which *allowed* him to succeed.

Shortly after graduation, he married his wife, Victoria, the daughter of his mentor in his combined studies in sociology and theology. Together the two had made the decision to return to Mississippi as social reformers. With a grant donated by the trustees of the college, they founded Children's Home for Orphaned Negro Children.

Ruthie woke Sally to help her get ready for the trip. "Reverend Beasley, he an upright and educated man. He done graduated from *col*-lege. Ignorance his enemy," she said. "He on the warpath against stupidity and stupidity running scared."

Baby threw up once, quickly, efficiently, expectantly in the toilet while she was getting dressed, wiped her lips, and reapplied her lipstick. Mr. Brumsfield had thought her idea about taking Sally to Children's Home was worth a try, but what had happened at their house the night before made Baby feel as if what she ought to do was dig in and keep Sally there at 12 East Percy Street with them forever—and she would have, too, if she didn't think it would cause Sally and her own girls more undue trouble. Now Baby was prepared to go. In the kitchen, she hesitated, waiting to walk out the door. The three girls were coming down the hall. She slipped the loaded pistol into her purse.

Claire and Jeana pressed against the screen, looking after Baby and Sally. "Good-bye, Sally!" they called and Sally waved shyly back at them.

"So long."

Baby and Sally walked side by side. Baby put her arm around her slight shoulders and guided her down the path to the car, steadying her other hand on her own stomach.

RIVERS BEND LAY thirty miles north of Eureka but safely southwest of Ruleton. Baby left the highway at the hamlet of Hushpuckashaw and drove another ten miles until she slowed at the border of the pecan grove that surrounded Children's Home. The silver mailbox that read REV./MRS. BEASLEY RR#7 revealed the way. The Beasleys didn't advertise the place as a home for Negro foster children and the grove helped hide the success they'd made out of the farm from view.

Baby glanced back at Sally, who was sitting up on the edge of the backseat to see out the window. "Here we are. This is it," she said.

"I don't see a home or no children neither," Sally said. "Where they live at? All I see's trees."

"They're pecan trees. This is the reverend's grove. There's a home all right. Children, too. Wait and see."

Baby turned down the tunneled drive. Children's Home rose into view—a sprawling white ranch with black shutters. The house stood on the opposite side of a circular gravel drive at the center of which grew a complex cultivation of flowers, perennials planted to bloom in turn, the colors picked to rise and fall and bud and fade into each other all summer long. Baby recognized cosmos and lady's slippers, taller daylilies clumped into bright batches of yellow and orange. Roses grew on a trellis in the full sun against the south side of the house, while grapes purpled in the sun, arching the latticed walkway that led from the front door across the lawn to the quaint brick chapel. Behind the chapel grew a small apple orchard, the trees stunted and low, limbs twisted. The reverend had even managed to graft a few orange trees. On the far side of the field bordered a canebrake. The yellowing slats had grown at least fifteen feet high and flourished thickly green, and close-ranked, good as any fence. The house and outbuildings sat up on a rise. Baby could see the trees that bordered the far side of the Hushpuckashaw River winding across the distance—the farm nestled in the bend of an oxbow, surrounded by the flow of its yellow water on three sides.

Baby circled the flowers and parked before the house. She glanced back at Sally.

"What do you think?"

"I never seen no place as pretty as this. How can I live here? Why would they let me do that?"

"You'll have to meet Reverend and Mrs. Beasley and see for yourself."

Baby climbed out and opened the door for Sally, but Sally still didn't move, not entirely trusting her eyes. Her thin, deerlike legs were tucked ready to spring beneath her. She looked as if she longed to run, but there was nowhere for her to go. They'd arrived.

Outside the car, Baby could smell the rich fertility of the fields— manure and the odors of animals, hot grass. A little boy sitting on a short stool in the open door of the barn wringing squirts of milk from a cow into a metal pail looked under his grip on the udder to peek at Sally. Other children who worked in the garden looked out at them from under wide-brimmed hats.

"It don't look real," she said. "Not real like I seen real."

Baby held out her hand.

Sally looked past her and Baby turned to see Penelope, the English teacher who had returned to work at Children's Home, where she'd once been a charge herself, step out of the schoolhouse. She wore a blue print skirt and a white blouse, her hair pulled neatly back into a bun. A tiny wooden cross hung on a chain around her neck.

"Good morning," Baby said and offered her hand. "You probably don't remember me. It's been years. I'm Mrs. Allen from the Welfare Office. Forgive us for disturbing your lessons."

"Mrs. Allen." Penelope smiled. She extended her hand. "Certainly I remember you. And don't worry about the lesson." She turned to see the row of faces jockeying to peer out the windows of the chapel. "My pupils are more than happy for the distraction. Who do we have here?"

"This is Sally Johnson." Baby stepped aside.

Penelope stepped up to the opened door and leaned down to look into the car at Sally, who had scooted all the way to the opposite end of the seat, her back up against the door. Penelope put out her hand. "It's nice to meet you, Sally. I'm Miss Penny."

Sally blinked at her.

Penelope smiled. "I know exactly how you feel. I felt the same way. I'll never forget the day I met the Family."

"Is Reverend Beasley here?"

"I believe he's in his study. Miss Victoria is inside as well. If you'd like, we'll watch after Sally."

Baby looked into the car. "Are you okay, Sally? I promise I'll be right back."

Sally kept her eyes on Miss Penny, then shifted them quickly to meet Baby's.

"Would you like to meet the other children?" Miss Penny asked. Baby nodded at Sally and turned toward the house.

Victoria welcomed Baby in. She wore a dress with a high lace collar. "Mrs. Allen," she said. "So good to see you again. Charles will be relieved. He just got back in from the fields. He's prepping his afternoon lesson in geometry for the older children. Mathematics was never his best subject, which is why he insists on teaching it. The man is a glutton for punishment."

Victoria knocked at the door of the study. "Charlie? Mrs. Allen from the Welfare Office is here."

The reverend pulled open the door. He still wore overalls. His reading spectacles rested tipped down at the end of his nose; he looked over the tops of them at her. A sprinkling of white lightly touched his hair. The office behind him stood crammed floor to ceiling with books, as if the place were a depository. A soft sagging chair covered by a patchwork blanket afforded the only space to read. The blinds had been pulled to focus the attention of the lamp.

"Mrs. Allen. To what do we owe this pleasure?"

"Perhaps I could speak with you and Victoria for a moment. I have a little girl with me. She's outside with Penelope."

"Hmm?" Reverend Beasley peeled off his spectacles and tucked them in the front pocket of his overalls. He negotiated the labyrinthine path between the piles of books and parted the curtain. Beyond him, Baby could see the other children outside, clustered now about Miss Penny. Coaxed out of the backseat, Sally stood in the center of them, listening, Baby imagined, as Miss Penny had them politely introduce themselves.

Still looking out the window, the reverend said, "We're at capacity. And even Claude won't graduate for another year. But you knew that, didn't you? And you still came." He paused, thinking. "This must be Letitia Johnson's little girl. I didn't know Letitia Johnson, but the word spreading fast is that she had a daughter. Isn't it amazing what one can hear even without a telephone?" He glanced around at Baby.

"I found her hiding out at their cabin Monday after the lynching. I've been trying to find her a foster home, but everyone's frightened. She's staying with us on East Percy Street. Last night the Klan paid us a visit. Fortunately no one was hurt. "

The reverend let the curtain drop. "Didn't I tell you this morning, Beth? We've been getting too comfortable around here of late. The Lord hasn't tested us in any significant way in quite some time. He told me this was coming—at matins, in my prayers, this morning. I knew it all day yesterday, like a hand on my shoulder, but I didn't know it was going to be you, Mrs. Allen. With her."

Reverend Beasley clasped his hands behind his back. He looked at his wife, who nodded back at him.

"Mrs. Allen," he said, "would you be so kind as to introduce Victoria and me to our daughter?"

chapter nine

OMFORT. THAT'S ALL Dorothy had needed. A little comforting to stop her crying. Someone to hold her. So Sissy had held her. She held and held her daughter, Dorothy. She wouldn't let go holding her. Tiny bubbles floating up, face mashed, fish-cheeked, blowing, magnified wide by the water, eyes blue, floating hair, the sudden screaming silence now in the aftermath of the dunking splash. *One, two, three, four* . . . Had she then? Sissy? For a fact? Was the image a remembrance? A recollection? She couldn't summon the moment exactly. Quite. She could not clearly recall what had happened that night.

She tried to. She tried her best to make the picture of what had happened exactly and there a picture suddenly was. Clear in her mind's eye as if it was happening again right then, right now, again. She watched the woman she saw as herself as if she were outside herself. The mother and daughter bathing naked together in the big white, claw-footed tub. The water running, pattering. The daughter crying, Dorothy distraught. The mother holding her. Comforting her. Sissy could see the woman; she'd been trying her best. A bath, she'd thought, might help. The consolation of warm water. The pleasantness of skin on skin. Mother and daughter. Was the baby still crying? Sissy listened. It seemed terribly important to her to be able to say to herself if what she saw and heard that night was real or not, no matter what she said to anyone else or what her husband, Clyde, told her to say.

They'd been in the bathtub together. The warm running water pattering into the drawn tub. She and Dorothy. Taking a nice long soak. They were in the tub soaking together. A pretty picture. A perfectly plausible picture. The fact of their bath together seemed tangible. Real enough for Sissy to get a grip on. To touch, *feel* even. Her skin pinked, the flush of heat. Then what happened? Had she fallen asleep? Slid underneath? She was so tired all the time, always now it seemed since the birth. Could she have fallen asleep in the craziness of all that crying? Her shrieks screeching up and down like an air-raid siren. Clyde storming in. What's that crying! Stop that crying! he yelled.

Clyde's yelling was something she could hear. She heard it as if it had really happened. She saw it happening. She felt the return of her alarm. She just needs a little comforting. Someone to hold her. I thought a warm bath might be a good idea. And so she'd tried to hold her, keep hold of her. Clyde had held her, too, trying. They both struggled to hold her. Slippery as soap! A fat little greased watermelon! A squealing porky pink pig! Oh! There she goes! Weeee! She slipped under, everyone splashing as if find the baby were a game they were playing with her, all three of them happily together, splashing. But when she bobbed up again Dorothy was screaming even worse than before. No holds barred! Shaking. Terrified. When she dunked under screaming at the top of her lungs the screaming stopped, but when she popped up, sputtering, coughing, she came unstuck, unplugged. A vomit of screaming sprayed by. Her face quivering out the fat squeeze of tears. Red-faced. Such alarm! Oh dear! The suck of water that was supposed to be air had scared her. She was only a baby!

Sissy grabbed her arm. She and Clyde fought hand over hand for control of her parts. Clyde got to her neck first. Who was pulling and who was shoving Sissy couldn't say. She needed to see it again.

The moment slipped from her grip, misted before her like steam from the bath. She was naked and the baby was naked and Clyde was soaked in his green-and-blue-striped Country Club tie and white shirt. Breathing hard. Struggling. Battling over their baby. Water sloshed over the tub and onto the floor. She shoved and Clyde banged down in the slick. *Damn!* he said. She searched underneath her bottom and legs frantically. When she got a grip on her, took hold and hauled her up to hug, comfort, at last, Dorothy hung dripping, her shock of white hair pinked, plastered to her head, but she did not cry. She was not crying anymore.

Sissy took that as a sign. Sissy stood from the tub pattering and wrapped her daughter in a fresh pink towel and carried her into their room and laid her on the bed. But Dorothy was so tired! The bath had worked. Done its job. She looked angelic, cherubic. So sweetly silent now. Sissy was afraid she'd wake her. She couldn't get her to wake up. Dorothy was so sleepy! Such a sleepy girl. She'd never been so quiet! So good! And Clyde was not yelling for once. Appeased by this silence, he'd gone pounding down the stairs. Sissy held her daughter then, just the two of them alone together on the bed, rocking. Sissy cuddled her, cooing, cradled her close. Rocked her and rocked her, singing *Hey, nonny nonny*. Nonsense. A lullaby. Such a good baby! Such a pretty, sweet, quiet, well-behaved girl.

That's all they'd ever wanted from her really. That's all. And now she'd learned her lesson. Sissy wanted to show Clyde now how good Baby Dorothy could be, but when Clyde returned, still breathing hard, soaked, the green-and-blue tie hanging twisted about his neck, he only looked at her. He was saying other things. The words spouted out of his mouth like silver bubbles that turned into sentences of dark mud. Telling her. He had it all figured out. It had been an accident, he knew that. He assured her. He told her she hadn't meant to do it really. He'd tried to stop her from drowning their baby. Why had she done it? he asked. He was trying to understand. He was being so understanding now. He wouldn't let them take her, Sissy. He was her husband, wasn't he?

Sissy stared at him. The story he told her about what she'd done to their daughter went in one ear and out the other. She didn't even feel concerned. She tried to see it the way he said it had happened. He told her what they were going to have to do. Dr. Jenks had arrived. Clyde had gone downstairs and called him to come alone. She'd drowned, the doctor explained, after examining Dorothy. That was his official opinion. Water had filled her lungs. They were tiny sacks. No bigger than this. He circled his hands. When the doctor turned her upside down, bath water poured onto the floor. The proof still lukewarm. Water had been the instrument. Clyde collapsed in a chair. Letitia had been bathing her! he confessed. He told the doctor their story, the sentences of dark mud snaking out of his mouth. Clyde detailed the events for him. He drew it as perfectly as if he'd witnessed the event. He had witnessed it. He had not changed his shirt. He dropped his face in his hands. *When I came home* . . . He grabbed his hair. Rage shuddered through him.

Sheriff Dodd stepped into the room to hear, listening silently, looking. He nodded. We'll pick her up. We'll take care of this. Sissy sat there on the edge of the bed. She was wearing a print dress she could not recall putting on. *Letitia.* Then she'd run away. A Negro, of course. Can you imagine how much she must hate us? her husband said. They hate us. It was his way of explaining Letitia's motive. But Sissy could find no room inside her head for the facts he unfolded. She tried and tried—Clyde had explained to her how hard she needed to try if she didn't want to spend the rest of her life on a place like Parchman Farm. Maybe they'd give her the chair. It wasn't really her fault. He said he didn't blame her. The crying was a lot.

But no matter what Clyde said, how many times he repeated it, the picture of Letitia drowning Dorothy wouldn't come. She couldn't even imagine it. Nobody asked her. She was obviously disturbed. Dr. Jenks was observing her. She was under close observation. She'd been understandably distraught at discovering her baby girl drowned floating facedown in the bathtub. Clyde had rushed to her side. Together they'd hefted Dorothy out and onto the bed.

Dr. Jenks understood perfectly. He asked no more questions. He'd been the Rules' family doctor for years. She hardly felt the prick. She was still struggling to get the pictures right in her head. The truth would not take hold. She could not hold on to it, slipperier than a wet baby even. She was thrashing about inside herself.

Letitia! How could she do such a thing? Sissy had trusted her. The betrayal was monstrous. Letitia Johnson had raised her, Sissy! She'd been Sissy's only nurse all her growing up. Sissy had suckled those same breasts. Her brain presented the evidence that Clyde had described of Letitia doing what he said she'd done and why. He had it all figured out. He knew how people worked. He said exactly how they would react. She heard someone begin to scream. Stop that screaming! Crying! But Dorothy lay silent. It wasn't Dorothy crying. Shrouded in the pink towel. Waxen cheeked as any doll. Squeaky clean. Sissy became hysterical. Clyde removed the body from the room. A strange icy warmth flowed through Sissy's veins. She could trace the progression of calm. She could have laughed. Dr. Jenks held her hand. She couldn't bear to look at him. She turned the other way and stared at the wall. She lay on her back on the chaise though she couldn't remember having sat. You're feeling very sleepy. She was! But she was thinking now wasn't the time to sleep. She had something important she had to tell someone, she was thinking, thinking she had to get up, she had to, when the trance of the tranquilizer took hold and knocked her cold.

She had violent dreams. Thrashing, still struggling to raise the baby. *A straitjacket might not be a bad idea. It's in her best interest. We don't want her to do herself harm.* In her mind, while she slept, Sissy kept swimming up toward the surface bright of unencumbered belief. How hard could it be? As easy as convincing herself that black was white and white was black, that day was night and night was day. People could believe any old thing and often did. If you could believe in God. What a ludicrous idea. A white-bearded twinkly-eyed Santa in the sky. Dispensing the prettily wrapped gift of eternal life! Free for the asking! All one needed to do was repent.

Simple as pie. Bother. Of course, this was separate from belief in the hierarchy of the church, which was more of a social concern. A class consideration. You had your Episcopalians. And you had your Presbyterians. Baptists. Methodists. Catholics, though they'd been kept to a handful in Ruleton. There was a world of difference between the sects that made perfect sociological sense. But that He would send His Son. Sissy submerged the truth. Held it under and waited for it to gasp its last. Stop thrashing. Go still.

Sissy lay in bed for the next few days with nothing better to do through the long hot afternoons alone in her room than try to hold on to her head. She felt it might roll right off her shoulders and bounce off the bed and bump onto the floor and go bashing down the stairs and right out the front door. And then what would she do! One couldn't just walk around headless. One couldn't even really lie propped up in bed headless. Could one?

All she'd needed was a little love. To stop the constant crying. Hold her. That's how it worked with babies. Sissy had wanted desperately to get the hang of it. That's what Letitia told her. "All she need a little holdin'. Rock her." And she'd tried to show her the miracle of gentling. It worked for Letitia every time. Dorothy going quiet in her arms. Immediately silent. Cooing quiet. Content. Comforted. At home. A good, well-brought-up little bundle of joy.

"You have been a comfort to me . . ." Sissy wished she could have said that to Letitia at least. Before. She should have. She never ever had, not once. It just wasn't *done.* Her brain spun. Continued to spin—the blur of a spinning yin-yang, a whirl of evil and good, world without end, amen. She shut her eyes and waited for it to stop. Dr. Jenks had visited her again just that morning. He'd been visiting twice a day since. She could tell he was growing tired of it. Bored. He liked to think he was important. His importance to the family had been acknowledged. He had taken his own Hippocratic oath: The life he preserved was his own, Sissy thought. But now that nearly several days had passed he didn't feel so important being there. She was almost calm enough, he thought, to attend her child's funeral, which was to be held on Friday—a week since her death. Clyde wasn't around to notice his good works. Clyde had already recognized his importance, by phoning him and entrusting the particulars of Dorothy's death to his care and discretion. But now Clyde wasn't there. He'd gone back to work at the bank. She noted the age in Dr. Jenks's black eyes, no accusation there. You'd never know he knew. The pricks let her sleep. He couldn't make it all the time. He had a practice to attend to. It wasn't so important that he give her the injections personally. He left Clyde the loaded syringes and told him how to inject her. How much he could use. The proper dose. Opium did have its dangers. Sissy didn't think she could shoot herself with the needle. Just looking at the sharp silver glint of the needle made her blanch and go watery, her limbs liquid. But without the ice in her veins, the heavenly warmth, she couldn't sleep. She hadn't slept under her own power since that night she'd lifted Dorothy out of the tub, dripping, heavier than she recognized her having been in her mother's arms. Face composed into a blubbering suck. Shadow blue eyes wide in terror or surprise—Sissy couldn't decide. Bluer than the blue dark bruise she had gotten getting born. Oh.

"You have been a comfort to me . . ." A comfort. That's what Letitia had been. But Letitia was gone. Letitia had disappeared. She'd never returned once she'd left the house to walk home that night that Sissy had unswaddled Dorothy and climbed into the warm tub to comfort her. Clyde wouldn't show her the newspaper. The newspapers vanished. He said he didn't want her to have to read about Dorothy. She'd been through enough. But Sissy knew. No use pretending she didn't. She knew. She'd known. She could not deny it. She'd understood the revenge such an accusation would ignite. Knew that Clyde was counting on it so that the questions would stop there. The assumption of guilt. Swift justice. The madness of the mob. No time for a trial. The deed done. No taking it back no matter how sorry one felt.

And now Sissy had no place to hide from the picture of what had happened to Letitia that she could imagine for herself. Her body—the face beaten and bloated, distorted by the swollen buffalo-thick tongue—dangled from a rope. Letitia had paid the ultimate price; she'd been sacrificed for Sissy's life. Dorothy's death. Sissy could not escape the imagined noose draped loose around her neck. Tiptoeing up to receive it. The hemp rough as it was snugged. Everyone looking up. She closed her eyes. The boot in her back. The kick that swung her out in the air and that moment when she fell. Yanked tight. She reached for the choke but her hands were tied. Her eyes bulged. Her brain burned. She was suffocating, jerking against the pain. Blackness and a million tingling pins. Her neck did not break. . . .

Letitia raised her, Sissy. She'd always been the one to comfort Sissy when she was a baby and then a girl and a young woman and then a married woman, too, when Letitia had come to work for her as a Tisdale. Sissy's own mother had many things to do. There were always important things to do. She ran the household staff at the house, for one. The Rules had a position to maintain. They entertained quite frequently. For another, she was a champion bridge player, her mother was, had been. Her mother had been serious about her game of bridge. So Sissy had suckled at Letitia's breast as a child. Letitia had been a girl herself, Sissy realized, counting back the years now. She'd lost the baby who had brought in her milk. With no use of it for her own she'd begun her sideline as a nursemaid. Her breasts mounded massive, enough to go around. She became a kind of golden cow—because she worked for the Rules and so was considered clean and reliable. She became quite in demand among a certain set in Ruleton. Sissy didn't know the story about how Letitia lost the first baby that had gotten her started down that path. She'd never thought to ask. She'd simply sucked without thought or consideration, pure satisfaction—a comfort. Sucked in secret until she was nearly five. She would demand the breast and Letitia could not refuse her, in the pantry pulling open her white dress and hauling out a breast, whichever Sissy wished, left or right, holding it raised for her mouth. As much as she wanted and as many times. The nipple stretched purple. Sissy pushed her back and sat in her lap and sucked. She sucked and sucked. The feeling of power the forcing gave her almost as satisfying as the sucking itself. A human pacifier. She would sit on her lap and look up at Letitia looking away as she sucked the sweet, water-white milk. Sometimes she would edge a tooth in just to see.

Then Letitia had had a second child, a daughter of her own. No husband she could name. But that was often the Negro way, Sissy knew, she'd learned as a girl. You couldn't think of them like people. Letitia made extra money on the side as a nursemaid the entire time that she fed her own daughter. Letitia had acted as nursemaid for Baby Dorothy, too. Sissy saw now again the saucer-sized nipples purpled and round ripe, leaking milk against her uniform, staining yellow, which Clyde couldn't stand. "Jesus, get her to clean herself up." Even in motherhood, Sissy's breasts paled in comparison. Hers were girl-tiny, pointy. Her chest hardly swelled larger than the just swollen pout of the pink nipples themselves. They had not grown significantly since the first budding when she was twelve. After Dorothy was born the nipples hammered against her nightgown. The nipples yearning pink as the pink wanting, wide-open mouth of her daughter, Dorothy. But they only eked milk. The ducts all but dry. Dried up. No explanation. Hardly a sniff. But Clyde thought that that sort of thing was "disgusting" anyway and she'd never told him about her "moments" in the kitchen with Letitia as a girl. "So primitive," he said. "Leave it to the mammies."

Though Dorothy was her second child, Sissy agonized through labor for twenty-six hours. She was small-hipped. She could have died. Out the window she watched the yellow sun rise and rise again. When Dr. Jenks had finally delivered her of the baby—a girl, he said—he'd had his nurse take her immediately away. He did not even try to set the baby on her breast. After her first baby, Robert, everybody knew. Sissy reached after her, but she was gone, hustled away. She was taken straight to Letitia and set sucking. Sissy couldn't help but fret. The first thing a baby chick sees upon hatching it takes as its mother. The thought didn't need to be logical. She *felt* it. Clyde was logical. Babies weren't chicks, Clyde would be quick to say. She thought of those bosomy black breasts. Letitia recognized as Dorothy's mother—not her, Sissy. Sissy had recognized the mother in Letitia, too. Felt that recollection. And the new baby's father? Clyde had gone riding that morning of the birth. He was impatient. He couldn't wait. Doing nothing all day. He was a busy man. Vice president at the bank. He couldn't bear her screaming, he said. Screaming and crying got to him in ways Sissy couldn't understand. They had with Robert, too. But Robert had been *his* boy. *My son!* Pride in that at least. The fact that he had a son to carry on his name for him worth the nights' suffering and Clyde gone all during the day. They'd taken word to him at the stable when he'd ridden in that it was a girl and Sissy'd been told that he'd gone galloping off again, the horse already in a lather. He had not come back yet to face up to the crying thing he'd help make that had gushed out between her legs.

The doctor had told the black nurse who assisted him to clean them both up before Mr. Clyde returned from his ride. Clyde couldn't stand to see her without her makeup. She had to make herself presentable before she faced him. She lifted her head off the pillow to peek into the compact the nurse fetched for her. She powdered her cheeks, applied rouge, eye shadow, and lipstick. She thought, peering critically at herself, that she looked as old and unhappy as any sideshow carnival clown. She almost drew red tear-shapes under her eyes. Clyde had been the one who told the doctor that she wouldn't be breast-feeding. Sissy had tried to convince Dr. Jenks that maybe she should try again. Maybe if she tried. But Clyde had made the decision. That was final. Letitia was already in their employ. He told Dr. Jenks what to do. Letitia parted her white dress and took out her breast. Fitted the baby's mouth to her.

When he arrived after breakfast, he stood looking down at Sissy. Mud on his riding boots. Still holding on to the crop, which he stood switching against his thigh. Well, we can always try again, he said.

Nights with Dorothy the crying got to him. He'd finally *hrrumpf* up and flick on the light. His face would blow red. What hair he had left wired wild. He looked as if he would explode. He exploded. She saw his head going off out the top as if he'd put a shotgun in his mouth and pulled the trigger. The fury of his brains launched in a wet, gray-green splat against the white wall. Dripping muck. The runny ooze of yellow. Clyde couldn't stand the sight of blood. Even a paper cut made him sick to his stomach. Dr. Jenks termed it his "condition." 4-F. He was too important to be spared for the war in any case, Clyde said, and everybody he told that readily agreed— even if they made him an officer. He was an *officer* of the bank, he said. Money. Money know-how showed the good sense of real command. Real captainship. That's why he'd married her, to go into banking, he said. Clyde considered himself a steward of the public good.

Now Clyde Tisdale stood next in line to become the newly appointed president at the Planters Bank of Ruleton—not just any old officer—as soon as Old Mr. Rule passed on. Through his relation with Sissy he would inherit the title of the position that he had already officially assumed. Old Mr. Rule, Sissy's father, still went in to the bank every morning, but everyone knew that he was retired. He had to be "reminded" of things. Mr. Rule was no longer all there. When they brought him to see his granddaughter, he nodded down at her. She didn't remind him of anything. He asked whose baby it was. He asked Sissy's name.

Sissy pressed her case. She wanted to try breast-feeding again. Dr. Jenks didn't venture a medical opinion; he didn't have an opinion. When it came to the Rules, Dr. Jenks did as he was told. Clyde couldn't stand the idea of Sissy suckling the child. The picture was repulsive to him. Revolting. He wouldn't suck her breasts either. They went unattended. Sissy had gone unattended. It seemed a miracle to her that she'd ever gotten pregnant even once. Her second immaculate conception as sterile as the first. He didn't really like sex with her like that. They didn't talk about it. What they did do wasn't *natural* either—what he liked, how he liked it—Sissy thinking: *primitive*. But that's what excited him. He got so excited. Shaking. White. Shuddering. Sometimes he would curse. Call her things. Whore. He rarely cursed in public besides an emphatic *damn*. He had an image to maintain. Bitch. Fuck. Whore. Suck my cock. That was how he liked it. He liked her like that. She was so slight. From behind she always imagined her hipless body, like a boy's. She couldn't help the thought. It made her feel embarrassed for him. Her bottom a boy's bottom maybe. He'd lived in Paris for some years. He had a special tube of cream that he would ream around inside her with his finger. The only other way he liked it was in her mouth. He would thrust himself in her mouth until he came, eyes closed, groaning, and gripping her hair as she gagged on him, but not between her legs where the babies came from. The few times she'd ever been driven to touch herself she would not admit that what she thought of was Letitia's breast in her mouth. The thought as disconcerting to her as if she'd committed a sin she would go to hell for, if she were religious but she wasn't. She said the words every Sunday in church. She'd memorized them from the time she was a girl so that she wouldn't have to read or think about them much. They bored her. Clyde bored her. In bed his stammered "wickedness" seemed passé. Sex bored her. Everything bored her. She was bored to death. Only the pain got her attention. Children were her pain. You had to have them. It was expected. Everybody had them. And her father, Old Mr. Robert, expected heirs—even if he couldn't remember his grandson's name, which was his name. Clyde had to try, no matter what he liked and didn't like. He tried, facing her, at half-mast, a thickening just better than limp to slip inside. Their trying was the price she paid, too, for being a Rule. That was all that was expected of her really. Babies. She knew it. She'd always known it. Since she was a girl. All through school. She saw herself as much of a golden cow as Letitia was made to be. So a cow without milk. A milkless cow. A sheeplike cow. Taking it. Udderly. She'd calved the girl.

But she felt it. She'd ripped badly. Slashed, an episiotomy to make way for the delivery. Dorothy at nine pounds fifteen ounces. Huge. A little monster. She'd lain breach for the longest time. She didn't want to come out. Then she had shifted and her head had emerged, pouring out of the water world she would shortly return to. Sissy pushed. She thought she'd pass out. She screamed, feeling the tearing. And then the lightning-bright slash. But Clyde hadn't cared. She hadn't healed, even begun to mend. Eight weeks at least Dr. Jenks said before she could resume "relations." And she thought giving birth was bad! The jingle of his belt coming down a few days later might as well have been the uncoiling of a whip with metal tips, a cat-o'-nine-tails, the sharp lash of him on her naked backside.

Clyde Clyde . . .

Dark so he couldn't see the blood.

He thrust away. He hadn't used the glide of the ointment even. He meant to hurt her. She knew. The blood the only lubricant.

He washed himself in the dark, too.

Letitia knew because it was Letitia who had to comfort her and tend to the tearing when she went away from herself in pain and blacked out—finding her facedown on the bed in the morning after Clyde left. She'd come to alone with Letitia in the room. Letitia had found her there. She cleaned her as if she were a baby and wrapped her small body in a silk robe. Clean cotton sheets on the bed. The sunlight streaming in. Good as any asylum Sissy could imagine herself confined in. She was coming unhinged. Clyde had gone on to the office afterward. He was always at the office these days, it seemed. Before when he'd spent the night away—she didn't care where—she breathed a sigh of relief. She'd let Dorothy cry through the night. Only on those nights when Clyde slept away did she fall through the deep well of her waking consciousness into some semblance of sleep. If not at peace, then at rest. R.I.P. Was this what it was like to be just dead? If so, it didn't seem so bad. Preferable even. She couldn't imagine what all the fuss was about.

May I see her? she'd ask Letitia. Not a request. It was her child after all. Her baby girl. Letitia brought Dorothy in and offered her to Sissy, but Sissy put up the flat of her hands. Just seeing the baby she could feel her nipples perking, eager, wanting their work, to do their mother's job. She dripped. Two drops. She stared at the spermlike liquid, pressed the robe to absorb the spot of fluid. No fountain. A leak. No. You do it. Clyde wouldn't approve. I just wanted to see her.

Letitia held her and Sissy looked. Do you think she'll be beautiful? Is she a beautiful girl, at least?

Yes'm. Beautiful as you and Mr. Clyde and Young Mr. Robert all is.

Sissy wasn't sure. I'm not so sure. Turn her this way. She looked at her. She looked fat. She was a fat little thing. Eyes the color of cubed pool water brightened the fat folds of her face. It must be Letitia's milk doing that. Though Letitia wasn't fat. She was solid. She was strong. In a kind of brute, animal way. She had the muscled beauty of an ox.

What's that bruise? Sissy pointed at the side of the baby's head. The fingernail like a pointer. She didn't touch.

It'll go away. It's just from being born. They's some knocks along the way in this life. She got her start.

I see. Sissy felt her own blood seep onto the sheets beneath her. Oh. That's enough for now. Please, take her away. I'll need a fresh robe and bedding.

Yes'm.

But the nights were worse. Once Letitia left for the day. They were the worst. They got worse and worse. They didn't get any better. When Clyde did come home. When the child started to cry. A baby's crying. Clyde had no patience. He wasn't built like that, he said. He had absolutely no patience. Diapers. Drool on his New York Hickey Freeman suits. But he had the least amount of patience for that.

Can't you stop her? he'd say. Get out of bed and stop her. Shut her up. I have to work tomorrow. I can't live like this.

Sissy hobbled down the hall to the nursery. Their son, Robert, slept in his own room in the opposite wing so that his precious sleep wouldn't be disturbed. He was a beautiful growing baby boy. Sissy waddled, holding on to the gash underneath, trying not to let it tear again, any more. She had not called Dr. Jenks to sew her back up after Clyde had finished with her. It would be too embarrassing. And Clyde might need her again. When the doctor had told her to wait before resuming relations, she had been relieved to hear the command. She would have waited an eternity to have sex with Clyde again. But Clyde had needed release. It had been so long for him. Weeks because when she was pregnant he couldn't bear to touch her. He'd been patient with her about that, he said. She shuffled down the hall and opened the door to the nursery. Alone, she stood looking over the railing down into the crib and tried to shush her. Shhhhhhhhhhh. It didn't work. Clyde would slam the door going into the bathroom. Damn it!

Shhhhhhhhhhhhhhh.

Sissy didn't want to touch her. She didn't dare pick her up, though she could smell the black stool of meconium laid in the room. The smell squatted in the air like a dark toad. The diaper needed to be changed again. Her nipples were pounding. Aching her. The pulse of another punishment. But her heart had the property of a wooden block in her chest. The block did not even feel heavy. It didn't feel at all. Merely inanimate. Impassive. Lumpish. It did not recognize Dorothy as a part of her, flesh of her flesh. She felt the old boredom returning, hooding her own eyes. She pulled the blanket over the baby's face to silence her.

Shhhhhhhhhhhhhhhhh.

The crying escalated beneath the blanket—Dorothy was screaming now, trying to catch her breath, gulping, scared at being covered, struggling, smothered—Sissy had scared herself at how long she'd held the covers over the fat face. Now her heart was pounding. She left the baby crying, closing the door behind her, and stumbled down the back stairs to the big kitchen and flipped on the stark white light. It was so bright at night in the big white cavelike echo of the kitchen. Letitia had left the tiles gleaming when she'd left to walk home that evening. Sissy heated a bottle of Letitia's milk. It bubbled boiling. Sissy started. She must have nodded off. Upstairs she could hear the wailing. She snatched the bottle out of the boiling water, afraid to try it on her own wrist. She had learned not to scald the baby. Scalding was counterproductive. Scalding the baby only made her crying worse. She set it on the counter to cool.

Shhhhhhhhhhhhhhhhhh.

Clyde started cursing. The curses were directed at her, not the baby. He didn't acknowledge the baby girl. It was as if it were she, Sissy, crying. She felt the tears. Sissy covered her ears and squeezed her eyes closed not to hear. The baby wouldn't take the bottle no matter how many times Sissy leaned over the rail and tried to poke the rubber nipple in her mouth. Maybe she was retarded? That bruise on her Mongolian-sized head could mean brain damage. The sense squeezed between the strong tongs of the forceps. Finally, at her wit's end at the baby's crying, Clyde's threats if she didn't DO something, she gave up on the bottle and hobbled back up the stairs, threw a blanket around the stinking baby and hustled it up into a blanket and swept down the stairs and out into the throbbing heat of the yard and across the lawn and put the baby in the car and drove in her robe to Letitia Johnson's cabin.

The cabin was hardly bigger than the toolshed for the gardens in back of their own house. The headlights shone brightly against the rough-hewn plank walls, revealing open knots in the wood. How could she stay clean in there? She wondered if Letitia could possibly be clean. Her salivaed breasts. She saw Letitia peek back the curtains. The lights shone on her clouded wide moon of a face. She blinked against the spotlight. She couldn't see a thing. Sissy beeped the horn to let her know who it was. She didn't want to scare her. The tablecloth curtain dropped.

Letitia opened the door and stepped down the stairs, wearing a homemade kind of shift. She walked slowly. Hurry, Sissy thought. She was as impatient as Clyde at insolence. She did not appreciate her help acting *smart*. Didn't she know that she wouldn't have come if it weren't an *emergency?* She should appreciate Sissy's position. She'd rather be sleeping, too, wouldn't she? She'd rather this baby had never entered their world. So impatient that she didn't bother to apologize for waking her. Letitia worked for her. Without her, Letitia had nothing. Was nothing. Letitia existed for her; she always had. When she thought of her own childhood, she thought of Letitia. The memories were the same. She assumed it was the same for Letitia. She imagined that Letitia thought of her needs and desires all the time. Sissy believed that. Sissy had been raised to believe it. Her desires held the preciousness of primary concern. Letitia's life had always revolved in orbit around hers. Hadn't her daddy given Letitia to her when she'd married? She'd accepted the gift. She believed Letitia appreciated that and how much she needed her— relied on her really, if she thought about it! The compliment implied by that. Her need. And she needed Letitia now. Again tonight.

She's hungry, Sissy said. I've tried everything. She'd rolled down her window, but she didn't bother to get out of the car. Dorothy lay in a blanket on the backseat. And I think she may need to be changed.

Letitia bent to look in at her. It ain't but four in de morning.

The baby doesn't know that, Sissy said. She was trying to be patient. Negroes, even the best of them, were always a little slow on the uptake. Sissy was also a little shocked—just short of letting herself feel offended—left wondering at Letitia's insensitivity. I'm having a very difficult time here, she said. She said it as evenly as she could. Trying to keep the tremor out of her voice. She was appealing directly to Letitia's sense of decency.

Letitia sighed. I'll take her inside where I can sit. Do you want to come in?

Sissy had never in her life been inside Letitia Johnson's shack before. She shook her head. Her daughter wasn't going in there either. She thought again of the grime. It scared her, that sort of filthiness. The depravity of it. How could they live like that? In such abject squalor. They might as well make their homes in teepees. No, she said. Feed her here. You can sit on the backseat. And then change her. And I have to have you at the house earlier. I've been meaning to speak with you about this. My husband and I have our own lives to live. This is becoming rather unbearable for us. Why should I have to drive all the way out here to this godforsaken place to beg you to take care of my daughter? You work for me. I need you at night, too. At least until Dorothy stops nursing.

Yes'm, Letitia said. I know. But I have a daughter, too. She ain't but a little girl. I don't see her all day already and . . .

Sissy waved away this argument. Letitia was missing the point. Letitia Johnson had raised her. Letitia's daughter was not Sissy's concern. That's not my concern. I really can't stand excuses, you know, Letitia. And neither can Clyde. We have a problem here. You are our nursemaid. I can't produce milk. We're talking about the life of our baby. I'm sure your girl can survive nights without you for a little while. It's not like I'm asking for the whole world.

Letitia opened the back door and sagged in. Yes'm. No'm. She raised the front of her shift and revealed the gargantuan heftiness of her whopping left breast. Sissy stared fascinated at it, horrified as Dorothy's jaw seemed to unhinge almost snakelike, frantically seeking the great thumb-sized nipple. She happily stuffed her whole mouth. Her tiny white hand pressed and kneaded the dark softness, more, more. She drank it in hungrily. Greedily. Obviously starving. Slurped. Burped. She farted. Letitia rubbed her eyes. She yawned. Feeding babies as natural for her as breathing. Sissy turned away. Tears stung her eyes. She made herself turn. But she could hear the soft sucking noises going on and on behind her back. The contentment that filled the cab. A moan of pleasure. The noises were so awful. Terribly sexual. Sucking and sucking. The wet satisfied sounds of the sucking drove Sissy crazy. She felt she might go running into the fields ripping at her own clothing, stumbling on her high heels, tearing out her hair. But she remained in the car. She glanced in the rearview mirror to sneak a peek into the backseat under the pretext of checking her face. She kept a spare compact in the car. Met Letitia's eyes waiting there. Calm as could be. Knowing. They'd known each other all Sissy's life. They were in this together, Sissy thought, softening. Feeling her calm return. Letitia had raised her like this, too. Comfort in that. She remembered . . .

What did you say your daughter's name was again?

Letitia broke the gaze. She looked over the moon-backed black fields. Sally, she said. My daughter's name is Sally. Sally. My Sally, she said.

chapter ten

T HEY'D LAID THE *big* _____ *on the floor*. They almost didn't have enough kitchen to keep him. *He'd lain lying on the floor.* Not now, but then, in a time ago that *was*, not *is*. Days before. In a place someplace Jakey was corrected again and again to call the *had been*. Jakey guessed he was still lying there wherever that is because, if not, then where did was go since he could still see it, feel it even better sometimes than the is of the instant before him? Almost as real as sitting in the rocker rocking watching his mama finish getting dressed for the funeral they are off to now.

They would go to the viewing his mama has said, Daddy, too. And then they will go to her funeral.

"Jakey, where are your shoes? Will you help Lee get ready to go when he wakes up from his nap?" The blue pants itch and the stiff shirt scratches at his neck. The heat makes it worse. "Come here. Quit fidgeting. Let me comb your hair."

"A viewing? Like a seeing? What will we see?"

"You'll see."

"Why? Where?" he asks.

"Where you see the person who's to be buried, that's a viewing. Before they close the casket."

"The dead person? That baby?"

"Yes. Dorothy. Dorothy was the baby's name. But she died. It's just so terribly terribly sad."

"Are you sad, Mama?"

"I'm sad about that. She was just a baby. She hardly had a chance."

Jakey thinks about how this is his chance to see a dead baby. He imagines her like the two-headed fetal pig kept pickled pink in a jar that he'd seen at the freak show at the fair. The skinny carny wouldn't let him go in the tent. You had to be twelve. But the carny had snuck it out. *Lookee here.* The carny held something behind his back so he couldn't see. *Letcha peek for a penny.* Jake turned over the penny in his pocket, rubbing it against the nickel—all the money he had. The carny held out his dirt-lined palm. He held the jar low. *Now you seen it long enough. I'm goina get caught. Less you gotcha another penny. For a nickel I'll letcha hold the jar.* Jakey had left the tent broke, his pockets emptied, feeling shaken. He felt as if he'd been held up-side down and emptied. He'd held the jar and turned the pink pig to see it all around. *Careful, don'tcha drop it now!* Two snouts. Two pig faces. Four pale blue eyes. The two pig heads had been joined at the brain. The two ears had two heads between them. The carny flipped Jakey's nickel and caught it, flipped and caught it. *Getcha some more money and come on back. We'll be here. I got other things I could show ya.* He winked. Jakey walked away with his hands deep in his pockets. He couldn't even buy a pink high cotton candy. But he knew. If he had had another penny he'd have taken it back to the carny.

Jakey feels a thrill now at the idea of seeing a real live dead baby for as long as he wants free.

Curiosity killed the cat is what his daddy would say and wink at him.

His daddy said Bigger. His daddy said *Negro.* His daddy didn't use the other word.

Why not, Daddy? Everybody else does.

They'd laid *Bigger* on the floor.

"There. You look so handsome. Now shoes. Find Lee's shoes too, please. You're such a big help to me. What would I do without you? Your father should be home by now. He promised."

Jakey had been peeking past the gap of the swinging door. The big Negro whom he didn't know then to call Bigger had come in through the side door making his daddy look like a boy as much like a kid as Jakey was to him. Like little Lee was to Jakey. Lee wasn't there to see. Lee had to take a nap. He was still a baby like that himself. But Jakey had turned five. He *would be* six at Christmas. Instead of a nap, his mama had sentenced him to one hour of "quiet time" while she rested upstairs. She lay on the bed with the shades pulled, the cool of a washcloth draped over her eyes. He'd gone up to ask how long again an hour was. He had to be quiet for that long until his mama said not to be quiet she answered was how long. Bigger had looked bad. Jakey had seen a real dead Negro once. He'd been in the back of a wagon before their house in Front Camp just lying there dead in the sun like he had nothing better to do and had no sense at all. There were shovels in there thrown in with him and a pick, too. He was being ridden to the cemetery at the edge of the camp to get himself buried. The way it looked, it looked as if he was going to do the digging and the burying, too, himself. His eyes had been shut with flat stones on the lids that wouldn't roll off, but his mouth hung with the tongue sticking out. A fly landed on his cheek and flew into his open mouth and crawled out again, walked up his cheek and disappeared up his nose. This one had not, but the Negro he had seen dead had looked shrunken. His brown face had gone gray, the color of a fire's cold ashes. Jakey had been with his granddaddy the Boss Chief when he saw him. Sometimes prisoners died. His granddaddy shrugged. It was all the explanation he had offered and that was all Jakey knew about it.

The other had been before Jakey had known to call Bigger Bigger. To him he'd been like the other dead one then. Once he knew who he was, he became Bigger. Or Calpurnia. Or Mason. Not the other his daddy wouldn't say. His granddaddy said it. His grand-daddy said he called a spade a spade.

"What day is today is?" Jakey asks. He's returned with his shoes in his hand.

"What day *is* it? It's Friday," his mama says. "It's still Friday and it's been Friday since you asked me ten minutes ago. It will continue to be Friday until midnight tonight, when it will become Saturday."

She gives him the press of her red smile, but her face is powdered serious for the funeral they are going to. Her green eyes shine out, extra bright, catlike, lined black with long lashes, faint purple over the lids. Jakey thinks how beautiful she looks dressed in a black dress. She has on black shoes and a wide-brimmed black hat. Her head tilts to look at him as he looks at her in the mirror as she clips on her gold earrings. His daddy is still at work on the road. He is supposed to be home by now again. When he comes home they will go. He is never home. Time is a problem for his daddy. His daddy is never on time. He missed dinner and then he'd shown up home with Bigger.

His mama keeps glancing at her clock. She glances at it again.

"What time is it *now?*" Jakey asks.

A clock has a face though it doesn't look like one except for its nose. And it's a nose that has hands. His mama asks, "Where's the little hand? Now where's the big hand?" Pointing all around at its face. There were hours, twelve of them. And sixty minutes. And sixty seconds. Jakey has had all this explained to him before. He can make neither hide nor hair of it. A red second hand goes by too fast to count. *Time stands still for no man—or boy either*, his daddy would have said and laughed if he were there and knew what Jakey was thinking about.

"I don't know," Jakey says. Looking at the clock trying to read it so hard makes his stomach funny. The hands keep pointing. If the clock unwinds it will stop, suddenly stuck telling the time. But that wouldn't be the real time of is. Like was again. The moment before it would be. Stuck on that meant forever if you didn't wind it again.

He had come in from wherever they came hunched, tumbling forward with his daddy squashed underneath him and Mason helping, too, and Nurse Hankins following behind in her not-pointy witch's white hat and a black bag she'd brought. Jakey hung back. Every time Jakey had ever gone to see Nurse Hankins she shot him in the bottom with a needle. And she never smiled or said she was sorry for shooting him either. Old Doc Evans handed out lollipops whenever he had to shoot them, which made it almost worth the pinch but not Lee's hollering. He did not want to get shot for just nothing. But he saw Nurse Hankins wasn't there to see him. It wasn't about him. He wasn't part of their plan. They hadn't planned on him. They had all come in hurrying in a hush, bunched, his daddy knowing their mama would be lying down. She always had to lie down after dinner. She would not be in the kitchen now that dinner had been missed, twice the effort. The time for dinner had come and gone. They did not talk, but started straight in to work.

When Calpurnia knew something he thought he was fooling her with, she'd say, "I know what time it is." But she didn't know the time. Cal couldn't read either. When she said this Jakey knew she knew something else.

I know what time it is, Jakey thinks. They'd laid him on the kitchen floor, his mama upstairs napping as usual.

Jakey sits up in the rocker, holding on to the laces as if they were reins. He's thought of something else. It needles him. He can't let it go: "If today is *Friday,* then why do I have to wear my *Sunday* clothes?"

His mama smooths her hands down her hips, looking over her shoulder at the back of herself in the mirror. She turns sideways and lifts her chest. "We dress up," she says, "to go to people's funerals."

"Why?"

"We do it to show our respect for the dead."

Jakey pictures the dead gunman in the wagon, the fly going up his nose. "How do the dead know about it? Why do they care if we respect them?"

"Not so much respect like that. But in their memory."

Jakey wonders if the dead Negro he'd seen had a memory of being dead. Jakey hadn't been dressed in his Sunday clothes then. He'd been wearing coveralls. He suddenly feels bad about it. His granddaddy had been wearing the gray suit he always wore. He looked ready to go to a funeral at the drop of a hat.

Jakey looks down at his own blue shorts and the white shirt and the blue Easter jacket. He can't tie his own shoes yet. He waits for his mama to notice and come tie them.

Jakey hadn't known the baby. He'd never seen her. How can he respect her or be in her memory either?

His mama picks up the clock and sets it back down. She sighs. "I knew it. Now we're going to be late. Your father works on his own time. Your father does what he likes. He shows no consideration for others."

"What time does it begin?"

"The viewing has already begun. The service is at St. Andrew's Episcopal at three. Then afterward we'll follow the hearse out to the cemetery. We should be back home by six, I'd imagine."

"Six," Jakey says. He tries: "Today is Friday. The month is July." He stops.

"How many *years* is it?"

"What? What are you talking about? This is no time to be fooling around. We've got to go. Now, no more foolish questions, please. It's very trying, Jakey. You can't imagine. Would you help me with Lee? He'll need his shoes. Cal!" she calls over the banister. "I need you up here, please."

Mondaytuesdaywednesdaythursdayfridaysaturdaysunday. He always has to start from the beginning again to get back at the day it had been. *Mondaytuesday.* July is the month. The year is whatever it was. It is the summertime. There is a big war over the seas even if he, Jakey, can't see it. The papers his daddy reads say it's true and they save tinfoil for the effort, too. It will be over soon, people say, and after that there will be peace on earth and goodwill toward man. I am a boy. My daddy is a man. Mama is a mama. Mamas are women, not girls. Lee is a baby still, but not the dead kind yet. His brother will always be a baby who can't get his shoes on his own. He is not really a baby though. He can find his own shoes, Jakey knows, when he wants. Jakey walks in with his laces still flapping and looks in the crib, but Lee is playing dead with his eyes closed. But Lee is not dead like the real live dead baby they are on their way in their Sunday clothes on a Friday in July to see at 3:00 for free if his daddy ever comes home. His daddy is working hard on the road. He says Boss Chief says they need to finish the job, that's why he's hardly come back all week. That's why he missed dinner the second day in a row. It was after dinner when Bigger drove off in the backseat to go to work with him. And now he's still not home.

Jakey had had his eye against the gap. He leaned forward to get a wider look to see closer if this one was dead, too, laid out like that and the swinging door creaked a crack. Calpurnia and Mason glanced right at him. His daddy turned from where he was kneeling over Bigger. His daddy didn't see him at first. He was looking higher, at his mama's height. His daddy looked down and saw him. He held a finger to his lips. He motioned him to come on in, whispering, "Let's try not to wake your mama. If we do there'll be hell to pay."

It was exactly what Jakey had been afraid of thinking when he saw what he saw then. Bigger lay on the floor. He didn't move at all, except for maybe a twitch. He was so big that he just lay there taking up the kitchen. "You didn't come home for dinner."

"I couldn't take him into the infirmary so I stopped and asked Nurse Hankins to come here. But we've got to hurry before somebody misses her. The door," his daddy had hushed him again.

Nurse Hankins opened her bag. She set out a little knife and a needle and thread on the tile.

Cal had already brought her a bucket and a sponge and the brown bottle that foamed when she poured it on their cuts or dug out a splinter.

Jakey had stepped all the way into the kitchen. He'd let the swinging door back slow. He pressed against it.

"Cal?" They had heard her voice at the top of the stairs. She was standing there.

They stopped. The clock tocked. His daddy glanced at Nurse Hankins. He looked at Calpurnia and nodded. She left the bucket. Nurse Hankins picked up a shot and stuck it in Bigger's giant arm. Bigger didn't yelp or even wake up. He just lay there being big.

"Yes'm?" Cal said, calling loudly back in the slap of the tiled kitchen. She parted the swinging doors, drying her hands on her apron, and stepped out into the shivery sound of the crystal on the sideboard.

"It smells like something died. Is he a dead one, Daddy? That's just what happens to prisoners sometimes granddaddy says, isn't it?" Jakey asked, whispering.

His daddy shook his head. "No," he said. "He's just hurt. We got to get him cleaned up. See just how bad it is." He pointed at the ceiling to listen.

His mama talked to Calpurnia from the top of the stairs down about cleaning the silverware. They'd done it just last week. "I want it done right this time."

"Yes'm," Cal said.

"And where's Jakey?"

"He with us helping."

"Don't you let him get polish on that shirt."

"No'm."

"That shirt cost six dollars. It came from Habscombs in Memphis."

"Yes'm."

"And you can tell Mr. Jake when he comes in that I will not be joining him for supper. He needs to learn manners. He can eat his plate from dinner."

"Yes'm."

"I wouldn't even bother to heat it up. Not that that man would notice the difference."

"No'm."

"I'm going to lie down for a bit again. I feel so exhausted. It must be this heat. Why don't you take Lee and Jakey out a bit later. Maybe play something with them, so long as they don't become overheated. But let Lee sleep. He needs it. He was so fussy at dinner. And remember, if he won't eat what's set before him, then he'll go hungry until we eat again at five. He's got to learn. Else he'll grow up like his father."

"Yes'm," Cal said.

Jakey listened to his mama's footsteps. They had all stopped to listen, except for Nurse Hankins, who was tending to Bigger. If his mama came down, there'd be hell to pay. His daddy had said it, but Jakey had been fearing it, too, when he'd heard and first peeked through the door. That day at dinner she kept looking at the clock on her arm, waiting, as if at any moment things were going to change and she wouldn't already act mad because he was already late anyway. Finally, she'd said, "Damn that father of yours." Jakey's mouth had ohed. Jakey knew how bad that was to say. To be damned. *God*-damned. But it would be worser yet if his mama came downstairs and saw what his daddy had dragged into their house without asking. She would not *tolerate* it. Jakey knew how hard their talking went back and forth until his daddy gave in. "Aw, hell, Jolene," his daddy would say, in a sort of begging way. *Hell* was a word Jakey had started to bravely use for himself, like his daddy did, who was a man, like men did. Boss Chief said other things. "F—" Jakey felt awe at the club of his voice. Jakey did not dare that word yet. But he was getting the hang of "hell" and "damn." He'd set his hands on his waist. "Damn!" And then he'd work up a good spit and spit it into the dust.

His mama hated spitting almost as much as cursing, more maybe because spitting was nastier even, she said. She never spit, though sometimes she cursed, when she got mad enough, *cussing mad*. She said she'd use soap to clean out that mouth of his if she ever heard him again. Jakey had learned to experiment with the dirty words around Lee when they played outside of earshot of the house.

"Aw, hell, Lee, that ain't the way." He had a vague idea what it was all about. "Damn that father of yours." *Goddamned* meant damned to hell. "A soul in eternal torment." He would lie in bed some nights with his hands locked behind his head trying to picture what such an awfully hurt soul might look like. What came to mind was the idea of a cottonmouth he'd seen one time caught crossing the road, run over, its middle crushed flat, but still stuck alive enough to writhe and strike furiously at the lagging other end of itself again and again, poisoning its own tail in an attempt to go on ahead and die.

Because he knew for a fact that hell was hot, Jakey imagined it like how the kitchen could get cooking on a day like that day in July. But that day dinner had been over, his daddy had missed it at work on the road, and the kitchen wasn't cooking. It was cool, maybe the coolest part of the house in the shade, facing north away from Front Camp. But it could get to cooking, quick, and would, too, if his mama found out about what his daddy was up to now. You would go to hell if you didn't behave.

It scared him when his daddy didn't do what his mama told him because that was wrong. At night, lying there, the idea of his own death and his call to Judgment quickened through him. Whenever Jakey thought of dying, thinking of the other he'd seen whose name he'd never know to call him who'd been dead and that fly going up his nose and not coming out again, he got an empty, hollow falling feeling in his stomach. His tongue dried, his own mouth going cottony-white feeling. Jakey was scared to death of hell. All that wailing and gnashing of teeth Pastor McCain got so excited about. Jakey bet it would be dark, shadowy with the flickering of flames, red devil shapes with pitchforks dancing.

Hell seemed a real possibility to Jakey in a way that heaven couldn't possibly. The ease and comfort of stretching out on a cloud did not appeal to his imagination in the least. Jesus was better in that regard. Jesus could get to him. Closer to what he could feel as real. Once, Jakey had seen a man-sized wooden Jesus nailed to the cross at the Catholic church when his father had taken him in to see it. The wooden Jesus had left an impression on him like his fear of being scared to death of going to hell when he died that he couldn't shake as easily as the notion of fleecy clouds and harps, naked "chubs." The hanging Jesus had been wearing a crown of pointy thorns. Red paint trickled down his cheek. His blue eyes had been painted sad, droopy, disappointed, looking down, right at Jakey staring up, his own mouth dropping open. They'd nailed him up there. Where? How? "Hammered through his hands," his daddy said, "here," using his middle finger of his left hand to point down at the flesh of his own palm. His daddy had to use his finger on the same hand to point to his palm because his daddy only had one arm. His daddy was a one-armed man. They couldn't crucify his daddy, Jakey thought with relief. They needed two hands for that!

Cal stepped back into the kitchen. No one had moved, waiting, except Nurse Hankins, who hadn't stopped moving yet—more of Bigger was hurt than wasn't and there was a lot of him to hurt. His mama's steps went lightly away from the stairs in the other direction. Cal did not meet Jakey's eyes, but Jakey watched hers closely to see. *I know what time it is.* She hadn't lied, but she hadn't exactly told the truth either. She'd acted dumb. His mama said Calpurnia was dumb. His mama said that word was a "common word." She said *colored* was more polite. She used *servant.* But Jakey understood that wasn't all the other meant. Calling someone it partly had to do with the color of someone's skin. She believed Cal was a dumb servant. How she'd handled his mama didn't seem so dumb, Jakey thought. Cal took a second bucket and filled it with water. She brought another rag. Sometimes things had two meanings. Things didn't always mean what they seemed, Jakey was thinking.

Mason stood at the back screen door, watching out. He nodded.

Nurse Hankins stood and foamed her hands with soap at the sink.

"All right then, Bigger," his daddy said. "This might hurt some."

Jakey stepped up to stand right behind his daddy, watching over his shoulder. He watched him squeeze the rag and begin to wipe Bigger's puffed face. He touched the cuts so gently. He was kind with the cloth. Once, horsing, scraping his knees and the palms of his hands bad on the gravel when he fell, his daddy had touched him like that. He'd done it so gentle. All the while he'd touched him he'd spoken to Jakey calmly, telling the story of his own fall as a boy. That time he told him about the time he fell off the back of the tractor when he'd lost his arm. Jakey had been so fascinated with listening that he'd hardly felt the sting on his own palms and knees, even when his daddy had to use the blade of his pocketknife to dig out the gravel under the skin. His daddy was always kind with him like that. His daddy had never once gone for his belt. His mama was the spanker. She would not hesitate to lay the flat of her hand or a switch or a wooden spoon or her hairbrush or anything else that came to hand to the backs of his thighs if he did wrong to show him the way. And his mama was a fierce hugger. She grabbed her sons to her and held on hard.

Jakey stood over his daddy's shoulder with his own hand covering his mouth and nose looking down at Bigger on the floor, seeing the cuts open up pink beneath the black skin coming clean. His daddy only had one hand to work on him. Cal worked on him, too. There was a lot of him to work on. His daddy was wiping Bigger's mouth where his lips were cut. He'd lost a tooth, a bloody stump beside the one front silver. His other teeth that hadn't been knocked out stood out to either side of his wide mouth. Jakey dropped his hand and tried to breathe regularly. He tried to breathe through his mouth at the dying smell on him like when he'd passed a possum rotting in a ditch. Jakey had made himself stand over the smell. A man-test to see if he could take it. He breathed in. He looked down into the mess of it. The possum was moving! He jumped back, nearly falling into the road himself. He regained his balance and marched back to stare. In horror, he bent closer—realized then that what he was looking at was a frenzy of maggots, clumped like boiling rice inside it, feeding. The squirming under the flap of dirty fur made the possum's guts wriggle, writhing to rise him again. The maggots had eaten out the possum's soft eyes and were busy ganging up on the tongue. Maggots dropped out like drips of drool. The possum grinning wider and wider as if being dead just got funnier and funnier.

Jakey felt a little faint, dreamy, smelling Bigger. But he wouldn't let himself look away this time either. Maybe Bigger had been hit by a truck, too. It would've had to be a big truck, a cotton truck. Jakey would have liked to see how the truck had come out of it.

Nurse Hankins picked up her needle and thread. She touched Bigger's split lip that his daddy had cleaned. Then she slipped the needle through it, drew the sides together, and pulled. She threaded it through and did it again, as quickly and easily as if she were sewing on a button. The lip closed. She poked the needle into the puff of flesh in the gash over his eyebrow.

Jakey stepped away. He'd passed the test. He'd seen enough.

Together his daddy and Cal cut and stripped away Bigger's bloodied uniform shirt. Old hurts had healed into the lash of long purple scars on his dark skin. The stuff from the brown bottle they poured gushed foam—doing its job, Cal always said when she used it on them. Next would come the monkey blood. Bigger winced, though his face was so fat with cuts and bruises it looked like one big wince already. Mason kept looking out the back screen door. Jakey noticed how close the car was parked. His daddy had parked the car so that the back door opened directly onto the side door of the kitchen. The car blocked the view from the rest of Front Camp. From the back door they couldn't be seen from the windows of his granddaddy's. Jakey knew that trick. Times he went out that way, too, sneaking. Now he knew his daddy knew it, too.

His daddy was pretty slick.

His daddy had been a famous man once upon a time.

Even more famouser than his graddaddy the Boss Chief, people said, outside of Parchman Farm, that is.

His daddy had been the tailback at Ole Miss. Everybody knew that. They knew him still mainly because they recognized his red hair and the one arm, which were signs that marked him like holes in the palms that Jesus had showed doubters like Thomas, the signs signaling people who he was even if they'd never seen him before. His daddy was Red Lemaster.

When they went all the way to Oxford for the homecoming game last season, everyone tried to shake his daddy's one hand with his mama beaming as she had when she'd ridden that float, Jakey bet. His daddy didn't have enough hand to go around. People slapped his daddy on the back. *Red!* they said. And they eyed him, Jakey, he knew, sizing him up, Jake Lemaster's firstborn son. He got the stuff? They always asked his daddy. We'll see. We'll see. His daddy grinned. With two arms, he ought to be twice the man! That was always how his daddy joked. Jakey could feel that it wasn't aimed at him. His daddy would say it and wink back at Jakey. Jakey could throw a rock hard enough to kill a blackird. If he could just hit one. He had to work on his aim. His daddy had had Joe Booker help him hang a tire up from the oak with the low limb in the quad. It looked like it was a swing, but it wasn't. The tire was for aiming. His daddy stood back in the grass and said, "Let her fly!" Jakey would shove the tire, swinging it, and his daddy would pump the football twice by his ear from thirty steps back and spiral the football hard through the air and straight through the swinging hole. "Your turn!" Jakey couldn't fit his hand around the ball. "Stand closer. Okay. Ready now?" His daddy swung the tire. Jakey watched it go back and forth. He threw. The ball wobbled through the air where the tire had been just a second before but wasn't anymore. "Close!" His daddy fetched the ball and tossed it lightly back at him. Jakey closed his eyes and the ball hit him in the chest and bounced off into the grass. "Open your eyes if you want to see what you're catching at!" His daddy waited until Jakey smiled at himself and picked up the ball to try again on his own. "Okay. Ready?"

Jakey stood looking as Nurse Hankins finished up the stitches.

His daddy and Cal wiped and wiped Bigger. He was cleaning up pretty good. He didn't look so hot. He looked cooler now. He didn't look quite so bad as he had when he came hunched stumbling in from who knew where. Though he was pretty beaten up, it didn't look like he was going to die. Jakey imagined that lying on the tile floor of the kitchen must feel like lying on a creek bed of cooling stones. There were no lights on in the kitchen now in the late afternoon. Above Bigger a fan twirled, winging air, a soft, gentle feathering sound, as if an angel were there, floating over them, keeping an eye out.

Bigger's eyes rolled opened, the yellows veined bloody as fertilized eggs. They just looked. Nothing registered in them. Not even fear. No recognition. Though this was the first time Jakey had seen him look to see where he was.

"You sit up, Bigger?"

"I don't know, Boss," Bigger said. "I ain't never tried yet."

"Let's give it a try then."

His daddy leaned back using all his weight to pull Bigger to a sitting position. Bigger was still in chains. The chains clanked and slithered.

Bigger looked around, sitting on the cool tile of the kitchen floor. He looked at Nurse Hankins and Cal and at Mason and he looked at Jakey. It didn't seem Bigger could be surprised by anything, Jakey was thinking. Like a bull led to stand in the killing box, blinking back through the slats—not knowing what it was waiting for and not thinking enough to care. You didn't want a bull to care. You didn't want a bull to see red. Bigger's eyes looked red.

His daddy held the chains so that they wouldn't rattle. The manacles on Bigger's wrists gapped. His wrists were that big. And his giant arms muscled up from his wrists, bigger even, the size of legs.

"I'm going to take off the chains, Bigger. We got to clean around where they cut. You try anything and I'll shoot you dead right here in my own kitchen. For a fact. We understand each other?"

Bigger held the stare, red-eyed. "I been done dead and back

again once in dat coffin box today. I don' want no more of dat bein' dead I can hep it."

His daddy used the skeleton key on his belt. The manacles cranked open. They'd been hinged wide as they'd go and the edges had rubbed into him. Bigger worked his grip back and forth over the cuts.

"He needs water," Nurse Hankins said. "He's lost a lot of fluid. I can't imagine how he's going to be able to work out on that road in this sun. He ought to be confined to bed."

"He's got to work," his daddy said, meeting Bigger's eyes again. "Work or go back in the box. That's the deal."

Nurse Hankins pursed her lips, but Bigger nodded to his daddy. "Oh, I can work," he said. "You jes watch."

Mason brought him water. Bigger drank now. He drank off the tin cup in one gulp. He drank off every cup Mason brought. Mason gave him a flat biscuit and then another to stuff in his wide mouth. Jakey wondered if he'd swallow them whole. It must hurt to chew with the stub of his tooth like that. But Bigger chewed and chewed, looking around the kitchen now. "Where is I?"

"Second Home." His daddy slipped out, careful not to let the screen slap. He left Bigger alone with Nurse Hankins and Cal and Mason and Jakey. Jakey wondered why Bigger didn't kill them all and get it over with. He didn't even need the cleaver on the block to hack them up. He could squeeze the life out of them with his big bare black hands. He could squish out their guts like soft mud. Rip them limb from limb. Jakey thought how he'd do it if he were in Bigger's place. And then he'd escape! He'd run out to the car and drive off. He wondered why his daddy believed Bigger wouldn't. When his daddy came back, he carried a gunman's striped uniform under his arm. "Biggest size I could find."

They all pitched in to help Bigger stand and Cal knelt down and stripped off his old uniform pants. Bigger stood before them naked and made with muscles like a statue in a book. Jakey looked. Cal didn't even seem to notice he was naked as she helped him into the clean uniform. His mama would say that that was just the way they were, no shame, and a lack of decency. Dressed again, Bigger stood before them, shuffling for balance. Beads of sweat popped out on his forehead. His jaw flexed. His face was still a mess of welts and yellowing hurts and the tooth missing, and though Jakey couldn't imagine how much it must hurt, he thought Bigger didn't look quite so bad now as he had when they stumbled him in and laid him in the kitchen looking dead.

"Better?"

"Better as I'm gone git, I reckon, huh, Boss."

His daddy picked up the chains and held them in the air between them. "I'm putting you to work on the road. We're going to move you to Camp One."

His daddy fixed the chains over the uniform as best he could so they wouldn't rub where they'd rubbed before and he could lead him out.

Bigger couldn't walk on his own. Mason crutched under his left side. Bigger's legs wobbled away from where he seemed to be aiming the bulk of his big body to go. The chains clanked when he lurched forward. It reminded Jakey of being a ghost, but the big man Bigger was too dark to be a ghost yet. He hadn't died. He was still a lot alive.

At the door, Bigger turned and nodded to them. The nod included him, Jakey, too.

"Cal?" They heard her on the stairs again. "Don't bang the silver!"

Cal pushed out without looking back at Bigger. "Yes'm," Cal said. "Sorry, ma'am."

Before she left, his daddy stopped Nurse Hankins, who had collected her black bag and washed her hands with soap again.

"I want to thank you for coming. That was above and beyond the call of duty."

"Duty to whom, Mr. Lemaster?" she said. Without another word, she stepped past him out the door.

His daddy watched her go and then he turned to Jakey. Jakey

thought maybe his daddy was going to say something about Nurse Hankins or tell him to be quiet, warn him not to tell, that if he did there'd be hell to pay. But his daddy only stood looking at him. He reached out and laid his hand on his hair without messing it. Then he went out the door. He helped guide Bigger into the backseat. Bigger sat with his wide shoulders filling up the window. His daddy shut the door and walked around to the driver's side. He took his sunglasses from his shirt pocket and slipped behind them. Mason came back in. He walked to the counter and flipped open the box of silver. Cal walked back in from reassuring his mama. She cleaned up the buckets and put away the brown bottle and took the bloodied torn uniform outside to the burn barrel. Back in the kitchen, without a word to Jakey about any of it—as if nothing had happened and Bigger hadn't ever been there—Calpurnia and Mason began to polish the silver, each fork, each spoon, every knife.

DOWNSTAIRS NOW, JAKEY hears his daddy come in—the crystal shivering again—hurrying without taking off his boots in the hurry he's in, the whole house shaking underneath him. He takes the stairs two at a time the way he tells the boys not to.

"Jake! Where have you been? We're going to be late. We can't be late for this! Think of the Tisdales. The Rules. Everyone will be there. We're too late to make the viewing now. We'll have to go straight to the church if we want a seat."

His daddy glances at him, already unbuttoning his khaki shirt. He goes past, his mama chasing him, dressed in her black dress. It reminds Jakey of the way a blackbird swoops to peck after a hawk. They take it into their room. The door slams. "You said you'd . . . !"

"Aw, hell," Jakey says, turning away from his parents' bickering. Hearing their voices rising. If he were outside, he would have spit. Lee rubs and rubs his eyes, just waking up to it, the voices yelling louder. Their mama has put him down dressed, but Jakey smells poop.

Jakey brings his little brother's shoes. They have buckles like a girl's.

"Well, come on," he says. "Let's get you changed. Daddy's home in case you haven't heard. Mama says we got to go show our respects. There's a dead baby waiting on our memory and the funeral's at three. We got no time to waste."

chapter eleven

Jake drove. He was mad and he sped down Highway 49 on the way south to Ruleton, where the funeral for Sissy's daughter, Dorothy, was to be held. He drove fast back toward where he'd just driven fast home from in time to wash up and dress in his suit and pick up Jolene and the boys. Why had his wife wanted the boys to go to the viewing anyway? How could they really even understand a funeral for a baby? It was about as much as Jake felt he could handle himself, knowing what he did about Sissy having drowned her child.

Since Tuesday when he'd missed the dinner Jolene had set for him in order to free Bigger from the box and had stopped by the infirmary counting on that look he'd caught in Mirabel Hankins's hazel eyes for help fixing Bigger up before he put him to work on the road, Jake had begun to feel differently about himself and his job on Parchman Farm. He'd obeyed to the letter the law Boss Chief had laid down about freeing Bigger, but he hadn't bowed to it. Jake had felt more like himself in the past three days on the road than he had in months; years even—trying as hard as he could.

Could Bigger *work?*

Bigger could hardly walk after what he'd been through, but he'd walked. He'd worked. When Jake pulled up in the state car with Bigger patched up in the backseat to begin serving out his weeklong punishment on the road, the call had faltered then fallen off as all the gunmen on the line stopped to watch. Even Joe Booker had forgotten for a moment that he was supposed to be driving the gunmen and turned with his hands on his hips. Jake left the state car in park and climbed out. He walked around and opened Bigger's door.

"'Preciate it, Boss."

Bigger reached up and pulled himself across the seat. He stuck his legs out and tried his weight on his feet, towering over Jake. His round face looked seamed together like a baseball, the bruises puffed and yellowing, the whites of his eyes burst red. His forehead gleamed from the effort of simply trying to stand, hanging on to the door in his clean uniform, swaying. Bigger looked out at the eighty or so gunmen looking back at him until Joe Booker remembered himself and turned back to the line.

"All right now. You know what the boss done said. We gone finish this stretch of road by Friday!"

The call went up—"I seen Rosie in my midnight dreams"—and the men facing Bigger gathered themselves, their picks and shovels scraping and clanging as they collected them to strike, shouting back: "*Oh, Lord, in my midnight dreams!*"

"Mose," Jake called and a tall, lanky trusty hustled over. "Put Bigger here to work at the head of the line."

"I can work," Bigger said, letting go of the door. He swayed for a moment and then lurched forward. He took a second pitched step, and then a third, carried forward by the weight of his own staggering momentum. Jake shut the door and set his boot on the running board to watch after Bigger as he struggled to walk the entire hundred-yard length of the line, jangling with every step.

The pick Joe Booker set him to work with looked toy-tiny in Bigger's hands. Bigger swung the pick up and brought it down to bust up the baked gravel. Rock flew. The other gunmen watched from under their caps, keeping an eye on him. Bigger brought the pick up and swung it down. Rock flew.

Joe Booker walked back to the car where Jake stood. He crossed his arms. Together they watched the big man go.

Bigger rounded out his stroke so that once the pick struck it swung back up in an arc. He brought it down again. He did not bother to rest between swings like the other gunmen on the line.

Jake tilted back his hat and squinted up at the sun. He swiped his brow. "How long you figure he can keep that up?"

Bigger swung the pick up and brought it down, spraying gravel and dirt. He'd begun to work up his own separate cloud of dust. It rose into the blue sky above him. Another trusty brought a wheelbarrow for him. He handed Bigger a shovel.

"I don't know. I seen a lot of fightin' men in my time. He oughta be dead, but he ain't dead. He went down, but he got up. That says somepin special about a man."

Jake fixed his hat. "You think we can really finish this stretch of road by Friday?"

Bigger shoveled up a mess of gravel from the shoulder and dumped it in the barrow. His face and arms were already covered ash gray. The color ran with sweat.

Joe Booker thought about that, watching the gunmen watch Bigger from under their caps. "I wouldn't a said so yestiday, Mr. Jake. But today a new day, and looks to me like we got a new man on the line."

Jake watched Bigger and then he glanced at Joe Booker, who was looking at him.

Back on the line, the caller shouted up the next chant, and the gunmen answered back even louder than before, loud enough for Bigger to hear, letting him know they were behind him:

> Been a great long time since Hannah went down.
> *Oh, Hannah, GO DOWN;*
> Been a great long time since Hannah went down.
> *Oh, Hannah, GO DOWN!*

With Bigger working alone in front setting the pace for the rest of them, Jake found himself out of the truck under the sun working right alongside the gunmen, directing and encouraging them. Boss Chief had demanded that that stretch of the highway be completed by Friday and, for a time, Jake had thought they might make it, as far behind schedule as they were. They had made unbelievable progress; they'd come close. All week Jake had felt as if he were marshaling his team in a comeback, down by seventeen points in the fourth quarter—three touchdowns needed to win and mere minutes to go. They'd charged back within a field goal of tying things up. Jake had stayed until the last possible moment that after-noon, but the clock had finally run out on him. And while the dead-line didn't matter in one way—certainly Boss Chief wasn't going to fire Jake for failing; he'd probably be pleased that his son had man-aged to make up as much ground as he had—in another, more im-portant way it did. Jake realized he'd cared. He'd had a goal to reach. The night before he'd actually gone up to bed before Jolene. Bone-tired, he hadn't needed even one drink from the sparkling crystal de-canter to help him sleep. That morning he'd awakened in the dark before the alarm at 4:53 A.M. raring to get back to work with Bigger and Joe Booker and the rest of the men.

Now in the car on the way to the funeral Jake tried to explain what he was feeling to his wife. He didn't want to argue in front of the boys any more than they already had. He used the most reason-able tone he could.

"I guess what it is is that it sort of reminds me of when I used to play ball. It gives me that feeling again like we're a team. I know that's silly. They're *convicts*. They don't have any choice. They're serving time—this is forced labor. We could drive them till they dropped. But even so we didn't have to drive them. Bigger rose to the challenge. Hurt bad as he is. And we've all been working to catch up to him. I feel like I've got some purpose again."

Jake nodded to himself. He'd come close to saying what the week working on the road since saving Bigger from the box meant to him. It wasn't Bigger's size so much as his will. He'd *willed* himself to work, to *live*. He knew Jolene would look at him incredulously and then laugh in his face if he went so far as to tell her that Bigger had become an inspiration to him.

As it was his wife kept her head turned when she spoke, watching the cotton flash by as if she cared to keep count of the seemingly endless rows. Her tone was flat, scathing. "You sound like a little boy, Jake. You don't need a hero. A colored convict for a hero is the last thing you need. You used to be a hero yourself. Now you have a job to do. The road still isn't done. Whose fault is that?" Jolene turned to look at him then. "You need to grow up, Jake. That's all you need. You're an adult and adults do things on time. Adults accept responsibility. They do things they don't want to do. You knew today was the day of the viewing and the funeral for us to pay our respects to that poor little innocent baby girl. And still you were late. You're always late for something, aren't you, Jake? You think the world revolves around you. You never consider the boys or me. Certainly you're not thinking of Sissy and Clyde and what they must be going through today. Think about someone other than yourself for once, Jake, would you, please?"

Jake was speechless. He opened his mouth to speak in his own defense. "I—" But then he clamped down on it, the muscles in his jaw tensing, his temples pulsing. The words he'd used to explain himself had rung true in his ears, but they'd been returned to him slanted, interpreted askew.

Jake glanced in the rearview mirror at sandy-haired Lee, who seemed not to have heard or even care to listen to what his parents had to say to each other, and then at Jakey, who was obviously brooding. Sitting on the seat with his feet sticking out, his jacket and white shirt tucked into his knickers, his hair slicked, and his mouth turned down in a frown, he looked like a little old man. Jakey looked straight back at him. Jake thought how his son's face looked shadowed some way, bruised. Jake felt an ache of recognition; Jakey was going grown up on him, that's what it was. Jakey was a worrier, his mother's helper. He was a thoughtful child; he thought too much. His older son's face showed the strain of conscience. Jake knew his son must be concerned about what he'd seen his father do in sneaking Bigger into their kitchen. Jake regretted burdening his son with the onus of such knowledge, which he imagined as the choice of whether Jakey should tell. But Jake was also aware that Jakey hadn't told. If he had, Jolene would have unleashed her wrath. She might even have gone so far as to tell Boss Chief. Jakey seemed to have come to his own verdict about what he'd seen. He had sided with his father, but Jake knew such decisions could exact a heavy toll.

Father and son's eyes met in the mirror.

"I apologize." Jake said it looking at Jakey. Lee, at three, remained blissfully oblivious, the first two knuckles of his pointer finger dug up his nose.

Jolene absorbed the apology as if it had been addressed to her and as if it was only natural and she was actually right about him. She faced forward, her hands folded in her lap.

THE PARKING LOT of St. Andrew's Episcopal Church in Ruleton was packed, jammed full. The overflow of cars had backed up and down both sides of Chinaberry Street and spilled down the tributary alleys and oak-shaded avenues of the surrounding blocks. But there was no one on the streets. The funeral service was set to begin, and the crowd of mourners had already settled into the pews. Jake pulled the state car up in front behind the length of the curtained black hearse from F. R. Lane Funeral Home. The wheeze and sigh of a somber organ prelude escaped through the church's opened doors. The greens and yellows and blues and oranges of the stained-glass windows glowed with the heat as if the glass were being blown from the inside. Friends of the Tisdales and Rules who had come to pay their respects stood in the vestibule. Not only had the Lemasters managed to miss the viewing because Jake had been late, now they wouldn't get a seat to see the funeral. Jolene wouldn't even look at him.

Jake opened his wife's door for her.

"At least it hasn't started yet."

He offered to help Jolene out, but she tucked her purse under her arm and stood on her own, smoothing her hips—looking elegantly slim in a black dress and black stockings and heels, her honey-colored hair coiffed and her lips bowed perfectly red. She straightened her hat.

"Come along, boys," she said and held out her gloved hand.

Jake opened the curbside door for them. "This side, Lee."

Jolene left him to park the car, towing the boys after her. Jakey looked back, holding on to his mother's right hand, Lee tethered to her left.

"Lee, please remove your finger from your nose."

Jolene smiled generously at the ushers handing out programs before the stone steps and they nodded appreciatively back at her. Her green eyes flashed and her pearl earrings and the matching strand she wore about her throat shone tastefully. Jake thought how Jolene had always sparkled in public. She was at her best on display, even at a funeral—made to ride the queen's float at any parade. Jake looked past his wife to see Boss Chief standing just inside the vestibule, dressed in the gray suit and black string tie he always wore. Hidden by the shadow cast by the archway, half of his big face was revealed in full sun while the other half loomed lost in darkness. His daddy's yellow eyes tracked Jolene's progress up the stairs, her shapely thighs slicing the slit in the front of her dress with each step as she climbed.

The acolytes, dressed in red-and-white robes, the tallest supporting a silver crucifix, flanked by two younger boys carrying the lancelike gold tasseled poles draped with the flags for church and state, led the priest down the sidewalk through a dappling of shade to the front of the church. They paused on the slate walkway before the steps, gathering for the procession.

Jolene herded the boys before her through the doors. Boss Chief leaned fully into the sun to kiss her offered cheek, resting his hand on her waist. He acknowledged Jake with the hint of a half-smile before turning Jolene with his hand on her back and guiding her after the boys into the church. Jake realized then that the Tisdales would have reserved one of the front pews for Boss Chief, if not for him. From inside, the sad strains of the organ prelude died, gathering silence. Suddenly the pipes swelled with the power of the processional.

Jake slammed the car door.

After circling around town for another five minutes, he found a parking space three blocks away at the crossroads where U.S. Highway 49 and Mississippi Highway 8 came to a four-way stop. The sign for PARCHMAN 12 pointed north and EUREKA 12 pointed south.

Jake pocketed the keys and began to walk quickly back toward the church. A car slowed to a stop at the sign before him. The late afternoon sun glinted hard off the windshield, flashing bright. He saw a hand raised in greeting, but he couldn't see who sat behind the wheel. It wasn't until the car lurched through the intersection and pulled over across the street from him that he recognized the dusty, old-timey Model T.

Mrs. Allen leaned on her arm out the open window. "Why, Mr. Lemaster," she said, "seems I can't go on the road visiting in Hushpuckashaw County anymore these days without running into you someway." She was not wearing a hat and a long strand of her blond hair had come undone. She tucked the hair back and smiled, he thought, not unkindly.

"Mrs. Allen," Jake nodded and touched his hat. "We're down to attend Dorothy Tisdale's funeral."

"That explains all these cars then," she said. "The Tisdales and Rules surely have a lot of friends. It has been over a week now, though, hasn't it? I must say I'm a little surprised they waited this long to get that baby girl in the ground."

Jake looked at her. He looked both ways. A truck passed and Jake crossed the street.

He leaned close to the window. "Well, everybody knows Sissy's delicate. They probably wanted to wait until she'd recovered sufficiently to attend the funeral. I imagine she's a bit distraught."

"I imagine she is a bit distraught, Mr. Lemaster." Mrs. Allen continued to look at him—fiercely now. She had dark blue eyes— storm blue. He thought then that as attractive as she undoubtedly was for an older woman, she looked unnaturally tired, drawn. She looked a bit wrung out. It couldn't just be the heat. By now everybody knew that she'd fired shots at the night riders who had torched a cross in front of her house for harboring Sally Johnson. What else Jake had heard about that night was that her husband, Gabriel Allen, hadn't been at home. The rumor going around about them was that she'd kicked him out of the house for having an affair. Jake knew he should be trying to wheedle information as to Sally Johnson's whereabouts as Boss Chief had told him to if he ran into her again, but instead he asked, genuinely concerned, "Mrs. Allen, are you all right?"

A car had to slow behind Mrs. Allen's car, waiting for Jake to stand so that it could safely pass.

"You best be careful now, Mr. Lemaster," Mrs. Allen said, watching the car go by before she looked him in the face again. "You'll get yourself run over sticking your neck out like that. By the way, did you happen to read in the *Tocsin* that Letitia Johnson's body was finally unchained and taken down yesterday? It seems our theological discussion devolved into a matter of real public concern. L. B. Ware sounded the hue and cry that after a week left hanging her body was becoming a countywide health hazard. Under such pressure, the city of Ruleton finally agreed to pick up the tab. They buried her in the pauper's cemetery."

Mrs. Allen searched Jake's eyes before giving him a tight smile.

"You'd best be on your way, Mr. Lemaster. You're going to miss your funeral," she said and pulled away from the curb so quickly that Jake had to jump back to keep from getting his toes run over. He watched her go, heading toward Eureka, before another car honked, and he realized he was still standing in the middle of the road.

JAKE STOOD AT the back of the church. His wife and Boss Chief and Jakey and Lee sat up front, in the third row back directly behind the Rule and Tisdale sides of the family. The little rosewood coffin sat before the altar. It was a beautiful coffin in miniature, made as well as a piece of furniture. The edges had been beveled and the corners showed a hand-carved scrollwork. White lilies lay piled on top of the lid, which remained closed throughout the service.

Sissy Rule Tisdale stood holding a silk handkerchief to her mouth, a black veil covering her face. Her other hand gripped the railing in front of her. Jake looked at her, trying to imagine her drowning her daughter. Her husband, Clyde Tisdale, stood to her right, both hands gripped on the shoulders of their son, young Robert, who stood before him. Old Mr. Rule sat in his wheelchair in the aisle. He looked slumped into himself. His mouth hung open, stringing drool. His nurse, a straight-faced, bright-skinned young Negro woman, stepped up and wiped the spit away.

When the crowd shuffled to sit for the eulogy, Jake slipped through the throng, nodding to folks he knew, and walked up the left side aisle to take his place with his family. He slid in beside Jakey and Lee. Jolene sat beside Boss Chief. When Jake sat, his wife continued to look ahead, but Sissy, who had turned in her seat to face the pulpit, glanced his way. Jake could barely make out the face he knew shadowed behind the veil. She seemed to be staring at him. He focused forward as Father James Fielding took the pulpit, but he could still feel Sissy's eyes on him even as the eulogy began.

"The burial of an infant is the most tragic of events—the potential of a life unlived," the priest read. He glanced up from his written remembrance and pushed at his black glasses. "Who knows who Dorothy Rule Tisdale might have become? It remains for us to keep the memory of the life she might have lived alive. The tragedy of her passing extends to her parents, who brought such a hope into the world and who nurtured that hope with all of their love. There can be no earthly explanation for such loss. Who among us can explain such an act? We might as well tear out our hair and gnash our teeth and ask: What justice is there in this world? And we might very well like to answer: none. Such is the Mystery of God, His Son, who is our only hope and salvation.

"Though Dorothy had an opportunity to flower, yet she had no opportunity to bloom. . . ."

Jake had heard enough. He turned slowly back to Sissy, whose face remained blanked behind the veil, raised to look up to the pulpit now as Father Fielding intoned. Clyde Tisdale had bravely fixed his visage, lifting the jut of his chin to clear the starched stiff collar of his white shirt, which edged above his pin-striped, navy-blue suit. His thinning blond hair was slicked straight back, his freshly shaven cheeks pinked by the heat. He sat by Sissy's side, shoulder to shoulder, but they did not touch.

Throughout the church rose the sounds of grief and lamentation—sniffling and quiet crying, respectful coughs, and the shuffling to escape the heat trapped in the sweltering church. Fans bobbed. Beside him, Jolene wiped at her eyes, trying to stop the run of mascara before it smudged. Boss Chief sat with his knees spread wide, his hands clasped in the attitude of prayer, but from where Jake sat he could see that his daddy was merely twiddling his thumbs.

Jake glanced down at Jakey, who was leaning forward in the pew to try to get a better view of the coffin in front of them. Jake took hold of the suspenders that held his knickers up and pulled him back in his seat. Lee sucked his thumb.

"God bless you, Sissy and Clyde. God bless Dorothy and keep her. She's in His hands now." Father Fielding searched the congregation. He nodded. "Amen."

The people stood, murmuring amens as he collected his papers and made his way back down to the altar.

The organ swelled.

At the end of the service, the pallbearers stepped up—young Rules and Tisdales, Dorothy's male cousins, as well as her older brother, young Robert. The six boys hefted the coffin by its brass handles. Jake helped Jakey step up on the kneeler so he could see, as they swept past, led by the acolytes carrying the crucifix and flags. Father Fielding followed, singing loudly in his just-off voice. Sissy and Clyde filed out after them, Sissy clinging to her husband's offered arm as if palsied. Old Mr. Rule's nurse wheeled him out next. The rest of their immediate family followed. The Lemasters sat in the last of the reserved pews and they were ushered down the center aisle after them, becoming part of the recession, too. They stepped out into the light. Jake held on to Jakey's hand, blinking, careful of the steps.

"I'm parked a few blocks away," Jake said.

Boss Chief turned on the slate walkway with his hands in his pockets. "I'm right here in front. Y'all ride with me. I'll drop you at your car afterward."

Boss Chief opened the passenger door for Jolene.

She cupped the curve of her dress under her bottom and sat and pulled her legs in. "Why, thank you." She smiled up at him and Boss Chief shut the door.

Jake sat in the back between Jakey and Lee. They idled eight cars back with the windows down and their headlights on, waiting to follow the lead of the hearse to the cemetery. The jam in the parking lot began to break up.

Boss Chief yawned and stretched his right arm over the back of the seat. "You wouldn't think it could get any hotter."

Jolene dabbed her eyes. She sat up on the edge of the seat and turned the rearview mirror to see.

"A tragedy," Boss Chief said, watching as she fixed herself. She licked a smudged tissue and wiped carefully under each eye.

"It's just so so sad," Jolene said. "Did you see Sissy? She's been rendered practically comatose. Lord knows what Dr. Jenks has got her on. Morphine? Opium? Her own maid." Jolene shook her head. "I heard Letitia Johnson raised Sissy, too."

"Well, it just goes to show." Boss Chief reached in his jacket pocket and gallantly offered Jolene the aid of his own pressed and monogrammed handkerchief, which she accepted.

"It almost makes you angry that they didn't have a chance to bring that girl to justice. Father Fielding's right. At least then we'd have had the satisfaction of some explanation. It all just seems so *arbitrary*, doesn't it? A trial would have allowed us to question how she could do such a horrible thing. Then we'd know something." Jolene fished in her purse for her red lipstick. She kissed in the mirror and drew her lips. She smacked the handkerchief and slipped the lipstick and the soiled cloth back in her purse. "The end result would have been relatively the same, of course. She would not have gotten off. Now that we've started lynching women, we can certainly electrocute them, don't you think?"

Boss Chief was looking the other way and Jake glanced out his window, too, at all the nicely dressed people they knew walking across the manicured lawn toward their gleaming cars. Neither he nor his father chose to pick up the thread of her thinking and contribute toward a conversation, but Jolene didn't seem to notice.

"What is this world coming to?"

In front of them the hearse moved forward, and they fell into line. The train of cars snaked its way out of Ruleton. Cypress View Cemetery lay at the edge of town on a long rise across from the yellow waters of the cypress-filled bayou. As they drove past, green turtles scooted off dead logs and plopped into the slough, and wood ducks zigzagged away into the thickly treed murk, negotiating the knobbed knees of the cypress sticking up like pylons. Beside the cemetery rose the neatly mowed knoll of an old Indian mound. They crunched onto the gravel drive through the gates and followed the hearse back to the Rules' family plot, which lay at the heart of the cemetery marked by a great obelisk that read RULE. A white-flowering magnolia had been grown to spread its limbs over the grassy spot. White dust from the parade of vehicles chalked the sky. Boss Chief pulled off the gravel drive, and they climbed out of the car into the heat and slammed the doors. The sun shone down on them. Cicadas revved the air. A large dark-green tent shaded the grave, and rows of folding chairs had been set out to seat the witnesses to the burial. The mound of earth from the freshly dug grave lay covered by a white cotton tarp.

Jake didn't have to face Sissy until after the rosewood coffin had been lowered into the ground and Clyde had stepped up and covered it with the first shovelful of dirt. When the dirt thumped onto the lid, Jakey finally piped up. It was as if he'd been asleep throughout the entire service and had suddenly been waked from the dream of it, startling up at the nagging question. He tugged Jake's sleeve. "Daddy," he whispered loudly, "what happens to her next?"

Jolene leaned across Lee to shush him. "Not now, Jakey."

Jake squeezed his son's knee.

The funeral ended with people paying their last respects to Clyde and Sissy. As they filed out of the cemetery and back to their cars that strung out along the length of the gravel drive all the way to the gate, they stopped to shake Clyde's hand and to give Sissy a parting hug. Boss Chief stepped up to pay his respects and then Jolene, who held Sissy for a long time. Now Jake could see Sissy's eyes clearly behind the shadow of her veil, but he hardly knew them. Surely this was not the bright-eyed girl he'd sparked. Her eyes were scrubbed raw, red looking, her mouth as pinched as a sixty-year-old woman's. In a week she seemed to have aged thirty years. Her movements, once skittish, had turned rickety. Her auburn hair looked dry, brittle.

When Jake stepped up after Jolene, Sissy said, "Jake Lemaster," and something like a smile touched her lips. "Jake," she said again and felt for his hand and latched onto it as if she'd gone blind and needed him to guide her. But when he hugged her, she did not hug him back.

"I'm sorry, Sissy," Jake said, letting go. For the first time since he'd arrived at the funeral for Sissy's baby girl, Jake felt an ache. His heart went out to her. He didn't know what had happened exactly, but in that moment Jake felt absolutely sure: No matter what Boss Chief had said, Sissy Rule Tisdale had not drowned her baby girl. "I really truly am sorry, Sis."

Sissy looked at him, but whatever remembrance suddenly seeing him appear in line before had brought to mind to make her speak his name with the hint of a smile had disappeared. No further recognition flickered across her gaze. She could have been staring white-eyed at a wall.

"Thank you for coming," she said, as if in hugging her Jake had leaned forward and pulled a string at her back to get her to repeat the memorized message that he'd already heard her say to others in the line in front of him. "Clyde and I appreciate your concern."

chapter twelve

B ABY SPENT THE rest of her Friday afternoon getting her paper-work caught up back at the Welfare Office in Eureka, although what she'd wanted to do more than anything was to go straight home and be with the girls. They would have to wait to spend the weekend together. After the week she'd had, Baby found herself woefully behind. But she was having trouble concentrating. Sally's folder sat on the edge of her desk and even while she focused on the file of the next case before her, she kept letting her eyes wander back to it. Baby finally gave in and opened Sally's folder again. She had typed Letitia Johnson under PARENTS and checked DE-CEASED in the box underneath it. Baby touched the mark she'd made. Not that she was worried about Sally in the care of Reverend Beasley and Victoria, but there was something. Something even beyond her continued concern for Sally's safety nagged at her. She broke into a cold sweat. She reached quickly for the handkerchief and pulled out the trash can from underneath her desk.

Baby sat back, patting her mouth. She closed her eyes and heard the train behind her. When she'd sent him packing, Gabe had taken the 9:15 that ran north, through Ruleton and Parchman on its way all the way up to Memphis. He'd left her their car; she had to have it for her job. The father gone. The mother left with child. *Men! They's a caution*—Ruthie's voice.

"The father," Baby said and felt the dawning. Sally had a father. She had a father even if Letitia Johnson hadn't had a husband, even if another man had conceived Sally. Sally wasn't an orphan. Not *officially*. Not yet. Baby was the official! She had the final say. Baby wouldn't sign off on her case yet. Even though she believed she'd found a good home for her, Sally's circumstances remained alive to her in a way that Baby couldn't completely explain—in a way other cases of the orphaned children she handled hadn't, heartbreaking as they often were. She saw again the grainy newspaper photo of Letitia Johnson and the hats of the crowd tilted back looking up at what had been done to her—witnesses held unaccountable, accessories after the fact.

Guilty.

At forty-one, Baby had not chosen to be left alone pregnant with this baby growing in her womb, nor had Letitia Johnson chosen to leave her daughter on her own. She and Letitia Johnson remained connected. Sally was the living connection. Their children had fathers—*accessories* themselves. Baby could account for that! Alfonse, Sally had called the man her mama had loved. Bigger, she said. He'd been sent to Parchman Farm. Surely Jake Lemaster would know who he was. He wasn't the father, but he could be a father to her if he chose to be. Going by an outsized name like Bigger, he ought to be easy enough to find. Baby was a parole officer at the prison; perhaps she could expedite his release. At least she could look into it. She felt that looking into it was the least she could do.

She would not let herself look for Gabe. Baby had too much pride for that. She had no idea where Gabriel had gone after he'd boarded that train, and she told herself again that she didn't care. Good riddance! She didn't know where he'd end up or what he'd do for a living now that he didn't have her to support him. She hoped she never saw him again! Her husband didn't know she was pregnant. He wouldn't know. She wouldn't tell him. She wouldn't take him back in any case, she told herself, even if he somehow found out, no matter what he said if she did happen to see him again, no matter how he held her, touched her hair—no matter how damn lonely she felt left alone on her own with the girls. No matter how much they missed him. No matter how many questions they asked. No matter.

"Take that, Gabriel Allen."

Instead of filing Sally's folder, she returned it to the right side of her desk under the brick-sized paperweight that read THESE MUST BE PAID. After pointedly sharpening her pencil, she opened her next case.

IT TOOK TWO knocks for Baby to think to look up. She glanced at the clock. On Friday afternoons, the welfare closed and locked its doors at 4:00, except at the end of the month when they disbursed checks. By 6:00, even Mr. Brumsfield had called it quits, doffed his pith hat goodnight, and walked home, leaving Baby and Gladys Pointdexter alone in the offices.

Gladys ducked in. "There's someone here to see you."

"A client?" Baby asked, immediately thinking of Mrs. Brim. On her journeys that morning she'd stopped by and given her the single jug of real milk she'd been able to procure. It was the only consolation she could offer her, explaining again the welfare policy on advances. Raymond, it seemed, had not moved from the rocking chair since her last visit with Sally. He only got up then to take the milk from his mother and carry it inside for himself.

"Actually," Gladys said, "no. It's not a client." She cast a glance back over her shoulder. Shielded by the glass, she whispered. "It's Mr. L. B. Ware from the newspaper."

"Is he here to apply for assistance?" Baby joked. "Doesn't he know we're closed? Why in the world would he want to see me?"

"I don't know. But he asked to see you, not Mr. Brumsfield. You know his editorials. Maybe he's going to suggest the state cut our funding again. Or take another jab at the new parole system. You'd better talk to him."

"Would you tell him I'll be right out, please?"

Gladys closed the door and Baby stepped up to the small mirror she'd hung by the coatrack. She tried to touch her hair into place, but after a day spent driving the back roads of Hushpuckashaw County, what was the use? To say she looked frayed would be a compliment. She thought of seeing Jake Lemaster in Ruleton again— of Jake's seeing her. She must've looked a fright; certainly he'd jumped to get away from her car when she'd pulled out! Baby shrugged, not even bothering to put on fresh lipstick. She snapped her purse closed and set it behind the desk.

Mr. Ware stood in the darkened reception area, his hat in his hands, and he turned when he heard her heels on the linoleum. He stood tall, shoulders back, with a full head of white hair and a handle-bar mustache. He wore a white linen suit that hardly showed a wrinkle, and as she stepped closer Baby took notice of the beautiful yellow-and-red polka-dot silk bow tie that seemed perched in front of his high starched collar. Baby thought the bow tie looked as if a carefully collected specimen of a monarch butterfly that had caught the measles had been pinned to his shirt with its wings arched, poised for takeoff. Of course she recognized L. B. Ware's name, but she had never met him face-to-face before. He ran his county paper out of a storefront office in Ruleton. Her mother had detested his columns—his political point of view had often left her fuming— and Baby felt much the same way about the editorials he wrote. In person, she was surprised to find him such a nattily dressed and cordial-appearing, handsome older man.

He smiled and bowed slightly. "Mrs. Allen. L. B. Ware, publisher of the *Hushpuckashaw County Tocsin*."

Baby offered him her hand. "I know you by your editorials, Mr. Ware," she said. "Shall we talk in my office?"

She sat across from him behind her desk. He held on to his hat and crossed a brushed white buck over his left knee. His canary-yellow socks showed a shade brighter than his tie.

"So, Mr. Ware. I must admit you've piqued my curiosity. Why in heaven's name are you here to see me?"

"Human interest," he said.

"You're interested in me as a human?"

"The information I have is that Letitia Johnson's daughter has been staying with you at 12 East Percy Street. I hear that you've found her a home. My readers are interested to know what's become of her, Mrs. Allen, as a sort of follow-up to the larger story. I'd like to know where and with whom you've placed the girl."

Baby looked at him more cautiously now, reassessing his ensemble and his chivalrous manner. She now recognized the butterfly tie for the elaborate lure it was. She wasn't biting. A train screeched and banged hooking up a car somewhere in the yard. Baby leaned forward and rested her forearms on her desk.

"I'm sorry, Mr. Ware. But that's official welfare business. I'm not at privilege to discuss the files of my clients. And, quite frankly, that's simply not the sort of public curiosity we care to indulge. But, so long as you're here, I can share with you a worthy bit of county news. I'm sure you're aware that night riders attacked my house Wednesday night. I suggest you write the truth about that—humans should be interested. A cross was burned in my front yard, Mr. Ware. My neighbors witnessed the entire episode—if you'd care to interview them—and Sheriff Burgess came out and filed a report. Windows were broken; windows I can hardly afford to have replaced. At the time of the attack, my girls and I were inside as well. It's a wonder no one was hurt. There's a bullet hole in the door of one of the vehicles, an old pickup truck. If anyone cares to actually look for the culprits and bring them to justice that ought to be evidence enough to convict them. You could write an editorial condemning those men, Mr. Ware. Or you could put word of the attack on the front page. I can see your headline now: Lynching Not Good

Enough: Klan Takes Revenge on Letitia Johnson's Twelve-Year-Old Daughter by Attacking the House of Woman and Her Girls."

L. B. Ware stretched a smile at her. "I heard about the incident of course. Terrible thing," he said. "Just awful. Horrendous." He shook his head. "A purported Ku Klux Klan action against a woman and her girls. But let me ask you one question, Mrs. Allen. Where was Mr. Allen when the 'attack,' as you term it, occurred? That's something my readers would like to know. Have you been left destitute? Are you helpless? In distress? A damsel in distress—or an especially attractive dame—always makes for good news. As do affairs. And lynchings."

L. B. Ware sighed. "Running a newspaper's a tricky business, Mrs. Allen. I understand your angle, of course. I do admire the impulse. We did report that an incident had occurred—a fire that breaks the blackout laws is news—as are the reports we've been receiving that the Klan has arisen to ride again during these troubled days in an effort to defend the home front while the majority of our able-bodied men are off at war. But we're not the *New York Times* or even the *Commercial Appeal*. A small paper like ours has to balance a responsibility with social reform with a clear understanding of the local demographic. Newspapers exist because of sales. Now that's a fact—call it *the truth*, if you will. I have to find news that sells without unnecessarily alienating the majority of my readership. Human interest is simply the caveman's mouth-slacked, gaping curiosity to know what happened. And then what happens *next*, until the thing runs its course. It's my job to tell them, to keep them abreast of developments. Telling them *sells*. And telling a story in a certain way sells better than telling it in another. What is the truth, Mrs. Allen? The *truth* is I can hardly make ends meet as it is!" He tried to charm her again with his winning grin. He splayed his palms. "As you can see I've been reduced to doing my own reporting."

"I can see exactly what you've been reduced to, Mr. Ware," Baby said. She stood. "I'm sorry I can't help you."

L. B. Ware looked at her and then he nodded. He stood. "I hope

I haven't offended you, Mrs. Allen. Truly, that's the last thing I wished to do by coming here to see you. The information I have is that Sally Johnson is no longer staying at your home. I assure you I'll have no trouble finding out where she is, Mrs. Allen. But since you were named as the agent on the case, I thought I'd give you a chance at the limelight—get your name in the paper. I could have made you the heroine of Sally Johnson's saga."

Baby smiled, matching his charm with a finely honed graciousness of her own. "I do appreciate the opportunity, Mr. Ware."

He smiled and tipped his hat. "I can find my own way out. Good evening, Mrs. Allen."

SATURDAY MORNING BABY woke at 6:00 as she did every morning of the week. She'd never needed to rely on an alarm, but then again she'd never been able to sleep in either, even when she had the chance. For a time she lay under the sheet, listening to the fussy screech of a jay outside her windows. The irritated cheeky chuck of a red squirrel answered it back, arguing the boundaries of the gnarled pecan in which they both lived. She smoothed her hand back and forth over the sheet on the empty side of the bed and then rose up on her elbow and leaned over to raise the blind on the day, a gloriously sunny morning. Through the screen it felt almost chilly, though by noon she expected the temperature would once again climb into the nineties. The heat wave had broken, but the dry hadn't eased one bit—not a sniff of rain in weeks. She wondered how dry and dusty it would have to get before the powers that be officially declared a drought. They were already conserving everything else for the war effort; why not just go ahead and add water to the list? In the years since the war started, privation had become the norm. In the Victory Garden they tended at the far back corner of their lot, she caught sight of Ruthie bent over, her big bottom in the air, weeding between the rows of string beans, taking advantage of the early morning cool.

Baby folded back the covers and rose to wrap herself in her robe. She clicked open the bedroom door. The girls were still asleep, but it wouldn't be long before Jeana realized it was Saturday and came running to sit with her. For the moment, she had the quiet of the house to herself. Baby treaded the hallway in her bare feet and stepped through the small living room, smelling the new paint and plaster stink about the picture glass that had been replaced. Hearing a faint crackling buzz, like the persistent irritation of a fly, she noticed the yellow glow of the dial on their old, cabinet-sized RCA Victrola, which Claire had been listening to before bed the night before. She flicked the radio off, feeling the heat emanating from the tubes inside.

None of their neighbors were up yet—their tightly rolled newspapers were still lying wherever they'd happened to land, aimed in the general direction of the porches by their sixty-year-old paperboy, Hollis, who wobbled by on his tall-wheeled bike trying to make his throws to the houses on either side from the middle of the street. Her *Hushpuckashaw County Tocsin* had landed in the hedge.

Baby retrieved the paper and scrolled down the rubber band. She opened the newspaper fully expecting to see a front-page story bylined by L. B. Ware exposing the whereabouts of Sally Johnson. But the bolded headline that greeted her that morning read:

HEIRESS DISTRAUGHT OVER DAUGHTER'S DROWNING TAKES OWN LIFE IN ESTATE'S SWIMMING POOL

Baby sat on the step.

Sissy's husband, Clyde Tisdale, had discovered his wife's body in the pool just before midnight when he'd gone to turn in and found she was not upstairs in bed, where he'd assumed she'd been since they'd returned from the funeral earlier that evening, helped there by Dr. Jenks, who had given her a light sedative to sleep. The death of Sissy's daughter had proven too heavy a burden to bear; as penned by L. B. Ware, "like Shakespeare's unfortunate Ophelia the watery weight of her grief and the sodden folds of her diaphanous dressing gown pulled her down to her own premature demise." She was thirty-two. Her husband, Clyde, and their son, Robert, survived her. Flowers were to be sent to the F. R. Lane Funeral Home. Her funeral would be a private affair.

No picture of Sissy's body accompanied the article. The photo of Sissy Rule Tisdale showed her as she had been as an eighteen-year-old debutante, with her hair curled, her face happy and eager, turned just so, poised with the promise of her coming of age in society, and looking dewy-fresh as a magnolia flower herself in an off-the-shoulders bell-sleeved white dress. It looked like a Hollywood promotional photo; the prettily smiling young woman shown in the photo could have been Judy Garland. The credit for the sitting was given as the Monticello Photography Studio, Memphis, TN. To set the scene, a second picture reproduced an oil painting of the Tisdale estate, noting that the original was kept on permanent display at the bank. The painting showed the stretch of pool and the extensive gardens that surrounded the grounds. The border of roses close in the foreground pricked gorgeously full, caught at peak bloom.

Baby sat on the front step dressed in her robe, her left hand resting lightly on her stomach. She didn't know what to feel. She had to admit she was shocked. Baby wondered who else this might touch. How would this affect them? It was difficult to say what it all meant. Or how people might react or where events might take them from here. Certainly she would have to warn Reverend Beasley and Victoria.

Baby stood abruptly, folding the paper under her arm, and reached for the screen door. Again, suddenly, she went woozy and the warning of a cold-hot sweat broke out on her forehead. Her stomach rose as she rushed down the hall. She dropped to her knees in the bathroom and grabbed the bowl in both hands, the photo of Sissy Rule Tisdale smiling sweetly up at her from the floor.

chapter thirteen

IT SIMPLY WASN'T the kind of work Tom Dodd preferred, given a choice. He'd been awakened by the call from Mr. Clyde Tisdale just past eleven o'clock. He listened, standing in the kitchen in his white T-shirt, which he could see had gone washed yellow under the arms, and his undershorts, black socks. He leaned one hand against the wall, his head down, listening. His wife had followed him down the hall. As sheriff of Ruleton, Tom Dodd wasn't often wakened to work in the middle of the night. His deputy, Ralph Simpson, could handle that sort of annoyance—the regular knife fights and shootings, routine domestic squabbles down in the Bottoms. That's what he'd hired Ralph for. The last time he'd gotten such a call at home had been the night Dorothy Tisdale had been drowned, just over a week ago. They'd attended the funeral that afternoon. The Dodds had a place to uphold. They were official dignitaries in the town. They'd sat two pews back from Boss Chief himself, Red Lemaster and that good-looking wife of his, their boys. Tom Dodd's wife had been raised Methodist, but they'd been talking about making the switch to the Episcopal church and welcomed the chance to go. St. Andrew's was undoubtedly the place to be. They'd simply giant-step the Presbyterians. They were getting there, Tom Dodd liked to think.

His wife, Doris, pulled out a chair at the kitchen table and sat and watched him listen. He shouldn't have confided in her about the night he'd gone out to the Tisdales to find Dorothy Tisdale drowned. He should have known better, but that one had gotten under his skin. She knew and now she looked scared listening to him talk to Mr. Clyde Tisdale on the phone again. Her hair stood wrapped in curlers as big around as Campbell's soup cans, her face wide and bland as a bunny's, slightly bucktoothed. Her daddy, Lanny Seton, had owned the Piggly Wiggly grocery in Ruleton and Tom Dodd had believed he was marrying up when he proposed to his daughter.

He kept his head down listening to Mr. Clyde Tisdale, still thinking of the other call. Even though Mr. Tisdale wouldn't say it over a party line, he could hear where this was going. Jesus! Letitia Johnson! Tom Dodd had known her for years and liked her. He used to stop for her on the road and give her a ride home from work if he was going that way and some days even when he wasn't. She'd never once been in trouble with the law. But he'd had to wash his hands of her. He'd led her from her house. Let McGales and them tear her out of the jail. He'd been terrified himself at the terror in Letitia's blanched face begging him as they pried her fingers off the bars. What else could he do? McGales had had those boys whipped into a frenzy. You can't beat city hall. You've got to pick your battles. But you could only stretch the truth so far before it'd snap back. And when it did! Watch out! A slingshot could kill as good as a gun. Tom Dodd could aim a slingshot near straight as a pistol. In fact, he might prefer it to a pistol, the Colt .45 he carried at his side. For one thing, you could never run out of ammo. As a boy, Tom Dodd had killed a mange dog with a slingshot—just some coot stray nobody'd give a damn about anyway, ribs showing and goop in its eyes. He'd cut the Y limb off a black locust and strung it with the slice of discarded inner tube. He picked up a smooth stone, round as a minié ball, and loaded it, pinched back the middle and squinted. He whistled the dog closer, *Here, boy!* Let her fly. One little stone! It conked him in the temple. The bald dog yelped and whined. It ran around in circles and dropped and writhed awhile, frothing, and then stopped, its tongue hanging sideways out of its mouth. The boy Tommy Dodd had run away from what he'd done and left the dog's body lying in the dust—nobody saw him do it and so it was almost like it didn't happen. Later that night alone in the dark he'd cried at what he'd done, but he'd never told anyone about it, not a soul. When he left the house later the next morning, he tucked the slingshot in the back pocket of his coveralls. If that passel of Rapchak boys from around Big Mound Bayou fooled with him ever again, they'd be sorry, sure. Carrying it made him almost feel not-small inside.

Tom Dodd glanced up at his wife again. Her daddy had been dead set against the idea of her marrying him. Tom Dodd's daddy had been the man what pumped gas and wiped your windshield at Jack Phillip's Texaco Station—in his blue work shirt with BOBBY scripted above the pocket. That was then. Now since the Setons had lost the store in the aftermath of the Depression, her old man had had to come to him time and again with his hat out, and Tom Dodd was not above letting him go on and beg. He made his father-in-law grovel. He could have bought her daddy a brand-new goddamned Piggly Wiggly, if he cared to. As sheriff, he had learned to keep a finger or two stuck in every pie, and in that regard it didn't hurt to go along with Clyde Tisdale or Calvin McGales, either one, no matter what time they called.

"Yes, sir, Mr. Tisdale," Tom Dodd said. He pushed away from the wall. "I'll be right there."

"Tommy," his wife said, sitting up when he hung up the phone. "What is it? What's happened now?"

Her breasts drooped low inside her tight-necked nightgown. They made her look as if she was carrying twins, but they'd never had children. This was not to say that Tom Dodd didn't have kids. He recognized a good number of his progeny around. Not that he'd claim them. With the money he'd made, he kept a mulatto woman, a high yellow who sometimes sang in the juke joints dressed in red sequins passing for a flapper from the twenties. She'd gotten herself arrested for doing the same with other white men who weren't as important as him and couldn't offer to pay nearly as well. Another plus for her was that he didn't send her to Parchman, where she would've had to work pumping a Singer sewing machine from dawn to dusk. She had Egyptian eyes and legs up to here. They called her Jasmine. She drove Tom Dodd wild in ways his wife couldn't begin to believe. Poking his wife was like sticking it to a cow. Not that Tom Dodd had ever fucked a cow. He wouldn't be caught dead fucking a cow. Or a colored, either, for that matter.

"Sissy Rule Tisdale's gone drowned herself in the pool," he told her. She'd find out in the paper the next day anyway. What was the harm?

She stared at him and then her mouth ohed. She covered it, hiding her front teeth. She shook her head and her eyes dropped closed, and she went still, transported by a kind of ecstasy of sadness. She dropped her hand and pronounced like some oracle, one of those colored washerwomen with the gray cataracted eyes who spoke the future for a one-pound sack of flour or a plug of tobacco: "This will be a curse on all of us. It is the beginning of our end. That Clyde Tisdale's a monster. He probably drowned his wife in the pool same as he did holding his daughter down in the bathtub. Don't be a fool. Don't get involved in this, Tommy. Think of your soul."

"Huh," Tom Dodd snorted. "What the hell, Doris. I *am* the *sheriff*. I have to get involved. Hell, I'm already involved. Anyway, I told you she drowned herself. No one else had to do it."

His wife's eyes rolled back in their sockets and she opened them to look at him. He saw the tears. Tom Dodd felt his disgust with her overwhelm him. "Why don't you go put on a goddamn bra or something," he said. He glared at her until she stood, her head hung, and then he turned to put on his uniform and fetch his gun.

MR. TISDALE HAD called him to come cradle Sissy's body up from the bed and carry her down the stairs and out to the pool. The pool had been Mr. Tisdale's idea. He hadn't explained himself on the phone, but when he said that's where he'd found her Tom Dodd saw at once how fitting it was. It made sense, given that the idea was that she had killed herself in grief over the drowning of her daughter in the bathtub. The story had the ring of truth. Even though what had really happened to her was clear to him from the vomit that had been cleaned off her nightgown. He saw the row of syringes on the bedside table before Dr. Jenks gathered them up, clinking, stowed them back in his black bag, and made them disappear. When Clyde Tisdale hauled his wife's body out of the water after Tom Dodd had thrown her in it, Dr. Jenks would step out on the patio and declare her dead from drowning and sign the death certificate—with him as the sheriff acting as the witness. Then they would call in L. B. Ware and go public. By Saturday morning everyone would know. Sheriff Dodd figured Clyde Tisdale was right; folks felt sorry for Sissy. They would understand.

Sissy was dressed in her nightgown and he could feel the roundness of her bottom through it, the thin elastic band of her panties. The nightgown was something, white satin and lace see-through. Probably from Paris, France, or someplace like that. It was a far cry from that collared potato sack his Doris wore to bed. He could see the pink of Sissy's nipples sticking straight out. Even after giving birth to two children, she still had the body of a girl, slight with slim thighs. She was still warm. He had his hand on her ass and damned if holding her like that didn't give him an erection. It was the closest he'd ever come to a white woman that fine looking.

What Tom Dodd had begun to think as he carried her out to the pool was how Sissy Rule Tisdale had never given him the time of day. Oh, she smiled and said hello. She had always acted polite enough. But she kept her distance. He was a gas station attendant's son, even if he had worked his way up to sheriff. She was a Rule with all the rights and privileges such a family title bestowed upon her. Tom Dodd had remained deferential. Even though he'd been a full-grown man when she'd become old enough to look twice at. At best these days, she'd been *Miz* Tisdale to him. But he'd watched young Sissy Rule grow up. He'd seen her with her pretty friends, but none prettier. And later with boys—and finally with Clyde Tisdale, the man she chose to marry. One time, soon after she'd made her debut, he'd caught her and Jake Lemaster in the backseat of Boss Chief's car parked in the dark off Bayou Drive. He'd seen someone duck in his headlamps when he pulled up and, for a moment, he'd wondered if the car hadn't been stolen from Parchman by an escapee—it wouldn't be the first time a convict had hijacked a vehicle. He unsnapped his .45 and slid it out of the holster. When he shone his light into the backseat, he saw that Sissy's blouse had been hastily buttoned back wrong. Damn if the boy hadn't been getting a little tit. Sheriff Dodd, she said, petting her hair. Lipstick smudged her mouth hot. He slid his pistol back in the holster. How you young folks? Nice night for a drive. He leaned on the roof. With his flashlight still shining down, Sissy noticed the buttons herself and raised her pretty hand to hide them. He'd winked at Jake. Drive careful now, son. He left them to it, shaking his head over young people today. He could admit now he'd been envious as hell.

And here she was in his arms. Her hair hung down, brushed long, silky, her head leaning back, lips parted. It was as if he, Tom Dodd, were carrying her to bed. He *was* putting her to bed. She'd be asleep a long time—until Judgment, Doris would say, acting the prophet again. The patio and pool remained dark—the only light came from a beam under the water that shot the pool through with a glittering greenish blue. Tom Dodd had never in his life seen a lit pool at night before. What would they come up with next?

Mr. Tisdale and Dr. Jenks had remained inside. There was no need for them to help. The story was she'd gone drowned herself. The lights in the study flashed bright. He could see them standing, talking, waiting for him to throw her in so that Mr. Tisdale could find her and call Dr. Jenks out to check—like they were acting out some kind of school play—but they couldn't see him.

He wouldn't be caught fucking a cow or a colored—or Sissy

Rule Tisdale. He laid her gently down on a lounge in the dark close to the wall of the hedge away from the emerald glow of the pool. She was turned as if merely asleep, her hair spread out behind her, her robe parted just so, the nightgown rising above her waist. He reached up and snagged the elastic of her underpants and yanked them down past her knees, off her ankles. When he saw her there, her patch neatly trimmed, he unbuckled his holster. Doris was wild as a bush down there—not that she'd ever let him see it. He was breathing heavily. He glanced back at the study and then quickly dropped his pants, his short, thick cock straining so that he thought the head might split. His heart pounded. His mouth had gone dry, but he managed a little spit. He slicked it on himself and knelt between her legs. She moved with the force of his thrusts as if she were actually fucking him back. "Oh, God," he said. "God." He thrust hard, biting his bottom lip. He came so swiftly—as if he'd never come before and the coming had been pent up in him all his life—he felt he'd been poleaxed. He felt rather than saw the flash. The force of it began in his toes and ended with him arched above her, feeling his mouth stretch wide. Sissy Rule Tisdale filled with his cum. A picture of her in the backseat with Jake Lemaster shot through his mind before he collapsed on her body, his face buried in her beautiful-smelling hair. *Peaches.*

Dr. Jenks would sign the certificate immediately without an examination and so he didn't even bother to wipe her clean. As sheriff, he would be in charge of the investigation. He pulled his pants up and buckled his holster. He wrapped her nightgown around her and tied her robe, cradled her up, and carried her to the edge of the pool. Standing over the shallow end, he thought better of it. Mr. Tisdale would have to go in for his wife if he insisted on all this playacting— he carried her to the deep end to make it more real for him. He didn't drop her. He knelt beside the pool and slipped her into the water. She sank facing up and then slowly rolled, her arms spreading like wings. With the robe billowing about her it looked as if she were an angel, flying. Then, in the raying light under the water, her feet dropped, her sheer nightgown floated up, and she sank naked to the bottom. He watched the striptease of her legs and ass and breasts turning blue, wrapped by the wrinkling bright. She sank until her tiptoes touched the bottom of the pool and then slowly, as Tom Dodd stood to go, her body began to rise, almost imperceptibly at first. He waited to watch the body surface, Sissy's lungs acting like balloons. He left her floating facedown on top of the water and started inside to give Mr. Tisdale his cue.

As he pulled open the back porch door, he saw Mr. Tisdale at the end of the hall. He was talking to mean-eyed Calvin McGales. Another man was with him. Tom Dodd recognized him. It was that big, handsome, shiftless son of a bitch, Gabe Allen. He nodded to them, avoiding that conversation, and walked into the study to help himself to a healthy shot of Mr. Tisdale's labeled whiskey.

chapter fourteen

JAKE READ THE news of Sissy's suicide Saturday morning over breakfast while Jolene sat at the opposite end of the table wearing a crisp-looking pink check gingham dress, last season's spring castoff, now designated as summer work attire. Saturdays were Jolene's chore days. Time to root out the last mote of dust that might be hiding in the immaculate house. Calpurnia had stepped into the kitchen to arm herself for the fray, collecting the mop and rags and bucket and bleach Jolene would direct her to use. Jake smacked the paper on the table and his wife glanced up at him. The boys looked, too.

"What?" his wife asked.

Without saying anything, Jake spun the paper around and slid the headline to her end of the table so she could read the story about Sissy for herself.

Jolene leaned close. "My God," she said and touched the edge of the white cloth napkin to her mouth.

"What is it, Mama?" Jakey asked. "Can I see?" He leaned over on his elbows as far as he could to stare at the upside-down picture of Sissy Rule Tisdale.

"Elbows off the table."

Jake scraped back his chair and stood from the table before Mason had a chance to take his plate, which he'd just served. His coffee steamed. He left his eggs, the pork sausages, buttered toast.

Jolene glanced up from reading the article. "What are you doing? Where are you going?"

"What is it, Daddy? What's happened, Mama? Can I see?"

"I can't believe this," Jake said.

"Is it that baby again?" Jakey's eyes rounded with realization. "It's that baby again, isn't it?"

"Believe what? What are you talking about? Sissy? You saw her yesterday," Jolene said. "It's unfortunate, but this can't be a surprise to anyone, not after what she's been through. Not after the way she looked yesterday. Like a zombie. And I can't say I blame her. Really. Can you? I mean the whole affair is an outrage, from A to Z. That Letitia Johnson will burn for this, too. The sin is on her head. If she hadn't gone and drowned that baby, none of this would have happened. Now sit down and finish your eggs."

"I'll be back."

"Where do you think you're going? You promised you'd take the boys fishing this morning, Jake. You're not getting out of that. This is no excuse. I have them all week. The least you could do is act like a father to them during the weekends."

"I'm happy to take my boys fishing."

"I knew something had to happen to that baby next. I knew that putting her in the ground couldn't just be it. This is it, isn't it, Daddy? Is this it, Mama?"

Jolene turned her attention back to the paper. She sighed. "It really is a shame, though," she said, admiring Sissy's portrait. "She was a beautiful, beautiful girl."

Mason stepped up to take Jake's plate.

"Daddydaddydaddy," Lee smiled, leaning close, his chin practically in his food, but Jolene was too absorbed in the article to scold him for it.

"Once your mama excuses you, you boys get ready. Jakey, would you help Lee find his shoes and get them on? Joe Booker and his boys are going, too."

"You're excused," Jolene said to the boys even though they hadn't touched their eggs either, and went back to the paper. She pinched up a piece of the buttered toast, her pinkie in the air, and leaned over her plate to take a neat bite while she read.

Jake was already on his way out, the crystal chattering as he fled the room. He stiff-armed the double doors and stomped into his boots, grabbed after his hat as he slapped out of the back, but left his pistol in its holster hanging on the peg.

Jake strode across the quad, kicking up dust. What grass there was left looked burned up as if a match had been put to it. He kept thinking of Sissy touching his arm, looking up at him, into his eyes, beseeching him, and saying his name, the spark of recognition that had come into her gaze before it faded, extinguished, that brightness guttered, and she'd fallen into a blind stare, gone into a monotone, dulled—and now she was dead. Sissy did not drown that baby, Jake knew. No matter what else he thought he knew, he knew that for sure—and neither had Letitia Johnson. Had Clyde?

Saturdays the administrative offices didn't open until noon. Boss Chief was upstairs. Jake took the steps two at a time and barged into his father's bedroom to see the woman slip behind the screen of the bathroom door—naked, her dark hair down long. Betsy Reed's neat clothes littered the floor. Boss Chief turned his yellow eyes from the full-length mirror before which he stood sawing his tie back and forth under his collar.

"It was once customary to knock, son."

Jake tried to shake off the shock of catching Betsy Reed naked in his father's bedroom—not that he was entirely surprised. "You . . . did you see the newspaper this morning?" he stammered.

Boss Chief carefully evened the strings of his tie, weighing one a little left and then the other a little right. He eyed the level, quickly knotted the tie, and left the strings hanging. "I got the call from Clyde last night after he found her in the pool."

"You believe Sissy drowned herself?"

His father turned to face him. "The older you get the more you act like a boy, Jake." He shrugged. "What do you want me to say? What do you want to know? Think about what you're asking me, Jake. I told you once before about the truth. Ignorance is bliss, for a fact. There's a good reason for doors. You should think hard about knocking before you go crashing through them."

The pipes creaked and water thundered, running in the tub.

Jake stepped close to his father. "You saw Sissy at the funeral. You led me to believe she drowned her baby girl. Letitia Johnson didn't do it either. I want to know the truth about all this. I want to know what's going on."

"Well, that's easy," Boss Chief said, nudging past Jake to pick up his jacket. "The *truth* is I don't know. And the truth is I don't want to know. I didn't *ask.*" He slipped his arm into the sleeve and pulled on the suit jacket. "But I'm curious, Jake. What would you do if you knew a different truth—say, that Clyde Tisdale had drowned that baby and then drowned Sissy? She didn't look too stable at the funeral. She was obviously drugged. She might've talked. She might've felt the need to unburden herself, tell someone that Letitia Johnson didn't drown that baby, how that little girl really died. Someone like you, Jake—someone she trusted intimately—someone she liked, used to love even. And then, if you knew, you might've felt like you had to *do* something. You would feel that way, wouldn't you, Jake? The old tailback for the Orange Bowl team? An all-American? Our hero. Go making a martyr of yourself. And what would you have done, Jake? Go to Sheriff Dodd? Tell L. B. Ware at the paper? Create a great big hullabaloo? Get yourself killed over this? And for what, Jake? You wouldn't have an audience that cared to hear—or care what you done—except maybe that welfare woman you been talkin' up. She'd listen. She'd be oh so sympathetic. And after you got her in bed and put yourself between her legs, you two could lie around in each other's arms and commiserate about the evil in this world—about what McGales and his bunch are going to do to that Sally Johnson, et cetera. But at the end, what would that change? Nothing. Now, that's the *truth*, Jake, and you know it. Everyone else is content to believe this story. They gone let a dead dog lie. It don't matter a'tall what actually happened. The truth is what folks agree to say it is, and we say that Letitia Johnson drowned that baby girl and that Sissy drowned herself in grief. That's what we choose to believe. Makes a pretty good story, too, don't you think?"

Jake had that sunstruck feeling again. He felt as if he'd stood too quickly and all the blood had drained from his head. The room dimmed. He sat back on the edge of Boss Chief's rumpled mattress. His daddy didn't reach out to help him. Jake could feel him watching him, his big hands caught at his lapels.

"I can't let you take over this place someday without understanding certain things, Jake. How does it go? 'When I was a child I played as I child, but when I became a man I got rid of playthings'? Something like that. I never was any good at those damn Bible verses."

"I won't work here anymore," Jake said.

"What did you say, boy?"

"I said I can't work here anymore. I quit."

Boss Chief laughed. "Boy, that's a good one, Jake. What's that wife of yours with all her Memphis-bought clothes going to say to that? And where are you going to go? I guess I could get you on helping Betsy's husband, Van, coach the football team over at the high school—he'd welcome you. Other than that I'm afraid the market for old tailbacks has long passed. Anyway, what have you got to feel guilty about? You ain't guilty of nothing. You'd be a fool to leave Parchman Farm, Jake. You still got you a bright future, especially now you're gettin' seasoned up a bit. You got everything here you could ever want, Jake. All the comforts money can buy, a nice home, servants. You got a nice-shaped wife. Two healthy boys. Most people would kill for all you got, Jake. They'll take it from us if we let them. You got to be strong. You're letting your scruples weaken you. They're getting in your way. Use a little common sense, son. You only get the one life, Jake. Parchman Farm is heaven and hell both. It's here. It's now, Jake. Just thank your lucky stars you weren't born a niggrah's all. God loves you, son. We've been blessed."

Boss Chief picked up his hat and walked around the bed. He opened the door and walked out, leaving Jake behind to think about what he'd said.

Jake sat on the edge of the bed with his face in his hand. The water in the tub cranked off, and he listened to the sounds of Betsy Reed bathing. The water lapped and poured again. He imagined it sliding off her long limbs. She was humming. She must have told her husband, Van, that Boss Chief needed her to come into work early—or stay late. What did he care if his daddy and Betsy Reed were sleeping together? Why should he get involved in any of it, any of this? As Boss Chief had said: You had one life. This was *his*. As Jake stood to go, he glanced at the small, sterling silver–framed photograph of his mother on top of Boss Chief's dresser. He reached up and took it and slid it into his pocket before following his father out of the room.

Jake took both of his boys. Joe Booker sat beside him in the front seat of the state car. Joe's youngest boy, Joe Junior—a particularly pugnacious-looking miniature of his old man—sat in the back sandwiched between Jakey and Lee. The cane poles stuck out the back window with the hooks caught in the handles, the cork bobbers trembling in the wind. They'd stopped and collected a can's worth of worms from under some rotting planks at the damp edge of the prison. The crickets Joe Booker raised for bait chirped and scoured the walls of the cage caught between his feet. Jake waved his way past the trusties at the gate, but instead of turning left toward Big Mound Bayou, their usual spot to fish for brim and perch, little sunnies, Jake turned right onto Highway 49, heading south toward Ruleton.

"New fishing hole, Boss?" Joe Booker asked, his strong arm resting out the opened window.

Jake let go of the wheel and handed across the copy of the newspaper he'd snagged off the dining room table as he walked out of the house. His wife had finished with it, her day of cleaning already in full swing, Calpurnia down on her hands and knees scrubbing the foyer.

Joe Booker had taught himself to read late in life. He read the article slowly, carefully, his brow furrowing. When he finished, he looked up. "What's it all about?"

"Damned if I know."

Joe Booker looked at him and then he nodded. "You saved Bigger's life. He'd a died in that box sho nuff without your help. I know he 'preciated that. But Jesus He the One s'posed to save the world. It's all down in writin' so you can read about it your own self."

Jake could feel Joe Booker looking popeyed at him.

"What I'm sayin', Mr. Jake, the Good Lord works in mysterious ways. You may have a job to do on dis here earth, but don' go be trying to put Him out of work."

Jake crunched down the long gravel drive and parked beneath the willows that shaded the Tisdale estate. Sheriff Dodd's shiny new black-and-white patrol car parked gleaming in the full sun at the front of the house. The state car Jake drove only had a radio receiver, but he'd read that the sheriff's new patrol car had come factory equipped with one of the two-way radios developed during the war. The Rules had always been big supporters of their town's sheriff's department.

Jake felt for the door handle. "Be right back, boys," he said over the seat.

"Where you going, Daddy?" Jakey asked.

"I just want to see something. I won't be but a minute or two—promise. And then we'll go fishing. I have a new hole I want to try."

"What's wrong with the old hole?"

"Nothing. I just want to try this new one's all." Jake grinned at his son. "Any more questions? Why don't you see if you can think one up while I'm gone, all right?"

Jake peeked around the side of the house; he wasn't properly attired to pay his respects at the front door. He'd dressed for the fishing trip, sporting dungarees and his faded blue practice jersey, his number, 7, in red big on his chest. He stepped up and rapped at the side screen. No one answered and he walked around back. The pool stretched before him. He wandered out onto the patio. It wasn't as if there'd been a shooting—or the event of a knifing like Bigger going after Alley Leech. He saw no blood or any indication of a struggle. The lounge chairs faced the sun. The yellow umbrella over the table had been brightly unfurled. Potted red geraniums and orange and pink hibiscus bloomed bright. Honeybees worked the stamens. Jake felt the morning heat beating down on the back of his neck. It didn't look as if anyone had committed suicide here the night before. The pool looked perfectly inviting.

Jake walked up to the edge and looked down into the water. The underwater light had been left on. It waxed dimly under the glare of the sun. Jake turned to face the great white house. With the sun shining directly on them, the windows blanked as black as if the house had donned sunglasses. From his left a mockingbird called, pretending to be a blue jay. Jake glanced that way. A satiny white strip of cloth caught underneath the hedge flagged his eye. He leaned over the lounge chair and picked it up.

"Jake."

Jake pocketed his hand and turned to meet Clyde Tisdale as he stepped out of the house. Behind him, framed by the French doors that opened off the patio, stood Sheriff Dodd.

Jake met Clyde's grip. "I'm awfully sorry, Clyde."

Clyde's jaw clenched and he nodded. He'd showered and shaved, the slicked wisps of his thin blond hair combed neatly back. He wore pressed khaki trousers and a pink golf shirt, loafers. "I should've watched her more carefully," he said. "I . . ." He shook his head. He coughed into his fist. "Drink?" he said. "I was about to pour another for myself."

Jake thumbed over his shoulder. "I've got the boys with me and my sergeant, Joe Booker, and his son. We're heading out to try a new fishing hole. I didn't get the news about Sissy until I picked up the paper this morning. I thought I'd stop by and see if there's anything Jolene and I can do."

"It's all been taken care of, thank you, Jake."

Jake nodded. "I wanted to offer."

"You were her first love, you know that, don't you, Jake? You two made a pair."

Jake looked at Clyde's pale watery-blue eyes. He ducked his head and stepped past him. Sheriff Dodd had disappeared. Out of sight underneath the shade at the side of the house, Jake reached in his pocket: fine silk and lace white panties—Sissy's, no doubt. He glanced up then to see Sheriff Dodd holding back the sheers in the living room, his small black eyes blazing at him like the bores of two pistols. Jake walked deliberately past and stepped again into the brilliant sunlight that bathed the front of the house.

"Daddy," Jakey asked him as soon as he slid behind the wheel, waiting with the question he'd thought up. "Why do they paint police cars black *and* white?"

JAKE BAITED JAKEY's line. He shook a cricket out of the cage into his palm. Then, with the cricket cupped like that, he pinched the dangling hook and, using his middle finger and thumb, worked the prong down under the plate of armor behind the cricket's neck. The point came out under its chin, oozing gunk. The cricket wriggled to get off, but it was stuck, arched to the curve of the hook. Jakey wouldn't touch the cricket for anything, its useless stingers sticking out like needles. He stared horrified at it while Jake worked the prong.

"There you go, son," he said to Jakey. He let go of the hook with the cricket skewered on it and the line swung out on the lead weight and plopped into the yellow waters of Indian Bayou, sending ripples out and out. The cork bobber floated above the line with the cricket baited on it.

Jakey stood gripping the cane pole tightly with both hands as he waited for a fish to strike and the bobber to dip under so he could yank the line.

Jake set his hand on his son's shoulder. "You all right?"

"Yes, sir." Jakey tried his best to turn the grimace into a smile.

Joe Booker threaded a worm on Lee's hook while Lee watched, absorbed. Joe Junior had already caught one palm-sized brim. They'd threaded it through the gills and left it swimming on the leader to take home and fry.

"You got things under control here I might take a walk."

"I 'spec I can handle these here boys."

Jake had chosen a fishing spot beside a picnic table set to overlook the bayou a block from Mrs. Allen's house on 12 East Percy Street. He strolled the quiet oak-lined sidewalk until he came in sight of the small, square white house with black shutters situated on the corner lot. From across the street, Jake could see the brand of the felled cross scorched in the yard.

The screen door slapped and Jake heard Mrs. Allen's voice. "Jeana, wait for me, please. Don't run out in the road."

Jake looked both ways before he crossed the street.

"Mrs. Allen," he called when he saw her emerge on the side steps with a picnic basket in hand, backing into the screen to hold it open. She stopped and looked at him.

"Why, Mr. Lemaster," she said. "What a surprise."

She turned and called back into the kitchen. "Come on, Claire."

"Here," Jake said, "let me give you a hand. Seeing as how a hand's all I've got to give."

Mrs. Allen glanced at him again when he said that. "I see you're out of uniform this morning, Mr. Lemaster. Am I to take this as a social call then?" She turned the basket over to him. "You can put it in the backseat of the Model T. It's in the shed there."

"My boys and my sergeant and his son, we've about fished Big Mound Bayou dry. We've been searching for a new fishing hole. I thought we might as well take a chance on Indian Bayou. And since I was in the neighborhood . . ." Jake felt the weight of the basket tug at his arm. "Feels like you got enough food in here to feed an army. Where you headed?"

"You did come down here to fish, didn't you?" She gave him a sugary smile without sweetness—no trace of humor showed in her eyes. "Where I'm headed, Mr. Lemaster, is none of your business."

Jake felt the rebuke. He tried again. "I didn't mean to pry. My boys' names are Jakey and Lee. I don't believe I've ever had the pleasure of meeting your girls."

"Jeana, this is Mr. Lemaster. Mr. Lemaster, this is my daughter Jeana. And the one perpetually late for the ball would be my older daughter, Claire."

Jake nodded to the girls in their matching white-collared, summer Sunday dresses. The younger one with black hair and green eyes looked him up and down as frankly as his own son Jakey might have measured a stranger. The older daughter looked like an exact replica of the girl her mother must have been. She had blond hair and the same storm-blue eyes.

"Have you seen the paper yet this morning?" Jake asked Mrs. Allen.

Mrs. Allen let the screen close behind her. "Claire, would you relieve Mr. Lemaster of that basket. It looks a little too heavy for him. Jeana, help your sister. You girls wait for me in the car."

"Yes'm," Claire said.

Claire took the basket and Jeana grabbed the handle on the other side. Together they lugged it unevenly down the path. Jeana sneaked a peek back over her shoulder at them.

"I saw it," Mrs. Allen said. She wore a sleeveless navy dress and she crossed her bare arms as if waiting for something. Jake noticed again how pale she appeared. He happened to notice then, too, that she had removed her wedding ring, revealing an even whiter band of skin. "Why are you here, Mr. Lemaster?"

Jake waited until the girls turned into the shed out of earshot. "Letitia Johnson didn't drown that baby. And I don't believe Sissy drowned herself either. But knowing that, I'm not sure what to do now. I couldn't imagine anyone else I could tell."

Mrs. Allen held her arms over her middle, searching him. "What kind of bait are you trying on me now, Jake?"

At Mrs. Allen's using his first name, Jake faltered. "It's the truth," he said.

"Haven't you heard, Mr. Lemaster? These days there's no such thing as the truth. Mr. L. B. Ware from the newspaper was kind enough to drop by my office yesterday evening trying to find out where Sally is and he took the time to explain it to me."

"I've heard a similar argument. Lately, my daddy's big on lecturing me about the truth, too. I found these caught in the bushes beside the pool at the Tisdale estate this morning on my way down here."

Mrs. Allen raised an eyebrow, looking skeptically at the pair of lace and silk panties. "A woman's underwear is hardly evidence of murder, Mr. Lemaster, if that's what you're suggesting."

"No. But it is an indication of what happened to Sissy last night. I don't have any doubt these are Sissy's, and I doubt very seriously that Sissy stepped out of her shorts before she waded into that pool to take her own life. I don't know *what* happened last night. But I know what didn't happen. The truth isn't what Clyde Tisdale says it is. These prove that. And that's truth enough for me, Mrs. Allen."

She continued to look at him. Jake held her gaze. "Baby," she said and offered him her hand. "My friends call me Baby."

"Baby," Jake said, taking it.

"We're headed to see Sally at Children's Home in Rivers Bend. She's living there with Reverend Beasley."

Jake nodded, accepting the confidence. "You know she can't stay there. Not after what's happened to Sissy. The Klan will be up in arms over this. Do you have a safe place to take her? You don't dare bring her back here."

"No. I know." Baby hesitated. She looked down, reminding Jake of the morning they'd met up on the road with the photograph of Letitia Johnson on the seat between them. She spoke up as suddenly again: "I thought I'd take her back out to Letitia Johnson's cabin for a few days. No one will think to look for her there."

"Tell me what I can do," Jake said. "Can I do anything? I could check on you two, if you'd like. I could bring out food. Keep you up-to-date. Let you know when it's safe for Sally to return to Rivers Bend."

Baby looked at him. "I can't *ask* you to do that, Jake," she said. "I need to go."

Jake watched Baby walk down the sidewalk toward the shed where the car was kept. When she glanced back and caught him looking after her, they both turned abruptly away.

chapter fifteen

GABE ALLEN RODE with Calvin McGales in McGales's beat-up truck. They drove chugging along with McGales fuming over the cud of a baseball-sized wad of tobacco. He'd bitten off a mouthful as soon as he'd climbed in the pickup and slammed his door to get shut of the Tisdale estate. The wad swelled out his cheek, rounding his jaw and making his long, skinny head look like a peanut squash. Gabe thought it was like getting a glimpse of someone's stretched portrait in the telling warp of a funhouse mirror— the comic reflection capturing something essential about who they were that was only hinted at by the features they regularly turned to face the world.

Like a waking dragon's eye, the sun glared red from underneath the dark lifting lid of the horizon. Gabe's own sockets burned rawly, red-rimmed, and he rubbed at them. He hadn't gotten a wink of sleep. Cotton loomed, assuming the ranked and uniform shape of rows in the fields to either side of U.S. Highway 49. Every once in a while as he drove, McGales would grunt again emphatically and then spit an exclamation point of tobacco juice out the window. He did not bother to dribble the prune-dark liquid into a cup, nor did he look to see if another car was behind them or if one might be speeding past in the opposite lane. He just spit and let the spit splat.

That was McGales. Especially when he was mad, and just now he was beside himself.

"That pantywaist gone give *me* fucking orders? He gone go fucking tell me let Sally Johnson go? He's as goddamn bad as that spoilt brat Jake Lemaster and you just wait till I get goddamn done with that whelp. Going athwart *my* fucking authority freeing that Bigger from the box! As if they's fucking somebodies can boss me around just cause they fucking rich! Who the fuck does that Tisdale think he is? I don't give a flying fuck if he is going to be fucking president of the fucking goddamn fucking bank now that his wife and that old fart Rule out the way. I wouldn't give a rabid rat's bald ass if he was the cocksucking president of the United States Franklin fucking Roos'velt hisself. Fuck that! As if all he's got to do is snap his fingers! Who is the Grand Dragon? Who is *the* fucking *Man* in this county now? You just go ahead and goddamn tell me that?" His cheeks worked furiously again and then he spat. Spat again. Gabe looked back to see the juice fly off. The solid-looking brown glop smacked the tailgate and splattered all over the already bird-shit-speckled bed of the primer-red truck.

"You fucking tell me that!"

"You are," Gabe said.

"Fucking A goddamn right I am," McGales said. He nodded. "And I'll do what I goddamn fucking please. I don't take orders from any fucking faggot bank president or no wannabe boy-boss neither. Mark my words! I ain't done with that Jake Lemaster yet! His time's a coming. We gone settle this thing once and for all. I'm just awaiting my opportunity. I'll bide my time. He can't go on hiding behind his daddy forever. And that Tisdale can't touch me no way. He don't got no fucking papers on me. I don't owe that money-lender one red fucking cent. *Neither a borrower nor a lender be!* I follow my own *rules*. What I fucking say goes. And what I say is: *An eye for an eye and a tooth for a tooth.* We root that pickaninny out this time for sure. Why give her up now we know she's at that preacher Beasley's place? The fact that Clyde Tisdale's wife gone and drowned herself ought to make him want to get that girl more, wouldn't you think? It sure as fuck does me. That's two of us and one of them. We got to even the score. But even if I didn't feel that way personally, I'm in a position of command. I got to consider the big picture. We done dropped out the undesirable material from the mass mobilization days, just like the Imperial Wizard commanded. Time has come for the Klan to rise again and I have been chosen to lead the charge! *May God give me strength and the wisdom to use it!* One little lynching done boosted new memberships twenty-three percent! Now, I ain't no banker—I may never been to no fancy fucking college—but my pappy didn't raise no idjit. Calvin McGales ain't no mo-ron. Tisdale's the fucking mo-ron. Men like to *do* things. Action's the key. All this sitting around talking about what we gone fucking do. It's worse than the goddamn army. *Hurry up and wait.* Same difference. *Strike when the iron's hot*, my pappy used to say. *Shit or get off the pot.* Now's the time. We can't wait. And we got our big meeting tomorrow night."

Gabe's knees pressed nearly up against the dash. He kept his hat on so that the raggedy wind from McGales's open window wouldn't muss his hair—even though the sputtering truck only made a top wind speed of thirty-two miles an hour. When they'd stopped in Ruleton the day before, he'd bought new pomade at the Rexall's: Sweet Water it was called—Elixir of Honeysuckle—*guaranteed to drive any woman wild.* There was a widowed schoolteacher who came around the shack to buy her jars of corn liquor. She had mousy brown hair and thin lips that she redrew heart shaped and juicy red. Her eyes peeked out from her round dough-white face shiny black as coat buttons. She wore false eyelashes, even Gabe could tell that. The way she looked stuffed into her dress, Gabe kept himself occupied just imagining how he'd work off the bind of her corset—the coming burst of her bust. Her breasts were her greatest attribute. They jutted out so big that when the woman spoke she seemed to be shelving her chin on them. Her bottom stuck out in back, bustle big. In fact, sticking out fore and aft as she did she was shaped a bit like a duck. But beggars couldn't be choosers, as McGales might say. Gabe had to admit he'd always had a hard time curbing his desire for women. If he had a weakness, he thought, women seemed to be it. It was just his nature, he guessed. And women had always taken to him as naturally. So it was mutual.

Gabe had offered her a jar for free; it hadn't cost him anything.

"It's on me," he smiled.

"A gift?" she asked, raising the lines of her penciled eyebrows, her berried lips kissed up. Coy, but she'd given up her name with a bat of her lashes: "Delilah. And yours?" she asked. She'd returned to lay her money down twice last week—a drinker of note or just plain interested.

"So, you're all alone out here?" she inquired the first time, trying to see into the doorway behind him.

Gabe had admitted that he was. "Alone and lonely," he said with a sigh. "Nothing but the skeeters to keep me company."

"You do your own cooking, too?"

Gabe had wagged his head sadly. "Aren't I a pitiful sight?"

The next time she came out she brought him something to eat. A little potpie she'd made herself, full of chunks of corn and maybe cabbage and some kind of ground gray meat.

"Well, isn't that sweet."

It was plain god-awful—he'd prefer to eat his own cooking in a heartbeat, fried fatback and brown eggs, grits—but after he'd thrown the potpie into the creek he'd scrubbed and saved the gleaming pan, waiting until she showed up again to give it back to her with a winning that-sure-was-good-thank-you grin.

Gabe was thinking now as he drove back toward the still with McGales that if he played his cards right Delilah and he might while away a little time. The next time she stopped by he was going to ask if she'd like to have a drink inside. He tried not to judge her looks against those of other women he'd been with—his wife's or even May Franks's. Why make himself feel any worse about how far he'd fallen than he already did? He had to keep occupied some way!

Selling whiskey and keeping an eye out over the slow bubbling still was not exactly taxing for as virile a man as himself, and Gabe had never been a drinking man, though he'd take a nip now and again just to be social. Drink did not tempt him the way he saw it did many a man—and woman, too—who came out to the still at all hours, driven there by their need. McGales's product was surely safe with him. Cards were more to his taste, seven-card draw or stud, but he was alone and no old boys were around to get up a game. You could only play at blackjack solitaire so long, he'd found. He wouldn't dare mention playing a hand—even penny ante just for the fun of it—to McGales, who was a hard-shell Baptist and a tee-totaler to boot. As a Klansman, McGales had sworn an oath to protect against the twin evils of gambling and liquor. But he didn't seem to see selling the rotgut stuff himself as contrary to the Klan's creed. McGales surely didn't think it was him society had to worry about! And even though the still was against the law, McGales didn't seem to see it as a gamble. He made sure to give Sheriff Dodd his cut. For him, the still was a surefire way of making money. It was strictly a matter of business and Gabe figured, by the number of jars and jugs that he'd sold in the past few weeks, that McGales must be a wealthy man, though you'd never think to guess it by the battered truck he drove or the slovenly way he dressed. No doubt every dollar McGales had ever made was squirreled away in his corn shuck mattress or stashed in the hollow of some tree. He wouldn't trust the Planters Bank of Ruleton with it, that was for certain.

Next to his efforts to revive the Klan, the still was McGales's major concern, but Gabe was simply minding the store. The duck-shaped woman was his only diversion. He felt entitled. Gabe had stopped trying to feel bad about what had happened with May Franks. Though he had to admit he still felt miffed at his wife. When she'd caught him lying about where he'd been that night and he finally fessed up, she'd acted as if she had had no idea about the affair! Gabe didn't advertise his tomcatting—he'd always been discreet; that was in the best interests of everyone involved—but he'd always been under the impression that he and his wife had had an *understanding*. After all these years, how could she not know? His wife wasn't dumb. It must be something else, but for the life of him he couldn't figure out what that something was. As far as he was concerned, theirs had been an ideal marriage. Baby's shock at his infidelity had surprised Gabe almost as much as the resolve she'd shown in throwing him out of the house she'd inherited from her mother.

Quite frankly, it was all more than he'd bargained for when he'd climbed down off the train in Ruleton. He'd boarded the 9:15 out of Eureka with every intention of riding out his ticket to Memphis. His plan had been to make himself scarce. Baby would miss him! His absence would stoke her already considerable desire. She'd come crawling, begging him back, once she'd realized the mistake she'd made in banishing him. They'd had a perfectly good arrangement. Gabe had assumed his seat on the train and leaned forward, lifting the shade to look out the window to see if she was in her office at the welfare sobbing after him. When he didn't see her, or the girls, he dropped the shade and sat back with a shrug, still buoyant at his prospects. Back in their bedroom at the house on East Percy Street gathering his things into the single overnight suitcase that he kept close now under his seat, he'd worked carfully to avoid meeting the accusation in his older daughter's blue-eyed glare or the hurt bruising his younger daughter's eyes, which he knew well were exactly as green as his own. Though he would undoubtedly miss Claire and Jeana, not to mention his wife and the comforts of their home that he'd come to take so for granted, lately he'd taken to imagining himself a lone wolf, a man made to roam. Gabe Allen had always felt undervalued. He knew what people said about him living off of his wife. Who people said wore the pants in their family. In Memphis, he decided to take a stand. He'd decided: He'd make his fortune. Gabe Allen had had a plan.

Then he'd run into Calvin McGales on the street—gauntcheeked, furiously seeking, with knots for biceps, and hard, bright, fierce ice-cube eyes. He looked as twisted to Gabe as the root of a scrub pine—misshapen, trying to get a grip on the hard life he'd lived. Word was out. Beau Biddle, the last man to mind McGales's "store," had been dippering off the profits. Over time, the man had become a regular sieve. He drank from the still as if it were a veritable fountain of youth—though at the end the rotgut stuff was what killed him dead, his liver bulging enormous as if he'd taken to watering a melon to blue-ribbon size inside his belly.

McGales and Gabe met on the boarded sidewalks of Ruleton and Gabe told McGales he was at "loose ends."

McGales eyed him up and down. He spat and wiped the juice off his lips with the back of his crooked hand. "I got a position open you interested."

Gabe told himself he didn't have much choice, no matter what his original plan had been. You had to remain practical in this life. He needed a place to sleep. His wife had only staked him enough money for a night in a hotel and one good meal. Standing on the sidewalk next to the live wire that was Calvin McGales, Gabe Allen quickly revised his previous ambition. He'd stay in Ruleton long enough to work up some cash to carry him on his way. But now, only a few weeks later, the truth was he already regretted taking McGales up on his offer of a job. This other business was more than he'd had in mind when he nodded yes. He'd only gotten involved with the Klan to ingratiate himself to his new boss. The night of Letitia Johnson's lynching McGales had positioned Gabe on the town square in Ruleton to sell to the crowd out of the back of the truck. They'd made a bundle, but Gabe had gratefully done as he was told and remained behind to guard his boss's investment when the crowd drinking in the square surged toward the jail.

The loose tools in the bed jangled as McGales bumped off the highway to double back toward where the shack and the still sat beside a spring-fed stream that ran into the Hushpuckashaw River.

His wife had only been trying to do her job. Motherless, the girl had needed a home. As for himself, truly, he didn't have a thing in the world against Sally Johnson.

The bullet hole was still in the door. Gabe tuned in to the lip pucker whistling of it as they drove. The whistle changed pitch depending on their speed, playing a kind of tune. When Gabe had suggested McGales putty it over and dress it with another slap of primer, not to hide it entirely but just not so as to seem like he was bragging about the whole thing, McGales had sneered, "That fatso Sheriff Burgess can't fucking touch me. I don't fucking care what he fucking says. Weren't me shot at nobody!"

Gabe had happened to be sitting in the passenger side seat of McGales's truck that night, and the bullet had come a little too close for his comfort. He'd heard the terrific bang of the bullet hit the door and felt the angry hornet's buzz of it sting under his seat. He still had a purple-and-yellow bruise that made the right cheek of his buttocks look as if he'd been hind-kicked by a mule. When they got back to the shack, Gabe had taken out his pocketknife and dug the .22 out of the cushion. His wife taking a potshot at him with the loving gift of the pearl-handled pistol he'd bought for her had brought the whole thing home to him in a way getting roped into going along for the night ride against his own house by his new boss hadn't.

McGales bounced the truck over the ruts in the well-run road. The shack stayed hidden from view in a copse of young, bright-leafed locust. The trickling sound of the stream was a comfort, but the pools bred roving hordes of mosquitoes. Idling there, Gabe slapped his neck. He looked at the blood on his wide palm.

"I'll come by tomorrow afternoon to carry you to the Lost Fifty for the big meeting. We'll gather there and wait for dark. Then drive out to that preacher's house in Rivers Bend and pay Sally Johnson a little visit. Pack up a few cases to sell; no sense missing an opportunity. The Invisible Empire ain't a goddamn charity."

McGales paused the chaw—the sign that his boss was through with him—and Gabe climbed out and slammed the shot door.

McGales ground the gears and swiftly reversed his way out of the woods into the daylight that had begun to green the open fields beyond. Gabe stood watching as McGales bounced the truck backward into the field, flattening the cotton, before he got the vehicle rolling forward again. The tools banged again as he jumped the water furrow. Dust climbed up behind his speeding away as if McGales were setting the road on fire.

Gabe turned and looked around at the damned mess he'd gotten himself into. This did not feel anything like a social occasion to him, but the first thing he did that morning was head for the still to draw a drink for himself.

chapter sixteen

Reverend Beasley nodded as he read the copy of the *Tocsin* Baby had brought for him packed in the picnic basket. "I see," he said. Victoria stepped up to read it, too. Penelope looked over the reverend's other shoulder, the sheet music she'd played at chapel hugged against her chest.

Reverend Beasley peeled off his reading spectacles. "But Sally belongs *here*," he said, already shaking his head. "She's a member of the Family now. The Klan is nothing new in Mississippi. We've dealt with night riders in the past. Years ago when they saw I could make this piece of floodland profitable they tried to drive us out. We are only too aware of the violent acts the Ku Klux Klan still seems all too capable of committing, but we will not yield in fear. We will not let ourselves be terrorized." He raised his chin. "God is on our side."

Victoria laid her hand on her husband's arm.

Reverend Beasley looked down at it resting there. Neither spoke, communicating silently. Then the reverend covered her hand.

"It has always been my belief, Mrs. Allen, that good swirls about us with the ever-present possibility for grace—whether we *believe* in Him or not. But if that's true, then the possibility of real evil must exist, too. The devil isn't some red-suited, pitchfork-toting jester we can poke fun at. His presence is manifested in cowardice and prejudice and fear and greed. But his principal agent has always been hate. Beware, Mrs. Allen. Evil isn't merely black or too easily white, because the devil is all too simply human. He's in us, Mrs. Allen, and we come in every color, size, and shape."

Outside saying good-bye, Reverend Beasley folded Sally close. "You come back to us as soon as you can, Sally. We'll be here waiting to welcome you. This is your *home* now," he said and laid the blessing of his hand on her head.

When Baby, Claire, Jeana, and Sally drove away from Children's Home, Sally knelt on the seat, the emptied picnic basket on the floor at her feet filled with her things, and waved so long to her family through the back glass of the Model T.

She waited until they'd turned through the tunneling of pecans and driven out of sight of the grove before she turned and sat.

"I don't know why I feels so surprised. I knew nothing that good couldn't last."

GOD HELP HER if she was wrong about Jake Lemaster was what Baby had been thinking over and over to herself all day. If Jake really had come by fishing to fool her into trusting him, then he'd finally found the right bait. She'd gone and swallowed the shining lure of sincerity she saw in his eyes hook, line, and sinker.

Baby lifted her mother's old suitcase off the bed.

"Let me put that in the car for you, Mama," Claire said, her blue eyes swimming.

Baby laid her hand on her daughter's cheek. "You be a help to Ruthie, hear? We both know what a handful that sister of yours can be." Baby looked seriously at her until Claire smiled. She ducked into her mother's arms.

Jeana and Sally were playing with Jeana's porcelain dolls on the floor of Jeana's bedroom. Ruthie had boxed plates and forks and spoons, one pot and a frying pan as well as Cream of Wheat and canned corn, powdered milk, coffee, Wonder bread, and peanut butter for Sally if she wanted it—the very idea of the oily stuff churned Baby's stomach. It was all the surplus food they had on hand. Baby laid the sheets she'd folded to take on top of the box and stepped up to the telephone table in the hall.

She asked Nelly Lands, Eureka's operator, to connect her to Mr. Brumsfield's residence. They weren't completely reliant on L. B. Ware at the *Tocsin* to get the news out. Nelly was privy to all the good gossip in Eureka, and no one was better connected. Baby knew that once Nelly overheard Baby report to Mr. Brumsfield that Sally was no longer staying at Children's Home, Baby could count on Nelly to help spread the word.

"Wonder about that Sissy Rule Tisdale, don't you think?" Nelly said while they waited for the Brumsfields to answer their jangling phone. "I heard from Miss Fletcher who got it straight from Franklin Lane at the funeral home that there's not even going to be a viewing. Course I can't blame Mr. Tisdale. After all that family's been through, the last thing they need is another public display."

"Hello?"

"There you go, Mrs. Allen."

"Mrs. Allen?"

"Mr. Brumsfield, I'm sorry to bother y'all on a Saturday, but you said not to hesitate if I needed to call."

"Has something else happened?"

"I wanted to let you know that I've removed Sally Johnson from Children's Home. After the events of yesterday, I was afraid of the consequences once the news of where she'd been placed got out."

Silence crackled the line.

"I was just on my way out the door to walk down to your house and tell you that I received a call from Mr. L. B. Ware earlier this afternoon. He wanted to verify the information he'd been given that Sally was at Children's Home. He's going to print it in tomorrow morning's edition. Of course, I told him I couldn't comment, official welfare business and all that. He said he was going to drive out to Rivers Bend to check for himself."

"Good."

"Good?"

"By tomorrow morning everyone in Hushpuckashaw County will know Sally's no longer there."

"But where is she *now*, Mrs. Allen? That's the other thing I wanted to talk to you about. I don't like the turn this case has taken. I'm thinking Sally would be better off in Sheriff Burgess's protection. Maybe it's time we turned her over to the custody of the law."

"Being in the custody of the law didn't protect Letitia Johnson."

Mr. Brumsfield sighed. "Mrs. Allen, I admire your dedication, but I can't have my agents unduly risking their lives. Let me remind you that you are a county welfare agent, not the Shadow."

"Mr. Brumsfield, may I speak frankly?"

"You're not speaking frankly already, Mrs. Allen?"

"I haven't wanted to bring my personal problems to the office. But perhaps Gladys has told you that my husband and I have separated."

"Well. Yes, Mrs. Allen, Mrs. Pointdexter did happen to mention that you and your husband were having some difficulties. But I'm not sure I understand what you're driving at. I thought we were talking about the fact that you've removed Sally Johnson from Children's Home. We were talking about whether or not we ought to turn her over to the protection of the law. What have your personal problems to do with Sally? What does the trouble with your husband have to do with any of this?"

"Mr. Brumsfield, I'm pregnant."

"You're pregnant?"

"Yes, and I must admit I haven't been feeling especially well of late. It's been a trial. I'd like to take off a few days, if you don't mind. I'm going to visit my sister in Memphis."

"Your sister in Memphis? What about Sally Johnson?"

"I can assure you that she's in capable hands, Mr. Brumsfield. I trust all of this will have blown over by the time I return."

Mr. Brumsfield coughed into the phone. "I see. Your sister's in Memphis. Very well, Mrs. Allen," he said. "I hope you feel better. Drive carefully now. You know where to call if you need me," he said, and then he said, "Nelly? Is that you I hear breathing in on our conversation? As long as you're still on the line, why don't you connect me to Mr. L. B. Ware at the *Tocsin*? He ought to be back from Rivers Bend by now. Let's see if I can make sure he gets a story right—for once."

BABY AVOIDED HIGHWAY 49, navigating the maze of even dustier back roads in an effort to make their way to Letitia Johnson's cabin without being seen. By the time Sally and she arrived it looked as if the sun that had been frying yellowly above Hushpuckashaw County without fail for weeks had been grabbed down and hurled smack against the edge of the horizon, the orange yolk dripping the black silhouette of trees that lined the river.

Baby turned down the dirt drive. *God help her if* . . .

Sally sat leaning her elbows against the front seat. "I never thought I'd be back here again," she said. "I know it's my house, but someway it don't feel like home no more."

Baby parked the Model T out of sight around the back of the cabin. "Why don't we take a quick look inside before we unload our things?"

She kept her purse tucked close underneath her arm as she stepped up onto the porch with Sally pressing close behind her. She unhitched the latch and peeked open the door. "Oh!" Baby's heart *tha-dumped* and she caught her hand at her throat. For a moment it had appeared to her as if the ghost of Letitia Johnson were hovering there, standing with her back against the wall in her white dress waiting on them, as if all along she'd known Baby and Sally would have to return to the cabin outside of Ruleton on the banks of the Hushpuckashaw River where they'd left her uniform hanging.

Sally stood on the porch behind Baby ready to bolt.

"What is it?" she whispered. "What do you see? Is it a haint? Reverend Beasley, he say there's no such thing as haints. He say the only Ghost the Holy One, but I'm not so sure. I mean I'm not saying Reverend Beasley wrong. And he sure not lying. But maybe he hasn't seen one for hisself yet is all. That's all I'm saying."

"It's just your mama's dress that we left," Baby said. "Everything's exactly as it was. Except for all the dust." Baby stepped up to the table and set down her purse. She swiped her finger across the top. "It's a wonder there's a bit of dirt left out in the fields to farm."

"It's what Mama always said."

"What do you say we get cleaned up in here a bit first? We'll need water. Would you mind drawing a bucket from the well?"

The sun had sunk down over the horizon in the west, raising a huge, harvest-sized full moon in the east. Sally went out into that hot groaning dusk, greenish yellow fireflies flashing on and off across the yard. Baby heard Sally dropping the boards that covered the well, and then the splash of the bucket, the squeaking of the pulley as she hauled the water up.

Baby set her hands on her hips. As a rule, she didn't think she had faith in the fact of haints either, but she found herself speaking out loud now to the presence she, too, felt hovering watchfully about the cabin. "Now, Letitia," she asked, "where do you keep your broom?"

JAKE LEMASTER USED one hand to undress her. "Jake," she said, encouraging him as he slid the dress off her shoulders and down over her hips. She couldn't imagine how she and Jake had gotten there. How had the two of them come to this moment? Gone this far? She reached up and pulled the pins out of her hair one by one, watching Jake watch her.

"You're a beautiful woman, Mrs. Allen."

"Baby," she said to him. "My friends call me Baby."

"Baby." Jake smiled.

"Can I help you with that, Mr. Lemaster?" She grabbed for the buckle of his holster. She dropped it along with his trousers to see him straining against his shorts. They kissed, began kissing. Then Jake bent to kiss her neck, her breasts. The tingle of his lips and his tongue and teeth on her nipples charged straight to her toes, electrifying her all over. Suddenly Baby wanted Jake inside her so badly that she felt the ache. He laid her gently back onto the bed and she reached for him. She couldn't believe how good he felt—how he filled her. They moved together, slowly at first. "Oh, Jake," she said. "Jake." She hugged him to her, thrusting up. She dug her nails into his back, reached lower and grabbed him from behind, trying to press him even deeper inside her—harder, faster. She was wet; sweat shone on her breasts. Her mouth went dry. "Oh, God, Jake," she said. Kissing him wildly now, madly, breathing hard, close, hot into him, back onto her. "Jake!" she called out, shuddering as she came, feeling the arch beginning in his lower back. The warning of worry about accidentally getting pregnant flashed through Baby's mind until she remembered that she already was. She held him close so that he came inside her, the luxuriousness of their lovemaking flooding warmly through her, the beauty of unhindered desire. After banishing Gabe, she had fully believed she'd never find that wonderful letting-go feeling with another man. She hugged Jake hard.

"Jake," she repeated. "Jake." She lifted his face in her hands to look into his eyes, recognizing again the sincerity she'd seen there. "Jake."

"Baby."

"Jake."

"*Baby.*"

"*Miss* Baby?

"*Mrs. Allen?*"

Baby startled in the dark. She looked around. Saw the home-made checkered curtains. Letitia Johnson's white dress hung from the nail on the wall.

Sally stood beside the bed, wide-eyed.

"Are you okay?" she said. "You was having you a bad dream,

Miss Baby. Calling out about 'make, make, make,' making something. All that moaning and with the crying out I figured you must be some kind of terrible hurt. Are you in pain?"

"Oh my," Baby said—as shocked at her own doings as she'd ever been. She sat up on an elbow, pushed her hair out of her eyes, held it. She laughed. She was sweating as if she really had overexerted herself in bed—though she wasn't exhausted. She wasn't at all tired now. She felt touched at the concern showing in Sally's face. "I'm sorry I woke you."

"I wasn't sleeping noways," Sally said. "I keep thinking of Mama. Like she's here or something. It feel like she is."

Baby watched Sally crawl back in her own bed. Through the thin curtains she could see the moon, as big around as a millstone now. The glow of it bathed the yard in a pale white light.

Baby wiped her forehead. Her stomach clutched, holding tight. And then she felt a sudden sharp stabbing, a carving pain. She felt as if what she ought to do was get up and go use the bathroom, but she didn't want to have to walk to the outhouse out back. She thought how she always had to remind Jeana to pee before she turned in. Baby flapped back the sheet to go.

"My God," she said and sat straight up. She yanked the sheet down. The blood blotching her lap looked black in the white light—her nightgown soaked—the wet of it seeping between her thighs.

"What now?"

She looked at Sally. Sally's mouth rounded when she saw. "I knowed you was hurt the way you was calling out! You been shot!"

"No." When Baby stood, the blood dripped down her legs. She pressed the folds of the nightgown against herself to absorb the flow. The bleeding didn't hurt too terribly, she could bear the knifing of the cramps, as if she were being raked from the inside out, but it made her feel terrible—she felt herself sinking with the knowledge of what it likely meant.

"Is it your time of the month?" Sally said.

"My baby," she said.

She shuffled out onto the porch holding the sheet close. If that's what this was, she couldn't bear to think of the possibility of leaving her baby in the fetid stink of the outhouse's bleak hole. Sally followed her onto the porch, looking after her.

Baby walked tenderly across the yard and stepped into the cotton, lifted the sheet, and squatted between the rows. She peed, letting the cramps work, waiting—until she felt the passing of a tiny but perceptible lump—before letting herself peek back the sheet. She put her face in her hands. She stayed for the placenta, hoping it would come. It came out in a clotted clump, purple and veined. The hunk of it scared her. Baby dug a hole in the middle of the row and covered the spot with dirt. Rather than burying her baby, she tried to imagine it as if she were planting a seed, hoping something good would grow out of this little death. She pressed her palms against the hot earth and prayed a prayer without words, the silence of it sounding back to her in the night noises of the crickets and bullfrogs, the whine of mosquitoes swarming her ears. If she possessed faith, it was the strong belief that God would care for this child that she would never meet.

Baby used a cotton leaf to wipe herself and cleaned up with the edge of the ruined nightgown. She stood, swiping at her eyes. As an agent for the welfare who had dealt with about every imaginable catastrophe in her visits into her clients' homes over the years, she knew perfectly well how common miscarriages were, for any number of reasons, especially in women of her age, but she'd never given a moment's consideration to the possibility of actually miscarrying herself. She'd been so awfully sick that she'd been absolutely sure the child growing daily inside her must be healthily alive. No matter the troubles a baby may have caused her, she realized she'd fully expected to carry this child to term.

Sally stood on the porch, arms crossed, hugging herself. "Oh, Miss Baby," she said, shaking her head. "I didn't even know you was big. I'm so sorry, I is."

"Me, too," Baby said.

chapter seventeen

"**W**ORTHLESS!" JAKE HEARD Jolene say about him still lying in bed with his eyes closed. She banged her dresser drawers and slapped down her hairbrush getting ready to go to church that Sunday morning without him before slamming their bedroom door behind her to punctuate her point. "Come along, boys. It's time to go."

"But where's Daddy?" Jakey asked.

"He's asleep."

"Isn't he going to church with us?"

"Apparently not."

"Who's a parent, Lee?"

"*Apparently.*"

"What does that mean?"

"It means he's pretending to be asleep. It means he's obviously not going to church with us this morning." Jolene raised her voice so Jake would be sure to hear. "But he's *not fooling me.* I *know* he's *awake.*"

"Who's he fooling then?"

"Lee," she said. "Shoes. Right this minute. We'll meet you downstairs. Calpurnia! What is it, Jakey? Hold the rail, please. I shouldn't have to remind you every single time. You could fall and split your head wide open."

"You can't get into heaven if you don't go to church, isn't that right, Mama? But even if Daddy doesn't go to church today, he did go to it at that funeral for that dead baby. That should count for something, don't you think, Mama? Do you think Jesus will count it?"

"*Dorothy*, Jakey. The baby's name was Dorothy. Not just 'that dead baby.' I've told you before. Please."

"Mama, do they have to put you in a box like they did her that time? I don't think I'd like being in a box in the ground with all that dirt holding me down. I don't think I could breathe."

They reached the middle of the steps and stopped.

"Jakey, what now?"

"I just thought of something. Maybe I should stay home, too. I don't think I want to go to heaven if Daddy doesn't get to go."

"Of course you want to go to heaven! Don't dare say such a thing. Heaven is where all the good people go. 'The righteous will receive their reward.'"

"Mama, are you going to heaven?"

"Well, I certainly plan to. I have been baptized and I have accepted Jesus Christ as my personal savior. I pray every day."

Lee pounded past the bedroom door in his hard shoes to catch up. He dropped onto his bottom and took his time bumping down each step, *thump, thump, thump* . . .

"Lee, do you have any idea how much those pants cost! Mason, did you bring the car around like I asked you to?"

"Yes'm. It's right out front." Mason unstuck the front door, ushering Jolene and the boys outside onto the front porch and down into their yard. The car doors opened and slammed. Jake sat up. Looking down through the white lace curtains from the vantage of the second-story window, he could see Lee and Jakey in the backseat of the family's Packard, Jakey still talking. Jolene had her mouth fixed—a bright, determined slash. She stared straight ahead as she drove them toward the gate.

Jake looked down at himself. He'd shafted through the hole in his shorts. He had a terrific hard-on. He'd had no intention of going to church that morning, but before Jolene had started banging and slapping things around to wake him, he really had been asleep. He'd been having a dream. "For goodness sakes," he said, feeling as guilty as a schoolboy entertaining a fantasy about his teacher. He tucked himself away and quickly stood, trying to think of anything else. Baby Allen was a respectable lady, a responsible married woman with two girls of her own. She must be forty!

In the bathroom, he stropped the razor back and forth several times, whetting the edge, before he shaved, careful not to nick himself. He dressed quickly in the khaki trousers and short-sleeve shirt with the Parchman Farm patch on the sleeve that Jolene had had Calpurnia clean and iron for him on Friday, ready for the new workweek to begin. He glanced back in the mirror one last time to comb his hair, thinking that he ought to get it cut. Before he left the bedroom, he pulled out the top drawer of his dresser and pocketed the little silver-framed remembrance of his mother that he had swiped from his father's room the day before.

Jake didn't bother having Calpurnia serve him breakfast, but he did have Mason help him strap on his holster.

"Tell Miss Jolene I had some business to attend to. I'll be home later this afternoon or evening. And tell her not to bother waiting dinner for me. Or supper either. I'm bound to be late."

Jake stomped into his boots and walked out the back door into the sunlit yard. No work details were sent out on Sundays—the gunmen given their chance to sleep in—and the quad remained deserted, desolate seeming. But Sundays were the best days at the prison for the gunmen, bar none, and spirits ran high all day Saturday in anticipation of the Sabbath to come. The Midnight Special that began its run in Jackson would arrive at noon carrying the wives and girlfriends of the gunmen. In the afternoon, after church services and sit-down family-style dinners in the camps, the gunmen would play each other in baseball. Ten teams from the fifteen camps made up the prison's organized leagues. The wives and girl-friends and other visitors who'd arrived on the train were invited to sit in the stands and watch the games. The gunmen could play ball on their camp's team or come to watch or tend to their garden plots or nap, as they chose. On Sundays things ran themselves. Joe Booker could handle things. No one would miss Jake.

As Jake strode across Front Camp toward First Home to retrieve his state car, he met up with the dog boys, Quirt Hanson and his gang of trusty handlers. Out most of the night keeping the hounds in shape was Jake's guess—the alarm of an escape hadn't been sounded. He would have been the first to hear. The happily panting blueticks and mixed redbones, a yappy beagle and a sad-eyed blood-hound tumbled past in a pack, held to their long leads by the trusty handlers so that they wouldn't go baying after every scent.

"Mawnin', Cap'n," Quirt called, grinning gray teeth, and doffed his sack hat, the twenty-four-inch, single-barreled .410 snake pistol jabbed in his belt. He had long greasy black hair and his suspenders had been belted two notches too high, pulling his baggy pants up over his belly, enough to show the whole of his blocky brown bro-gans. One of the trusties brought up the rear, dragging a dog-sized coon by the tail, its little humanlike hands hanging down over its head as if it were begging to give up, but Jake could see it had been treed and shot dead.

Jake watched them go. He opened the door to climb into the car, but stopped, the razored hairs along the back of his neck prickling with the feeling of being watched. He turned and searched the win-dows of First Home. The curtains at Boss Chief's bedroom window rustled ever so slightly, as if a breeze had blown them, but that July Sunday morning was every bit as stiflingly still and hot and dry and dusty as it had been every morning for weeks.

Jake climbed into the state car and shut the door. He picked his sunglasses up off the dash and slid them on before starting the en-gine and backing out of his space. As he passed the infirmary on the way toward the front gate, he happened to see Alley Leech, carefully stepping down into the yard. He took small, tender steps as he started away from the building, hunched forward, his bandaged sternum visibly padded underneath his untucked uniform shirt. A Negro gunman attended him, but when he tried to take hold of Alley's arm to help him along, Alley yanked it away. "Don't you goddamn touch me," Jake heard him say.

Certainly, as Mirabel had foretold, Alley Leech had been way too mean to die, but it seemed as if he was even in far too foul a humor to take his convalescence lying down.

When he looked up and saw Jake in the car slowing before him, he scowled, his distaste rising raw as a welt on his face.

Jake stopped, idling, and rested his arm on the window. "Alley," he tried. "Good to see you back on your feet."

Alley's face twisted into a sneer. "That big nigger you saved won't think so. You may got him out from the box, Mr. Jake, but I aim to have my satisfaction. I won't be denied. Justice is on my side. And so is Cap'n McGales."

"Now, Alley. Bigger spent six hours in the box and served out a weeklong sentence at work all alone on the road for what he did. I'd call that even, wouldn't you—especially given how I hear you taunted him."

"He ain't dead."

"No, but look on the bright side—neither are you. But you might be if you mess with him again. Bigger doesn't seem like the type to take this lying down either."

Alley Leech almost smiled then, his face smoothing over like a wicked child's with a secret he thinks is terribly funny—the eight puppies he's strangled clumped in a single shallow grave dug under the porch.

"Don't worry about me, Mr. Jake. I got my revenge all planned. He was Letitia Johnson's man. Now he gone have to live with it what all we gone do to her little girl. And ain't a thing in the world he can do about it stuck in here."

From behind his black glasses, Jake stared hard back at Alley

Leech. "If I were you, I'd watch myself, Alley. And you can tell Calvin McGales I said the same. If you boys aren't careful, you'll end up being guests here at Parchman Farm your own selves. Believe it or not, there are laws against killing and threatening people in this state. I'll witness against you myself. And when you're found guilty and I process you into the penitentiary maybe I'll put both of you in the cage at Camp One, make Bigger your trusty. See how you like that."

"That'll be the day!" Alley Leech beamed happily as if Jake had told a good one. He went just short of clapping his hands in delight. "I'll see Judgment first!"

At the front gate of Parchman Farm, Jake showed his face to assure the guards.

"Mornin', Boss." They raised their rifles and waved him past.

Jake turned out onto Highway 49, heading south. Though he knew he'd have to return to Parchman Farm later that night, he left feeling as if he'd quit the prison for good. He did not look back.

chapter eighteen

THE FOX HUNKERED at the edge of the field to watch the cabin. It was not cool, but it was cooler than it would be later in the day. He'd caught the smell of food. It was coming from the cabin again. He raised his nose in the air and licked his teeth. He whined and then pricked his ears. An armadillo waddled by as uninterested in the fox as the fox was in him. Nearby, a red-winged blackbird bent the top of a tall tuft of johnsongrass, chirping. A grasshopper whirred and the fox trapped it quickly between his paws. He bent to sniff and lick it, nibble its head—a crunchy snack while he watched, eyes up, shining, alert.

At the sound of the humming tread, he flattened himself against the hot clods, chin on his paws. The dust climbed into the sky behind the machine. When the machine rolled to a stop in the yard, the dust that had been trailing it caught up and swept past, hazing a hot cloud that slowly drifted over the little house. A man climbed out. The man had one arm. He looked to have lost the other in a trap. The fox did not know this man; he'd never smelled him before. But the fox could smell the oil on him—the smell meant the thing that flashed and banged. He saw it strapped to the man's hip and he knew to fear the danger of it as much as the stretch of dirt that the machines rolled by on. When the man banged the door, the fox's muscles bunched, wired to flee, but he didn't move a hair. The man thumped up close to the cabin. He took off his top. The man rapped the wood and turned to look out over the fields. His black fly-eyes silvered sun. The house opened and the girl stood framed by the darkness behind her. The fox raised his nose to smell her—and sniffed the tang of something else—his whiskers quivering. A drip of wet broke out on the black tip.

"She said you'd come. I got her to lie down. But it still won't stop like it ought to. Hurry, quick do something."

"What happened?"

The man followed the girl into the shadows. The cabin door closed behind them.

The fox waited, his muscles slowly relaxing. His tail whipped and wagged. He picked the hopper up with his teeth. This was all very interesting—he was always curious in goings-on around his den—but though he smelled food, he didn't foresee a meal here. He'd been hunting since dawn, and he had his mate and pups to feed. He rose and trotted down the row, following his nose.

The fox stopped. He doubled back and sniffed the earth. He pawed the pile, smelling pee and blood—the telling tang he'd scented when the girl had come to the door, but not her. The other he'd smelled before. The fox dropped the grasshopper and buried his nose, snuffling. He dug out the hole. He nipped up the dirty lump he'd uncovered, held it, pausing, ears perked again. He hunched flat and twisted to snap back, snarling, as the blackbird swooped over him, red wings flashing. The fox snatched up the lump again. Crouched beneath the canopy of cotton, he tipped his head back and gulleted the morsel. He took the meat in his mouth.

At the far end of the field, the fox broke from the cover of cotton and bounded across open ground, racing toward the thick tangle of brush that grew along the bank of the river. He ducked under a lightning-struck tree and wriggled beneath the arm-sized vines of

poison ivy and the mess of ferns that hid his den, and dove under-
ground, disappearing into the cool earth. His pups greeted him
warmly, whining and licking his chops to see what he'd brought
them, welcoming the meal. The treat he threw up at his mate's feet.
She nuzzled the fur at his neck, thanking him before she ate.

chapter nineteen

A T STAKE WAS first place in Parchman Farm's camp league of ten teams. Camp 1 had a commanding 3–0 lead in the bottom of the eighth inning of their Sunday game against Camp 5. With two outs and two men on, runners at first and third, Bigger stepped up to the plate. The thirty-six-inch lathe-turned bat looked like matchwood in his great hands. Joe Booker acted as the unofficial coach for Camp 1. Officially, he called the first base line for both sides. But that didn't stop him from cheering on his team. After all, the games were supposed to be just for fun—serious as they always were—Sunday afternoon entertainment for the families and girl-friends of the gunmen who played, though they attracted a large crowd of convicts and trusties as well.

"Come on, Bigger, rip the cover off!" Joe Booker yelled. "Put this game away for good!"

Bigger had already hit two home runs that day on Straight Ball Willie, by far the most feared pitcher on Parchman Farm. In the second inning, Bigger had hit the very first pitch Straight Ball had challenged him with. He hit it so hard that it lined straight back past the mound at almost the same angle that Straight Ball had pitched it and shot past the outstretched mitts of the second base-man and then the center fielder and over the fence into the tangle of woods bordering the curve of the Hushpuckashaw River beyond. But at least the trusties, armed for their search, had found that ball.

Bigger's second home run had come in the fifth inning on a 2–2 count with one out and one man on. Joe Booker had been thinking that if Straight Ball were a swifter pitcher he'd keep working his junk, keep Bigger off-kilter. Bigger was a fastball hitter. But Straight Ball had his pride. Since Bigger had cut Alley Leech and survived the box in Camp 5, he'd grown an even larger reputation in Camp 1, enduring the week's worth of punishing work he'd been put to all alone ahead of the line on the road. Though Straight Ball and Bigger had been teammates before the incident with Alley Leech and Bigger's transfer to Camp 1—the combination of Straight Ball's pitching and Bigger's hitting largely responsible for putting Camp 5 in position to defend first place in the league—now Straight Ball looked to be aiming to take his old friend down a peg or even two. He was out to show Bigger who was who. They'd eyeballed each other hard over that second at bat. Then Straight Ball wound up and kicked his leg high, then snapped it down, defying Bigger's prowess with a blur of his own pure speed. To Joe Booker's trained athlete's eye, Bigger had seemed to begin his swing even before the ball left Willie's forked fingers. He met it squarely, waist-high over the middle of the plate. The bat went *crack!* And the ball had rocketed high over the right-field fence. It sailed over the tops of the trees, cleared the river, and landed in the shade of the trees on the opposite bank. The yellow river was rumored rife with the nests of water moccasins and not one of the trusty shooters would dare the swim. They'd left that second ball for lost. The man on base had come home, batted in by Bigger, who stomped heavily on the plate as he came across it, huffing up dust. 3–0.

Now as Bigger stepped up to the plate for the third time, Joe Booker was thinking rather smugly that the defeat would be a good lesson for Camp 5—that maybe it would teach Calvin McGales and that gang a thing or two about messing with Camp 1—put the nail in their coffin, so to speak. But he'd had no idea!

Joe Booker began to clap. "Let's go now!" All the spectators started clapping and yelling and cheering. Bigger took two looping practice swings facing the mound, and then he stepped outside of the box. And that's when Joe Booker looked up past Bigger to see Alley Leech gingerly climbing the bleachers behind home plate to take a seat, shooing away the attendant at his side. Joe Booker had gotten the warning that Alley Leech had set himself loose from the infirmary that morning, but he never would have thought to imagine he'd actually show his face at one of their games. One entire bleacher was reserved for the families of the colored convicts. It was packed. The overflow clung to the backdrop and strung out all down the length of the waist-high fence behind both teams. The other bleachers were reserved for whites. Alley Leech sat on those peeling green bleachers all by himself, hunched over his wounds, looking pitiless and vengeful and remorseless as he ever had, long, stringy yellow-haired and grub whiter than anything Joe Booker had ever seen dare the light out from under a rock. Joe Booker began to worry. From where he stood behind first base it looked to him as if Bigger had grown a second head—Alley seemed squatted at the perfect height to turn and whisper directly in Bigger's ear. The wives and girlfriends and trusties and other gunmen were cheering and hollering at Bigger's next at bat. Joe Booker saw Alley Leech raise his hands to either side of his mouth, but from where he stood Joe Booker couldn't hear what Alley Leech yelled. But everyone knew that it was Alley Leech who had set Bigger off before.

Fortunately, Joe Booker didn't think Bigger could hear him either. He didn't think Bigger knew Alley Leech was even there. Bigger hadn't so much as glanced back. He was focused forward, fixed on the task at hand, batting in these extra runs and putting the game on ice.

On the mound, Straight Ball glowered at Bigger from low under his striped prison cap. Straight Ball nodded and spit, hitched his pants. "Anytime you ready, nigga!" he called out. Joe Booker let himself be swept up in the excitement of the moment, banging his wide hands together as loudly as if he were clapping two boards. He was cheering himself hoarse.

This was it!

Bigger calmly stepped in the box before home plate and planted his enormous feet, right elbow high, bat back, waiting, ready.

Straight Ball Willie nodded and assumed his stance, hands behind his back. He shook off signals from his catcher until he got the pitch he wanted to throw, eyeing the zone.

Joe Booker began to clap even louder, faster, his hands blurring before him as if he were working the speed bag. Everyone was screaming. Going crazy now, frantic with it, on the edge of their bleacher seats. "Let's go, Bigger! Come on, Bigger!" Joe Booker yelled over the infielders' chattering beside him, *"Comeonbatter, comeonbatter,"* and the family of fans stomping the bleachers. The pitch popped the mitt behind Bigger, who did not even swing. He stood like the granite statue of a batter. "Strike!" the umpire called. Those for Camp 5 whooped. A general groan rose from the other families in the stands.

Bigger stepped out of the box once more. Straight Ball waited to get the ball back from his catcher. "You see the way it is now, nigga!" Straight Ball called out. He grinned and spat. "De bigger dey is! You going down, boy!"

Bigger stepped back inside the box. He spread his feet and raised the bat. Waited in a crouch for the next pitch. He took a ball high to the outside. And then a second called ball, a breaking pitch down low and inside—Straight Ball trying to brush him back from the plate—but Bigger didn't give up even the inside edge and didn't flinch at the pop in the mitt so close behind his knees.

Straight Ball Willie nodded. Bigger stepped out and back into the box. Got set. Everyone knew the fastball was coming. You didn't have to be a genius to guess it. From where Joe Booker stood, he could see the fork of Straight Ball's fingers gripped inside the web of his mitt. It was a straight challenge—the third time the charm. Straight Ball wound, snapped the leg down, hurling his arm, and

Bigger began his swing. The bat smacked and the ball soared, a white speck rising against the summer sky. Everyone tipped their heads back to watch, straining to see. The ball rose and rose. It was still rising. Joe Booker shielded his eyes. Everyone was looking away. "Going, going . . .

"Gone!" Joe Booker yelled and jumped with both hands over his head.

And that's when Joe Booker heard the screams, Bigger already in the stands.

He'd followed through with his swing, letting it turn him all the way around on his heels, took two giant steps as if he were racing for third base, and leaped the waist-high fence behind them, still gripping the bat. Alley Leech didn't even have time to cover his eyes before Bigger leveled off another of his home run swings at his head.

Bigger got in four or five more fast whacks before anyone had time to react and then he thundered up two more steep steps and leaped off the back of the bleachers and disappeared. Just like that.

Gone!

"What! Huh!" The trusty shooters were caught off guard, everyone looking the other way at the high home run ball that had undoubtedly salted the game away, too stunned and heavy from their Sunday sit-down dinner of fried chicken and the fun of the game to shoot. Then the trusties began shooting wildly, yelling, but Bigger had been unchained for the game, and he was perfectly free to use the unbound strength of his big arms and bigger legs. He appeared again a hundred yards away from the bleachers, running hard, racing for the trees, in the opposite direction from where the trusties had been headed to help search for yet another ball. The river was right there. It would occur to Joe Booker later that Bigger could not have done better if he'd planned his escape from A to Z.

It had all happened so quickly. And Joe Booker felt himself moving through a gummy molasses of slow motion, submerged in the silent rising air bubble of it himself, popping out into the sweltering summer heat to yell. "Hey!" he heard himself squawk, flapping his arms. And then he took off, running. He jumped the waist-high fence. All of them were in the race to catch Bigger now, but boy could that Bigger *move!* Could he go! And he had one hell of a head start. Joe Booker had never seen a man go so fast. Joe Booker stopped running when he reached the woods, tasting the iron in his lungs, hands on his knees, cautiously looking down at the snaking roots at his feet and the vines that hung down from the trees, just waiting for a water snake to slither off a limb and drop onto his back from above. He glanced out over the river and the seemingly endless stretch of the brilliantly lit cotton fields beyond. Bigger must have already forded. He was nowhere in sight. The water flowed by without a ripple or a splash. They'd have to set the dogs on him. Joe Booker spit and spit again, trying to get the blood taste out of his mouth.

The other trusties came across the finish of the race to catch Bigger far behind Joe Booker's own distant second—third, fourth, fifth, sixth, seventh—leaning on trees or falling on their knees, dropping onto the ground, beat enough for a second to forget that any fat limb could be a death-sized moc, any dulled, fallen leaf an arrow-headed copperhead waiting to strike.

"Sound the alarm, C. K. Even Bigger can't run like that forever. He may a got away, but they ain't no way he gonna escape. He gots twenty-two thousand acres in front of him. He won't get far."

Joe Booker walked back to the stands, everyone standing around the stumped body horrified. It was surely a mess—a sight worse than what Bigger had done to Alley Leech the first time, except that Alley Leech was plain dead and so couldn't feel a thing. That was one plus, Joe Booker thought. The stub of Alley Leech's neck yawned back from the ruined head still pumping blood. Booker, though a boxer himself, cringed remembering the pop at the impact of Bigger's first leveled swing.

Joe Booker heard a grumble from above. The sky was perfectly blue—not a rain cloud in sight—but a drop splatted his forehead. *The devil's beatin' his wife.* Joe Booker reached up the flat of his hand

and wiped it away. He looked down at the hair on his forearms standing straight up, teased by the electricity in the air, the tartness of a storm tasting up the buds on the back of his tongue.

Joe Booker turned and began to jog toward Front Camp. What he needed to do, he thought, was find Mr. Jake, and quick, too. Bigger had gone and done it now. McGales would get what he'd wanted from the start—the big man's hide. The bunch of them would hunt him down like a common coon. They'd tree him. They'd show no mercy. Bigger'd be lucky if all he got was shot, Joe Booker knew. He'd seen it all before. But he could still hope. Hope for Bigger was all he had.

At the back door of Second Home, Mason shrugged. "I don' know where the captain gone. All I know is he gone for the day. Said he'd be late." Miss Jolene and the boys had just returned from an after-church outing. She had no idea about Mr. Jake either. "Your guess," she said to Joe Booker as she removed her hat, unwinding from around it a sheer scarf that had protected her hair from the wind on their drive, "is as good as mine. And I don't care to guess." Joe Booker flinched at how coldly furious she was at returning home to find her husband gone. "In fact, you can tell my husband when you see him that I don't care if he ever bothers to come home again. I've plain had it with him. I've prayed and prayed about this. I want a divorce."

Joe Booker stood on the back porch before the slammed door. Mr. Jake certainly had problems of his own. But Joe Booker didn't see as he had any choice.

He turned away from Second Home and started reluctantly across the quad. First Home stood before him. There was no hope for Bigger now, he knew. Not none.

Boss Chief himself would give the orders now.

chapter twenty

B OSS CHIEF ORDERED Quirt Hanson to set the dogs. Then, straightaway, he sent for Calvin McGales. McGales roared up to the quad before First Home in his wreck of a pickup stirring up the dust, happy to join in the hunt. From the glassed gun cabinet in the parlor, Boss Chief chose his .375 double rifle. The gun, which bore the stamp of Harrison and Richardson, had been an extraordinarily extravagant gift from an Englishman named Sir Henry Cassells, a colonel in charge of prison camps as part of Her Majesty's forces in India, who had paid a visit to Parchman Farm before the war and returned to his post well pleased with the lessons he'd learned. The African safari gun was made to halt a charging elephant or rhinoceros dead in its tracks. Boss Chief broke down the breach and dropped in two of the five-inch shells—the diameters of the brass casings as big around as half-dollar coins—and locked them home. He carried along two more bullets just in case. The solid lead sagged his pockets.

"If you want something goddamn done right . . ."

They met up at the ball field to see Alley Leech's body for themselves and to let the hounds get a noseful of Bigger's scent. Quirt and his trusty dog handlers had to pull back hard on the leads to keep the animals from lapping up the blood that had pooled out of

Alley Leech. Flies swarmed and swirled, already busy trying to nest their eggs in his ears and up the nostrils of his nose. They landed on Alley Leech's cheeks and tickled across his opened eyes, which had been shaken so hard by Bigger's swings that they looked liquefied in the sockets.

Boss Chief covered his nose and mouth with one of his monogrammed handkerchiefs. "I reckon he's dead all right."

"Heah, boys!" Quirt called to his dogs, jammed two fingers under his tongue, and whistled sharply. The pack perked up, scrambling over each other and tangling the leads to circle about Quirt's knees, threatening to trip him. Quirt bent over and unclipped the bloodhound. The dog snuffled its big nose to the dirt, its tail wagging. He sniffed and snuffed where Bigger had jumped down off the bleachers. The hound raised his sad eyes and bayed. He panted happily up at Quirt. "Go on, boy!" The dog jumped and turned a full dopey circle before he fixed his nose on Bigger's trail. He ran off, doing a funny bunny hop with his back feet.

"That's it, boys! Cut 'em loose!" Quirt said and the other handlers unclipped their leads. The bloodhound bayed *follow me;* and the whole ragtag bunch raced off gleefully, baying and yipping and barking—none the worse for wear it seemed for having been out hunting the night before. They made a beeline for the woods.

Boss Chief shouldered the rifle on its leather strap. For the hunt, he wore what he always wore, his gray suit and black string tie. He looked up from under his hat to gauge the angle of the late-afternoon sun and noticed for the first time the brilliantly white anvil-shaped thunderheads that had begun to pile high on the horizon to the northeast. Boss Chief eyed the sky and then peeked at his gold pocket watch. It was indeed past 4:00, but they had hours of light left yet. They hadn't been blessed with a significant rain in months, and they were due for a good soaking, but the bottoms of the clouds still looked too fluffy and nice to guarantee a storm. He tucked the watch away.

"Two cold beers we bag him before dark," Boss Chief offered

McGales, knowing full well he wouldn't accept the bet. It was a wonder to him how sanctimonious about his teetotaling the new Grand Dragon of the Invisible Empire could act given the common knowledge that he owned and operated the local still. Boss Chief had no illusions about his fellow man, but he found he was not above needling the Grand Dragon at such hypocrisy.

McGales shrugged. He spat. "Everybody knows I ain't no drinker, nor no goddamned gambler neither. I'm the type gone make good on a shore fucking thing. I'll reap what I sow. But I'll tell you goddamn what, if we don't find this Bigger by dark, you want I'll scare up some of my boys to help protect the population at large. What if that big nig's out for revenge in Ruleton over what been done to Letitia Johnson? I'll bet he's headed that way! A stud buck that size could go to despoilting half the white women in the town before we shoot him down. Who knows what kind of chaos his escape gone create? Catching this run-amuck nig's got to be our number one fucking first pri-orty now. Godallmightydamn! Can you imagine the mob that's gone want a piece of this action? He gone done beat a white man to death with a fucking *baseball bat!* There ain't no escaping that, no matter how fast he can run, and I already spoke to Sheriff Dodd. He gone be looking to get up a posse. I can help."

Boss Chief weighed what McGales had said—in begging license to leave if they hadn't caught Bigger by dark, the Grand Dragon was asking him to endorse the actions of the Klan in the name of the public good. McGales was nobody's fool. No doubt he saw Alley Leech's murder and Bigger's escape as godsends to seize on in helping him drum up new members for his cause. Boss Chief understood that McGales stood to gain from the day's events, but if this Bigger did somehow manage to escape the boundaries of the Farm, he would gladly use whatever help he could get to catch him again—counting the Klan's. As superintendent of the penitentiary, Boss Chief was well aware that, ultimately, he would be held responsible for how this entire affair wound up. He could not afford to take any chances. He had a standing of his own to protect.

"If we ain't bagged him by dark," Boss Chief nodded, "you on."

The dogs had reached the woods, leaving Quirt and his handlers far behind. The pack raced into the shade under the trees. Their baying faded as they dropped down the bank.

"The river'll give 'em a little trouble," Boss Chief predicted, "but they'll pick up his track before too long. How far you figure he'll go downstream before he'll climb out?"

"I ain't a betting that big nig can even swim," McGales threw in. "But he's such a goddamn giant maybe he can just wade the fucking thing. If they don't find his body washed up bobbing nose down in a eddy behind a log on the bank maybe they'll find him with six or seven mocs nursing on him like he got teats." McGales used his finger to claw out the used chaw. He flung the wormy-looking clump to earth. He reached in his back pocket for another plug. "But I sure as hell fucking hope not. I got *bigger* plans for him," he said, all the creases in his face wrinkling the wrong way at his own pun. Boss Chief was startled to realize that it was Calvin McGales's smile.

The hunting party strolled toward the woods—they had ten trusties with them. Joe Booker came armed, too.

"Remember, boys," Boss Chief said. "Any of you catch sight of him, fire a round. Take 'im alive if you can. If you can't, take the shot. I'm partial to writing a pardon letter to the governor for the trusty what brings him down."

Though nowadays Jake usually handled this sort of thing for him, Boss Chief had been on countless manhunts in his time on Parchman Farm. There had been a time when he had actually enjoyed such pursuits, but they'd become rather routine—the outcome all too predictable—and he had known to come prepared. Boss Chief reached in his inside jacket pocket and pulled out a silver flask, a gift of appreciation from the governor to mark his thirty years of public service. Engraved on the flask was a finely wrought tableau of a foxhunt. Mounted hunters in jackets and caps, one raising a bugle, stood watching after an entire yapping pack of beagles flooding down an embankment after a bushy-tailed fox, who had obviously tiptoed across a log that stretched between both banks to lead the hounds over and then swum the creek to get back to the other bank again. The lesson on the flask was clear-cut: Once the dogs bayed by hot on the trail, the fox would assume his old track going back the other way, double-crossing the hunters. Boss Chief unscrewed the cap and took a healthy swig. Joe Booker was hanging back a bit behind the trusties, reluctant no doubt to be on the chase after Bigger without Jake.

"Now, Joe," Boss Chief addressed him, "where you figure my boy got off to so fast and early this mornin'. He was dressed in his uniform and toting a pistol as if he were actually going off to do some work. I was hoping maybe he was headin' out to finish that road single-handed that y'all fell short on Friday."

"I don' know, Boss. He never said nothin' to me 'bout it nohow if'n he did."

"No?" Boss Chief stowed the flask. "Well, it don't matter," Boss Chief grumbled. "We don't need him to take care of this. In fact, he'd probably just end up gettin' in the way of what got to be done. I shoulda followed my own mind when it came to this Bigger in the first place. But won't he be surprised when he finds out what's been going on? That'll teach him to go off without leaving word where he's gone."

They stepped under the canopy of the sycamores and cotton-woods, the mess of locust and willows, and slid down the bluff—grabbing after the whips of limbs to slow their descent. Quirt and his boys waited on this side of the yellow mud running river. The dogs were racing up and down the bank, frantically trying to find the scent they'd lost. A little beagle yelped and twisted, licking at his leg. The men spotted the snake then that none of them had noticed when they'd walked right past it before—fat and rusty red-brown and stubbed-looking and stinking as a fish rotting on the bank. The spade-headed moc yawned, wide-white, and struck the dog meanly again in the chest, and then again in the side of the head. The dog was snarling and snapping at the snake, trying to get it by the neck to shake it to death, but before he could one of the trusties stepped up with a twelve-gauge and let go a blast from the waist. The snake jumped high and plopped heavily into the bushes. Dirt rained the leaves.

"Damn. Dougy," Quirt said, laying the strop of the thin horse-whip he carried across his own thigh to rebuke himself as he worked his way back through the vine-thick poison ivy. The dog was whining, limping. It retched and retched again. The side of its head had already ballooned. The beagle threw up hard, frothing, and then sat down and then tried to stand, already drunk from the poison, half blind. He looked up at Quirt smiling a lopsided grin, panting sheepishly. Two bloody dots showed in the bloating meat of its hind leg. The other two fang marks holed its neck. Quirt looked down at the dog and then he nodded to the trusty who'd shot the snake. He turned away, not watching his man take aim with the other barrel. The blast boomed between the banks, the report of it echoing sharply back to slap them again and again as it carried away down the river between the bluffed banks. Quirt used the crop to pick up the arm-long snake. He held it for them all to see—the damn thing still undulating though its fist-sized head had been blown clean off. The pack of hounds circled back to look up at it. They whined over the size of the hole blown in the beagle. Quirt flung the stinking snake into the yellow water and they watched it flow downstream, sinking slowly from sight.

"Collar the dogs. Blue," Quirt said, singling out the nearest of the gawking trusties, "you throw some dirt on Dougy. We'd best work 'em up and down the bank ourselves until we catch the scent. I don't aim to lose another hound."

Boss Chief stood his ground while McGales went to picking up his boots and looking underneath them, as if a water moccasin or a cottonmouth or a copperhead might be stuck to the soles.

"Hell," McGales said, searching out in a wider circle now, his rifle pointing down, levered loaded to fire.

"You can go on home you like. Put your feet up. Wait till dark to do your part."

"No, sir. I ain't that fucking afraid of snakes. There's a chance you might just catch him before then. I'll go when the time comes. One way or a goddamnnother, I aim to have me a hand in this."

A howl went up from sixty yards down the bank.

The dogs scrabbled about in the yellow mud, looking back at Quirt. They strained against the slips, anxious to take the plunge and get on with the chase.

"Let 'em swim!" Quirt Hanson yelled as he stood up from the giant footprints they'd found in the mud.

Unleashed, the dogs splashed into the water, paddling hard with their heads up, noses in the air. The slow current swept them along and downstream a ways before the first of them, a bluetick, touched on the opposite bank. He climbed out and shook himself off in a spray. Immediately, he put his nose to the ground again, his stub tail working behind him. He took off, yodeling. A redbone mix and then the bloodhound splashed out and shook. One by one, the dogs gained the bank. They took off howling and baying and yapping, too. Soon they were out of sight in the brush that led back up into the sunny, wide-open fields.

"Well, boys," Quirt said. "I don't see no bridge, do you?"

Quirt waded in, his long-barreled .410 pistol held high above his head, his trusty handlers following his lead as if he had them leashed. The water pushed against Quirt's knees and then his crotch, wetting it as if he'd pissed himself, and then his waist. The pushing water darkened his chest. Before he had to start to swim, Quirt pooched his cheeks out to hold on to his air in case he dunked under doing his doggy paddle. The water swirled about him wetting his shoulder-length hair, but he never lost his bowler or got his gun wet. His men splashed and coughed and joked and cussed after him, loudly defaming God and His water moccasins, too.

"But, Mr. Quirt, I can't swim!" the gawking trusty named Blue who'd been ordered to stay behind to dig the shallow grave for the beagle called after him. He stood left on the bank with his arms hanging down forlornly, the outsized sawed-off double-barreled ten-gauge he chose to bear obviously too heavy for him. He had a nasty razor scar on his cheek.

Quirt slogged up on the opposite side, his blocky, now black brogans squelching water and mud, and called back across, "Then you better learn to walk on water quick, boy! Or get down on your knees right there in that mud and start praying to Jesus I don't put you back in the cage. You know what them gunmen gone do to a trusty man gone back in?"

Joe Booker stepped neatly out of his pants and shoes. He bundled everything up and quickly tied it to the barrel of his rifle, as if he were going hoboing.

"Just fuck it." McGales shrugged off his suspenders and dropped his pants. Underneath he sported a full-length red union suit buttoned all the way up to his skinny neck. He put a toe in to test the water, the nail horny and yellow and so long it curled clawed over the end.

"McGales," Boss Chief grinned. "You look like a plucked pullet."

Boss Chief took out the flask and tipped it back again. He saluted the men with it. "I already had me a bath this mornin', thank you. I'll get a truck and a few more boys and meet you on the other side."

The trusty named Blue who couldn't swim waded in and then stepped quickly back out again. "I'm gonna die, Boss!"

Joe Booker had made the other bank. He swiped himself dry as he could with his hands and started to dress again.

In the middle McGales dunked all the way under. Only his twisted hand sticking up with his rifle gripped in it proved that he hadn't drowned. And then his head poked up, water running in rivulets off his hat, still chewing the chaw, and then his shoulders appeared, and then his waist, and his legs, walking. "Ain't that deep," he said. He had his soaked coveralls and boots with him bundled under his other arm, but he didn't slow down to put them on. His bare feet slapped through the mud past Joe Booker and then after Quirt, who had already disappeared up the bluff through the brush.

The remaining trusty took a run at it with the hefty-looking shotgun he hugged close before him. He charged in and sloshed forward two or three steps, wading in almost up to his waist, before he pitched forward in a kind of halfhearted dive and sank straight under, as if the big gun he had hold of was actually an anvil. He spouted up, flailing wildly, eyes rolling wild. He tripped and fell backward to his neck and splashed up again, only to find himself standing in knee-deep water. He looked as shaken as if an alligator had him in his teeth from underneath, but he was doing it all to himself. The trusty surged forward again and flailed his way to the middle of the river, but this time when he dove under he didn't surface. Joe Booker gave him a slow five count before he gave up and swam back after the man, soaking his clothes, which he'd been careful making his own crossing to keep dry, and shot his hand under and grabbed his collar. He turned and ferried him across and dragged him out onto the mud. The trusty gasped like a bellied fish. He coughed hard and spurted up a little fountain, before he rolled onto his side and gave up the river he'd drunk. Through it all he'd somehow managed to keep hold of the oversized shotgun, blunted ugly and mean looking in its own way as the water moccasin that had struck the dog.

"You gone be all right, Blue," Joe Booker said. He left the trusty there and turned after McGales and Quirt and the dogs. The hounds sounded tinny in the distance.

Boss Chief, too, turned away from the trusty left breathing flat on his back on the opposite bank. He thought to remind the boy about the other kinds of snakes that might be slithering about—that'd get him up, fast! As he began to screw the top on the flask, he regarded the scenario depicted on it again. Boss Chief was alone now, left to his own devices, and he glanced around the woods about him, just wondering. He appraised the trail down which they'd just come. He took a last quick nip off the flask, shrugged the strap of the rifle off his shoulder. He started back up the bank with the .375 cradled under his arm. When he topped the bluff, he stopped and looked down on the smoothing yellow flow. He was searching for telltale bubbles. He closely inspected the reeds that poked up along the bank, watching for one to twitch. The yellow water made it impossible to see the bottom.

The cotton on the other side of the river stretched to the horizon, parceled by the network of irrigation ditches, revealed by the bright green grass that grew high on both sides, and the shallower cuts of the water furrows. Boss Chief followed the raggedy swatch of red that was McGales in his long johns bushwhacking straight across the rows to catch up to the pack. He listened carefully. By now, Boss Chief could hardly hear the dogs. A yip here, a yodel there, but the hot-on-the-trail baying of the pack had fallen off. They'd lost Bigger's scent again. It was going to be a chase.

Boss Chief started back toward the ball field. This hunt was going to be anything but the routine rounding up he'd come to expect. His old blood quickened. He reached again for the flask.

Before the bleachers, a gang of gunmen gathered about Alley Leech's body, which they'd rolled onto a tarp to heave into the back of the wagon.

"Just go on get him in the ground get it over with. No need for a marker or the preacher either one, I don't guess, not after what he did to his own son. Nobody will ever come looking to find him and far as I know Alley Leech never cared about being a Christian."

Boss Chief watched them load the body. The pussel-gutted gray mule spewed a fart and splatted a load, giving Alley Leech his send-off. The gunman climbed up on the bench seat and took up the reins. He clucked and the mule pulled, clopping off.

Thunder rumbled. The sun still shone brightly on the ball field, but over the tree-lined horizon, the white cumulus clouds that had been piling up higher and higher on top of each other had begun to darken forebodingly. They looked angry now, swollen and bruised on the bottoms, casting a shadow over the land. Some might imagine humpback whales or camel shapes in the clouds, pyramids perhaps, but the threatening bulk of them reminded Boss Chief of two locomotives hurtling full speed toward each other. The heavenly crashings of a storm now looked imminent. Boss Chief raised his chin to catch the sweet scent of the coming rain, but the stagnant air smelled of the dry, scorched grass that surrounded the playing field, baked dirt. The air about him had gone still as if the day was holding its breath to see what would happen next.

Boss Chief started for First Home. He needed to phone Sheriff Dodd and clue him in about the escape, commandeer a truck, and gather a gang of trusties before he rejoined the hunt. Behind him, the river continued to flow by undisturbed. From where he lay underneath the murk, Bigger no longer heard the muffled voices, and the dogs had run off, yowling, the trusties' frenzied splashing long gone. He took a deep breath and rose gigantically out of the river like some storied swamp monster, dripping yellow mud. He'd gone under nearly a hundred yards upstream from where he'd waded in after racing out across the field as fast as he could and jumping in an irrigation ditch to mask his track before retracing the same straight path back to wash away his scent in the river again. He pulled from his mouth the reed he'd broken off to breathe through but held it in his hand in case he had to dunk quickly under again. Bigger squinted up at the late-afternoon sun shining darkly from behind an eclipse of clouds to make sure of his directions. The river wound south-southwest.

It was as if he'd been on the road at work again alone in front of the other men and had heard the caller's chant, "I seen Rosie in my midnight dreams," and had shouted back in time with them, *"Oh, Lord, in my midnight dreams!"* The news had come to him just like that—almost as if by magic—Alley Leech's thin voice, talking, taunting him again, telling about the horrible things they were going to do to little Sally when they got hold of her that night, but hearing his Letitia's voice right there, informing him what had to be done now—as if a mockingbird had perched on his shoulder to whisper instructions in his ear while he stood in the box at bat waiting for Straight Ball to deliver the pitch he'd been waiting for: Her shack she'd left behind for Sally and where he assumed her daughter must still be living lay along a bend of this river miles downstream from here, just outside of Ruleton. The pact Bigger had sealed with Letitia Johnson as he'd waded into the stands to begin it by putting an end to Alley Leech was that they would not get Sally.

He'd give them a run for their money. He knew it was only a matter of time before half the white men in the county dropped everything and armed themselves to get busy looking for him to exact their revenge. He knew just how badly they'd want to get him, how afraid they were of his color and his size and his strength, and all they'd want to do to him to make themselves feel better about their fears, making an example of him for others who might dare to step out of line—hanging the best of it.

Standing on the bank, Bigger knew exactly what he had to do. When the hounds' handler realized Bigger had fooled them, he'd gather the pack and they'd return to the river where he'd given them the slip in an attempt to refresh his scent. Bigger turned and headed upstream toward the northern boundary line of Parchman Farm, leading the search away from Letitia's cabin, careful to leave his footprints in the mud of the bank for the trusties to track, just to be safe.

chapter twenty-one

IT HAD FALLEN to Gabe to get everything ready for that night's big Sunday meeting, now being threatened by a storm. Far to the northeast end of the county, lightning forked the mouth of the cave-dark sky. The rolling rumble of thunder that followed long-shuddering seconds later boomed as loudly as if cannons were being fired from a battlefield terribly nearby but just out of sight over the horizon. Though the sun still shone on the shack by the still, the air down by the creek had turned almost cool. The breezings that announced the coming rain felt to Gabe like a blessing.

The shack beside the still served as the temporary Klan den. "For the time being," McGales had explained to Gabe when he'd showed him around his new home the first time. "Rome wasn't built in a fucking day. Once we get the membership back up, I got plans to fund me a palace like the one the Empire built for the Imperial Wizard down in Jackson." On the walls inside, a crisp new American flag had been tacked up side by side with a larger, frayed old Confederate one. Someone had framed up a passable drawing they'd done of Robert E. Lee. The blood-drop emblem and the night rider on the steed they'd painted directly on the weather-grayed cypress planks. The shack was supposed to be his new home while he worked selling liquor for McGales, but as the temporary

Klan den it was used to closet the requirements set out in the ritual-istic Kloran that he and McGales would transport out to that night's outdoor meeting place, a field acknowledged by those in the know as "the Lost Fifty." It was not McGales's land but that of a local farmer, Maynard Fletcher, who, though he wasn't a sworn member of the Klan, was sympathetic enough to the cause to leave the center of one of his cornfields laying fallow for them. On top of the folding card table that served as their altar sat a Bible left spread open to chapter 12 of Romans, a naked sword, a Coke bottle of water, and a sterling silver cross that looked valuable enough for Gabe to believe it had been swiped from a church.

Gabe was busy trying on the robe that had been lent him, a musty castoff from McGales's neophyte days in the Klan. Moth-eaten and more of a waxy candle color than pure white, the bottom hem left off above Gabe's knees, making him look as if he were sporting a skirt. The hood would not stay up so that he could see through the eyes. The tip slouched. He was supposed to look the part of a ghoul, but he thought the getup made him look more like one of Snow White's dwarfs—Dopey, most like. He stared back at the image of himself in the cracked piece of mirror tilted on a shelf over the wash pan where he was forced to shave. He leaned forward and looked into his own bottle-green eyes watching back at him through the round cut holes. "Boo," Gabe said. He pulled off the hat. He never had liked to play pretend. That night they'd hold their spook-fest, a gathering of the dissatisfied from the other side doomed to walk the earth for a certain time before they died and went to hell for their sins. At least that's how Gabe conjured the scene. Because there was nothing else at all funny about the situa-tion, it amused him to do so. Let them get together and put on cos-tumes and make Halloween-scary speeches about the "niggrah situation" or the conspiracy plans of the pope, the undeniable su-premacy of the great white race. That was their business. But Gabe didn't want anything to do with it if he didn't have to. But, of course, just now he had to.

It was already suppertime, and he expected McGales to show up at any moment. After dark, Klansmen would begin to trickle in from all over Hushpuckashaw County. Gabe had spent his afternoon packing the mason jars he'd filled fresh from the still that morning. When McGales arrived, they'd load the crates of moonshine into the littered bed of his rusting truck, liquor being the fuel such gatherings ran on. Long about midnight, when the time came to ride out to Rivers Bend, the boys would be raring and ready to go.

Gabe pulled the robe off over his head. He folded it and hid it away in the bottom drawer of the battered dresser. He had begun to realize just what a snafu he'd made in dillydallying around with May Franks. Sitting around the shack all day every day with nothing better to do than swat away mosquitoes and count killed flies gave him too much time to think was what Gabriel Allen was thinking. He was thinking that if he had his druthers he'd rather be at home with Baby and the girls. Truth! He carefully calculated begging his wife to take him back. But the more he came to see his infidelity like he imagined his wife did, the more concerned he became about his chances. He remembered the reproach clouding his wife's beautiful face that night when he'd ridden out to 12 East Percy Street with McGales and those other boys. If she had known it was her husband she was shooting at, she might have taken more careful aim.

Gabe sat himself on the edge of the cot in McGales's mildewed shack and put his face in his hands to try to come up with a way to redeem himself in Baby's eyes. How could he make it up to her truly? He really did love her, he thought. He loved Claire and Jeana, his girls. He could admit he had some bad habits. But habits could be changed, couldn't they? The real difficulty Gabe could foresee, the dilemma he recognized and couldn't see his way around, was that even if he did amend his habits, he would still be himself. He'd been Gabriel Allen his entire life and he wasn't sure how he would become someone else now, no matter how hard he tried. He didn't want to feel how final this answer was, but the realization of it felt like the end of something to him.

As luck would have it, at that moment the duck-shaped woman pulled up in the clearing by the creek. No doubt she needed to pick up an emergency jar to see her through the storm. Gabe clomped out onto the front porch, where he posed a hand against the support to greet her—feeling exactly how much like Clark Gable he must look. The rain purpled the sky over Ruleton now, the wash of it painted in a perfect brushstroke from cloud to treetop horizon. A gust of wind teased up the woman's skirt as she climbed out into the clearing and she fought to keep it from shaping so closely about her. Gabe smiled and smoothed a hand back over his hair, glad he'd used the oil that kept it just so. He justified his further interest in slipping that brassiere of hers off with a shrug: might as well make the best of a bad situation was his thinking on the matter just then. He'd suffered enough. After all, his wife was the one who had kicked him out of the house. A man had needs—that was plain. And Gabe felt plainly in need of a little female companionship to while away the time. And the woman—what was her name again? She seemed willing enough. Oh, she wanted it all right! And Gabe was just the man to give it to her. If his wife ever did consent to take him back, then, he promised himself, he would do everything in his power to turn over a new leaf.

"How you?" he said. "Delilah." He gave her an even bigger smile, pleased with his own powers of recollection. Face-to-face, her name had instantly leaped into his mind.

"You can call me *Di*, Gabriel." She actually batted her fake eyelashes at him. "You poor, poor man. I just couldn't stand to sit home and think about you out here all by yourself subsisting on your own cooking. I brought you another potpie!"

"Well, you shouldn't have." Gabe's stomach gave a loud intestinal grumble, protesting fiercely at the very idea. He figured he'd better pull something fast to get her into the shack quick before he had to take a taste in front of her. Maybe if he left the god-awful concoction on the porch he could kill two birds with one stone—surely the offal whiff of it would call to a grubbing possum or some stinking skunk, and be the end of them, too. "That was awfully thoughtful of you, *Di*. Won't you come inside? I was just about to have a little nip myself. They say a little *aper-i-tif* is good for the digestion."

She looked shy of a sudden. He thought she might break out a fan and go to cooling her cheeks. "Oh, I'd like to, but I swan you know how folks talk about a widow. I mean, this is such a secluded spot. There's not another soul around for miles. I mean, we are all a-*lone* out here, aren't we, Gabriel?"

Gabe grinned. He pushed away from the post. "Why, Di, we most certainly are."

The brassiere was a struggle. In all his experience, Gabe had never wrestled with such a creature before. Like some tentacled octopus, it seemed to have no less than eight clinging arms. He couldn't get the sucker off. No matter how he tugged and pulled, the clasps held fast, barred to keep those humongous breasts bound. And the coming storm had brought on an early dusk, his view of the goings-on in the cabin dimming. Once she'd stepped inside, he had not even had time to light a candle.

She was huffing and puffing, blowing in his ear. Rain pelted the roof. The tattered curtains that hung down over the windows fluttered in and then sucked sharply back out again. He gritted his teeth, looking over her shoulder trying to see. The last hook gave and her bounteous breasts bounded free. Lord, they hung durn near to her knees! The pink nipples stretched big around as cup saucers! Gabe buried his face between them, pillowy soft. He sighed. He felt he'd arrived. He could've gone right off to sleep. But she wanted to kiss. She herself must've had onions for dinner. Gabe decided to go for her underwear. After all, he was on the clock, so to speak.

She moaned. "I'm not that kind of girl. What kind of a girl do you think I am?"

He had never seen such a configuration. The bra was child's play compared to the snaps and buttons that served as the body armor of undergarments underneath. By the time he got her garter unhooked and struggled her girdle off and made it to the next stage, finally tugging her diaper-sized panties down, he was about worn out. He got the next part over with as quickly as he could. He lay slumped on top of her, breathing. She looked up at him sparkly-eyed, pooched her berried lips, and gave him a quick peck.

"I'm afraid your dinner will be cold, Gabriel."

She dressed herself again, standing naked before him now without the slightest hint of embarrassment. She had the tiniest feet! In the high heels, they looked like hooves. Gabe was beginning to get an odd feeling, as if he'd been tricked by this Delilah somehow, though he wasn't quite sure how since he'd gotten what he wanted, when he heard McGales's incontinent old truck gas its way into the yard.

"You eat every bit of that potpie. Now that we're properly acquainted, you'll need your strength," she winked. She kissed Gabe on the cheek and raised an eyebrow asking permission before she lifted one of the freshly filled jars out of one of the crates. She clicked out onto the porch, ignoring the truck, and hugged the jar bumpered between her breasts as she ducked into a sudden gale of wind that swept the fields flat and bent the trees surrounding the clearing, making them look as if they'd been skinned inside out, showing the pale undersides of their leaves. Gabe grabbed for the support.

McGales slammed the door just as the first heavy drops began to dent the dust. The swiftly moving clouds now lidded over the clearing—heavily blued on the bottom, fixing to burst. Ruleton had disappeared behind the wall of water roaring toward them, the forward edge of it misting away the fields. In that twilight, McGales appeared grainy, his face told by shadows. Gabe could see that his coveralls were bespattered with mud and that his long-john sleeves, pushed past his knobby elbows, were dark, already soaked. McGales looked like he'd been through the wringer. Not only that, but he was working the cud of tobacco even more energetically than he had that day in the truck riding back from Mr. Tisdale's, railing against the president of the bank who'd ordered him to leave Sally Johnson go and cussing Boss Chief's spoiled son, Jake Lemaster, and bragging about how he'd get even with him for letting that convict go out of the box he'd put him in. Gabe felt something inside him go empty-light at the sight of McGales all fired up like that. He knew him well enough by now to be afraid of what it might mean.

Delilah blew him a kiss before she hiked her dress, showing a thick ankle, and climbed in her car. As she drove out of the clearing, she *boo-booped* her horn. She waved.

"I got everything ready to go for the meeting," Gabe said quickly to his employer before McGales could say anything to him about his entertaining on the job. Gabe practically had to shout to be heard over the wind and the sound of the rain closing in on them.

McGales looked at the potpie on the porch. He grabbed it up without asking and forked up two fingerfuls. He chewed the pie on the opposite cheek from the wad, his mouth open enough for Gabe to marvel at the skill it took to spit from the one side while swallowing from the other.

"There's been a change of plans," McGales announced.

Gabe absorbed this information. "You still want me to load the liquor?"

McGales gulped. He sucked between his teeth with his tongue, considering something. Suddenly, the sky curtained down on them. Standing underneath the overhang of the porch, Gabe looked out in awe. He'd never seen it come down so hard all at once. "Directly," McGales nodded and forked up another bite of the pie that now served more like a soup, the gray matter dripping from his fingers. "Reminds me of Mama's cooking." McGales smiled wistfully then from underneath his streaming hat as if the sun was out and there wasn't a cloud in the sky, childlike and almost merry, happy as Gabe had ever seen him.

chapter twenty-two

BABY LAY PROPPED up in the bed in her ruined nightgown with a bloodstained sheet pulled up about her waist, eyes closed, and Jake stood beside her, holding her hand. Since Sally had met him at the cabin door that morning with the news that Mrs. Allen had lost the child with which he learned she'd been pregnant, he hadn't let her get up out of bed for any reason. He'd stood by Baby all day. The only time he stepped out of the room was when Sally tended to her in private. But simply keeping her still hadn't stopped the now uncontrollable bleeding that had begun that afternoon as inexplicably and without warning as the miscarriage had the night before. Baby continued to bleed without stop, an insidious flow—worse than an obvious cut or gash because when what Jake understood now to be her hemorrhaging had begun it had not seemed dangerous enough to warrant his rushing her, without argument, straight to the hospital in Ruleton.

Baby would not hear of leaving Sally at the cabin by herself. "We can't take Sally. It isn't safe for Sally to go out on the roads now and Sally's the reason we're here. I'll be fine, I think. I think I just need to lie still a little longer like this maybe. I think it's stopping. It may have stopped."

Above them, the heavy rain continued to hammer the tin roof, sounding thunderously loud in the close cabin. Each lightning strike brightened the place as if it were actually wired for electricity, the thunder that they expected to follow immediately afterward cracking loudly enough to make them jump.

Suddenly, Jake felt like a fool. All afternoon, they'd been listening to the storm building; the cloudburst had not taken them by surprise. Jake fully realized then that he might already have waited too long to try to save Baby's life. After months of dry, the downpour would turn the accumulated inches of dust on the back roads into a morass of mud, making them impassable. He should have acted. If this entire business with Letitia Johnson had taught him only one thing, it was that. *He* was responsible—he couldn't blame Baby's stubbornness. Baby wasn't thinking straight. Sally could take care of herself. Jake called on his memory of Bigger; he couldn't stand by and watch Baby die under the guise of having done all he could by being there in the cabin with her. Jake could no longer fool himself.

"We're going," he said, reaching for his hat on the chair. "I'm taking you to Mirabel Hankins. She lives this side of Ruleton just on up the highway from here."

Baby shook her head wearily. "No. We can't leave Sally. I'm not leaving Sally," she said.

Sally pleaded with her once more. "Please, Miss Baby, please go."

"I'll be fine," Baby said. "Fine," she said again, dreamily. She sounded far away.

Baby's eyes drooped closed, and Jake felt her grip go slack. Her head lolled against the pillow.

Jake bent and draped Baby over his shoulder, gathering the sheet. Baby startled. "I'm *not* leaving Sally." She rallied to struggle weakly against him. She knocked Jake's hat off onto the bed and it fell to the floor. He turned for the door.

Outside, the storm-dark sky glowed strangely green, eerily orange, the cotton in the fields before them undulating like a great gray sea. Though the lightning flickered in the distance and the terrible crashing sound of the thunder had dimmed—the disturbance raging now to the south—the rain poured down, unabated.

Sally splashed past to open the door for them. She was clutching Baby's purse and her heels.

"I couldn't think what all else she going to need," she said, shaking her head at herself. In the thin dress, she looked as soaked as if she'd been dunked.

Jake settled Baby into the car. Her head rolled back against the seat, her lips parted. He tucked her legs into the car and fixed the slipping sheet about her waist.

"She going to be okay. Don't you worry, Mr. Jake. You'll see. I just knows it. Nice a lady as she is," Sally said, "it can't end like this."

Jake took Baby's things from Sally and put them on the floorboard before he turned back to her. "Do you think you could make it back to Children's Home on your own? It's no more than a day's walk downstream from here. If we're not back by day after tomorrow, I want you to try. Stick to the river. You won't even have to cross. Could you do that?"

"I can do anything. Don't worry about me, Mr. Jake. Go on now. Get her to that nurse. *Go.*"

Water flowed down the windshield of the state car as if Jake had driven under a waterfall. The receiver tuned to Parchman Farm squawked, blaring static from the storm. Jake couldn't make out the garbled broadcast, and he reached down and turned off the receiver. He flicked the wipers, which fought frantically to clear his view. Before the headlamp beams, the rain looked drawn down in lines.

Jake fishtailed around the yard without getting stuck and aimed the car at the road, picking up speed—the vehicle swerving back and forth so that he had to saw the wheel wildly to keep them on course—and nearly ran headlong into the flooding ditch that bordered the fields on the other side. The car stopped just in time. Jake let out his breath. He raced the tires to get them going again. The rear wheels whirred, digging in.

They hadn't even made it out of sight of the cabin. Glancing in the rearview mirror, he could see Sally standing small in the yard, watching after them.

Baby looked to have passed out. Now that he'd made the decision to go, Jake knew he didn't have a moment to waste. He shouldered the door and stumbled out into the slop, frantically searching for a board or a downed limb, anything that he could wedge under the back tires to give the tread purchase in the slick, found a rough plank from a shattered packing crate floating in the ditch and jammed it under the left back tire. He climbed back in behind the wheel and swiped the rain from his face. He revved forward and then rocked the car back, forward, tires whirring, and back, then forward again until he bumped out of the rut. He used that momentum to keep going, spinning forward. They crawled ahead slowly, as if towing a great weight.

"Baby?" he said, glancing her way. Her eyes were still closed. "Baby, are you awake?" The windows fogged with his breath and he had to steady the wheel with his stub while he circled the glass clear with his free hand.

When she answered him, her voice sounded farther away than before. "I feel so tired suddenly, Jake," she said. "I don't think I've ever felt so tired."

"The highway's just up ahead," he said. "We're almost there." He looked carefully at Baby. Jake had once witnessed a gunman who'd accidentally cut his femoral artery with a scythe blade empty himself of blood in a matter of minutes. While Baby hadn't cut a major artery, she had lost a lot of blood—and she continued to bleed. Her face ghosted white. If she went into shock, she might never wake up. "Hey," he said. "Baby," he said gently. "Why don't you try to stay awake? Let's talk. Talk to me," he said.

"What would you like to talk about, Mr. Lemaster?"

He turned to find her looking blue-eyed at him again.

Jake faced the road. He nodded. "That Friday night Letitia Johnson was lynched, I was standing on the front porch of Second Home with my foot up on the rail when McGales and Alley Leech and that gang drove past in that rattling pickup, hurrying to get to Ruleton so they wouldn't miss out on the fun. I knew exactly what was going on. The lines at the switchboard had been jammed all day with the news that Sissy's baby had been drowned and that Letitia Johnson was being blamed. And you know what I did about it? I strolled back inside and poured myself another drink. That Monday morning I met you on the road I was lying up in that cotton truck nursing another hangover. I should've gotten shut of Parchman Farm years ago." They drove in silence, the noise of the rain pounding down. "I love my boys," Jake said.

Baby rested her hand on Jake's thigh; he felt it there hot as an iron.

"That morning on the road when I drove up in my old Model T with Letitia Johnson's picture faceup on the seat between us I was feeling so sorry for myself," Baby admitted. "Maybe that's why I spoke out the way I did. What was done to Letitia Johnson was just so awful, and I was feeling overwhelmed by my own troubles— Gabe and this pregnancy we hadn't planned. I was thinking that we were all of us guilty. Every one of us."

She paused, looking ahead, without taking back her hand.

"If we can help Sally safely through this it will be a start," she said finally. "We can all hope for a new start."

Jake didn't dare to slow at the crossing. He swerved out onto U.S. Highway 49, skidding, the tires sliding for a grip on the gravel, flinging mud, stuck stones pinging up inside the wheel wells. On more solid ground—ground Jake had worked every inch of from here to Ruleton—he felt confident enough to gun the accelerator. The state car shot down the long, straight road, throwing up a trail of spray. The highway was completely awash and Jake could feel the big car streaming, the dial of the speedometer climbing close to seventy. Jake didn't know what it was like to fly, but it felt to him, right then, going seventy on that wash of highway, as if they were flying—negotiating thin air with flaps and rudders, soaring free of the road.

The car swooshed forward. Jake glanced at Baby, but she was resting her eyes. Her hand relaxed on his leg.

"Only a little longer," he said, hoping to assure her. "We're going to make it," he said out loud then, doing his best to reassure himself.

chapter twenty-three

WELL, IT WAS all too close for comfort. It made him uncomfortable as hell, and that's what Tom Dodd had stepped backstage again that evening to try to patiently explain to Mr. Tisdale, who continued to act as if he were the director of the entire production. Standing in the wings of the study, Sheriff Dodd felt as if he were awaiting his cue to go back on and fulfill his admittedly minor role in this home-staged passion play. But Tom Dodd needed to have Tisdale understand before he was called on to perform again: him running around loose out there, playing an ill-defined role . . .

"Don't worry, Sheriff." Tisdale lurched up from the red leather chair in his study to pour himself another bourbon. He wore a maroon velvet smoking jacket over his regular clothes. The ceiling fan blurred above them. The humidity was the real killer. Tom Dodd swiped at his temples. The windows of the study had backed black, mirroring the light. The diamond glitter of the crystal chandelier that hung over their heads reflected in the glass. Distant lightning cracked and the lights dimmed and then flared bright again. Rain rushed down, making a hushing sound. Dodd guessed they must have gotten five inches already. Tisdale hardly seemed to notice. He didn't seem to care what was going on out there or even to be aware that the long dry had been broken. Tom Dodd thought he must be about half-lit himself. He watched him sip his drink and then sit back. Mr. Tisdale was obviously in the mood to pronounce, but Tom Dodd wasn't in the frame of mind to listen.

"They'll catch him, of course. Of all people, you should know that, Sheriff. Why get yourself all worked up in a lather over this? They rarely get far. Rarely do these escapees threaten the general populace. By morning we'll most likely find him dangling from the limb of some venerable ole oak hisself."

"Not him. That Jake Lemaster's who I'm talking about. He's trouble. Believe me. I know."

"But why is he? I hate to be obtuse, but I'm afraid I still don't understand the danger. He doesn't know anything. You saw him when he came out here Saturday morning. He's no tailback hero anymore—'the fiery, red-haired leader of Ole Miss's 1935 Orange Bowl team.' He's a one-armed man now for real's all he is. A common cripple. A drinker from what I hear. He's grown sentimental about Sissy, whom he sparked with when she was a girl. Sentimental over the woman he no longer even knew. He didn't know her. *I* knew her." Clyde Tisdale was shaking his head. He rattled the ice in his glass.

"Trust me," Tom Dodd said.

Tisdale stood to pour himself another three fingers. He'd already offered Tom Dodd a drink, but the sheriff insisted he was on duty. He had work to do.

"Stop acting so guilty, Sheriff. You *are* the law. Between us— you, the sheriff, me, the banker, and Jenks, the physician—we form a kind of civic trinity. Tomorrow we'll put Sissy to rest and that'll put an end to this whole rather unfortunate affair. As I've argued before, we have more to fear from Calvin McGales and that fanatical bunch of sheet-wearing Boy Scouts than we do from Jake Lemaster. Jake isn't white trash. At heart, Jake's a reasonable-enough man. I imagine he'll do what his daddy tells him to—since his return to

Parchman Farm he always has. That makes Jake Lemaster one of us. He's on our side."

"I just—" Tom Dodd mashed his mouth. He'd been out to visit Jasmine early that afternoon to try to set his feelings straight. He'd lain with her, but for the first time in his life he hadn't been able to command an erection. He lay looking down at himself, the skin hooded over and wrinkled at the top, gray looking without the red-hot pump of blood, soft and blind as a mole. *Oh, baby, it happens*, Jasmine assured him, getting up out of bed to lounge languidly about the cabin, casually lighting up one of the Lucky Strikes from the carton he'd brought for her as if the travesty hadn't even occurred. *You just tired maybe. Maybe you gots a lot on your mind. You an important man.* But Tom Dodd had not felt important or tired either one; when Jasmine said that, what he had felt like was punching her. He sure felt like punching somebody someway. He'd grabbed his pants, dressed in jerks with the buckle jangling, and smacked out through her screen door still stuffing in the tail of his uniform shirt. He was afraid that he was irreparably damaged in some way. He'd broken his tool.

Ever since the night of Sissy's suicide he'd been feeling strangely about matters of the flesh. He had a hollow at the pit of his stomach. He kept picturing Jake with Sissy's panties in hand as he walked around the side of the house from the pool. Their eyes had locked. Jake Lemaster knew!

And just what if it got out that he, Tom Dodd, did not fuck cows or sheep or coloreds, but *dead* people—and not just any old dead person, either, but the recently expired Sissy Rule Tisdale! In that gorgeous lace and shimmery silk nightgown. She *trimmed* down there! Her pussy hair as neatly coifed and prettily cared for as the money-pampered rest of her. His wife's was all a tangle—she kept a genuine rat's nest. He made a point of turning off the lights when he poked her; he couldn't bring himself to look at what he was doing to himself. But he'd looked, eyes bulging, at Sissy lying there with her luxurious auburn hair spread out behind her on the lounge—the very image of a Hollywood movie starlet. The prettiest white woman he'd ever been with. Those lips saying yes to him, yearning yes, *do it*. Tom Dodd felt himself growing then, the old mole up and on the move, burrowing hard against the front of his trousers, his renegade member rising against his will. He turned away from Clyde Tisdale to stand facing the blanked black windows as if in contemplation of the rain—surrounded by the smell of books and leather, good bourbon, the rich smells he so desired. *Her* smell.

Tom Dodd couldn't help himself. He felt he'd let loose of the reins, his reason gone galloping off without him. He felt the stampede terror. The whole thing didn't seem real. Really, truth be told, it felt to him like a kind of nightmare that he'd had but couldn't recall being a part of, the film footage of an underwater scene in which Sissy turned and slipped out of her robe flickering in the lights of the pool, suspended there—lithe-limbed and white-winged as an angel—one of those avenging kind. In this vision he had of her, Sissy Rule Tisdale's eyes glowed a flaming frozen blue. But it hadn't happened like that. Obviously, it was a hallucination of what he'd done. That was it. He tried to believe that. The memory was only the stuff of his pornographic imagination. There were some things you ought not to admit even in private to yourself. He would never confess. He'd die first. He'd take it to his grave with him. But what he could let himself feel about it was how much he hated Jake Lemaster. He saw Jake looking at him that morning—and seeing Jake see him again he blamed Jake Lemaster. It was quite a trick, he knew, but if Jake didn't know, no one would know. He'd take care of Jake, by God.

Tom Dodd coughed and hitched at his trousers before turning back around to face Tisdale, who was looking curiously at him over the tops of his gold spectacles.

"Are you okay, Sheriff? You seem . . . unduly pressured."

Sheriff Dodd had dropped his hat on the chair when he'd entered Tisdale's study. Now Tom Dodd picked it up, ready to go. "We got a murderer out there on the loose in Hushpuckashaw County. Boss Chief called and I spoke to Calvin McGales before he left on the hunt. It was his sergeant that convict killed. Now it's my job to help find him. Folks are in a panic. I've got to go. I won't rest until he's caught. That's what I draw a salary for."

Tisdale had managed his feet again. He set down his glass on the sideboard and clapped. "Bravo. Quite a performance, Sheriff. I can tell you've been rehearsing for years." Tisdale used silver tongs to drop in two cubes of ice. "But you edited your lines. I know as well as you that McGales doesn't give a damn about Alley Leech. And I told him that going after that girl was a mistake—he would have made it too easy for people to feel sorry for her. That would have worked against us in the long run. This is the chance he's wished for all along. What does he want you to do? No, don't tell me. Let me guess. McGales wants you to deputize that mob of miscreants who're going to show up for his scheduled cabal to form up a posse to help you catch this Bigger. Am I right?" Tisdale swirled his ice around in his drink. He looked down at the cubes as if disappointed in himself. "I prefer to drink my whiskey neat. But this heat. This rain's hardly cooled things off a'tall." He poured a dollop. Took another sip. Nodded. "Sure you won't join me in mourning my wife?"

Tom Dodd felt the heat building under his collar. The back of his neck prickled with the flush. "You're missing the point, Mr. Tisdale. No matter what, Alley Leech was as white a man as you or me. That's what this is all about. I'm happy to be able to do my part."

Tisdale smoothed his chin. "Let's get one thing straight, Sheriff Dodd. In my opinion, poor white trash of Alley Leech's sort—or types like Calvin McGales for that matter—are worse than most Negroes. At least the Negroes acknowledge their proper place in the social order. Some poor whites, Sheriff, have delusions of grandeur." Tisdale held Tom Dodd's gaze. He sipped his drink, his lips curling up about the curve of the rim. He lowered the glass and turned back to his chair. He lounged back, crossing his right leg over his left, raised one arm behind his head, and rested back against his hand. He gestured at Tom Dodd with the glass as he spoke. "You see, Sheriff, McGales's problem is he thinks all this is only about what happens here in Hushpuckashaw County. That he can go on killing these Negroes at will. But the world is becoming smaller and smaller. The war's bringing a certain consciousness home. Do you realize that in certain arenas overseas, Negro soldiers are actually being permitted to fight side by side with whites? Lynchings as a way of enforcing our social code are passé. Worse, they're *blasé*. Such overt acts of violence aren't the way to go. Not anymore. That time has passed. You can no longer hope to control the Negro with mere force—or simple fear. Economic power is the key to his continued subjugation; the trick will be to make him believe he's actually a part of our American dream—that he's getting his due, his piece of the apple pie, all the while we're charging him an outrageous percentage on cheaply held loans he can hardly afford in the first place or using him for fodder in our mills up north. The Negro is no longer a strictly regional concern. But cretins like McGales can't see it. They are driven by baser desires. They are the original Cro-Magnon men, Sheriff. Hairy and dumb. They rely on their clubs. Of course, violence will always have its place—men like McGales have their practical uses in the scheme of things—but the days of such acts of vigilantism are numbered. For all I know tonight's could be the last lynching we'll experience in our lifetimes! We have the electric chair for the more obvious cases we need taken care of—and the claim of impartiality on our side if we can prove, for instance, that this Bigger beat another man, any other man, to death with a baseball bat. Can you *imagine?* That's horrific. Any jury—even a mixed one, if you can envision such a thing—would condemn such a brutal act. The coming battle about race will be fought over the moral high ground. It doesn't matter what we believe about racial equality. Why, Sheriff, do you realize that in a hundred years the Negro population in the Delta will have outnumbered that of the white? It's simple arithmetic, unavoidable as the bottom line. If every colored family has ten kids and a white family in the higher social echelons raises, on average, only two-point-three. And those ten Negro kids have ten Negro kids. And so on." Tisdale shrugged. "You can't hang them all, Sheriff. After us the *deluge*, huh, Dodd?"

Sheriff Dodd stared at Tisdale's drunken grin.

"I'll be here at one o'clock tomorrow to escort you to the cemetery, Mr. Tisdale."

He settled his hat and reached for the door. He hadn't really been listening to Tisdale's highfalutin lecture; he'd only paid Tisdale half a mind. At any rate, such far-flung theories concerning the future didn't hold water with him. It didn't take a professor to figure out that all that really mattered was the here and now. And just now, here tonight, Tom Dodd figured, he had enough to think about.

Sheriff Dodd took the front steps, hunkering to try not to get wet. He climbed into his still new-smelling patrol car and slammed the door. He shook off his hat, trying not to drip on the seat. A bright flash lit up the sky before him, the crack of thunder pealing close over his head.

His headlights shone the way as he crunched the private drive of the estate—sticks and limbs downed by the violence of the winds strewn in his path. Out on the public road, puddles ran deep from one gushing ditch to the other. The sheriff sprayed through them, his wipers flapping to clear the windshield. After the call from Boss Chief, he'd had his deputy, Ralph Simpson, set up the requisite roadblocks to cut off the main routes to and from the prison— standard operating procedure in such instances—and they'd broadcast word of the escape over the news. Ralph's oldest boy, Hanford, was manning the desk at the jail. Sheriff Dodd radioed in on the two-way and found out the phone had been ringing off the hook with clues of false sightings.

"Every niggrah of a size in the county's become an escapee named Bigger," Ralph's boy said. "He's been spotted from way up Hushpuckena all the way on down to Black Water Bayou and in about every hamlet and town in between."

"But no word from Boss Chief that he's been caught yet?"

"Not yet. No, sir."

At the junction with Highway 49, Tom Dodd glanced both ways before turning south, heading toward the Lost Fifty, where McGales and his boys would be waiting for him to deputize them. He didn't give a good goddamn what Tisdale had said. With the way things were going, they could use McGales's boys—that's what the Klan was for! People thought the Klan was a hate group, but that simply wasn't true at all. The Invisible Empire had always served with the public's welfare first and foremost in mind. The beauty part of deputizing them all to help string that murderer up, he thought, was that it was legal as hell.

A car raced toward him from the opposite direction and slapped past, smacking his front windshield with a wave of water—just begging for a speeding ticket. Tom Dodd locked the brakes, recognizing the green state car from Parchman Farm in his rearview mirror.

"Well, I'll be damned."

He hit the lights and reversed direction in the middle of the highway. He floored the patrol car—hearing his siren's wail—Jake Lemaster fixed in his sights.

chapter twenty-four

THE COTTON TRUCK Boss Chief had commandeered upon his return to Front Camp lay listing to its right side, beached on its chassis, mired to its axles in mud. Unfortunately, he couldn't cuss anyone else for plunging the truck into the ditch; he'd been the one driving.

He took account of the egg on his forehead—a crack spanned the windshield glass where he'd smacked it when they'd crashed— before he kicked the door open and climbed out on the running board to survey the mess they were in now. The collision of trains he'd pictured in the clouds that afternoon had foretold this wreck in the rain. The bottom had fallen out of the sky just as they'd pulled out of Front Camp to join the hunt, and it had taken nearly an hour of getting stuck and unstuck, slipping and sliding through the worsening muck, having the trusties pile out to push every hundred yards or so, to travel less than one mile before he'd gone and stranded the truck for good. And the heavens didn't look as if they were through with them yet, the rain still bucketing down as hard as it had been when the clouds had first burst. It hadn't let up one bit. Worse, Boss Chief guessed, he'd lost his bet. They hadn't caught Bigger, and with the deluge had come an early dark. At the first gloaming, McGales would have left to go gather his Klansmen. Boss Chief tried to ignore the dull ache that throbbed his head and cocked his ear to listen for the dogs, but all he could hear was the rain pounding the earth and the roar of the river before them that they still had yet to make it across. Watch the goddamn bridge wash out with the luck they were having today, he thought. The slow, shoving flow had risen to within a foot of the raised planks. If the bridge did wash out, they'd be forced to slog all the way down to Highway 49 to cross. They'd lose even more time. Dusk had descended upon them; it would be night soon, true dark. This little escapade was turning out to be a regular disaster—this Bigger giving them more trouble than Boss Chief had bargained for. He should never have listened to his son. Loosing Bigger from that box had pried open the lid on a whole host of ills. He touched the egg gingerly again. This Bigger was becoming a real pain in the neck.

"You wait 'til I get a hold of you when you get home, Jake."

Disgusted, Boss Chief turned to glare at the trusty shooters who'd scuttled to the high end of the tipped truck's bed in the aftermath of the crash to keep out of the gushing ditch that frothed about the wheel wells. They crowded crouched together under a single tarp they held umbrellaed over their heads. Immediately, the trusties inspected their shoes or the sky and checked again on their rifles and shotguns, keeping as busy as they could so that they would not have to lock eyes with him. It began to hail. The minié-ball-sized bullets of ice shot off the windshield as if they were being fired back at the sky. The cotton in the fields before them wilted, cut down in the fusillade that stopped as suddenly as it had begun.

"Sergeant Shepherd!" Boss Chief yelled for McGales's night man from Camp 5. "Take some help and hustle on over to Camp Fourteen and saddle up some horses. We ain't goin' nowhere in this here truck tonight. It'll take a team of eight mules to haul it out once this road hardens up."

Boss Chief watched Shepherd slog off with three trusties in tow. Camp 14 was the closest camp, but it would be slow going on foot, sinking knee-deep with every step. He ducked back inside the cab of the cotton truck to wait. He'd get wetter soon enough. Boss Chief settled himself, mopping his face, relaxing at the angle of the tipped truck as if he were lain out on a chaise longue, and reached again for the silver flask that he'd been sure to top off when he'd gone back to the house to phone Sheriff Dodd, though he had not thought to pull on his boots. What had he been thinking?

"Don' tell me I'm slipping?" He bobbed the flask and wiped his lips with the back of his hand.

A trusty with water running in rivulets off the spout of his soggy hat leaned down to the window. "You say somepin, Boss?"

Boss Chief didn't even hear him.

He was thinking that Bigger must have been hiding on the bottom of the river breathing through the tube of one of those reeds. He'd doubled back on them is what he'd done—that's why the dogs had lost his scent so quickly. Otherwise they would've bagged Bigger by now, rain or no rain, big as he was. He shook his head at himself again, thinking of his conversation with Jake. Eyeing those reeds, he should have known to trust his instincts—he should always do what his gut told him to do. If he had, he'd be at home in his robe with his feet kicked up, congratulating himself on another job well done. And he had other business to attend to. Betsy Reed would stay late again if he asked her to.

With nothing better to do while he waited, Boss Chief broke down the breach on the double rifle .375. Boss Chief fully appreciated the firearm. He alone understood how fine an instrument the Harrison and Richardson was. The gun was intended for work at close range, but he could gauge the drop of the heavy bullet from a hundred yards to knock out the bull's-eye using the gun's open sights, which he actually preferred as a way to show off his good eye. Boss Chief, as everyone on Parchman Farm knew, was a crack shot. As a young buck desperately in search of his way in the world, he'd competed in county shooting matches to work up the stake of cash that had given him his start.

That was the thing Jake would never understand about him,

Boss Chief thought, tipping the flask again. How he'd gotten his start, become the man he was. How could he? Though they were father and son and shared blood ran through their veins, they were as different as night and day. The difference, as Boss Chief saw it, was in how they'd been raised.

Boss Chief had laddered his way to success, clawed his way up out of the seemingly bottomless pit that had been his childhood. Both of his parents had been killed by the yellow fever that had swept the Delta when he was a boy. For a time he'd lived with an aged aunt. At the age of seven he'd left to work on a crew that gypsied around picking cotton—an orphan responsible for himself. So what? He had never yearned for pity. The need for pity did not drive him—fear did, Boss Chief was well aware. His wish had been that Jake could feel just a smidgen of the abject terror he himself had felt as a child: his loss of innocence the deep understanding that there was no guarantee you would survive this thing they called making a living—*life*. While Boss Chief had known from the day of Jake's birth—his wife Catherine's death—that he couldn't actually take his son back and inflict upon him the childhood he himself had suffered through, he'd done everything he could to make things hard enough on the boy to scar him, leave an indelible mark. Yes, maybe he had lurched the clutch of the tractor on purpose that day to shake his boy up—Jake had been daydreaming again and he'd warned him twice already to pay attention—even if he hadn't intentionally meant to cast him under the churning blades of the disk. He had meant to teach him a lesson. *Happy families were all alike*—all the same. Doughy and undriven, the members of such unions never amounted to much more than smiling, content drones, simply happy. Tragedy alone motivated greatness. Oh, Jake had suffered calamities of a sort—his mother dying before he ever got to meet her for one, the loss of his right arm for another—but it seemed to Boss Chief that they were the sort of misfortunes that, in the end, had merely had the effect of turning Jake back in on him-

self. He'd overcome the loss of his right arm, for instance, by becoming a championship tailback. People had cheered his personal
victory; they'd loved him for it. Red Lemaster had become the stuff
of local legend, a hero—an *all-American!* But once he'd lost the big
game at the Orange Bowl that had been the end of that. What next?
Unlike his father, Jake did not have an ax to grind. He did not exist
to wreak his revenge on a society that seemed ganged up against
him. He did not *need* to win in larger and more significant ways than
playing the young man's game of football, earning the sort of victory
that would set him apart, raise him to the status of Boss Chief.
Boss Chief had wrested such a victory from life. He alone was comfortable admitting that in the beginning his fate had been more akin
to that of the niggrahs with whom he'd grown up picking side by
side. They used to lynch gypsies, too! He might have met just such
a fate! But he'd long ago left that particular fear far behind, buried it
deep inside. *Devil take the hindmost* was the McGales-like *An eye for
an eye and a tooth for a tooth* maxim that he recognized he'd lived his
life by. He, Boss Chief, trusted in his superiority absolutely—*he*
was the *truth* he believed in most. His drive and intelligence and
ambition and all that he'd accomplished in his life separated him and
set him distinctly apart. His crudities, his crassness, a cultivated
earthiness of manner were simply his bridge back to his beginnings;
his manner of companionship, his way of communicating a kinship
with poor whites while accentuating the fact of his disassociation,
his ultimate claim of dominance. The way Boss Chief understood
his power was that he had the common touch. Not that he had ever
thought of himself as a common man—far from it. Again: He was
no egalitarian. Boss Chief did not consider himself to be one of *them*.
But he did hold close to the notion of himself as American by birth
and Southern by the grace of God: He had come up the hard way,
like a lot of folks in his home state, and he understood and appreciated their communal concerns. He knew the McGaleses in his world,
recognized the Alley Leeches in the crumbling gumbo buckshot he

himself had been dug up and molded from—baked hard. He could actually relate, while his boy, Jake, merely found himself acquainted with such men.

If Boss Chief had any regrets in this life that ached him as deeply as the loss of Jake's mother, it was this confusion he felt whenever he got to dwelling on the notion of their son. The fact that Jake was his only heir was a problem that Boss Chief still couldn't quite work his mind around. For the longest time now, and especially in the last few months hearing the reports that his son lay up in the cotton truck half-drunk whenever he did show up for work, he'd felt what Jake needed, at the age of thirty-three, was a good whipping. He would've liked to have yanked his black leather belt out of his pant loops and bent the boy over his knee—whop the hell out of him. Wake his ass up! Boss Chief found the problem of what to do about his son paradoxical. He loved him. He believed that he did. But he had never believed in pure softness. He'd learned that it was a mistake to think with his heart. Love had to be earned and forgiveness in this life was not an option. Your enemies were your enemies. It would not do to offer them the other cheek or turn your back either. Boss Chief had never been very religious, but he attended church. He listened to what the preachers told him about what Jesus did. But to his way of thinking you couldn't count on what Jesus said; Jesus had not wanted anything in this world! All He'd had to do was fix it so that He got Himself nailed up on the cross to make His point. His Father did not seem to care so long as He did that. And He wouldn't help Him down! The Boy had asked! Forsaken? He was simply doing all along exactly what it was His Father had meant for Him to do! Jake had not earned his father's love in any such manner. Jake had not sacrificed himself up for him! As a father himself, Boss Chief had done the best he could for his son. He'd done everything he could think to do. If Jake had been any other man in his employ, Boss Chief would have sent him packing years ago.

How could Boss Chief leave the empire he'd built to him? He

tried to imagine Parchman Farm with Jake in charge—Jake believed in the new parole procedures and even the idea of rehabilitation! Oh, he and that welfare woman would make a pair all right—they were goddamn made for each other! There was a movement to train prisoners for life outside of the penitentiary, give them a skill they could rely on when they were set free. But Parchman could not operate like that! Such a practice would ruin the prison; send it spiraling into the red. Parchman Farm depended on the free labor to operate in the black. All a gunman needed to be trained to do was to work a hoe. It was antebellum for a fact; and it worked for sure. Anyway, Boss Chief was not about to coddle guilty men. What could possibly be the point of that? They owed a *debt* to society. They'd been sent to Parchman Farm to pay. And pay they would! Boss Chief was there to collect.

He'd toast to that!

Boss Chief raised the flask just as Shepherd galloped up and slowed, rounding about with the horses, a big stallion roan for Boss Chief tethered on a line.

"'Bout time," Boss Chief said, taking a last quick nip before he screwed on the cap. He checked the bump on his forehead in the rearview—it was already yellowing a bruise. It hurt to squash his hat down over it. He allowed Shepherd to maneuver the roan broadside to the truck before he opened the door. He stood on the running board and waited for Shepherd to swipe off the saddle before he creaked his formidable weight into the stirrup. Another trusty handed Boss Chief up the Harrison and Richardson and he slid the rifle into its scabbard. He didn't have to worry about jostling the sights—they'd been grinded to fit. He took seven men on seven horses and left the remaining trusties to walk back.

"All right." Boss Chief wheeled the stallion and set off, leading them at a gallop. They rode hard as a cavalry down the black road, kicking up mud, making their own thunder now in the rain, the pounding of their horses' hooves on the boards as they crossed the bridge that looked more like a raft floating on top of the dark swirling Hushpuckashaw. Safely on the other side of the river, Boss Chief divided them into groups of two and three.

"I already told Quirt's bunch: I'm partial to writing a pardon letter to the governor for the trusty that brings this Bigger down."

Boss Chief reined in and turned. He sat and watched the trusties he'd directed splash off out of sight.

"What now, Boss?" Shepherd asked.

"I got a feelin'." Boss Chief nudged the roan down off the road into the shallows of floodwater that had risen over the stretch of plain, smothering to the tops of the knee-high cotton growing low in the swags. He led the way on the sunken turn row with Shepherd plodding behind, trusting the high-stepping horse's sense of solid ground underneath his hooves, following the flow downstream.

They rode for a long while through the watery void, leaving the boundary of the farm far behind. They rode for some time, lightning cracking and flashing before them, showing the way. In that flickering light, Boss Chief recognized the gray-weathered cabin in the flooding fields. He spotted the pinprick of candlelight and homed in on it. Letitia Johnson had been Bigger's woman; Bigger had been Letitia Johnson's man.

Boss Chief reined in his mount, reached down, and unbuckled the rifle. He slid the .375 out of the scabbard.

"What is it, Boss?" Shepherd asked, catching up.

"The girl," Boss Chief said and spurred forward.

He rode up to the cabin. The windows shone faintly orange and wide-eyed as a jack-o'-lantern pumpkin, lit by the candlelight from inside. Boss Chief dismounted and dropped the reins, left the roan waiting, stamping still. Around back, Boss Chief came across the well-traveled Model T, which he recognized as the car that welfare woman drove. He might've known she'd have a hand in this. He crept past the well and stepped up to the back window. He was tall enough to peek in over the sill. Through the slit between the curtains, he saw the candle dancing shadows about the wick. Shepherd splashed up to the well and Boss Chief turned and raised his hand for him to stop. He pressed his back against the wall and worked his way around the side of the cabin. He creaked up onto the front porch pointing the rifle before him. Boss Chief clicked the latch and nudged the door. He waited and then he pressed the barrel forward. There was only the one room. Two beds. A maid's uniform hung from a nail on the wall. He crouched and checked underneath both beds. There was no place else to hide for a man the size of Bigger, much less the little girl. He stood, looking for possible clues. The sheets had been stripped off the mattresses. He looked more closely. A stain darkened the ticking. It came away on his fingertips—still wet—bright red in the cast of the candle's light. *Bleeding like a stuck pig* was his first thought. And then he saw Jake's hat—unmistakably Jake's, trampled underneath his own feet at the foot of the bed, with the blood on it, too. Boss Chief felt as if he'd been sucker punched in the heart. What in the hell was going on? Where was that welfare woman, whose car was parked out back by the well? And Sally Johnson, where was she? His hunch had told him she'd be hiding here and that Bigger would come to save her. Alley Leech had to have been taunting him about what McGales and his boys were going to do to her that night. It all made sense; it added up. But what about Jake? Was he having an affair with that welfare woman—is that why he'd come here without telling anyone? Were they using this as an assignation place? Had Jake stumbled onto the escape? Had Bigger murdered his boy? But there was no sign of a fight. The struggle that had occurred looked to have taken place on the bed.

He spun, raising the .375 waist high to fire, but it was only Shepherd, who'd scraped up on the porch, dragging his leg along behind him.

"Don't shoot, Boss!" he said, cowering with his hands thrown up in front of his face.

Boss Chief left the candle guttering on the table behind him and grabbed Jake's bloodied hat. He shoved past McGales's sergeant, taking it with him. Around the back of the cabin, he slid his rifle into the scabbard, put his foot in the stirrup, and hauled his bulk into the saddle. He turned the big roan and switched its flank sharply with the reins, launching himself at full gallop into the pouring dark.

chapter twenty-five

IN HIS RACE to save Baby's life, Jake hardly gave a thought to the car hurtling toward them in the opposite lane until they'd rocketed past each other, going in opposite directions, speeding through the wash of each other's wakes. But less than a half-mile down the road, Jake was forced to take into consideration the red flashing lights in his rearview mirror. He recognized Sheriff Dodd's new black-and-white cruiser. The sheriff was riding hard on their tail with the siren wailing for them to pull over. He seemed ready to bump them from behind if Jake didn't comply. Jake braked as quickly as he dared on the rivering road. He didn't want to take the time to stop, but he figured that as soon he explained about Mrs. Allen, Sheriff Dodd would pull out in front of them with his siren wailing, leading the way to Mirabel Hankins's.

Sheriff Dodd pulled in close behind them, but he took his own sweet time climbing out of the cab into the rain. Jake had no time to wait. Baby lay slumped sideways in the seat beside him. Despite his holding up his end of the conversation to help keep her awake, she seemed to have gone off to sleep again. He left the car running, the wipers flapping frantically back and forth.

"Sheriff!" he began, but the sheriff didn't even look up. Sheriff Dodd stood behind the silver star on the door of his patrol car, settling his hat. He looked both ways up and down the highway as if he were about to cross the street, but when he stepped out from behind the door Jake saw that he had his pistol leveled at him. He grimaced at Jake. "Get in the car," he said.

Jake stared at the pistol. He motioned at the state car. "I've got Mrs. Allen from the Welfare Office with me. She's lost a child. She's bleeding to death. You've got to help us."

"I'll shoot you where you goddamn stand," Sheriff Dodd said. He cocked the hammer back on the pistol, a hogleg Colt .45. The storm had swept the roads clear of vehicles. They stood alone on that long, dark, straight stretch of highway, and there was something in the sheriff's eyes that Jake hadn't noticed before. Instinctively, Jake raised his left hand. Sheriff Dodd stepped into the road to go wide around him. He held the pistol on Jake as he bent down to look in the car at Baby. In the soft nightglow of the dash lights, with her long blond hair framing her face, she seemed a sleeping beauty, but she was pale as death. She looked dead.

"She could die without your help, Sheriff."

Jake's voice brought Sheriff Dodd's slated eyes back from wherever they'd been. In the headlamps' glare, his face appeared shadowed grim, deep-socketed, the skin stretched tight, shrunken about his skull. He gestured Jake's left hand higher, and then waved for him to raise his stiff-arming stub, too, before he reached down and slipped Jake's own Smith .38 out of its holster. He waved Jake around in front of him, training both pistols on him. "Get in the car. Now."

Jake didn't move. And then, blinded by the brights of the cruiser, he stepped carefully around the back of the state car, knowing something had gone very wrong.

"You should've left her goddamn panties where they lay," he heard the sheriff say. It sounded as he was speaking through clenched teeth. He was breathing hard as if he'd run a hill. Jake heard the click of the hammer being cocked—his own pistol being used against him—the barrel aimed at the back of his head. He heard the shot go off. He jerked and dropped. And then another. The third banged close enough that he felt the powder sear his ear. And then Sheriff Dodd bumped against him where he crouched against the hood of the patrol car and Jake spun and the sheriff rolled off and fell on his back. He'd been shot point-blank, as he'd meant to shoot Jake. Baby stood hunched against the trunk of the state car. Clenched in her fist was a silver .22 pistol. Looking down at the sheriff lying there with his eyes wide open staring up into the rain, she swooned and dropped onto the gravel shoulder beside her spilled purse, the flag of the bloody sheet unfurled behind her, naked from the waist down.

Jake checked the sheriff's pulse before wrenching his own hot pistol out of his grip. He quickly stepped over the body to wrap Baby back up in the sheet and load her into the car.

As he ran around to the driver's side, he stooped and gathered up her purse and grabbed the pearl-handled .22, which had skittered to the pavement when Baby collapsed. It rubbed against the remembrance of his mother that he'd forgotten was in his pocket. His ears were ringing like an alarm at the shot with Jake's own pistol the sheriff had touched off close to his ear. He saw again Sheriff Dodd's black eyes blazing down on him from behind the living room curtains of the Tisdale estate the morning he'd stopped by and discovered Sissy's underwear in the bushes at the foot of the lounge. A shudder shook Jake as if a rabbit had run over his grave. He still didn't know what had happened to Sissy that night—maybe he'd never know for sure—but whatever had happened, Sheriff Dodd had paid for it with his own life.

And Baby had saved Jake's.

Now Jake sprayed gravel as he sped back onto the highway, racing again to try to save hers.

chapter twenty-six

THEY ROUNDED THE bend and there he was. Ever after, Joe Booker would think how strange that moment still seemed to him. Bigger had had the jump of an unheard-of head start and the rain to cover his trail, but *there he was!* just around the bend, standing to face them on a knoll high on the bank above the flood—huge. A colossus. His great muscles bunched and gleaming in all that wet, his silver tooth shining. Was he smiling? Was that a grin? Had Bigger been patiently waiting on them to catch up? The county line had been right there! But maybe he simply hadn't known how close he was to escaping from Parchman Farm.

The downpour the thunderstorm had brought had dwindled into a drizzle, but the river beside them continued to rush by, choked and swollen, the runoff straining between the trunks of the trees. Such a swift swooshing flow of water could easily sweep away a dog, and Quirt Hanson had clipped the hounds back to their leads to splash behind them through the shallows, trusting his own instincts since the dogs had lost the scent.

When Quirt saw Bigger standing there on the muddy rise—the Samson-like storybook strength the man displayed made Joe Booker want to go rubbing his eyes like a child—the first thing he did was loose the dogs to bring him down to size.

"Sic!"

In the kerosene-reeking sizzling bright smolder of the torches the trusties carried—the far-flung flashes of lightning backlighting the scene—the dogs swarmed over the giant man. It was something to see. The dogs tore in snarling and leaped at Bigger's throat and Bigger, unfazed and unarmed—he had not even snatched up the weapon of an ass-jaw-like club to defend himself—grabbed them with his bare hands and swung and flung them howling like lost souls into the outer dark. He stood his ground as if he'd been treed, but he had not been treed is what Joe Booker would always remember about the man Bigger, whose called name had been Alfonse. He did not try to make a break for the county line or take a last-ditch dive into the flooded river and swim for it, sweeping by as even a cornered panther, sensing its end, might well have done. He did not look hurt. Bigger did not appear to have stopped because he'd been wounded or run out of steam. He'd simply stopped and turned to face them. He *had* been waiting! It had been Bigger's decision. Bigger's choice. Joe Booker and the other men stood in awe of him.

It was the trusty named Blue who'd nearly drowned when fording the river—the very man Joe Booker had swum in for and raised up himself—who took the shot with that mean-looking, double-barreled, sawed-off ten-gauge he'd been lugging all afternoon. While the dogs occupied Bigger from the front, he snuck around in the dark on his flank, climbing close as he dared, and shot Bigger from behind with both barrels square in the middle of his broad back, blowing out his enormous heart. The big man's body stood even after such a terrific blow, hollowed but remaining invincible somehow, terrific even in death, the dogs whining, licking their wounds, defeated and whimpering about his feet—the river roaring silence in the echoed aftershock—and then Bigger toppled, fell forward in a whooshing hush that Joe Booker would describe each time he recounted the tale had sounded like the toppling of a massive hundred-ring, ages-old oak, the trusties stepping quickly back so that they didn't get crushed or trapped by his fall.

And then, though he'd *sho 'nuff* given them a run, the hunt was over, as quickly and as violently as it had begun.

Still, no one moved.

Joe Booker was the first to step close. He knelt in the mud. He had to use both hands and lift with his back to roll Bigger's body faceup.

"How 'bout that shot?" the trusty named Blue who'd bagged him from behind bragged, big-toothed, grinning. "I gone be paroled into the world, a free man! Boss Chief said he'd write the letter for the trusty what took the shot and brung him down! I knewed ole Bessie here gone come in handy!"

Joe Booker stood and whirled on him, only a hair slower than he used to be with his fists, delivering a roundhouse knockout punch that lifted the coward into the air and left him flat on his back on the mud, out so cold that his feet didn't even jerk. Joe Booker glared around to see if he had any other takers—not one of the others who'd witnessed what the now snaggletoothed trusty had done dared a word—but there was nothing at all Joe Booker could do to stop what happened to Bigger next when the trusties Boss Chief had sent out to search, alerted by the signal-loud doom of both barrels, galloped up on horses.

Quirt Hanson was the only white man present. "Little help," he said, not looking around at them.

Quirt hog-tied Bigger and cinched the coiled rope around his thigh-sized neck and waited for the trusties to pull up the slack. They'd yoked two horses together to drag him back through the mud and slime to Front Camp. Whatever else they did to Bigger now that he was dead, Joe Booker knew that in the morning they'd find what was left of him dangling from some tree, hung proper for everyone to see—just as they had Letitia Johnson. They'd leave Bigger there for days, until the jays and the blackbirds had plucked out his eyes and the body began to stink for miles, possums sagging the limbs above him trying to reach the feast. It was always the same.

They'd called off the dogs, collared back to their leads. One rider had already been dispatched to find Boss Chief and give him the news that Bigger was dead. Another left to spread the word county-wide, letting Sheriff Dodd and Captain McGales know, too, calling off the search. They'd know where to find the body. They'd take possession of it at Front Camp. They'd get their chance at Bigger now.

Joe Booker turned to start his own long walk back, slogging home through the mud. He marveled over that last home run Bigger had hit over the right-field fence. That ball had *soared!* It didn't *never* want to come down! He wished Mr. Jake had been there when they caught up to him to see Bigger stand up to them like that—it might have helped in some way after all he'd done to try to save him—but Joe Booker had worked hunting down escapees on Parchman Farm for twenty years. He was an old hand. It might've helped someway, but what he knew about having Mr. Jake there was that it wouldn't have changed Bigger's end one bit.

chapter twenty-seven

"'T̲HE FUCKING FUN ain't fucking through yet!" McGales said and slapped Gabe on the back. "I tempted you fellas out in this storm with the promise of a hanging and I aim to goddamn de-liver!" McGales worked his chaw and spat a black, snaking stream. When he smiled, the strings of tobacco hung like baited worms off the points of his yellowed incisors.

If McGales had looked merry earlier that afternoon tasting that god-awful potpie of Delilah's, now he seemed downright gleeful. Maynard Fletcher, who owned the Lost Fifty, had slipped and slogged the corn-maze path to bring them the news about Bigger passed to him by a trusty on horseback. Shotgunned to death was the news the armed men had cheered.

"Start a few more jars around, Gabe!" McGales called out, mak-ing sure the host of newly sworn in and potential Klansmen who'd been milling restlessly about the Lost Fifty in their robes waiting for Sheriff Dodd for the past hour heard him loud and clear. "It's on me! Get you a free fucking snort, then we'll go!" McGales turned away from the gathering and raised his eyebrows significantly at him.

Gabe understood. McGales acted as if he were tickled to death at this development, but with Bigger already dead, the big night the Grand Dragon had been betting on was shaping up to be something of a bust: All that was left for them to do now was to drive up to Parchman Farm and help string up the corpse.

Following orders, Gabe opened the next case of jars and began unpacking them from the straw. By now most of the boys were already three sheets to the wind. Many were drinking two-fisted. They looked like normal-enough folks, Gabe was thinking as he passed the jars into their reaching hands—without the full disguise of their masks to show how they really were. His own too-small robe bound about his arms and shoulders, making him feel roped into things. Hades itself couldn't get any hotter, Gabe felt, sweating as he worked to keep up with the demand for McGales's liquor. In the aftermath of the storm, the ground seemed to seethe about their feet, steaming mad.

The majority of the men grinned and laughed at the news Maynard Fletcher had brought them as they gathered about Gabe, actually as happy as McGales was pretending to be at Bigger's premature demise, but a few showed their disappointment openly, stomping around in the mud, down in their cups, lamenting the fact that they hadn't played a part in the actual kill.

"I knew we shouldn't wasted no time waiting for the sheriff. What's McGales thinking? Any case, who gone convict a white man of shooting a runaway in Hushpuckashaw County? What's he mean by 'legal' anyway?"

"All right, boys!" McGales yelled, stepping up onto an empty crate to get their attention. His new catalog-bought green robe shimmered in the flickering torchlight. The men quieted and turned to look up at him. When he had everyone's attention, the Grand Dragon reached up with both hands and affixed his mask.

"Follow me," he said, staring down round-eyed at them, his voice muffled behind the cloth.

"Hot damn!" some of the boys called, grabbing their masks, too, and others, "About time!"

McGales hopped down off the crate. "Load that last case in the truck," he said to Gabe. "And don't forget the fucking cash box. You ride with me."

They pulled out onto Highway 49 in a convoy nearly thirty cars long with McGales and Gabe in the rattletrap pickup leading the way. They were just shy of the Ruleton city limits when McGales slowed the truck.

"Now what the fuck?"

The first thing Gabe saw as they pulled close was the flashing lights of Ruleton's two police cruisers parked off to the side of the road—the new one Sheriff Dodd's, the humble other the battered black-and-white that he'd hand-me-downed to his deputy, Ralph Simpson. McGales pulled up beside the cruisers and parked. As Grand Dragon in command of a well-armed company of Klansmen, he assumed he had every right. The spotlight was on Sheriff Dodd, who was on his back with his arms and legs flung out to the sides, his head nearly in the running ditch. At first glance, it appeared to Gabe as if he'd stepped up to try to stop the storm that had blown past and gotten himself knocked flat.

McGales creaked open the rusting door of the pickup and slammed it sharply behind him. Deputy Simpson actually had tears in his eyes. He stood snuffling into his fist. Even Gabe knew that nobody expected much from Ralph. He'd merely been Sheriff Dodd's lackey, a once full-time unemployed drinker, and a cheap part-time hire.

"Jesus to God almighty in heaven, Ralph!" McGales said. "What the hell gone happened here?"

"I wish I could tell you, Mr. McGales. I was a-cruisin' up and down this line of highway keeping an eye out for that escapee like Sheriff Dodd told me to," Ralph sniffed. "I stopped when I seed the sheriff's lights, and I found him here like this my own self. Kilt. And now what I'm gonna do? Poor Sheriff Dodd! I'll have to tell his Doris. They ain't no one else to do it. A man never felt no heavier burden! You know they never even had no kids. And now she'll be left to fend for herself. All on her own! Oh, oh," he said.

"Well, hell, Ralph." McGales snatched off his mask and spat at Ralph Simpson's boohooing. "Get aholt of your fucking self. Christ. Didn't you see nothing else?"

"Only Jake Lemaster in that state car going the other way."

"Jake Lemaster?" McGales stopped chewing. The stilled chaw bulbed his cheek, big as a baseball. "Is that right? You sure?"

"Yes, sir. It was him in that green state car all right, no doubt about that. I figured it had somethin' to do with the convict he was going so fast. And I hadn't come across the sheriff yet so I didn't think nothin' about stopping him to ask if he'd seed anythin' suspicious his own self."

McGales cut his eyes at Gabe. Then he pushed past Ralph. "I best take a closer look. See exactly what we got us here."

He squatted beside the body. McGales counted, hanging his head as he held Sheriff Dodd's wrist, and then he gave a sigh as if he were oh so tired and sad. "Sheriff Dodd's done gone to a better place all right. Ralph ain't fucking lying about that."

Gabe stood behind McGales, looking over his shoulder. There wasn't a mark on the sheriff that he could see. Maybe he'd been struck by lightning is what Gabe Allen was thinking until McGales turned Dodd's head by the chin and Gabe saw for himself the two tiny holes just behind his left ear. McGales covered the holes with his first two fingers. "Twenty-two," he said, naming the caliber. There was something about the fact of the .22 that troubled Gabe, but even though the bruise on the cheek of his right buttock was still tender to the touch, he couldn't quite place the reason for his discomfort.

McGales held up Dodd's own unfired .45.

"What we got us here," he pronounced loudly to the Klansmen who'd piled out of their vehicles to huddle around him, "is a cold-blooded murder. They can't be no fucking doubt about that."

Dodd was dead all right. Dead as a doornail, Gabe was thinking. What he'd first taken as a shadow underneath the sheriff, he realized then, was really a pooling of blood. Gabe felt his stomach go creamy, churning squeamish on him. He turned away from the scene and pushed his way back through the ghouls who were craning forward to see. Gabe grabbed off his mask and retched in the ditch on the other side of the road.

McGales stood and put his hands on his hips.

"Now why wouldn't Jake Lemaster stop, I ask you that? He had to've seen the sheriff's lights. Am I right? How could he miss Dodd a-laying here in the road like this? It weren't raining that hard!" McGales looked up at the Klansmen gathered about him. "But Jake Lemaster didn't stop. Far be it from me to accuse Boss Chief's son of murder, but we do have an eyewitness—the goddamn deputy sheriff no less—who saw his boy speeding away from the scene." McGales rolled the chaw around, letting that sink in. "Why ever he didn't stop . . . I'd like to ask Jake Lemaster some questions, wouldn't y'all? I believe Jake Lemaster owes us some answers. I don't care whose only son he is. You boys go on ahead and load Sheriff Dodd's body in the back of my truck. We'll go on up to Parchman Farm and present the evidence to the Boss Chief hisself. I for one can't imagine a greater breach of fucking justice. You just can't go murdering the goddamn sheriff now! He represents law and order. It's law and order that's been killed here tonight! This breaks all the fucking rules! We'll find the person responsible for Sheriff Dodd's death. As Grand Dragon, you got my word on that."

"Sounds to me like we might could have us a real live hanging tonight after all!" a man yelled out from the crowd.

"Why not?" another voice answered him back. "We got men enough to form a posse and the new sheriff right here to swear us in!"

"I guess McGales does got him a point," someone else said, trying to sound reasonable. "Why didn't Jake Lemaster stop?"

"I used to like to watch that boy play ball. If I'da only knowed. Some hero Red Lemaster turned out to be, huh!"

McGales winked at Gabe as he emerged from the knot of men he'd left abuzz behind him. He wore a smirk on his face, pleased as punch at the turn of events. The night now seemed to be going his way. He hid his pleasure behind his mask.

"Gabe, you bring up the rear in Dodd's police car. You fall in behind me, Ralph. Stick close now, boys!" he called back. "Close up the ranks! Stick together, just like we fucking drilled."

McGales acted certain of himself; Gabe wasn't so sure. Jake Lemaster certainly had some questions to answer about his part in all this, no doubt about that; but to Gabe, McGales's bid seemed a bald-faced ploy. Boss Chief's son! *Ho, boy!* If McGales had seemed mad to Gabe before—cussing crazy—now he seemed poised to go over the edge. As big a chaw as McGales could unquestionably cheek, Gabe feared he might be biting off more than he could chew.

Gabe stood back as four Klansmen lifted Sheriff Dodd by his arms and legs and shuffled him along with his head hanging down. They had to swing him on the count of three to heave him high enough to land him in the bed of McGales's truck. He sat propped against a bald tire with his head gaping back as if he weren't dead at all but simply in the throes of a blinding drunk, grinning as if they were going off to have a fine time now.

The sheriff had left the keys in the ignition of the new-smelling cruiser, but for the life of him Gabe couldn't figure out how to turn off the flashing lights. He felt a little silly as he pulled out after the last car, whorls of red spilling over the wet black fields that lined either side of the highway that led to Parchman Farm.

chapter twenty-eight

T HE LIGHT OVER the back door bulbed bright and the curtains parted at Jake's insistent knocking before Mirabel Hankins answered, her neat white nurse's cap exchanged for can-sized curlers. The sleeves of her silk, rose-flowered kimono yawned wide. "Mr. Lemaster?" She lifted her pince-nez glasses from the chain about her neck, her eyes growing wide at the sight of Baby slung over his shoulder. "This way," she said and stepped back, opening the door wide for them.

Jake stepped quickly inside and followed Mirabel through the kitchen and down the hall, explaining about the miscarriage Baby had suffered the night before and the hemorrhaging, which had begun that afternoon.

"In here." Mirabel directed Jake to lay Baby on her own bed. They used the pink pillows and shams to raise her legs. "Fetch me a blanket out of that cedar chest. And towels from the bathroom closet. And bring me a bag of cotton balls from under the sink. There should be two bags. Bring them both."

"Is she going to be okay?"

Mirabel ignored Jake's question. She covered Baby with the blanket and doubled it back to her waist. She began to massage Baby's lower stomach. "Her uterus," Mirabel explained. "Get me those towels. I need those cotton balls. Close the windows. There's another blanket."

Mirabel did not stop her massage and Jake knew better than to ask for assurance again. After he'd returned with the cotton balls, he fetched another stack of towels without having to be told.

"Is there anything else I can do?"

Mirabel didn't pause to look up. "I'll call you if I need you."

Jake collected the bloodied sheet. Back in the kitchen, he stoppered the sink and ran the cold water, dunking it. The sheet billowed with air, ballooning, and the fresh water turned pink with Baby's blood. The red washed off of his hand, but her blood had dried on his shirt and the trousers of his uniform, staining them.

Jake pulled out a chair at the table. He sat there for a long time with his knees spread wide, drumming his fingers. He rubbed his eyes. He heard the clock on the wall click. With his eyes closed, he listened to it go, time moving incrementally forward. It seemed slow, but it was growing late, already past 9:00. He had no idea what time they'd arrived. He lost track of time. He pictured Dodd's black eyes. He started to find Mirabel Hankins standing in the doorway, watching him. She stepped past him to the sink.

"Maybe I ought to open up a clinic, Mr. Lemaster, as much business as you've been bringing my way lately."

Jake waited while she ran the water and soaped her hands. "I've packed the uterus," she said without looking up. "There's not much more I can do but keep an eye on her. She's not out of the woods yet—infection's always a risk—but the bleeding has stopped. The massage seems to have helped. There are no guarantees, but at this point, I'd be willing to say her chances look good." Mirabel turned back to him then, drying her hands. "She's lucky you got her here when you did, Mr. Lemaster."

"Is she in shock?"

"Her pupils aren't dilated. She only fainted. She's weak from loss of blood. She's just exhausted. She'll need two or three weeks' bed rest to get her strength back up."

Jake felt the relief, almost gladness. He sat back in the chair. A smile widened his face. He ran his hand through his hair.

Mirabel trained her hazel eyes on him. "You don't know then?"

"About what? What now?" Jake said.

"It's on the radio. The whole county's been up in arms. I was listening when you knocked."

Mirabel led him into the living room. She pulled the cord on a lamp and fished a bottle and two glasses from underneath the stand her gramophone sat on. She flicked on the radio, and the tubes hummed, warming up, as she set the glasses side by side on the coffee table. She splashed a swallow for herself and poured a full shot for Jake.

"Drink that," she said. "Nurse's orders."

Jake sat on the couch. The strains of Jack Benny's orchestra swelled the room. "Tell me."

Mirabel sipped her own drink.

"Doc Evans wasn't on the grounds so I was the one who pronounced Alley Leech dead. Oh, he was good and dead, all right. This was just before it started to pour. It was Bigger who did it. Then he made a run for it. They just called off the alert a little while ago. Apparently, Quirt Hanson and his dogs finally tracked him down. The report said he was close to the county line when they caught up to him. He was killed before he could cross."

Jake blamed himself. He should've known it would happen—the way Alley Leech was talking when he left Parchman Farm that morning. All of a sudden, Jake felt bone tired, exhausted from it all himself, his shoulders sagging.

He remembered the glass, but left the shot untouched. He stood.

"May I use your phone?"

The operator in Eureka connected him with Mr. Brumsfield. "Yes?"

"Mr. Brumsfield, it's Jake Lemaster."

"Jake Lemaster? Boss Chief's boy? The red-haired, one-armed tailback? Orange Bowl '35?"

"Yes sir," Jake said, "that was me."

"Was? Who are you calling as now, Mr. Lemaster? Is this some sort of a prank?"

Jake quickly explained about Mrs. Allen. "She's here at Mirabel Hankins's outside of Ruleton."

"My God. But she's going to be all right?"

A pause crackled the line that ran the length of Highway 49 from Eureka to Ruleton, then Mr. Brumsfield said: "And Sally Johnson?"

"She's safe."

"Tell me what I can do, Mr. Lemaster."

Jake turned, holding on to the cord. "I remember from your campaigning during the last election that you're a lawyer."

"As director of the Welfare Office, I don't practice law anymore, but I have a degree in jurisprudence, yes."

Jake glanced back at Mirabel to make sure she was listening, too. He had to assume the operator was. Jake told Mr. Brumsfield what had happened on the highway on their way to Mirabel Hankins's, imagining the posse that would form once Sheriff Dodd's body was discovered along the highway. Jake had seen Dodd's deputy, Ralph Simpson, coming his way, but there'd been no time to stop again and plead his case. They'd be in a lather looking for the man who'd killed him. Jake could not imagine how he could begin to explain to a mob Dodd's inexplicably trying to murder him over a pair of women's underwear, but he also knew he had no choice but to drive back home that night and face up to this. After what had happened to Bigger, he made a promise: They would not get Baby.

Mr. Brumsfield asked Jake to leave the evidence with Mirabel Hankins. "I'll take this to Judge Haskell's tonight. Sissy's to be buried tomorrow afternoon; we can try to obtain a stay. It may well be that we can have Sheriff Burgess from down here in Eureka deliver the warrant. Burgess is an honest man, and the county coroner's a friend of mine, a classmate. There's a new forensic lab in Memphis. Science can be used to solve such cases now. It's a wonder. You'd be surprised at what they can detect. We'll do our damnedest. We haven't lost this one yet. There's still a chance. You know, Mr. Lemaster," Mr. Brumsfield continued, "I was in the stands that afternoon at the Orange Bowl. That was a game I'll never forget."

Mirabel assured Jake that there was nothing more he could do for Baby, who lay on the bed sleeping underneath two blankets—in that close heat a little of the blood had returned to flush her cheeks.

"She just needs to rest now, Mr. Lemaster. Don't fret unduly. You got her here in time. In a few weeks, Mrs. Allen will be up and about again, driving the dusty roads in that old Model T. You just worry about taking care of your own self. Whatever happens, don't you dare turn your back on that Calvin McGales. Alley Leech was a nasty enough piece of work, but McGales is the type of viperish soul who'd turn and strike his own tail for lagging behind."

chapter twenty-nine

THEY LAID BIGGER in the yard.

He'd lain before Jakey in the kitchen just Tuesday. And now here he *was:* is, dead! Not in the has been, though he had been alive then, or the even was, but here in the very now all over again.

Jakey rubs his eyes. He stops and unstops his ears. Like the wings of coming cicada, that veined clear and humming slightly, the faraway whir and sliding grinding sound of grain pouring fast down a metal chute—the rev and vroom of trucks and cars far away that first found him sitting up straight in the dark as if he were going to lift his arms and go walking off in his sleep, the swarm growing closer, and closer, and then up close, hovering, rumbling his room with their own persistent thunder—making their own grumblings, beyond the storm's: loud and growling, not only their wings now, but their razor jaws working, stripping everything in their path, a seething black cloud. Jakey knows the word *plague* from Sunday school. Pharaoh got his! Moses and his serpent turned staff taught him that: *Let my people go!*

The men who have landed in the quad cloud up close like that, too, shadowy dark in a bunch but rising bright-winged in white robes, haloed brilliant as if they've burst into flame before the string of headlights lined up shining behind them. They stand in a line before Bigger's body, which lies roped behind the horses, with their arms crossed over their chests. They look huge, their tall hats throwing pointed shadows across the yard. Scary. They do not move. They just stand there, staring, silent—straight-faced, angry-eyed— while the other men in their day clothes walk around, looking curiously back over their shoulders at them, which makes Jakey feel a little better about his own fear. He's never seen such a thing. He wonders if it's some joke, grown-ups dressing up like that, like Halloween, but inside him it doesn't feel funny. It's as if he's awakened into a nightmare: *Ghosts are real!*

Altogether they are too many for him to count, like a hatch of flies come the sun, like bees in a comb. Like ants crawling over each other to go back and forth in the corked glass house his daddy helped him build and pour the crumbly dirt from their fields into before it dropped off his dresser and shattered and his mother screamed, "Cal!" and "Never again in my house!" blaming his father. Jakey tries to come up with a number he can name. He holds ten fingers against the screen, trying to match them to the many men he sees, the voices he hears. More men come, driving up the lane from the front gate. More and more of them. Most of them carry guns, Jakey notices. He flashes his fingers. Ten and ten and ten and ten and ten and ten and ten . . . But the final figure for the number will not sum. He does not know what time it is either. *Dark*-time. He knows *night*. But it is Sunday for sure because of church, he feels. Or yesterday it had been if by now it is already tomorrow, meaning today. Of this alone Jakey feels absolutely sure.

Bigger!

The tail of one of the two horses used to tow him back to Front Camp raises and splats a load loud against the wetter mud, gas spews.

A man comments on the tune: "Sounds to me like 'Yankee Doodle.'"

Men laugh. Chuckle.

"Hell, Herm, how'd you know? You can't even whistle 'Dixie.'"

Jakey holds the high ground, upstairs looking down from the

window of his room, *the catbird's seat* his daddy would call it and muss his hair if he were here to help him look, listen, but he's not here. *Where is he?* Jakey feels suddenly afraid for his father someway beyond his own fear, though he does not know what that way is. All these men! His daddy will be angry at them for what they've done to Bigger after risking the trouble of having his mother discover he'd brought him here to their kitchen to have Nurse Hankins fix him up. He hasn't seen his daddy since they left for church that morning without him. Somehow he managed to miss dinner again even though he had all day to try not to miss it is what his mama said. Jakey and Lee and their mother ate in a harder and stiller silence even than the quiet they'd driven back home through to find him gone in. Whispers and whispering that would suddenly stop when Jakey pushed through the swinging door into the kitchen—Mason peeling away at the potatoes as if he hadn't been speaking at all. Jakey knew that trick; he felt the hurt of its being aimed at him. They ate peas and fried chicken and mashed potatoes: Sunday dinner. *Who likes peas?* is what Jakey was thinking when his mother lurched up from the table so suddenly he thought maybe she was going to be sick on them herself. Jakey hadn't even seen her begin to cry. She sobbed into her napkin and left the room. He hadn't seen her get hurt. Maybe she'd bit her tongue. His daddy wasn't there to hold her shoulders and Jakey didn't know whether they had permission to be excused to see if she was all right. He and Lee sat there without speaking, afraid to break the riddled silence, talking with their eyes. Lee looked to him to say the word to get down—take responsibility for suffering their mama's blame if he made the wrong decision. Finally, Calpurnia parted the kitchen doors. His mother hadn't come back for them. "Go on. Get down," she said gently. "You fine." She removed their plates. "Let's go on get ready for bed." Upstairs, the door to his mama's room faced shut. She did not come out to kiss them good night. Cal tucked them in.

Now Jakey hears his mother yank open her door. She stomps angrily halfway down the stairs to call over the banister, "Mason!" and

"What is the *meaning* of this? What are these men doing in our yard? Do I have to take care of everything myself?" He hears his mother stamp back up the steps. The door to her room slams.

That day in Sunday school pretty Miss Acres with the yellow curls had learned them about Abraham and how he'd raised up his knife to sacrifice Isaac his son because God told him to. And Abraham had been going to do it, too! That's how the story went. He raised his knife with both hands over his head ready to plunge it in. But then a ram had appeared in the thicket. And so God let Abraham off the hook because he had shown faith. God told him to butcher the ram instead of his son. But Abraham had been going to stab his boy or maybe slit his son's throat, offer him up, sure enough! That's the faith part, Jakey guesses: that Isaac's father had been willing to go so far. It prickles the hairs on the back of Jakey's neck thinking of his daddy and what he might be capable of doing if he believed it enough.

He wishes his father would come home *now*.

At the edge of the crowd, Quirt Hanson's hounds pull up onto their hind legs, held back by a trusty holding on to their leads, and then drop back, hacking dry at being choked, and then licking their chops again, wagging their butts for someone to pet and praise them, while Quirt himself ambles up to a group of white men milling close beneath Jakey's window.

"Damn near to the line," he hears Quirt saying—seeing Quirt accept the jar. "Like a bar. Damn near big as a bar, too. Biggest sort of bar."

"A black bear?"

"No, one of them grizzly bars you hear about out west. That thar kind of bar. Fierce. Big."

"Well," a man says. "I guess he ain't so fierce. He don't look so big now."

No one says anything and then someone says, "I don't know, he looks pretty big to me."

"Fierce, too."

"You hear what he done to Alley Leech. By God . . ."

And: "It was almost as if he was waiting on us, I swar. Jes standin' thar big as a goddamn bar. He chose that ground. Thing I can't figure's why . . ."

"He just didn't know. How could he a knowed? Did he have a map? Could he a read if he had? He didn't know the line was there."

"Couldn'ta knowed. That's right. Jes dumb luck. And that was the end of it."

"Poor Dougy," Quirt says, taking the jar back. "You wasn't thar. I'm tellin' you, the biggest kind of bar. Brave. You ask Booker. He don't knock your lights out straight, he'll tell you."

"I'd like to see him knock out my lights."

"You don't think he could?"

"I'd like to see him touch me."

"Ask him then."

"He may been pardoned, be a free man, a sergeant here, but he's still a nigger. He can't escape that. There ain't no escaping that."

"Oh, that. Well, go on ask him then. You just go ahead."

"They shore poured Alley Leech into that grave all left of him."

"It's been a wet day all around."

"When it rains it pours. You done nursin' that jar? I'm feelin' a mite parched."

"Hard to tell what to make of it."

"A real soaker. It'll be days 'fore I can get my mule back out in the field. I'm thinking about building an ark. Two by two."

"Brave. Big. Chose his ground. And Dougy dead. He weren't no ordinary hound by no means. You know, I used to sneak 'm inside sometimes fore my wife she . . ."

"Get me that jar, Quirt. Good Lord. You're half in the bag as it is."

"And Dodd, too. And now they say Jake Lemaster."

"It's been a dark day, for a fact."

"Two mules, two snakes, two . . ."

"You would take two mules, too. What they gonna do?"

"Pull, I reckon. Plow."

"Far's I'm concerned, we could just leave the snakes. Wouldn't hurt my feelins none."

"Jake Lemaster couldn'ta shot Dodd, though. I'm just here to tell you—no matter what McGales is sayin'. That's pure tripe. That's the silliest goddamn story. Why would he do it?"

"Someone saw him driving off!"

"Who did?"

"Ralph Simpson did."

"Ralph Simpson!"

"And anyway it was a twenty-two that killed him. I saw the wound with my own eyes. What's Jake tote?"

"Well, I don't know about that. Thirty-eight Smith most like."

"Well, McGales."

"McGales!" Quirt says.

"Hold on now."

"McGales!" Quirt says again. "The Boss Chief the big boss man and he don't take no truck with no Klan. What the Boss Chief says on Parchman Farm goes. Not McGales. McGales! You wait till the Boss Chief gets here, then we'll see what's what! Who who!"

"Hush now. He'll hear you. That McGales got a temper on him."

"That's just like you, Quirt. That there come from McGales's still. And he givin' it out free as rain. What do you have to say about that? Like you to look a gift horse in the mouth."

"I say pass me that jar back you got no use for it. What the hell I care where it come from? Long as it does its job."

"You sure done yours. You tracked him down all right. Think of it as your re-ward."

"The thing about an ark is it's got to be so dang big. How do you think ole Noah did it?"

"I 'magine thinking about the end would be a real motivator. Get left, get drowned. Simple. Get to work. Figure it out."

"You got a point. Jesus, Quirt! Give me that jar. You gonna go blind."

"Don't care if I do. I seed all I need to see. Don't believe me ask

Booker you ain't afraid of a 'nigger.' Poor poor Dougy. You shoulda seen him standing thar. Never sawed nothing like it afore. It was as if . . ."

Jakey hears his mother come back out of her room and go quickly clipping down the stairs. It's her high shoes he hears, the swish of her dress—she's put on her clothes to face the men. The front door unsticks beneath him. He can imagine her with her hands down on her hips, waiting for them to finally notice her. He sees the flash of the bulb light. The porch yellow lit.

"Miss Jolene . . . !"

"I have children asleep upstairs! This is a scandal. You take that dead Negro out of this yard immediately! This is a complete outrage! You men are crazy! Are you drunk? Is there a man among you sober? Have you men gone completely insane? Where is Boss Chief? You wait until he hears about this atrocity!"

The men crunch gravel, walk up to talk low to her, seriously, the low burble of their murmurs, explaining. Being reasonable. Jakey knows the tone.

"What?" his mother is saying. "When? Jake? They say it was Jake?" he hears his mother's questioning wail, the beginning of a lament.

And then, just like that, as if with a snap of the fingers, his daddy appears before them, driving up in the state car, coming on slowly past the front gate and down the drive, no doubt seeing the men gathered in Front Camp before Second Home who stop their jawing, the gathering going silent, nudging each other to look at him coming—the line giving way, the men stepping back, bowing out so that he can see Bigger trussed up in the yard.

"*Daddy!*" Jakey calls, feeling the rousting alarm at his father's finding Bigger who he lay in their kitchen who's landed lying caught in their yard now, and turns away from the silvery screen, already running for the door, lost already in a long tunneling of running. Wheeling as if in water, treading, no purchase, he begins toward the idea of the stairs holding to the feeling of some fear, the vague instinctual idea of a son's saving his father from it all if only he could.

chapter thirty

JAKE STOPPED BEFORE Second Home and put the state car in park. Men stood about the yard—jars openly in hand—as if the prison quad had been transformed into a country carnival fairground and they were waiting for the robed Ku Klux Klan members rowed at attention to perform a marching drill.

Before them Bigger's body lay roped to a pair of horses. Jake's heart sank.

Beneath the porch light Jolene stood, looking down on him. He recognized that glare—*hell to pay*—but there was fear for him in her face, too, and Jake suddenly felt sorry for her. Hell, for both of them. He hoped that the boys were fast asleep. At the gates of Parchman Farm, the flashing red lights of the patrol car had alerted him to the fact that Sheriff Dodd's body had undoubtedly been found.

The one other person Jake had expected to see waiting for him at Front Camp and didn't was Boss Chief. But there was no turning back now.

Jake shouldered out of the car and stood before the crowd, which was turned silently to face him as if they expected a speech. He slammed the door and walked deliberately along the ranks of cars and men walling off the quad as if he were out on the highway directing work on the road. After all, he *was* second in command at Parchman Farm.

As he passed McGales, Jake could feel the Grand Dragon's eyes burning bright, fierce with scorn from behind his green mask. He ignored his glaring and stopped to look down at Bigger's body. Whatever else this mob had in store for Bigger, the shooting and the fact that he'd been dragged back to Front Camp through the mud by the throat seemed to Jake to have exacted retribution enough. Bigger's eyes bulged like boiled eggs and his tongue swelled the hole of his mouth. Jake felt something collapse inside of him. Seeing into Bigger's strangled face, Jake's own throat closed up. He didn't trust himself to speak. And it wasn't only sorrow; anger throttled him. He felt the rage. It had been a bloody and brutal week. Jake hated the hate it seemed he could no longer escape.

From behind him, Jake heard Ralph Simpson clear his throat. "Mr. Jake," Ralph said diffidently. "Excuse me. I'm awful terrible sorry about this, but I'm afraid I got to place you under arrest for the murder of Sheriff Dodd."

"Got Dodd's blood on him for sure," someone said.

"Looks like he gone butchered a hog."

And another man swore softly, "*Jay*-sus. McGales ain't even lying."

Jake glanced down at his ruined uniform. He turned to Ralph. The Grand Dragon stood solidly shimmed in behind him, arms crossed over his chest, showing the Klan's determination to back the deputy. The men gathered about the quad had packed closer, waiting to hear what Jake had to say in his own defense. Jake had one chance. Without a word, he reached in his pocket and pulled out the silver, pearl-handled .22 pistol. The crowd gasped. Then the mob erupted, clamoring, the men all talking all at once as Jake turned the weapon over to Ralph.

"I goddamned knew it!" McGales crowed over the hubbub. He tore off his mask and spat. Stepping forward, he snatched Jake's

.38 out of his holster. "You a goddamn murderer! You a goddamn *murderer!*"

"Where's Boss Chief?" Jake asked Ralph.

Behind him McGales was bawling, "Your daddy can't save you now. It's murder. *Murder!* What more proof we need? We got all the evidence we could want right here!" he said, pointing the barrel of Jake's revolver at the .22 Ralph Simpson held. "*An eye for an eye, a tooth for a tooth!* I say we save the county the expense of juicing the chair!"

"*Daddy!*" Jake glanced up as Jakey burst through the front door of Second Home. "Daddy!"

"Hold on there, little buddy!"

Jake saw Quirt Hanson weaving back and forth, making feeble gestures after the boy, but a group of men standing at the foot of the stairs caught his son back before he could break free into the quad.

"That's my wife's pistol," a man piped up. The genuine surprise that filled the voice quieted the clamor, the men craning to see who had spoken. Jake looked up at the big Klansman who stood a full head and shoulders above McGales—the robe cutting him off at the knees. "That's my wife's pistol." He grabbed off his hood to take a better look, revealing himself to be a handsome man with a square jaw. He had green eyes and curly black hair, the features of Baby's younger daughter, Jeana. Without ever having laid eyes on him before, Jake recognized Baby's husband, Gabriel Allen.

McGales looked as if he'd swallowed his chaw—truly dumbfounded. "What the fuck you talking about, Gabe? Just looks like it. Can't be the same gun."

"It is. Nickel-plated. Pearl handle. Twenty-two. It's hers all right. No mistake about that. I bought it for her myself when she took that job at the Welfare Office. I'd recognize it anywhere. It was a gift."

"Jake here stole it then or bought it or your wife threw it away and he found it." McGales waved the .38 at Jake. "He handed that gun over to Ralph. He's got Dodd's blood all over him. That's the twenty-two the bullet holes that killed Dodd come from." McGales turned to address the mob. "I got the body right in the back of the truck any you want to take a good look and I *guaran*-goddamnfucking-*tee* you they gone match up!"

"She didn't sell that gun."

"Gabe," McGales warned, shaking his head.

"I can prove it!"

"*Gabriel!*"

"She had it just a week ago because she took a shot at us that night we burned the cross. Look at the twenty-two hole in McGales's truck door." He faced Jake. "What are you trying to pull?"

Jake offered himself up to the deputy's custody, beseeching him to act quickly before Gabe could say anything more about whose pistol it was. "Ralph, you best take me on in right now. Let my daddy know where I am and then I'll make a statement about what happened tonight. We'll get this mess straightened out."

"You ain't going nowhere!" McGales said. "Ralph, listen to what I'm telling you now! *Gabe!* That's enough!"

"She kept that pistol safe in the closet of our bedroom. I knew her kicking me out couldn't have been all about May Franks. I may be dumb, but I'm no idiot. You're *screwing* my wife!"

Gabe lunged at Jake, and the men bunched behind him surged forward to grab him, shoving Jake backward over Bigger. He smacked hard against the flank of the first of the yoked horses still chained to the body, and fell. The horse shied, rising, spooking the other, and the frightened pair lurched forward, yanking free of the trusty who had hold of the reins, and exploded across the yard. Jake covered his head and rolled to get out of their path. Bigger's body shot past.

"*Whoa!* Whoa now! Look out!"

"Get Jake!" McGales screamed to his Klansmen. "The murderer's attempting to escape!"

Jake felt himself caught up by many hands, their roughing and grabbing and punching at him like being trapped in the tumble of a breaking wave. He was as much at the mercy of the mob as Letitia Johnson had been. Something bashed his face, a rock, and he felt the numbing shock of his teeth razored off. He literally saw a bright flash of stars. He was struck down and yanked up again. A slug doubled him over. He was being pummeled, beaten, and kicked. Jake scrunched into a ball and felt himself hauled up under the arms and by the scruff of his neck and shirt and the hide of his hair, raised aloft on the shoulders of the crowd. Shouts filled his ears. He imagined he heard Jolene screaming, Jakey yelling, "*Daddydaddydaddy!*" He wanted to assure his son that everything was going to be all right. He thought to tell him how much he loved him. But his mouth wouldn't work right and the chaos of noises that swirled around him bled together, pounding in his ears. He felt himself swept away on the tide of violence, the sound of his own lynching trapped in his brain like the whole of an ocean in a too-tiny shell. The old oak with a low limb that stood at the center of the quad had been used more than once to weigh the scales of justice at the prison.

"You a goddamned traitor's what you fucking is!"

And that's when Jake heard the report. As the men were lifting Jake to fit the dangling noose, he saw Gabe stumble back. McGales stepped closer and fired a second shot and then a third, yelling, "He was trying to help Jake escape!"

Ralph Simpson still had a grip on the little .22. "Hold on now, McGales!" he said. "You can't just go shooting citizens at will."

McGales turned on him, too. "Who the fuck you think you talking to?"

Ralph quavered with the pistol before him. "I mean I can't just let you . . ."

McGales clubbed Ralph. The .22 popped harmlessly into the air as he fell. Fangs of tobacco juice had leaked down on either side of McGales's mouth. At the sound of an answering shot being fired, the crowd broke underneath Jake, dispersed, dropping him flat in their hurry to take cover—every man for himself.

The two horses rumbled the quad at full gallop, dragging Bigger's body bouncing and tumbling behind them over the muddy yard. It swung back and forth like a wrecking ball, flattening bushes and splintering a bench. The horses rounded before First Home and started back, making another pass. Their eyes rolled wild. McGales leaped back to avoid being run down, the horses pounding the stretch of open ground between him and Jake.

Jake slipped the noose, his head still swimming. He crutched up leaning on the knuckles of his left hand. McGales stood alone on the other side of the lane. Jake launched himself out of that three-point stance, rocketing forward as if he'd trapped the snap from center and was going straight up the middle as fast and powerfully as he could, keeping low as he'd always been coached, his shoulders squared to the hole, breaking through the line of scrimmage into open field, sprinting toward glory, racing straight at his goal that was McGales.

McGales saw him coming. He raised the .38, the chaw stilling, rounding his cheek behind the smirk of a grin as he took careful aim at Jake, an easy target, and then jumped as if a switch had been thrown on him, his body surging from the full charge of the bullet from Boss Chief's .375 Harrison and Richardson. Boss Chief had ridden back into Front Camp in time to witness the final moments of the melee. In that same instant, the Klansmen who had taken cover behind the wall of their cars and trucks let loose a withering fusillade. Just as he had in his dream that had visited him three nights in a row the week before, Jake met the bullets and kept running, churning, knees high. He'd reached top speed. Sheer momentum carried him over McGales's body for the score, falling with his left arm raised as if to acknowledge his fans. The roaring in his ears was the last thing Red Lemaster would ever hear, sounding forever now like the long-lost cheering of the crowd.

chapter thirty-one

FOR SACRIFICING HIS life in his "final big play, racing unarmed into the fray at Parchman Farm," L. B. Ware proclaimed Jake Lemaster a hero on the front page of the Monday, July 24, 1944, edition of the *Hushpuckashaw County Tocsin*. A CHAMPION TO THE END the headline read, and his athletic accomplishments were duly noted. The accompanying photograph had been dug up from the archives of the *Mississippian*, the Ole Miss student newspaper. It showed "Red" Lemaster in full uniform, down on one knee, resting on his stub, wearing the jersey with his since-retired number 7 on the chest, a football tucked underneath his left arm. Black streaks high on his cheeks underlined the game in his eyes.

"A son of the Confederacy—a celebrated Ole Miss Rebel—Jake Lemaster gave his life protecting us and ours in the line of fire here at home, even as our country stands mired in the midst of a world war against tyranny and subjugation, the likes of which humanity has never before known."

The publisher ended his tribute on a mournful note—with a final slow tapslike trumpeting:

"And what more can we ask of our heroes? What more, but their lives, can they give?

"We will miss him: Our all-American Jake Lemaster—the Red

Fox—the fiery-haired, one-armed quarterback of Ole Miss's 1935 Orange Bowl team."

The burial was scheduled for 3:30 on Wednesday afternoon at Cypress View Cemetery and would be preceded by a 2:00 funeral service at the First Presbyterian Church in Ruleton. The viewing would be held at F. R. Lane Funeral Home. Times to be announced.

And just like that, Baby thought, the heroics of Jake Lemaster would be lain safely to rest, the public's memory of him kept alive and well: to the majority Jake would remain unchanged, the same hero he'd always been to them. L. B. Ware made no mention of the Klan's involvement in the final confrontation at Parchman Farm or of Calvin McGales's stature as Grand Dragon in the realm of the Invisible Empire. It was as if in death a wand had been passed over his life. Magically, any hint of such an association had disappeared. Apparently, McGales had simply "run amuck," going on the shooting spree that had ended in the taking of the life of her husband and assaulting Ruleton's deputy sheriff before Boss Chief brought him down and returned law and order to the prison. The incident had become merely a "disturbance" in the wake of Sunday's escape attempt.

Confined to her four-poster bed back at home on East Percy Street, Baby began to rifle the pages of the paper, the words blurring before her.

On the back page, she found the one-paragraph obituary for Gabriel Julius Allen. Mr. Brumsfield had passed along a picture of Gabe, which Baby herself, as the wife who had "survived" him, had been called upon to supply, and which she still held dear, and Baby felt a mournful pang full of something like regret looking closely again at the photograph. She touched Gabe's smile. She could yet recall a time when she'd loved him, when she'd believed he loved only her, when the four of them had made a family. Claire and Jeana had taken the news of their father's death hard. He'd left for who-knew-where on that train—lost to them—but not *dead*. Baby had not been able to arrange to have him buried until Friday. The bloat of bodies had overwhelmed the F. R. Lane Funeral Home. Gabe would be the last of them to be lowered into the ground. They'd have to wait his turn.

Sissy Rule Tisdale's funeral would go off without a hitch. Scheduled for that afternoon, her funeral would remain a private affair. No mention at all was made of the warrant Mr. Brumsfield had sought from Judge Haskell to delay Sissy's interment.

Confronted by the evidence Jake had left behind at Mirabel Hankins's for Mr. Brumsfield after he'd told the story of what he'd found over the phone, Clyde Tisdale had scoffed. "A pair of women's *under-*things? You *can't* be serious. What if they are Sissy's? One of the dogs must have dragged them out into the yard! Would you gentlemen besmirch her memory further? Would you make a laughingstock of my family? This is an outrage!" The stay was denied. By then Mr. Brumsfield had learned the body had already been embalmed. No trace of evidence existed of which the new forensic lab in Memphis could make sense. Charges were not brought. Whatever had happened to Sissy the night of her death would be lain to rest in the Rule family plot.

It fell to Sheriff Burgess to investigate Sheriff Dodd's death, but after Jake died valiantly trying to stop Calvin McGales, no one was willing to seriously blame him for the murder—Jake dead regardless, only his good name to be preserved. The case would remain forever unsolved: "Inconclusive Evidence" the official term Sheriff Burgess would stamp on his final report. The county took care of disposing of the murder weapon.

The last clue in putting together the series of events that had transpired in Hushpuckashaw County as a result of the lynching of Letitia Johnson that Baby read that afternoon in bed was about the recapture of the prisoner Alfonse—no last name given—commonly known as "Bigger." His only known next of kin, Sally Johnson, a charge of the state once again officially in the foster care of Reverend Beasley of Children's Home, had claimed his body and he'd been buried there on the grounds in the orchard overlooking the bend in the river.

Ruthie had frowned considerably at Baby's asking Mr. Brumsfield to take her to Jake Lemaster's burial, leaving the bed she'd been confined to by Doc Evans. Ruthie would hardly even allow Baby to feed herself. She spoon-fed her soups, heavy with chicken and beef broth to help her "get up her strength."

"Only if you promise you'll stay in the car. You gots to promise me now."

"I promise," Baby said.

The welfare had paid for the wheelchair, which Gladys Point-dexter had rented from Eureka Drugs. Miss Honey fanned a good-bye from the shadowed cool of her screened-in porch as Mr. Crosthwaite from across the street helped Mr. Brumsfield shift Baby from it into the passenger seat of the shiny black Oldsmobile.

"Thank you, Howard," she'd said to him. Mr. Crosthwaite squeezed her hand.

They met up with the other mourners at Cypress View Ceme-tery. Mr. Brumsfield parked the Oldsmobile on the edge of the gravel road facing the hearse. "I'm not messing with Ruthie. This will have to be close enough."

From the passenger seat, Baby could gaze out across the rolling expanse of the cemetery's lawn, green from the recent rain. The throng of folks that had come to pay their last respects to Jake Lemaster had gathered in a semicircle about the grave. A stone's throw away, beneath the twenty-foot-tall obelisk that read RULE, the family plot where Sissy Rule Tisdale had been lain quietly to rest two days before lay hidden heaped underneath a pyre of white flaming lilies. The ever so slight rise, taken as high ground in the Delta, offered a panoramic view of more common stones. Calvin McGales's and Tom Dodd's plots remained out of view entirely, rel-egated to the piney, scrub edges of the cemetery.

Jolene had chosen to wear a fashionable knee-length black fitted dress. She wore her honey-colored hair up, and a black lace veil hid her face from view. She stood before her husband's open grave with one hand on each of her sons' shoulders. The boys had been dressed like little men, their hair slicked neatly back, dressed in blue sports coats that they wore over their knickers. Each sported a green-and-blue-striped Ruleton Country Club tie. The older boy strained so far forward against his mother's hold that Baby thought he might actually try to leap into the hole. Suddenly, the boy turned and smothered his face against his mother's waist.

The rosewood coffin sat beside the hole, gleaming bright, well wrought as a Chippendale hutch—no expense spared in sending Jake off.

The gathering was waiting for Boss Chief to arrive. He pulled up behind them. His wide shoulders and great head and tall black hat seemed to fill the Packard. He'd driven by himself from the First Presbyterian Church, where the funeral service had been held. Baby glanced back to see him stab his hand inside his breast pocket. He pulled out a silver flask and tipped it straight up. His Adam's apple glugged, pulling hard, before he screwed the top back and stowed it. He climbed laboriously out of the car to stand, glaring at the mourners trying not to stare back at him, and puffed out his chest, smoothing his large hands down over his lapels to snug his bolo tie. As he stumbled past Mr. Brumsfield's car, he happened to glance their way. He stopped and leaned close to look in at them. His yellow eyes slid over Mr. Brumsfield but snagged on Baby. He held her gaze and then he tipped his hat, acknowledging her. "Mrs. Allen," he said. Boss Chief straightened to plow his way over the mess of graves to get straight to his son's, which had been set to the left of another with a gleaming black granite stone. Baby figured it must be Jake's mother's, Boss Chief's wife: CATHERINE MCCRAE LEMASTER. From the dates, Baby realized with a start that she'd been only twenty-three when she died.

Baby waited until they'd lowered Jake into the ground and his father stepped up and threw down a shovelful of dirt on the lid of his casket before she reached out and touched Mr. Brumsfield's arm. She faced forward, ready to be taken home.

"Could it get it any hotter?" Sally Johnson sighed to herself, knowing for a fact *it could*. She reached for the lever that controlled the air conditioner on the dash of the Galaxie 500, keeping her eyes on the road—people parking in the slanted spaces before the stores and walking about—wary for the safety of others. "Don't fail me now, Henry." She'd adopted the name for her car after that Ford man, the father of the assembly line, and the sobriquet was not always complimentary. She shifted the blower to full speed and flapped the low-buttoned front of her blouse, trying to fan the cool. The winking digital gauge beneath the shimmering green-and-white sign for the Planters Bank of Ruleton alternated between the temperature, 101, and the time, 3:22. The smiling face of Robert Tisdale, the bank's president, smiled pink-cheeked down at her from a full-color billboard. PUT A FRIENDLY FACE ON YOUR FINANCES! the slogan said. Sally read the fine print underneath it: *"Extend Your Credit Line! Low-interest loans now available!"*

As she passed, the date flashed August 13. It was Friday. The digital did not need to tell her the year was 1990, but calculating the bad luck signaled by the combination of that day and date and hearing the slow whirling falter and ticking of the fan—the imminent failure of the air conditioner—Sally knew that the car she was driving could *up and die on her* at any moment. The 1975 Ford had become something of a white elephant—fifteen years old with 192,431 and four-tenths miles on the odometer. It had outlived its time, if not its usefulness. Sally had just turned in her receipt for new tires. She and her husband, Dr. Gerald Ross, had bought the vehicle new from the dealer in Greenville. In the years since she'd driven it off the showroom floor, Sally had put the majority of those miles on the car as an agent making home visits for the Welfare Office. The once-black plastic dash underneath the windshield glass had blued and cracked from years of facing such heat, the blaze of countless days of the Delta's summer suns. At fifty-eight, as director of the Welfare Department for Hushpuckashaw County, Sally knew she could have enjoyed the relative comforts of one of the latest state vehicles. Nowadays, the welfare had a fleet of look-alike "official" white Tauruses in which the agents visited their clients. But Sally still chose to drive her own old Ford and to be reimbursed for her mileage, waiting two weeks for the state's check, the way things *used to be*.

Not that the way things used to be was *all that!* She was well aware that the younger agents called her "Old School" behind her back. But Sally didn't mind—herself, she was inclined to take the recognition of her age, which she considered to be the hard-earned wisdom of the hands-on way she'd learned to do her job, as a compliment. She'd had time-honored teachers, her mentors: Baby Allen and Mr. Brumsfield and Reverend Beasley. Mr. Brumsfield and the reverend both had since passed on. Baby, now eighty-seven, had never remarried, but by now she'd been made a great-grandmother seven times over, and she spent part of each winter with her daughter Jeana in northern Florida. Her mind was still sharp, though, her memory of the era she'd lived through acute. She knew *the business*—kept abreast of the politics down in Jackson, "the welfare wars," as she called them, the fight against state budget cuts and for the support of federal programs—and Sally remained mindful of her experiences. Baby still lived in the little white house at 12 East Percy Street with the help of a full-time nurse named Rachel, who was good enough, at times, to remind Sally of how great Ruthie had been. These days, when Sally visited, she and Baby sat together outside openly socializing side by side swinging on the front porch swing, sipping Old Crow bourbon. Things had certainly changed. Her own mama's lynching—forty-six years in the past—had been one of the last such travesties in the state until the 1960s when the hate had boiled up to the surface and erupted anew. The Invisible Empire had shown itself again, renamed the White Knights of Mississippi. It was if the revived corpse of the long-buried Calvin McGales had staggered up from the grave, stomping about with his hands held out straight, like some sort of stinking, coming-unwound horror-show mummy to terrorize the state again. But no matter how clichéd the robes, the manifestation of evil they symbolized was all too real—the bombings and shootings and hangings had taken a heavy toll. Sally heard herself say, "Um." That had been a bad time, but good had come of it. Any war, any struggle worth the price, demanded sacrifice. Sally knew. Their work was not finished, not by a long shot; Sally did not believe in kidding herself—she wore glasses now, bifocals, but not the rose-colored kind—but things were better. They would "overcome."

Sally's enduring wish was that her mother could have lived to see it—see her now. *Who'da thunk it?* She often recalled the question Baby had posed to her all those years ago, testing her client's self-esteem as they drove the back roads to find Sally a foster home: "What do you want to be when you grow up?" Sally's answer had come to seem to her like fate: "Maybe I'll grow up and go to college. Work for the welfare, just like you."

As director now, Sally could easily have justified returning to the cool of the brand-new centrally air-conditioned offices recently built for them in Eureka, across the street from St. Peter's Episcopal Church. She had work enough to keep her busy behind her desk all day long, evenings and most weekends, too. But that was not the way Baby Allen had done things in her tenure as head of the welfare after Mr. Brumsfield retired and it was not the way Sally Johnson did things either, not the way she ran "her shop": Old School. It was personal—what made her who she was, *Sally Johnson*. Folks knew about her and her mama, and the dusty, "dirty-white," beige, great white whale of a Ford had become her calling card, as that dusty old Model T had once been Mrs. Allen's. People knew she was coming when they saw the dust trundling up behind her, the signal that help was on its way. They kept their eyes peeled for her, and Sally did not like to disappoint them. Even though these days she wined and dined state senators and members of the legislature, phoned back and forth on a first-name basis with the governor, and made countless speeches before assemblies, in many respects, going out on the road was still the most satisfying aspect of a job she still loved.

The raggedy cool air from the blower rattled the sheets of the paperwork beside her on the bench seat. She slid slowly to the end of Main Street and stopped at the red sign. She used that four-way pause at the crossroads of U.S. Highway 49—twelve miles north to Parchman, twelve miles south to Eureka—facing off against a pickup truck, a cotton picker rolling forward on her right, to leaf through the paperwork she'd brought. She had one more visit to make that Friday. She had an orphaned girl to see. Her mother had passed away from breast cancer. Her name was Amanda Ann Phipps. She was just fourteen.

Sally turned south, gaining speed as she accelerated beyond the city limits of Ruleton. The cotton on either side of the highway striped green to brown and skipped twice green again before lining brown. A sign for the Billups Plantation flashed past on her left. Four square, twenty-acre catfish ponds shimmered bluely as a mirage to her right, catfish the newest cash crop in Mississippi—King Cotton had long since been dethroned. Texas and California both produced three times the cotton the Magnolia State did these days. A green Deere tractor had been backed up to the water. The pump attached to it threw a rooster tail of spray high into the sky, aerating the pools.

Sally slowed, her right turn signal ticking, and bumped off onto the dirt road, feeling the queasiness, a sudden shifting in her perspective. *Of course.* She'd known where she was going. Where she'd come from, where she'd been. She knew exactly where she was, though she had not had occasion to pass this way in years. Only then did she realize that she must have been subconsciously avoiding it, detouring any other way around. She eased down the dirt drive and pulled over and stepped out to stand beside the car.

Before her sat the cabin she'd been born in—which her mother had owned along with twelve acres, the inheritance her mama had left her, and which Sally had sold years ago to establish the stake of the fund that had paid for her to go to college at Tuskegee herself. The cabin she'd known lay covered over in kudzu, lost to the vines, a mere ruin now. The roof had caved in on the river's side. The stone chimney alone stood exactly as it had then, untouched, impervious to time, implacable. *Strong.* Impossible to believe, looking at the remnants, Sally thought, that real people had once lived here— she and her mama, and Alfonse, too. Like the foundations of the slave cabins she'd witnessed for herself, the weathered shack stood, a kind of testament—concrete proof of who she'd been, *was.* Who I is, who I *bees*, she reminded herself. Beyond the inheritance that had *got her* her education, this was the legacy Letitia Johnson had left. Sally would never forget.

That night she'd been hiding in the depths of the well, clinging to the knot above the bucket, waiting for the men to go. She'd heard the big white man she feared as the Boss Chief go galloping off in the rain, but the speckled white-looking pink-scabbed black man she'd glimpsed in the flickering of the candle's light had stayed, lurking about. Sally waited him out. But once she'd climbed back over the lip of the well, she had not waited for daylight to start her trek to Children's Home. A gut feeling had driven her on. She'd walked and run, slipping and splashing through the flood of mud, slapping mosquitoes all the while. For a time she'd felt that little fox that had tried to make off with her lunch shadowing her steps. When she bent to pick up a rock, he fled. She never saw him again. She'd arrived at Rivers Bend the next morning to find Reverend Beasley weeding in the early cool, the smell of rain still strong in the garden. When he saw her, he stood and opened his arms, welcoming her home.

Sally turned to scan the horizon, the hub of the rows of cotton that rayed out from her in every direction. Remembering the girl who needed her, she climbed back into the cool of the car and put the Ford in drive again. Fourteen-year-old Amanda Ann Phipps lived only a few miles down this same stretch of dry, dusty road that her own mama, Letitia Johnson, had hoofed home on barefooted from the Tisdales each afternoon, her white shoes in her hand, ordered not to "muss" them.

Sally glanced down at the flowing, patterned slacks and brown leather sandals she wore. The short-sleeved tan silk blouse. Her gold and jade bangle bracelets jangled and her wedding band flashed as she lifted her hand to flip down the visor to shield her eyes against the glare of the sinking sun, wondering what in the world ever had become of her mama's uniform, which she'd left behind her in the cabin that night, so neatly hung.

Why I Wrote This Book

WE WERE HEADED to my grandmother's in Indianola, Mississippi, for our annual summer visit. We swept out of the hill country and the land flattened out. We were in the Delta now, our mother informed us. But even I knew that. You could see forever; it felt like it did where we lived, in the craggy West Virginia hills, where the summer sun could angle off a holler dark enough to bring out fireflies by two o'clock in the afternoon. I pressed against my window to watch the rows of smoky green cotton go wheeling past. We rolled to a stop at a sign that said to in a spot that claimed itself to be a hamlet. The brick of the building beside us was a hard red in the late afternoon sun. We drove out the other side of the crossroads, leaving the tiny town behind. More cotton fields swept by on either side. There were tractors in the fields. After getting stuck behind a car for nearly twenty miles, Dad said, "Why is it that everyone in this state drives in the left lane?"

"What now?" Dad said when traffic slowed yet again. And that's when I saw them—heard them first, really, with the windows all rolled down: the chant. Maybe it even went like the one I would use more than twenty years later in my second novel, *Cotton Song:*

Well you won't write me, you won't come and see me.
Oh!
Say you won't write me, you won't send no word.
Oh!
Said I get my news from the mockingbird.
Oh!
Said I get my news from the mockingbird.
Oh!

"It's a chain gang," my mother told us. "From Parchman."

"What's a parch man?" my little brother asked, sitting up, wide-eyed, pixielike.

"It's a prison," she said. "It's where the bad people are sent."

All the bad people that I saw in the row at work with the hoes and scythes were black. I remember that. And I remember, too, that all the white men in the sheriff's outfits had rifles or shotguns slung under their arms.

The prisoners wore yellowing white-and-black-striped uniforms and leg irons. They did not slow their work for us. They chanted the chant and shouted it back and their hoes and their scythes worked in rhythm to the song they sang. They did not bother to look at us looking at them. They acted as if we did not exist. I pressed against the door with the window down and hardly a stir of air and stared through the mounting dust with my heart going fast.

You couldn't call my grandmother Granny. Though we liked to try every chance we got. "Hey, *Granny!*" we'd cry out, standing in her kitchen doorway. She'd turn from the stove or the sink and grab her red flyswatter, which she left hanging on a peg by the door. You had to be fast if you didn't want to get switched—out the front door and down the sidewalk on East Percy Street, skipping pecan shells in your bare feet. But Grandmother was always faster. The swatter left a sharp square sting of holes on the backs of our bare white legs. Our grandmother was not kidding about being called Grandmother—although she was sort of joking around. (Our mother said that when she was a girl and got in trouble our grandmother would make her go out to the hedge between her and her next-door neighbor Miss Honey's yard and cut her own switch and bring it back to her to take the whipping. She told us that Grandmother said that that would give her plenty of time to think about what she'd done wrong.)

Grandmother was retired by then. The silver retirement bowl had a place in her china cabinet in the dining room. The little dining room was off the flapping door from the kitchen and was glassed off by French doors from the living room. When you walked in, the bone china in the cabinets made a shivering sound. The see-through drapes always hung shut and they'd yellowed some from the constant sun they took. The silver bowl said she'd been the director of the welfare offices in Sunflower County, Mississippi, from 1942 until 1967.

GRANDMOTHER HAD WORKED for the "Welfare," as she called it, and she said her job was "to try to help folks." Grandmother had helped Mary Appleberry by giving her a job in her home. Mary Appleberry had worked for my grandmother since before I was born. In fact, she'd been there when my mom brought me home from the hospital in Greenwood. Family legend has it that when Mary Appleberry first saw the premature runt I turned out to be she tried to make my mother feel better about me. "Don't worry, Miss 'Lizbeth, some of the ugliest babies grow up to be the most beautiful children." Mary Appleberry was tall and thin and had a wide, friendly, freckled face. Her skin was a bright coppery color. She wore a white uniform dress to work every day because she chose to, and she always called my grandmother "Miss Mary."

Every Christmas since I could remember, Mary Appleberry had sent us a big freezer bag full of pecans, which she'd gathered out of

Grandmother's yard and shelled herself. She did this for us for years even after my grandmother died. Because my grandmother was gone, we had no idea that Mary Appleberry had passed on. We didn't know until one Christmas when the pecans didn't come.

IN THAT HOUSE I only heard the word *nigger* used once. It was in Grandmother's living room. It may well have been that summer we heard the chain gang on the way to her house. I know for a fact it was cocktail hour. Grandmother always had her bourbon at 5:00, even years later when I was in college and she had to go into the hospital for weeks at a time because of the emphysema that would eventually kill her. When I visited her there, she would nod at the cabinet in which her robe hung. She kept the bottle of Old Crow on the top shelf. She drank a jigger of it with water, and she'd have me pour a tall drink for her. When I handed it over, she'd lift the oxygen mask and blow out a little puff of breath, as if she'd arrived at the end of a long, uphill race. "Thank you, dear," she'd say, but only after taking the first sip.

It was my grandmother's sister—my auntie—who said it, I remember. There was no heat in the word when she said it. It was something like a plain fact—"The nigger didn't come cut my yard today"—which, to me, made it somehow worse. What I also remember is my grandmother's silence, the rattling of ice in the air-conditioned cool. I believed it to be the kind of pointed ignoring with admonition in it, giving her sister time to rethink what she'd said—like asking my mother to take a long walk out to the hedge to cut her own switch.

GRANDMOTHER DIED IN 1985, when I was in my first year at the University of Iowa's Writer's Workshop. I wished to be a writer. When I first started writing stories I often wrote them about Mississippi. The place where my mother was raised and where I'd been born and where I'd returned every year since I was a child remained vivid in my memory. It was *more real than real* was the feeling I often had when I was at work at my desk. I recognize now that it was my imagination I was getting in touch with.

While I was at school that first semester, my grandmother sent me a five-dollar bill in a plain white envelope. Enclosed with the money was a little note on a yellow grocery list. "For ground chuck," it read. "Ground chuck is the meat made from a steak. Ground beef is just plain hamburger."

The note was signed, appropriately enough, "Love, Grandmother."

MY MOM CALLED with the news late one winter's night. I lived in a one-room, second-story apartment above a pizza shop on the square in Iowa City. The digital clock on the building opposite my front windows flashed minus twelve and then minus thirteen. The wind whipped the wisps of fallen snow and buffeted the glass, making it groan. Pigeons lived in the wall beside my bed. I could hear them cooing. Sometimes one would fall between the joists, and I would hear it flapping to try to get up as it went down and down. A week or so later there would be that too-sweet smell.

Even in those days I went to bed around 9:00 because I got up at 4:00 A.M. to write. At that time, I was working on my first novel, *Road of the Sun*, which, as many of my early stories had been, was set in the Mississippi Delta. I would finish it two years later, the year I left Iowa, and I'd end up burning the completed manuscript in the public park before I went. It was 512 pages long, and I had a good fire going when the ranger walked up.

"You can't burn trash here," she said.

"It's my first novel," I answered.

The ranger looked at me, thumbs in her holster. Then she nodded. "Let me help you," she said, and grabbed a stack of pages off the pile.

It felt like a dream, but I wasn't asleep. In the dream that wasn't a dream my grandmother was in the room with me. The apartment I rented came furnished, and in it was a frayed old wingback chair similar to the one in my grandmother's living room. Grandmother was sitting in the chair. I remember she was wearing the rose-flowered housecoat she'd taken to wearing in her last years—sitting in her own wingback chair back home on East Percy Street, smoking a cigar-brown More cigarette held between gnarled, arthritic fingers stained yellow from the smoke, and watching *Wheel of Fortune*. She said she'd come to tell me how much she loved me. She said she knew I loved her, too—and so not to worry if I couldn't make it to her funeral. She understood.

And that's when the phone rang. I heard my mother's voice, talking, telling me what I already knew. I sat dry-eyed as she told me. We talked about when the funeral would be. I told her I'd be there. I wouldn't miss it for anything. When I hung up the phone, I switched on every light in the apartment. Of course I looked under my bed. I even looked for Grandmother in the coat closet.

It snowed two feet that night and on into the next day, a regular blizzard—the way it can in Iowa in the winter—and the world was a wild, white mess for almost a week afterward. It took me nearly that long to dig my car out of its iglooed space on the street. They buried my grandmother without me there, and I felt terrible about it all that day and the next and the next and the next . . .

I wasn't able to make it back down to Mississippi to pay my respects until summer recess.

When I rode into Indianola, the first thing I did was drive straight to Grandmother's house on East Percy. No one was living there, though I knew my aunt was trying to sell the place, but the front door remained unlocked. I stepped in and shut the door behind me. It was hot-smelling; the air conditioner had been turned off, the windows closed, and the place was awfully close, sweltering even—heavy with the suffocating smell of cigarette smoke.

I walked into the living room and stood for a long time beside my grandmother's wingback chair. There were caterpillar-sized burn holes in the arms of the chair and in the carpet at her feet from where the ashes from her cigarettes had fallen. The dining room shivered as I passed down the hall. I stepped into the little kitchen. The red flyswatter still hung by the door. Outside in the pecan tree, I could hear a jay fussing. A red squirrel chucked back. I toured the bedrooms that had been my mother's and my aunt's. Miss Honey next door had died years ago and an up-and-coming couple had bought her house and remodeled it so that it was unrecognizable to me. It looked like something out of an architectural magazine. They'd dug up the hedge where my mother used to cut her switches. They'd put a tennis court in the backyard.

I walked to the end of the hall and into my grandmother's bedroom. My mother had told me this was where she'd died, in the glass-paneled room overlooking the backyard with the tractor tire filled with sand where my cousins and brother and I used to play summers when we visited that she called the "sleeping porch," not in the hospital, where she had refused to go at the end even though the doctors might have been able to keep her alive a while longer. The bed was perfectly made up, and I thought again of Mary Appleberry, who I imagined had been the person to wash those sheets my grandmother had died in, to scrub out the stains and to iron them straight afterward and to stretch them over the mattress and smooth over them the worn thin, nubbled white spread that had once been my grandmother's mother's when she'd lived back in Kentucky.

And then it happened. I jumped, my heart leaping into my throat. Even though she'd been dead for months, my grandmother's bedside alarm clock had gone off, buzzing insistently for her to get up. She'd set it for 2:25 P.M.—to wake her from her afternoon nap. It must have been going off like that every day, I thought, ever since the night she'd come to me in Iowa City to tell me I didn't need to come to her funeral because she knew I loved her.

I reached over to shut the alarm off and then I walked around and pulled the cord.

Granny, I thought sentimentally, feeling the tears well, and like a fast slap, I felt the sting.

Grandmother, I corrected myself.

Laughing then, I wept.

IN MY EXPERIENCE I've found there are lots of reasons for writing a novel that may never make it into the actual book. These are some of the reasons why I wrote this particular one, which is based on my grandmother Mary Steele Nabors, the first female director of the welfare offices in Sunflower County, Mississippi, whom I miss more than I'll ever be able to say.

cotton song

a novel

TOM BAILEY

READER'S GROUP GUIDE

1. Discuss the recurring appearance of the red fox at Letitia's house. Why is the fox associated with this location? Why does the author include such gory details of this same fox collecting the remains of Baby's unborn child?

2. What do you think of Sissy Rule Tisdale? Is she a sympathetic character? Why do you think the rest of the Rule family seems so absent from her life?

3. What do you think really happened the night Dorothy Tisdale died?

4. Discuss Boss Chief's philosophy of right and wrong. Whose rules does he follow? How does he see his role as head of Parchman Farm? What factors influenced his chosen path?

5. What, if anything, is the significance of the song lyrics throughout the book? Did you find them meaningful?

6. Discuss the contrast between Alley Leech, whose crimes and general behavior define a villainous man, and Bigger, of whom we hear reports only of kindness and nobility. Why does the author contrast these two characters so vividly? Do you think his point is overstated? How do these extremes of character serve the story?

7. Everything we know of Jake and Jolene's relationship indicates that his careless and sometimes neglectful attitude toward her and her wishes is habitual. Why does she put up with it?

8. Boss Chief says of his late wife, "I might even've been a different man with her at my side." What kind of man might he have been? What sort of regrets, if any, do you think this statement implies?

9. Do you think Jake would have made a good boss chief? Did he have what it would take to reform the prison?

10. Discuss the different ways sex is discussed in the book—from the adolescent excitement of Jake and Sissy, to the matter-of-fact romps of Boss Chief and his secretary, to the "magic" between Bigger and Letitia, to the violence between Clyde and Sissy, and even the "unspeakable acts" between Alley and his son. What role does sex play in the telling of the story? How important is it in defining relationships in the book?

11. In reliving her daughter's drowning and its aftermath, Sissy wishes she had taken time to tell Letitia, "You have been a comfort to me." Do you think this would have been as important to Letitia as Sissy seems to think it would have? What does it say about Sissy that this is the primary regret she expresses in her recollections?

12. Do you think that Clyde Tisdale is inherently a bad man? What factors might motivate his behavior toward Sissy?

13. Most of the adults in the book seem to have chosen their paths, but the children—Jeana, Jakey, young Robert Tisdale—still have their lives before them. What do you think each will make of the events of the story? How might these events alter their fates, if at all?

14. Discuss Calvin McGales's motivation in leading the Klan. What drives him? Does his role and behavior in the KKK bear any similarity to the way he carries out his bootlegging business? Why do you think he was chosen as a leader above other Klansmen? What

qualities of his make him a desirable candidate for the Klan's membership and mission?

15. Although Clyde Tisdale defines the Klan as the greatest danger, his foil to the Klan's rule is a "civic trinity" of himself, Sheriff Dodd, and Dr. Jenks. Is this ruling class any better for Ruleton? Do you think Clyde honestly thinks it is? Does he even consider the welfare of Ruleton? Does anyone?

About the Author

TOM BAILEY was born in the Mississippi Delta. Growing up, he lived in North Carolina, Alabama, Florida, Virginia, and West Virginia. He is the author of the novel *The Grace That Keeps This World* and a collection of short stories, *Crow Man*, as well as *A Short Story Writer's Companion*, a book on writing short fiction. He is also the editor of *On Writing Short Stories*. The recipient of a Pushcart Prize, an NEA Fellowship, a Newhouse Award from the John Gardner Foundation, and the 2006 Mississippi Institute of Arts and Letters Award for Fiction, Tom Bailey teaches in the creative writing program at Susquehanna University in Selinsgrove, Pennsylvania, where he lives with his wife and three children.

Also by Tom Bailey

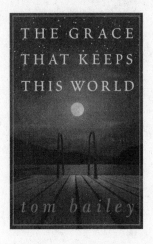

In his novel about family, community, and the shared values that underlie human relationships, Bailey weaves a tale of profound loss, human fallibility, and the love—romantic, neighborly, or familial—that can sometimes blur our line of vision.

THE GRACE THAT KEEPS THIS WORLD
$13.00 ($17.00 Canada)
978-0-307-23802-3

Available from Three Rivers Press wherever books are sold.